It is now three years since the Battle of the Wide Plateau (Vol 1—*Murder in Hattusas*) put Tudhaliyas on the throne in the realm of the ancient Hittite Empire, yet instead of feeling secure, he feels menaced. His chief spy, Satipilli, has vanished, and trouble is brewing in the west, possibly from Ahhiyawa. The Mittani are threatening Ishuwa on the eastern border, seeking revenge for their humiliation in the civil war. All this requires reliable intelligence reports. Tudhaliyas is forced to turn to the unknown faces of Mokhat and Palaiyas and asks them to go to the west, to Millawanda, and discover what has happened to Satipilli, the chief spy of the Hittites.

On their journey, at the outset they are followed with someone trying to kill them; with each failure, their attempts become more desperate. The assassins follow Mokhat and Palaiyas but are then dissuaded just before Millawanda; but they suddenly reappear in Egypt. Somebody doesn't want them to complete their mission.

At the close of the Old Kingdom in 1417 BC, Madduwatta, the Governor of Lukka, a vassal of Tudhaliyas, has plans of his own. How is he implicated in all this? He has his eyes on Arzawa. He badly needs friends, and will ally himself with anyone prepared to help him achieve his goal. But who has stirred him up? Who has gone to these lengths to create a rebellion for the Hittites? Meanwhile, Ahhiyawa is in the grip of a Civil War, with two brothers fighting it out for the throne. The outcome of the conflict will impact on their neighbours, Arzawa, the Hittites, and the Governor of Lukka.

From Milllawanda, Palaiyas, a Prince of Tiryns, decides to go home to make peace with his father, the king. While in Tiryns, he's abducted by his uncle, Electryon, the king of Mycenae, and brought to account for his desertion from Keftiu (Crete); then forced to complete his tour of duty. Mokhat follows him and rescues him. After fleeing to Khemet (Egypt), stopping at Ugarit, and then being captured by pirates near Lukka, they finally discover the truth in Ura.

In this adventurous romp through the ancient Mediterranean, Mokhat discovers love, and Palaiyas is ultimately reunited with his wife and child in Hattusas—all in a search for Satipilli, the missing chief spy of the Hittites. This is the 2nd Volume of the Hittite trilogy. Volume 3 is scheduled to be published in 2012.

# Madduwatta's Rebellion

## Sasha Garrydeb

**Historical Novel**

**Volume 2 of the Hittite trilogy**

**London**
**2011**

Published in Britain in 2011
by ABC Publishers
24 Treadgold Street London W11 4BP

e-mail: abcpublishers@ntlworld.com

A CIP catalogue record for this book
is available from the British Library.

ISBN 978-0954814472

Printed by
ABC Publishers,
Notting Dale,
London W11 4BP.

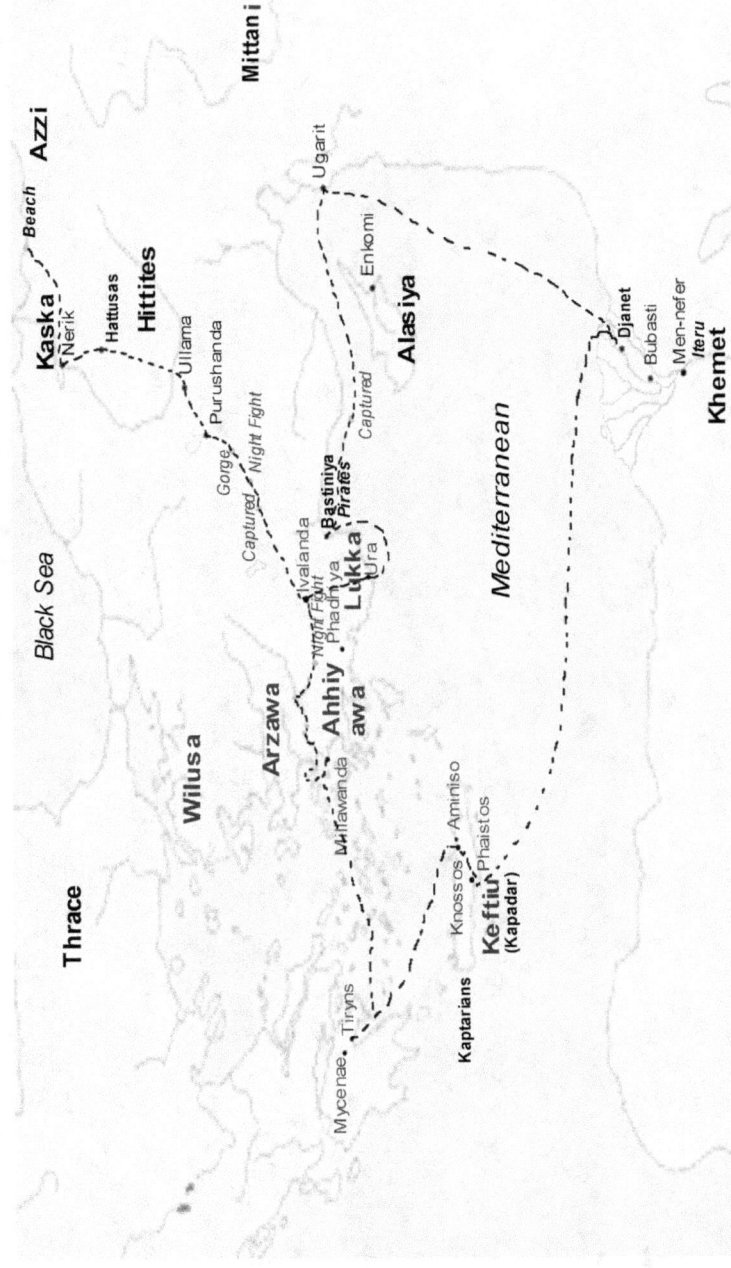

# CHARACTER LIST (main characters in bold)

**Mokhat**—brother of the Kaska ruler, sent to look for Satipili
Kasalliwa—king of the Kaska, Mokhat's older brother
**Palaiyas**—Prince of Tiryns, companion to Mokhat
Alkaeus—father of Palaiyas and king of Tiryns
Amphitryon—brother of Palaiyas
Alkmene—Elektryon's daughter
**Mahera**—Palaiyas woman who has his child
**Narmus**—Captain of convoy and works for Satipilli
Melinar—Narmus' second in command
**Ulurra**—slave given to Mokhat, she's Narmus' sister
Genger—Leader of the Gimirri raiding party, the wild men
Savanghi—known as Scarface, the tormentor of Mokhat
**Tudhaliyas**—King of the Hittites
Nikal—Queen to King Tudhaliyas
**Satipilli**—Tudhaliyas' chief spy, missing while on a mission
Kishnapili—General leading troops to the Ahhiyawan border
Tipali—Kishnapili's deputy
Mekiner—Tipali's deputy
Onasiyas—Captain in the Hittite army who speaks Ahhiyawan
Feliyas—Captain in the Hittite army who speaks Ahhiyawan
Captain Nikmed—Master of the ship out of Ugarit
Aranare—Minoan (Kaptarian) resistance fighter
Captain Mengebet—Egyptian who rescued them from Keftiu
**Madduwatta**—Governor of Lukka
**Daubum**—Madduwatta's chief spy, nasty piece of work
**Napat**—false Shepherd, a Saka from Central Asia
Parmodius—dead King of Millawanda
Famemnon—new king of Millawanda, brother of Attarsiyas
Attarsiyas—younger brother of Famemnon
**Sflokos**—Ahhiyawan spymaster
Elektryon—King of Mycenae, uncle to Palaiyas
Saustatar—King of Mittani muscular and his son
**Artatama**—Crown Prince of Mittani
Wassukkani, capital city of Mittani.

# Glossary

Cubit = 0.46m or 18 in. League = 5 km or 3 miles
The shekel was the state currency (named after the
Babylonian shekel)
    40 mina = 1 shekel usually in copper or silver
    2 weight mina = 1 Kg

Ahhiyawa = Mycenae
Ahhiyawans = Mycenaeans

Millawanda = Miletus
Keftiu = Crete
Kapadar = What the Minoans call Crete
Alasiya = Cyprus

Atana Potnia = Mycenaean version of Athena
*manes* = spirits of the dead

Khemet = the ancient Egyptian name for Egypt
Pharaoh Amenhotep II (1424-1401 BC)
Djat = First Minister to Pharaoh
Djanet = Tanis
Waset = Thebes
Mennufer = Memphis
Iteru = Nile
Ta Mehu = Lower Egypt
Retenu was the ancient Egyptian name for Canaan

## Part of the Hittite King List

**Old Kingdom**
Muwatallis I (c.1422-1420 BC)

**New Kingdom**
Tudhaliyas I (1420-1400 BC)

# Background

The story is set in the tumultuous period of the Hittite Empire in what is now Turkey, at the tail end of the Middle Kingdom and the start of the New. The year is 1417 BC, three years after the civil war that brought King Tudhaliyas to power. The time is after the winter solstice. The kings are real.

# Chapter One

Along the dark ill-tempered shoreline, waves pounded angrily onto the shifting shingles of the wintry southern coast of the Black Sea. High on a grey pebbly beach in the lee of a cluster of oversized boulders, two freezing figures waited in ambush.

'I wish that filthy scoundrel would hurry. It's the middle of the night...' Palaiyas was intent on whispering the obvious, 'and I'm not likely to be of any use to a woman if parts of me freeze and fall off.' Palaiyas squatted behind a large boulder enveloped in his black cloak, massaging his hands to keep the circulation moving.

'I'm just as cold as you. Stop complaining!' Mokhat tried to keep the smile from engulfing his face and looked sharply askance with his dark eyes at his companion, from under his cloak....'*Shhh*! Quiet...! Someone's coming!'

The ambushers heard sandaled feet pounding a steady rhythm on the scattered shingles, getting ever closer to where they were hiding. Mokhat made out the shadow of a bent figure rounding a nearby spur loping towards the boulder where the two men lay in wait—and as the quarry ran by—Mokhat was the first to pounce. The taller Mokhat aimed himself, arms outstretched, at the individual's shoulders whilst the more muscular Palaiyas dived for the victim's legs. The trio tumbled hard onto the pebbles and the panicky victim tried desperately to free himself from his attackers.

'*Ouch*! *You dirty shit.*' Mokhat felt a bite on his arm. He yelled, '*Hold the bastard*!'

'*Argh...HELP*!' screamed the quarry. Fabric tore in Mokhat's hands.

'*Keep still or I'll cut your throat*,' Palaiyas shouted.

Mokhat finally managed to get his arm round the individual's throat, although in a twist, he had landed heavily on his back with the prey on top. Palaiyas was on his knees, splaying himself on top of the struggling target with his knife near the victim's nostrils.

'Keep *still*.....damn you,' Mokhat hissed menacingly into his enemy's ear as the last vestiges of the desperate struggle ebbed away from the despicable lout. Mokhat released his grip and Palaiyas scrambled up, pulling their quarry to his feet with him, his dagger under the victim's chin, drawing a droplet of blood. Even in the darkness, fear and belligerence sat uneasily on the wretch's half hidden face. The wind tore cruelly at their cloaks. 'You know who we are?' Palaiyas asked with a loud snarl.

Mokhat jumped to his feet, brushing his cloak down, rubbing his bitten arm. 'Oh, he *knows*! Come; let's get back to the cavern! I want to get off this forsaken beach, and out of this filthy freezing wind.'

Out at sea the storm was picking up and the dark sky grew ever more menacing. The blustery weather buffeted them, tugging at their cloaks, tearing at them in all directions, making the going difficult. Despite the darkness of the bulbous clouds, a sort of dawn was trying to break through from the east. Seagulls squawked piercingly overhead as they fought against the wind that was pushing them out to sea, trying desperately to get inland, flying ever higher over the long meandering shoreline.

Palaiyas took charge of their now cowering captive, holding him by the scruff of the neck, prodding him forward with his dagger in the small of his back, marching him up a ravine towards the nearby hills. A few drops of rain landed, threatening a deluge, but the swift moving clouds made that difficult. After a dozen more paces, Palaiyas tied the captive's hands, while Mokhat held his own knife at the traitor's throat. They continued walking on in silence for some time, with the storm howling like a demented banshee all round them, before reaching a natural cleft between an indented limestone formation. Palaiyas, scowling with disgust, pushed his captive into the hollow between two ridges towards a dark medium sized opening. The smell of dampness overwhelmed their senses just before they rushed inside, past the hobbled horses near the entrance. In the clammy cave Mokhat unfurled some tinder from a cloth beneath his cloak, then quickly set to with flint stones and got a fire going. He'd previously gathered and prepared the wood for this eventuality. At first, it was a reluctant glow, but as the tinder caught and dry twigs were added, it burst into flame. More twigs and a blaze began to make itself felt. Ghostlike shadows danced on the dank sand coloured walls setting the ambience into its proper gloom. Mokhat added more twigs and piled a split log on top.

'Over there, *you!*' Palaiyas ordered and pushed the surly captive down hard, forcing his back against the soggy cave wall, hands still tied behind him.

3

'I'll get us something hot to drink,' Mokhat told his companion. 'We've picked a nasty night for catching this turncoat.' Their captive grimaced at hearing those words applied to him. He stared sadly at his torn cloak. His fear-laden eyes were frantically searching to and fro for a way to escape his dilemma. Mokhat filled a bronze pot from a water-skin and set it hanging over the fire.

'Look at him,' Palaiyas scowled. 'He's trying to find a way out. No my disgusting little fart. You're for the high jump.' He spat at the man. Then he wandered over and kicked him hard in the thigh. Staring at him hard, he shouted, 'Why did you do it?'

The captive looked down averting his eyes. Despite the cold, a bead of sweat dribbled down his forehead.

'I asked you a question......' And Palaiyas kicked the man again in the same spot. 'When your superiors speak to you, you *answer*.'

'Come and watch the water boil,' Mokhat suggested to Palaiyas. 'Let me have a go at him.' Mokhat rose from the fire and sauntered over to sit beside the captive. He turned the man's shoulder away from the wall and cut his hands free. The captive rubbed his wrists but didn't look at Mokhat. 'We knew *someone* was giving the Azzi military information. Now we've *got* you. Don't bother denying it. What *I* want to know is—*why*?' Stubbornly the captive kept silent. 'Look, you can talk to me or you can talk to him,' Mokhat motioned at Palaiyas.

The frightened middle-aged man looked at his muscular tormentor by the fire and made a decision. 'I...I... had *no* choice.' He stammered, then paused and stared at the dirt on the cave floor still rubbing his wrists. Tears began to well up, silently running down his cheeks. After a long pause..., 'When the Azzi...first invaded Kaska, they took my brother prisoner. He was in charge of a squadron of cavalry on the border. They worked on him, tortured him, until he could hold out no longer, and it was he who revealed...that I worked as a scribe in the Royal Archive. Then....their spies put pressure on me to get them information—or I would never see my brother again. I said no! They tortured my brother some more and he told them where my village was...and they sent a raiding party to get my whole family...*all* of them. My mother, father, sisters, uncles...*all* of them. What choice did I have? So as soon as the military lodged their tactical plans in the royal archive—as they're required to do by royal decree—I memorised the dispositions and passed them on to a waiting Azzi spy. That's where I was going tonight when...well...anyway... here I am. Now you know! What will you do to me?'

Mokhat felt almost sorry for the man. 'You know who I am?'

'Yes, your highness. I've seen you in the palace.'

'You must tell me the whole truth. Are there any more traitors working with you?'

'No!'

'You are sure—absolutely *sure*?'

'*Yes*, your highness, I swear it!'

'Right! We're taking you back—back to Nerik. You must know there's only one penalty for treason....but that's for the king to decide.'

The man hung his head, wiped his tears with the cuff of his sleeve and mumbled, 'Yes, I know! All I can say is....I had *no* choice! I'm sorry your highness. I...I did it to save my family.'

Mokhat sighed, 'Surely you must know that your family is doomed no matter what you do. Once you've served your purpose, they would be killed. It's just how the Azzi are. You could have saved *yourself* if you'd used your common sense. As it is....' He left the sentence hanging and got to his feet.

Palaiyas had been quietly making a hot chamomile brew. As the prisoner's story unfolded, his eyebrows went high. Finally rocking back on his haunches, he burst out,

5

'Well done! I could have sworn he'd never talk right to the end. I thought I'd have to really work him over to get him to talk.'

Mokhat came and took the bronze mug held out for him. 'Pour another one for our prisoner. He's saved us a lot of unpleasant work.'

Palaiyas did so, though reluctantly. 'If I had my way we'd finish him right now and save ourselves more trouble.'

Dawn reached for them with its slender fingers, as shafts of light danced playfully near the cave mouth. Palaiyas went to put the woollen girths and colourful saddlecloths on all three horses near the entrance of the cave. They had optimistically brought three horses, anticipating a successful outcome to their venture.

Mokhat helped to secure their meagre travel goods onto the horses and then doused the fire. 'Come, it's time to go,' he called to the prisoner. Palaiyas unhobbled the horses and led them out of the cave. The wind had died down somewhat, but a stiff breeze forced them to wrap their cloaks tightly around them. Mokhat held two of the horses, while Palaiyas jumped into the simple saddle of his grey stallion. Two small brown pillows stuffed with horsehair held his thighs in place, front, and back. Mokhat forced the captive onto a bay mare, handing the reins to Palaiyas, and then he mounted his own black stallion.

The long journey back to Nerik was a cold affair. The snows that winter had been the worst in living memory. The winds howled and the slippery ground made every effort to unseat them, sliding, tripping or skidding the horse's hooves on the frosty landscape. Cold, hungry, and extremely tired, they finally arrived at the royal citadel at Nerik late that evening.

The trio found the king ensconced warmly in the banqueting hall, eating an evening meal with his family and a number of senior officers. Hot food assailed their nostrils and all three stomachs returned a mating call that seemed to echo round the hall.

'I see, brother, you've caught who you went after.' King Kasalliwa's brown eyes looked closely at the captive. 'I know you,' he boomed. 'You're from the archives.' The king scratched his dark beard and then nodded to his guards, pointing at the prisoner. 'You know what to do with him.' The palace guards sprang to and frogmarched the prisoner out of the hall, down to the deepest dungeons. The traitor taken care of, the king returned to his seat.

'Got any food to spare?' Mokhat asked, throwing off his cloak. Palaiyas was already warming his large frame at the fire.

'Sorry! Both of you must be frozen!' The king rose and ushered Mokhat towards the open fire. 'Go...warm yourselves. There's enough food here, or there ought to be for a normal pair of men. Oh! And well done!' He patted Mokhat on the back and nodded to Palaiyas, then returned to his seat, picked up his goblet and waved it in the air until a servant rushed to fill it. 'A cup of hot wine will put the pair of you right—then I've got another job for you. A big one.' He stared at his younger brother's sharp face, and those dark eyes—and his demeanour had a strangely serious ring to it.

While warming his backside at the fire Mokhat looked harshly at his older sibling as he listened to those words. He shrugged, brushed back his long black hair, and looked sideways at Palaiyas. He decided to wait until after he had filled his belly before inquiring further. In a hungry frame of mind he might be tempted to agree to anything.

A little while later Mokhat's brother said out loud as if he wasn't talking to Mokhat, 'The Hittite king has asked for your services again.'

An hour had passed and Mokhat sat satiated, relaxing with a goblet of wine. He received this new information with less than enthusiasm. 'Any idea what he wants?'

'Not the slightest—except he says it's extremely important. A task for which he can't use his own people. He's offering us grain and other trade goods—if you accept this assignment.' The king smiled to himself at the bribe. 'It would ease our provisioning efforts, especially with this war against the Azzi. Think about it! Now you've closed the leak from our archives…there's nothing left but hard fighting. You might be better out of it!'

'Out of the mud and into the shit, heh? I think I'd rather do more fighting.' The scowl on Mokhat's face said it all. 'The last time I tried to save the Hatti king's neck, I landed myself in the middle of a full scale battle—a civil war no less.'

'Yes, but look at the benefits that came from that escapade. We've had peace with Hatti for over three years. Trade is booming. It's got the Azzi so envious that they've decided they want a piece of the action.' The king thumped the table with his fist.

'It's brought us peace on one side and war on the other. I don't call that much of a benefit,' Mokhat responded.

'Would you rather have war on both sides….with the Hittites and the Azzi? The Azzi we can deal with—the Hittites are a different proposition altogether. We could end up losing to them. They have far more resources.' The argument started off as banter, but somewhere along the way it had got serious. The king's face looked grim. 'Are you refusing to go?' The king's face took on a darker disposition. He was puzzled as to why his younger brother was being so resistant. It wasn't like him to refuse a challenge.

Mokhat hesitated, and then answered calmly, 'Not at all, my liege.' The anger on his brother's face was clear. 'I am yours to command, brother. If you wish me to go…I will of course go. I'm merely pointing out that we didn't get the freedom from strife that we anticipated from the *escapade* you mentioned.'

'We don't always get what we anticipate. That we're at war with the Azzi and not Hatti is a big blessing and I thank Illuyankas for his kindness in that respect.' Suddenly the king smiled and relaxed. The minor confrontation between the two siblings was over as quickly as it had begun.

The tension in the room eased and Palaiyas' grim clean shaven features relaxed, allowing him to breathe out the tension. He poked Mokhat, who was sitting next to him, in the side with his elbow. He'd actually put his hand on his dagger just in case. Only the gods are privy to what he thought he could have done with a simple dagger. Now he raised his goblet in one hand and brushed his neck length hair backwards with the other, then took a long swig of the warm wine. Others in the room had sensed the rising discord between the brothers and had fallen silent. As the discord had ebbed, so the hubbub increased and the talk and laughter became over loud. The music rose in volume attempting to compensate. Lutes, panpipes, zithers, and drums filled the air with melody.

The king of the Kaska looked at Mokhat and affirmed, 'That's settled then—you leave in the morning.' There was no further arguing with his tone of voice.

\* \* \*

Without much enthusiasm Mokhat watched Palaiyas steer his grey mare across the shallow iced-up stream leading to the North Gate of Hattusas and his heart sank. He hadn't seen the Hittite capital in over three years but the memory of that "escapade," as his brother had put it, lingered strongly. He felt overly guilty at his reaction when he withdrew from the Battle of the Wide Plateau, at the height of the civil war. They had orders to pluck Tudhaliyas out of the front line, but Mokhat had felt an overwhelming, yet shameful, sense of relief at being able to leave the front line himself. Even now he was not sure if the panic that gripped him then, was craven fear or pre-battle nerves. He had not mentioned it to Palaiyas for dread of him thinking he was a coward. Palaiyas would not call him a coward, but he might think it, and that would be just as bad. The memory of that "escapade" was the main reason he had not wanted to deal with the Hittites again. He was not overly confident in what he might discover if he dug too deep within himself. He was a priest to the Kaska, but with a shallow conviction for that calling, and had not been as thorough in his examination of himself as he should have been. The next time…who knows?

'I wonder what happened to Mahera.' Palaiyas, now in full armour, voiced over his shoulders, more to himself than to Mokhat.

'Who?' Mokhat wasn't listening, deep in his own reflections.

'*Mahera*! The woman I left behind. She was pregnant —remember?'

Mokhat kicked the sides of his horse to catch up. 'Ah, yes, Mahera! The little one will be three years old by now. You don't even know if it's a boy or a girl. You'll have to see her; see if she wants for anything. It's your moral duty.' Mokhat was still preoccupied and was mouthing platitudes. It was the priest in him inattentively speaking.

Palaiyas responded irritably, 'You needn't remind me of my duties. I fully intend to visit her.'

Palaiyas' tone of voice brought Mokhat out of his reveries. 'Sorry! I wasn't preaching. I was only half listening. I didn't mean to tell you your duty. I know you're a good man and will do all that's needed. I apologise.' Mokhat's sincerity was evident.

'Oh! It's all right. I'm just oversensitive on the subject. The last time we left I didn't even say goodbye—

just vanished as if she didn't exist. Now I feel guilty. Of course I'm going to go and see her. In fact, you go on up to the Grand Citadel and I'll go and see her right now, as soon as we get through the city gates, assuming she's still living in the same place.'

Tall thick grey walls fortified the twin hills Hattusas stood on. The Hittite capital had been chosen for its natural strength backing onto gorges and crags to the north, whilst on the open southern crest of the hill a massive stone wall topped by crenulated ramparts interspersed at sixty-five cubit intervals by large projecting rectangular towers, protected the city's approaches. An access road swung sharply into a thirteen cubit wide lane, set between the two flanking towers, whilst the gate itself was set back eight cubits into the protecting bastion towers. An arched gateway framed by huge irregular blocks of masonry extended from the outer to the inner side of the whole system, traversed by a tunnel leading to the Upper Town.

The twin bastion towers now loomed ahead as the two riders approached across the snow covered landscape. On either side of the tunnel entrance stomped a number of sentries holding scimitars, scrutinising anyone wishing to enter. They tramped around in their heavy cloaks and cloth-wrapped legs, trying to keep from freezing. Sentries in bright yellow heavy wool tunics rushed to bar the gateway as Mokhat and Palaiyas drew near. Seeing the Kaska uniforms approaching, they brought their spears on guard. '*Halt and state your business,*' the senior guard shouted.

'*We've been sent for by the king,*' Palaiyas shouted back.

'Just hold on there! We'll send an escort with you to guide you to the palace,' responded the senior guard.

Mokhat told the guard, trying to keep his voice even, 'We know were the palace is.'

'That as may be, but I have my orders. No strangers in foreign uniforms unescorted within the city gates.' With that he called to another sentry at the rear to sound a signal on a conch. Within a short time six riders came through the tunnel gate to escort them up to the palace.

The close watch on their movements put paid to Palaiyas' search for Mahera. A flash of anger at being thwarted rose and passed in an instant. He thought, *so much for my good intentions.* He regained composure and whispered to Mokhat, 'Something serious is afoot. Some kind of trouble!'

Mokhat gazed around as if trying to extract the information from imperceptible clues around him, then nodded. 'Probably something to do with why the king's asked for us.'

Shortly thereafter, they were escorted along the main thoroughfare crossing from east to west. Snow covered squat square houses standing uniformly on either side leading to the Upper City. The group of horsemen passed through the now familiar narrow corbelled arches of the citadel gates, flanked by its portal sculptures. The arches opened into the lower paved courtyard holding stables, an armoury, various guardrooms, and then on further to the official access to the Upper Palace proper. Their escort halted at the stables while Mokhat and Palaiyas continued to the palace entrance.

Just as they dismounted, the biting northerly wind sent another flurry of snow sideways into the quadrangle.

'It's the worst winter I can remember,' Mokhat shouted over the wind at Palaiyas.

At the top of the main staircase an old man with white hair waited, face beaming a welcome. As Mokhat carefully climbed the stairs he was shocked to recognise the old man as Kantuzzili, the king's uncle. He looked much older than the last time Mokhat had seen him. He stood imposingly in a yellow kilt, white cotton blouse, and a dark fur cloak. Only three years had passed but the affairs of state had taken their toll. Behind a face full of ridges, was the unmistakable twinkle of bright intelligence set in blue eyes, staring out at Mokhat.

'Welcome, and doubly welcome, Prince Mokhat. I see Palaiyas is still with you. I expected no less. Come inside out of this cold. The king waits impatiently up in the antechamber. He's most keen to see you again.'

'It's good to see you as well, prince. My brother, King Kasalliwa, sends his felicitations.' Mokhat and Palaiyas followed the elderly prince up the wide stairs and along the corridors to a private room behind the throne room. Ranks of bronze torch-holders lit their way.

They found Tudhaliyas sitting at a table, pouring over a wax tablet, shaking his head. He spotted Mokhat behind Kantuzzili and rose to his feet. 'I'm happy to see you, Prince. It's been a long time. Why haven't you visited? The Queen often asks of you. Warm your selves by the fire.'

'Sire,' Mokhat kept a stern face. 'We are at war with the Azzi. The battle prevents us from making social visits.' He welcomed the invitation to warm himself and stood facing the king with his back to the fire. Palaiyas joined him, wondering what his friend was up to. The Kaska prince and the Hatti king were supposed to be close friends and allies, yet Mokhat behaved as if they'd just met.

In turn, the tall Hittite king felt the detachment in Mokhat's voice, almost as a slap, rather than the expected warmth from a friend and comrade. Mokhat was correct but distant. Tudhaliyas looked puzzled at the Kaska priest, but then forced himself to brush it aside. 'Well anyway, you're here now. When you've chased the chill from your bones, sit and I'll explain why I asked for you. I'd like you to go to Millawanda.'

The bemused shock on Palaiyas' face said it all. His mouth was open and his eyes almost popped out of their sockets in surprise.

# Chapter Two

'**G**rey is the time left unto you; bleak is your future,' a shadowy spectre whispered in the old man's fading ear. 'Why do you linger?' Death hovered impatiently by the dying man's shoulder barely able to contain itself. '*Charon is w-a-i-t-i-n-g......*'

Bemused, gazing through his closed eyelids into a far-off lifetime past, his mortal coil slowly unravelling, as were his wits, the old man gave a rattling sigh to signal he was ready to cross the Styx and move on.

A gruff military voice whispered near the bed, 'He's going! Where in Hades are his sons?'

'General, I sent for them five days ago. They must be on their way. The frost...the snow...they must be having difficulties getting here.' The chamberlain's narrow face winced. He knew they would blame *him* if the king died without his sons present at his bedside.

'They should've been here by now,' the burly general's strong features were set grim. His fingers rubbed the coins he held, ready for the eyelids; money to pay the ferryman across the Styx.

Fourteen elderly green-robed priestesses of Diwonusojo, armed with wands tipped with a pinecone, and all wreathed with vine and ivy, chanted in a corner of the king's bedchamber, tearing unenthusiastically at their hair. The *maenads*, members of the orgiastic cult of the nature follower Diwonusojo, were always likely to wake the dead, rather than ease the soul's transition to the netherworld. Only on this occasion, the general had instructed the "mad women" to keep their chanting low—on pain of death. The general wished King Parmodius a peaceful passage. It was the least he could do for a close friend, a comrade-in-arms, and a generous benefactor. 'Those two sons are never around when he needs them—and Famemnon is to inherit—Diwo preserve us.'

'It could be worse,' the chamberlain observed.

'*Worse*? How worse?' the general spat out.

'Attarsiyas might have inherited the throne of Millawanda,' the chamberlain told him. 'Then there really would be chaos.'

'I'm sorry to say, but you're right there,' the general agreed, easing his face into a reluctant smile. 'At least Famemnon is prone to listen to advice when he gets into deep shit—Attarsiyas just plods right through it.'

'You're going to have to make sure Famemnon stays in power. We're relying on your steady hand, General, at the tiller of Millawanda in these difficult coming months. Attarsiyas is ambitious.' The tall chamberlain looked hard at the general trying to fathom if he had registered his concern.

The general's face returned to its deep frown, 'Where are those sons of his?' he asked for the umpteenth time. 'They should have been here by now.... Yes, yes! Don't worry so! I heard what you said. I'm just more vexed with the present crisis than any coming future problems. That's all!'

Just at that moment the racket produced by the chanting *maenads* rose to a pitch and the general's face transformed into fury. He marched over to the nearest and cracked her on the head with the butt of his dagger. She dropped onto the tiled floor as if pole axed. The rest of the devotees stopped dancing and cowered backwards at such a sacrilegious assault. They raised no protest but glared menacingly at the general, who snarled at them, 'I warned you. Either show some respect for the dying—*or get out,*' he shouted. All around him a frightened hush clamped down. People stared first at the general, then at the *maenads,* and then at the dying king—but nobody interfered with his admonitions. Either they were too cowed, or simply

15

agreed with how he dealt with the outrageous "mad women."

A guard hurried into the bedchamber and snapped a silent salute. 'General,' he whispered, 'a squadron of horse has just been reported by the watchtower coming in fast from east—along the sacred way.'

The general's face relaxed. '*At last!*' he exclaimed with relief.

*       *       *

The squadron was led by Famemnon and Attarsiyas, each racing the other over the slippery snow at a reckless pace. At that speed, both were a danger to themselves and their horses. Competitiveness between the two brothers had become far more serious in recent years than was healthy for either. Ever since childhood they had competed, and been encouraged to do so. But there was friendly competition and aggressive destructive competition, and the latter had taken them both to the brink on many an occasion.

They were far out in front of their escort, racing each other to reach Millawanda, not to be at their father's deathbed, but to be the first through the town gates at any cost. A silly thought that he might become the next king, ran through Attarsiyas' mind; if only he could be the first through the gates instead of his brother. He simply could not see himself taking orders from Famemnon. Bowing and scraping to someone he had grown up with, and often bested. Why should *he*, Attarsiyas, play second lyre to his brother, simply because he was born a few years later—a mere quirk of birth. Did his merit count for nothing?

Famemnon was just a horse's head in front in the race and Attarsiyas whipped his steed cruelly to try and restore the lead. Behind them, another of their bodyguards fell of his horse and hit the ground as his horse stumbled and slid on ice, but the two brothers were entirely oblivious of their bodyguard's predicament. The town gates had been ordered thrown open. Famemnon raced up the hill, through the gates, just in front of Attarsiyas, and Attarsiyas howled loud in anguish at having lost the race—and in his own mind, the crown. They galloped through the empty frozen streets towards the citadel, pulling up at the last moment in front of the main stairs leading to the heavy doors. Grooms waited to take the horses. Famemnon jumped down and raced up the few stairs, followed by Attarsiyas.

The general waited out in the *megaron* by the round hearth in the centre of the brightly coloured square room. He tried to distract himself by staring at the bold red and blue patterns on the floor and the large lion painted in front of the throne. The guards in the vestibules sprang to attention as the two princes ran through the entrance making for the bedchamber, but the general rushed to bar their progress with his body, in the hope of restraining the two princes. He knew of their reckless character. Knew of the turmoil and noise that followed in their footsteps. He was determined to quieten them before they approached the deathbed. 'Your *highnesses*! About time you appeared. What kept you?' The general was angry, and the question lacked the usual regard for their princely status.

Attarsiyas glowered at the old soldier for his impertinence and was about to push past but Famemnon put his hand on Attarsiyas' shoulder and restrained him. 'I'm sorry,' Famemnon looked penitent at the general. 'The weather made travel difficult and by the time the news arrived, we were deep in a skirmish with some bandits. We got here as fast as we could.'

This seemed to mollify the general and he lowered his voice. 'He's hung on *desperately* waiting for your arrival. Go to his side! Make your peace with him—and for Diwo's sake, try to restrain your usual commotion! Remember he's dying!'

In anger at the general, Attarsiyas muttered under his breath, 'Interfering old fool,' as he followed his brother. Famemnon had nodded to the general in acceptance of the strictures and led his brother through two more rooms before entering the bedchamber and quietly making their way to the king's bedside. Many tall bronze braziers round the room lit up the solemn scene. The two sons of Parmodius knelt on either side of the bed. The general bade the chanting *maenads* cease their racket, which they did.

Famemnon, being the heir apparent, knelt at the right side of the bed, to be at the dying king's right hand, and Attarsiyas on the left hand side. Parmodius felt their presence and opened his eyelids. His tired bloodshot eyes cast firstly on Famemnon, and lingered there. He stretched out his trembling right hand and placed it on Famemnon' head. 'You are to succeed me,' he said with just enough strength that those present could hear. Then his arm dropped from exhaustion. He next turned to Attarsiyas and saw the anger in his younger son's face. He shook his head and opened his mouth to say something...but a convulsion arrested his voice and death grabbed its chance...making off with the king.

Famemnon stood and gazed sadly at his departed father, reaching over and kissing him for the last time on the forehead, then slowly backed away and looked around at those present. He stretched out his right hand and the general placed the two coins in it. Famemnon turned and gently laid the coins on his father's eyelids. Turning to those present, he raised his arms and all knelt in the presence of their new king—all except Attarsiyas who was still on his knees looking at his dead father. Tears flowed down his cheeks as though from a little boy.

'*All hail Famemnon, rightful king in Millawanda!*' shouted the general in acknowledgement to his new sovereign. Those present joined in solemnly, '*Hail King Famemnon, our sovereign lord!*'

\* \* \*

For the next few days, Attarsiyas followed the rituals and kept himself under supreme control, until Parmodius' funeral pyre had died down. Then, still seething at what he perceived was an obvious injustice to the rightful heir to the crown of Millawanda, namely himself, he began plotting. Tradition had made Famemnon the heir to the throne, but natural justice always favoured the strongest, and that was surely himself. Attarsiyas had always been encouraged to hold a high opinion of himself by the departed Parmodius in an effort to balance the favoured birth of his brother. But somewhere along the twisted path, the princely youth had taken this to mean he would one day be chosen to rule in his brother's stead. In Attarsiyas' twisted mind, he was a cut above his brother, which is why they continually, and more recently, destructively competed with each other.

Subsequent to the funeral, Attarsiyas gathered his band of sycophantic followers and grasping hangers-on, and was seen to gallop out of Millawanda with this group of young firebrands, heading back east, to where he felt more secure amongst his other army cronies.

\* \* \*

The old general marched into the *megaron* audience chamber and found the young king pacing up and down near the circular hearth, fists clenched by his sides. The colourful frescoes on the walls belied the king's mood.

'You sent for me, sire.' The general reached out to warm his hands on this cold day.

The king glared in the general's direction and his face softened. 'Yes, I did. I think we're heading for big trouble. I've just been watching my brother riding out with a bunch of hotheads. We need to talk. I know his companions...

which means the situation is bad. He's surrounded himself with disaffected officers who are itching to stir up trouble—and grab some loot in the process. They will stop at nothing. My brother made it quite clear the other day; he intends to fight me for the crown.'

'Are you sure he's not merely throwing a tantrum, sire?' The general knew the king was right but he wanted to steady the conversation.

'I know him...he *means* it. If it was just between him and me, then I could handle him as I have in the past, but this is different. It isn't simply me and my brother anymore. This is for the crown of Millawanda. This is treason against the state.' The king's agitation increased and his voice rose. '*We will be fighting for our survival.*'

'I fear you're right, sire. This morning sentries found two senior officers dead in their rooms. Murdered; allies of yours, sire. A calculated action designed to be provocative. He's virtually declaring war; civil war that is. Those that rode out with him just now are his close allies, traitors, inside the citadel walls.' The general finished and stood calmly, waiting for the young king to ask for his council.

'You were lucky he didn't come after you in the night,' the king retorted.

'I've been expecting something of the kind, sire, so I've slept in the same quarters as your bodyguards as a precaution.'

'Wise choice! It's time we called the King's Council and involve all those loyal to us. Will you fight for me?'

The question took the general by surprise. He didn't hesitate. 'Just say the word, sire! I served your father faithfully and my sword is yours on my oath.'

'Good! I knew I could rely on you, but I just wanted to hear you say that.' The king's face broke into a smile. 'It reassures me. Now we must clean the stable. All those who are hesitant, need to be added to the manure pile.'

'I agree. Your majesty, your army must be asked to take the oath of allegiance once again.' The general set his face. 'I'm sorry to ask this of seasoned soldiers, but we must know who we can trust. I will dispatch riders to the army throughout Ahhiyawa demanding the senior officers perform the oath, and send written assurances back to Millawanda. Those who refuse will have chosen your brother. We need to eliminate them swiftly.'

'Make out a Proclamation naming Attarsiyas traitor to the crown...include a copy with the dispatch riders. Oh! And ready a dispatch to Mycenae. The Wanaka will need to be kept informed. We may have to call on his help, if things turn nasty.' The young king raised his hand and cocked his ear in the direction of the entrance. 'What's all that noise?' he demanded.

Shouting and the clash of bronze upon bronze was heard near the entrance. The commotion arrested both men in their tracks. The general pulled his sword and stood in front of his sovereign. Bodyguards appeared from the next room fanning out in a protective arc, figure-of-eight shields raised, swords drawn, facing the uproar. The pandemonium and the clash of metal increased as it drew closer.

'Go fetch more soldiers!' the general shouted at one of the bodyguards.

More yelling and screaming emanated from the combat, for it was now clear a battle was in progress at the entrance and the clash of arms increased; then it began to subside and after a few more moments it ceased altogether. The general nodded for the officer in charge of the bodyguards to hold his stance and he cautiously moved towards the entrance to determine the cause of the ruckus.

The next room was clear but the walled courtyard was littered with dead and dying soldiers. Swords and shields lay strewn on the snowy ground. Large patches of red blood splattered the white snow. Some of the enemy were being put to death before the general intervened.

'Stop!' he shouted at a group of palace guards who were engaged in the grisly task of finishing off the wounded. 'We need prisoners.' A number of the enemy had been disarmed and were being held against the far courtyard wall.

'General, sir, would you at least permit us to exterminate *these* dogs?' one soldier asked, readying his sword. His reinforced boars' tusks helmet on at a crazy angle.

'Just hold them there,' the general commanded, zigzagging his way past dead bodies towards the prisoners, careful not to slip on the ice. 'Bind their hands tightly and then bring them to the king. His majesty would like to question them.' The general made his way back to the king, followed by a group of the palace guards prodding the sullen straggling prisoners with their spears. More palace guards appeared and penned them in with swords point.

The sight of the general with prisoners, released the tension in the *megaron*. The king's bodyguards surrounded the prisoners, taking over from the palace guards, hemming the villains in tightly. The king walked over slowly peering at the captives.

'Damn it! I know these men. They rode *in* with me and my brother.' He locked eyes with an older man standing out front. '*Why* have you chosen treason against your *lawful king*? Speak up.'

The man cast his eyes down and hung his head, refusing to answer. He wasn't being stubborn; he simply was at a loss. His commanding officer, Attarsiyas, had given him an order and he'd carried it out. Disobeying a prince of the realm was beyond him.

The king didn't see beyond treachery and grabbed a sword from the nearest bodyguard, running the captive through. 'Disloyal imbecile!' he exclaimed. The rest of the prisoners shrank from the king, fear on their faces. The young king glared at them, 'If you don't speak, the same fate awaits you. I won't tolerate treason. Why have you turned against me?'

One fell on his knees, followed by the others. 'Mercy, your majesty,' they cried in chorus.

'Now it's *your majesty* is it? Only now do you remember who I am!'

One bold young soldier kneeling at the front spoke for all, 'We had no choice, sire. All those that rode in with you, and some others from this palace, stood holding their swords, readying to slaughter us if we'd refused. It was die then, or die later. We throw ourselves on you benevolent mercy, sire.'

The general strode up and took the man by his hair, 'Why didn't you surrender, or even ride out, after Attarsiyas departed? Heh!'

Gasps came from the kneeling captives. The thought hadn't occurred to them. They looked at each other sheepishly. The king nodded to the officer in charge and then turned away. The guards immediately cut the jugulars of the prisoners.

The king said angrily, 'I need men who will *die* for me not men who want to *kill* me.'

\*    \*    \*

Attarsiyas and his rebellious band rode furiously across the wintry landscape, towards the east, to the Lukkan border. Before the old king's demise and on his orders, he and Famemnon had been trying to destroy the Lukkan pirates on Ahhiyawa's southern border; and to a large measure they had succeeded. They'd managed to drive them off Ahhiyawan territory further down the coast past Ura with help from the Ahhiyawan navy. Earlier, the Lukkan governor had used a ruse to get them out of Ura and so they'd holed up in the small port of Bastiniya. Now he was planning to turn things on their head and buy their help against his brother. In effect to turn them into his own mercenary navy. Every little helped. First though, he veered a little northward to provide employment for his pigeons.

What Famemnon had failed to notice while they were battling the Lukkan pirates, or dismissed as usual petulant behaviour, was his brother's frequent absences from the fighting. Attarsiyas would go for days without appearing for briefings or reporting for duty. All the while he was plotting future treason. He knew his father was not long for this world, and he was preparing to acquire the throne. He was busy making alliances, promising advancements, buying commitments, anything to gain allies. If he could now alert his carefully placed co-conspirators amongst the rest of the army, before his brother called them to order, he'd stand a better chance of gaining more recruits to his cause. He'd worked hard to lay the treacherous groundwork for the past two years to ensure he could count on a substantial part of the army when the time came to strike.

Putting together a pigeon communication network, one *not* under the king's control, was a crucial part of his rapid reaction, which was intended to give him the edge over his brother. He'd secreted his pigeon roost in an abandoned farmhouse in a secluded valley, guarded by a small staff of dedicated followers. This was now his destination. It required a half a days detour to reach the pigeon roost, time he could ill afford, but it would ultimately save more time in the balance.

It was a wintry twilight when the band of heavily armed riders reached the farmhouse. They dismounted, cold and frost-bitten.

'Welcome, your majesty,' the commander of the little garrison greeted his future king. 'Come inside; warm yourself.' He led Attarsiyas inside, followed by the other members of the renegade band.

Attarsiyas smiled at the regal greeting and went to the roaring fire in the middle of the room, sitting himself down on a stool, staring into the fire. 'Well! Are you ready?' inquired Attarsiyas.

The young commandant joined him. 'Yes your majesty. All the pigeons have been trained and practised, and are ready for your orders.'

'Good! Then send the agreed messages. Oh! Don't send any to Millawanda. I think that would be a waste of time by now.' A cynical smile played on Attarsiyas' face. 'My parting present to my brother may have alerted him to what I'm about. He will have taken measures.' He chuckled at his own wit. 'I doubt my assassins will have succeeded, but I simply couldn't resist the gesture. They might've....' He shrugged.

The commandant of the little garrison smiled with his chosen "king". 'What about Madduwatta, sire? Do I send the pigeons to him also?'

'Only the pirates! Leave Madduwatta out of it! I'm going to see if I can get the pirates to harass Millawanda. Lukka maybe later—I still have plans for that place.'

# Chapter Three

The scribe felt uncomfortable, 'Your worship, this may be a bit strong?'

'I didn't ask for your opinion!' Madduwatta answered irritably. 'Just write it as I dictate, or I'll find another scribe. Now you've made me lose my train of thought. Read the last bit back to me.'

"In light of your vassal's treachery and my willingness to be of assistance to you, I feel sure you will look favourably on any trade with Lukka. Beware of Famemnon and his treason." It was the latter phrase which had prompted the scribe's unseemly outburst.

'Yes. Just add that I will keep him informed of any further developments by the incoming king of Millawanda. Address it to Wanaka Elektryon in Mycenae. Then give it to me and I'll seal it.' Madduwatta waved the scribe away, scowling in his direction. *What impudence,* flittered through his mind. *I'll have to find another scribe; this one presumes too much. How dare he question my judgement?*

\*   \*   \*

'There you are!' Madduwatta's preferred wife complained, pushing through the massive door, helped by the guard on the inside. 'I never see you anymore. You're children have forgotten what you look like,' she remonstrated.

'Don't exaggerate! You like the jewellery all my hard work brings, don't you?'

Lawaiya pouted demurely seeking to wheedle herself into his attention, past his official duties. She stood behind her spouse, tussling his hair. 'Husband, I need you, your children need you.'

'You have me, but don't fuss so! You're my favourite of all my wives, not just some other harem wench—mother of most of my children.' Madduwatta reached round and pulled her on to his lap. She kissed him hard and he put his arms round Lawaiya's waist. She stroked what was left of his hair while he nibbled at her neck, both getting aroused. Suddenly he pushed her away gently but firmly, forcing her to her feet. 'This won't do. I've more work to do. Tonight wife...tonight! I will send for you.'

She stood looking down at him, unsmiling, trying to show hurt, but she saw the look on his face and retreated, blowing kisses at him seductively. She would get her revenge later.

Madduwatta rose and went out onto the balcony, looking into the far distance—more plots going round in his head. The weather was fine and the sun warming. He'd heard tales of the cold that had settled the north, but that didn't concern him. His ambition was to rule—not as a vassal to the Hittite king, but in his own right. He wanted to be king—no matter where—but a king, with all the power for himself. He had toyed with the idea of grabbing Lukka and setting himself onto its vacant throne, but...the pirates...the pirates wouldn't have that. When Muwas lost the Hittite throne three years ago, the pirates had gained power and virtually taken over Ura. Muwas had supported the Lukkan king. The then king had been forced to flee to Alasiya, and Tudhaliyas had appointed Madduwatta governor of Lukka. The trouble was that recently, the pirates had been pushed out of Ahhiyawa to a port further down the coast; out of Ura with a ruse dreamt up by Daubum, and were now ensconced in Bastiniya, proving to be even more troublesome.

True, the capital Ura was under Madduwatta's control, but the pirate faction still held great sway in parts of

Lukka and they didn't recognise any fealty. Madduwatta had cultivated Parmodius, his neighbour to the east, and in the latest engagements Parmodius' sons had overwhelmed the brigands in some furious fighting, ejecting the pirates from Ahhiyawa. Then again, the old king was on his deathbed, not expected to recover. Madduwatta knew the king's eldest son, Famemnon, would never be amenable to his future plans, and so he was now in the process of undermining his credibility. If the king in Mycenae felt his new vassal was plotting against him, he would make moves to remove him. A risky strategy if he was unmasked. Millawanda could easily oust Madduwatta from Ura—but high stakes called for high risks. Secrecy was of the utmost at this stage...and then there was that troublesome scribe?

He called over the guard at the door. 'The scribe who just left—get rid of him...you know what I mean!'

The guard nodded and left to carry out his Governor's bidding.

# Chapter Four

The tall and muscular Hittite king looked intently with piercing eyes at Mokhat and Palaiyas, his strong jaw reflecting determination. The bright light from the fire danced playfully on their taught faces. Long black slightly curly hair swung forward as Tudhaliyas reached out to the nearby table and scooped up a pair of baked pottery items. He opened his hand and displayed two seals. 'The larger one is my Royal Seal which will identify you to my secret network in the west, telling them you act on my behalf and that they must do as you ask. The second seal is from the Khemet Ambassador to this court, Prince Hapu, and does the same for their secret network. He sends his best wishes and hopes you use it well.'

'But majesty, why would we need such things?' Mokhat interposed, adjusting his position on his seat.

The king's features flashed a fleeting anger at being interrupted, but then he controlled his temper. Breathing deeply, he leaned back on his chair. 'I'd better start at the beginning. A week ago, word arrived from the west that Satipilli had disappeared. That is when I sent for you. Satipilli is the head of my spy network. Recently he'd reported strange goings on in Ura, between my Governor there, and the younger son of the king of Millawanda. The reports suggested a bizarre conspiracy...but then the reports ceased. A pigeon arrived with news that Satipilli was nowhere to be found...and that is contrary to his habits.' Tudhaliyas suddenly looked tired and paused for a while, leaning forward and gazing into the fire. He drew breath and resumed, 'That's it. I can feel something is wrong—something serious. I can't send anyone who is part of

Satipilli's network because I don't know how far it's been compromised. If *they* can disappear my best agent, then the rest of the undercover network must be compromised. That's why I sent for you. I have to find out the truth of what's happened to my chief spy. The western provinces are delicately balanced with Arzawa and Zapislla seeking to expand at their neighbour's expense, and Lukka always wheedling for more autonomy. Ahhiyawa, on the other hand, has always been both friendly and predatory. When Parmodius was on the throne—I could rely on his friendship, but now... I'm informed his two sons are at loggerheads and there may be trouble. I need to know where that's going to end. This is of vital importance. Peace is balanced on a knife's edge in that region and I need good intelligence if I'm to act rationally. If I have to send troops to the west, you may be sure it will rekindle Mittani interest, and that will affect the Kaska. Your brother has already realised this. Satipilli's mission was crucial for both our realms—now he's completely vanished...nowhere to be found at all. I must know what's happened. What did he find out that warranted his disappearance. Who disappeared him? I'm hoping he's just out of touch—but I have to plan for the worst. Who's outwitted my chief spy? What's going on out there that I'm not supposed to know? I need answers to all these questions—and I can't use my own undercover network. It's probably been exposed. That's why I need fresh faces—faces *I* can trust. I need to know why he's vanished. I fear the worst. If I don't stem this disaster, I may as well say goodbye to the western Hittite interests. You're my only hope. Will you help me?'

Mokhat looked questioningly at Palaiyas, seeking guidance from his friend and companion. Both their lives would be under threat and they would have to rely heavily on each other. Both needed to be of one mind on this.

Palaiyas returned the look and slowly nodded.

Mokhat straightened on his chair and breathed slowly. 'We will go, sire, and determine the truth of the matter.' He took the proffered seals from the king's outstretched hand. 'Communication will have to be by pigeon. I assume you have them in place where we're going.'

The king smiled. 'Rest assured they're in place and at your disposal. One more thing! Although Governor Madduwatta may be conspiring with the Ahhiyawans, he is *my* vassal, and supposed to be loyal to me, so when you get there I would treat him as an ally and call on him to assist you in your task. Be cautious of this scheming governor, but get him to help you if you need it. If he's reluctant in any way, that should make you weary, but make it *clear* that you speak on *my* behalf. That should do the trick.' Tudhaliyas stopped, looking momentarily weary, then finished with, 'Well, thank you both. That's lifted a load off my shoulders. When you leave, it would be better if you slipped out quietly. Spies are everywhere! To that end we have a couple of yellow tunics. In those Kaska outfits you stick out like a couple of wolves in a goat herd. We thought it best if you were disguised as a couple of ordinary soldiers and left Hattusas with a squadron of cavalry heading west. A Kaska priest and an Ahhiyawan soldier—far too conspicuous. When you're a good distance from the capital, we have prepared a similar Ahhiyawan outfit for you Prince Mokhat. Two Ahhiyawan soldiers going back to Ahhiyawa won't be noticed so much.' The king stood, prompting his guests to do likewise. 'Now, I've prepared a feast on your behalf and you look as if you could use some warm food.' He led the way next-door where a large table was laid with all sorts of steaming meat, bread, and vegetables. The queen sat on a couch, toying with some dates, and turned as the guests entered.

Mokhat immediately went and bowed before Nikal. 'It's a pleasure to see you so well, my lady.'

Nikal sat demurely, dressed in colourful fine cottons, looking like the Queen she was. 'Prince Mokhat. I've been so offended that you have not visited for so long.' She tried to look offended with those big brown eyes, but failed utterly, and instead, a broad smile spread on her attractive angular face. Sweeping her long brown hair backwards, she lifted her head to look at Mokhat. Then turned to Palaiyas, 'Please, Prince Palaiyas. Won't you come and pay your respects?'

Palaiyas looked startled at being addressed by his correct title. He had been holding back, standing with the king. Now he moved forward and gently took Nikal's hand, bowing. 'Your majesty. I see my secret is out and I commend *your* spy network.'

'You're not offended are you? We only found out recently of your lineage. Your father has been making inquiries...even this far. The king at Tiryns seeks reassurance that you are alive.'

Again this took Palaiyas by surprise. He made an effort to disguise his shock. 'I'm sorry my family's affairs have intruded this far east. Now we're going to Millawanda, I will be in a position to deal with it.'

'Then you've taken the commission?' Nikal queried.

Mokhat and Palaiyas looked at each other, and nodded in unison.

'I'm so pleased,' she told them. 'Tudhaliyas thought you might refuse. It will lift the burden from him. He's been so worried over this state of affairs.' Then she sighed, 'It's all of a hundred and forty seven leagues to Millawanda.' She looked at Palaiyas, 'but then you know that, don't you?' She looked disconsolate and asked them, 'When do you leave?'

The king came and sat by his queen. 'In the morning,' the king told her. He put his arm around Nikal, in an effort to console her; then smiled and said, 'But tonight we dine and make merry.' Tudhaliyas waved at a group of musicians barely visible at the far end of the room.

A gentle music emanating from string and woodwind flowed across the hall. Fruit was placed on the table and wine was being poured as they sat down.

Mokhat and Palaiyas glanced appreciatively at the banquet and both couldn't help salivating in anticipation. A large variety of roast meats, bowls of peas and beans lay spread before them. Unleavened bread and plates of pancakes. Figs, apples, apricot, pomegranates, and medlars. They had travelled far through the wintry landscape and were bone tired. However, they beamed appreciatively at all the food that was available to them.

\*   \*   \*

The morning was crisp with an overnight layer of snow covering the palace courtyard. In the stable, the squadron was readying to go out on patrol into the west with its two new recruits. The horses had good blankets over them as did the soldiers. Mokhat and Palaiyas were secreted in the middle of the column as the squadron commander led his troop out under the narrow corbelled arches of the citadel gates. Predawn, two by two they trotted through the quiet narrow streets down to the Lion Gate. There, the squadron commander exchanged words with the captain of the gate and the night gate was unsealed. The squadron was allowed to pursue their bearing to the south, parallel with the rising dawn.

Mid morning they swung west, hoping the deception had worked. Before long, after some hard riding, they traversed an ice encrusted wooden bridge crossing a minor tributary of the Marassantiya River with no sign of anyone following. Thereon, the squadron commander eased the pace allowing the horses to recover. A while later, the squadron stopped for a morning break, sheltering under bluff from the biting wind.

'I think we managed that without letting the cat out of the sack,' Mokhat jested with Palaiyas as they sat wrapped in blankets round a fire, drinking a herbal decoction.

'What cat? Did you bring a cat with you?' Palaiyas joined in the banter.

'I think you're right, highness,' the squadron commander clipped in. 'Nobody saw us leave. Not that early.'

'No disrespect, my friend, but spies don't sleep all that well,' Palaiyas told him. 'They learn to sleep with one eye open. I'll believe we're in the clear when we reach Millawanda without any trouble. Even then...'

Mokhat nodded and told the commander more kindly, 'I fear my companion is right. This matter is serious, and it does take a special type of person to infiltrate another's realm. They can't afford to miss a trick. They will have had someone watching the exit gates and taken note of an unscheduled squadron leaving. I would have, had I been assigned to that role.

'It makes me thankful that I've this simple job of running a squadron,' the jovial commander laughed. 'I thought my life was full of twists and turns, yet here you tell me that I've got it easy.'

Mokhat raised his bronze mug in mock salute, 'Not exactly easy, but certainly less stressful. Let us drink to less stress...'

'To less stress,' Palaiyas and the commander both joined in.

Rising to his feet, the commander prompted, 'And now your highnesses, I must urge we continue our journey.'

The rest of the squadron doused the fires and remounted. The squadron commander picked up the pace and they rode hard throughout the whole day so that by evening they were able to make camp in a forest clearing for the night, utterly exhausted. By mid afternoon of the next day, they had come to the main Marassantiya River, roaring ever downwards to the Black Sea through the snow swept countryside. To date the journey had been uneventful, but that was just about to change.

Mokhat couldn't contain the shock of seeing the downed bridge. 'Curse this for bad luck,' he exploded. 'Now what? How are we to cross?'

The commanding officer stared at the wreckage of the destroyed bridge and scratched his head. 'Can't understand it. The reason I brought you to this bridge is because it has never been shattered in my lifetime—even during the winter rains. It's one of the strongest on the river. No matter how formidable the floodwaters are, this bridge has always been able to withstand them. But look, two whole spans have gone. Blessed me if I know what to do? The next bridge is one and a half days ride downriver. If this is down, then the one downriver is probably down as well.'

Palaiyas pointed at a group of people on the other side and then waved at them. They waved back frantically, almost desperately. 'There's a couple of wagons stranded over there. What about cutting some timber and spanning the gaps?' he suggested to the commander.

The commander looked at his troop and made a decision. 'By the gods, you're right. It's the only way we'll make the crossing. The thirty or so cavalry were ordered to dismount, tether their steeds, and find timber to cut down. A little further down there were quite a few sturdy trees on their side of the riverbank and the soldiers lay into them with gusto. Physical work gave them warmth from the chilling winds of winter. The cutters cut, whilst the strippers cleaned the logs. Horses were used to drag the timber to the bridge, and within a couple of hours, enough was at the riverbank to begin the process of spanning the first break.

Mokhat advised, 'There's little point in risking your men's lives by having someone swim to the middle pier as per usual construction. I propose we lower the first log onto the middle pier with a rope. Tie the rope to the far end of the log and stand it up; find a boulder to jamb this end firm, then lower it by using your men to the middle pier, then we can lash them together as we go. The wind isn't too bad. Let's hope they don't bounce into the river. If we go easy, it might work.'

'Sounds feasible; I'm willing to give it a try,' agreed the senior officer.

A log was stood upright and a number of soldiers held a long rope, lowering the log gently as they could to the middle pier. 'We don't have enough rope to do that with each log,' reported the warrant officer in charge.

'Send one of your men across the log we've just dropped—get him to untie the rope and bring it back. We'll use the same rope over and over. As the span gets wider, it'll be easier with every log we put in place,' Mokhat counselled.

Palaiyas wanted to be in the thick of it. 'I'll go. It should be enough for me to walk across to the middle pier.'

'No, your highness! One of *my* men will do that. No sense risking the mission at this early stage.' The commandant had an imploring look on his face which Palaiyas couldn't argue with.

'As you wish,' Palaiyas conceded.

The selected soldier scrambled gingerly across the log and undid the rope at the other end. When he returned, the next log was dropped in place, but it bounced a little sideways. The group on the rope pulled it into position. 'Steady lads, go easy, and be accurate,' encouraged the warrant officer.

Log after log was positioned in this manner, until ten logs had been laid across to the middle pier. The logs were then lashed together as best they could, some with strips of cloth, others with sinewy branches.

The squadron commander walked across, head down against the lifting wind, and pronounced his satisfaction with a job well done. Mokhat and Palaiyas joined him. 'Now for the final span,' the commander told them. 'Right lads, bring the logs over, and let's drop the next one in place. Let's hope this holds.'

The next log just barely spanned the gap sitting on the edge of the bricks of the middle pier. They pushed as hard as was possible to give it a better grip, eventually pushing it onto the far span. The same brave soldier scurried across and untied the rope, bringing it back for the next log. There followed more logs in the same manner, until finally, the warrant officer stood on the other side of the river, grinning. 'Well done!' shouted the commander to all his soldiers. 'I'm proud of you all.'

It was precarious and impermanent arrangement, but would do for the mean time until a proper repair was put in place.

'Well, your highnesses. That's the best I can do,' offered the commander. 'I don't know if your horses will cross, but at least you'll be able to. If you wait until the wind dies down—it'll make it easier. This is as far as my king ordered me to take you. Once I see you safely on the other side, I'm ordered to return to the capital. The warrant officer will bring your pack-horse across. I wish you well and a safe journey.'

They waited until the wind calmed somewhat and then Palaiyas tore a strip of rag from his kilt and tied it round his horse's eyes, talking ever so gently to the horse all the time. Then he led the horse to the first timber span of the bridge and gently and gingerly walked him out to the middle pier; stopped there for an instant and finally led him over the final timber span to the other side of the river.

Mokhat waited until Palaiyas was safely across, then he covered the eyes of his own horse and followed Palaiyas. The burly warrant officer tagged on behind Mokhat with the equally blinded pack-horse. When they arrived safely on the other side the non-com handed the reins to Mokhat. 'I'll report the bridge down to the maintenance people when I get back. I wish you well once more and a safe journey.' He then retraced his footsteps leading back a number of those poor souls who had been waiting to cross. Both Mokhat and Palaiyas waved back to the departing soldiers, watching them mount and ride back towards Hattusas.

A wail rose from those at the nearby wagons. An argument had erupted between the two drivers and fists were being used. What looked like a burly bearded shepherd intervened between the two drivers with his crook, as Mokhat and Palaiyas watched in astonishment.

'Shall we break it up?' Mokhat invited.

'What for? That shepherd fellow looks like he's dealing with it. We'd better mind our own business. There'll be plenty of time to look for trouble later on.' Palaiyas looked suspiciously at the shepherd. 'Don't like the look of that fellow,' he ventured. 'When he thinks we're not looking, he gives us a mean glare as if he would happily kill us. Where's his flock?'

Mokhat shrugged and reminded his companion, 'We have a long way to go.' Mokhat was still inclined to give others the benefit of the doubt. 'Best mount-up and keep going. We might make Ullama by nightfall. I'll take the pack-horse.' Even now, the priest in him had not become over cynical, and he always endeavoured to give others the benefit of the doubt. He'd seen the sly looks the shepherd gave them, but was prone to see it as an innocent stare, rather than that of malevolent intent.

Some time later near dusk, in a wooded area just before they reached Ullama, both travellers changed their costumes into the thoughtfully provided Ahhiyawan uniforms, concealed on the pack-horse. This done, two freshly metamorphosed Ahhiyawan soldiers emerged.

Palaiyas smiled at Mokhat's transformation. 'You look the picture of a new recruit to our army,' he joked.

Mokhat was scratching at his left greave where it chafed him. 'We've changed too early. This'll get us into more trouble this far east.'

'Trust me!' Palaiyas was confident. 'It'll throw off any followers. The Ahhiyawans are respected as fighters. We'll have less trouble dressed in these uniforms.'

The two figure-of-eight shields were packed in such a way as to disguise their shape and were left on the pack-horse.

'Why the tusk-boar on the helmets?' asked Mokhat as they left the tree line, more for the sake of conversation than information.

Palaiyas tut-tuted. 'What does it say about a soldier if he can display on his helmet so many trophies from one of the fiercest of beasts to roam the wilds? I would have thought it was self explanatory!'

The light began to fade by the time they came to the closed gates of Ullama and they were challenged aggressively by the sentries from above. 'Who goes there?' yelled down the officer in charge.

The two Ahhiyawan soldiers neared the gate. 'Just two weary soldiers looking for food and a bed for the night,' responded Palaiyas as innocently as he could.

When the sentries spied the uniforms, they pointed their bows menacingly at the strangers.

'There's no need for that!' Palaiyas tried to look and sound offended. 'We mean you no harm. How can two tired soldiers be a threat to you?'

'Get off your horses. Come forward!' shouted the gate commander. Then he shouted inside, 'Open the gates!' His head disappeared, and a little later he reappeared at the gates.

Both of the duo did as ordered and led their horses to the officer in charge. Mokhat pulled out the royal seal and

39

pushed it at the officer's face. 'Do you recognise this?' he asked quietly.

'What is it?' the officer queried, taking it in his hand for closer scrutiny. Suddenly realising what it was he looked startled. Then he shouted, 'Where did you get that?'

Mokhat looked calmly at the officer and said, 'From his majesty in Hattusas. He placed it in my hand just two days ago and bid me speak in his name. He commands his subjects to help us in anyway we ask of them. Are you going to offend his majesty by disobeying his wishes?'

From hostility to surprise…the officer made an effort to stand to attention. 'No sir! I'm in his majesty's service… *and yours to command.*'

'Stand easy. No need to go overboard,' Mokhat calmed the officer. 'Now, what do you say to some grub, and a bed for the night, heh? And I shouldn't need to mention this, but keep the royal seal just between us two, understand?'

'My lips are sealed. I haven't seen anything, I promise you.' The officer winked at Mokhat, and led the way briskly inside.

# Chapter Five

'**H**ave we heard from Mycenae yet?' Famemnon demanded of his intelligence officer.

The man stood with his head bowed before his sovereign and shook his head, 'No sire! Odd as it may seem, not a word. They're keeping strangely quiet. I've sent a number of messages by various means—and we've had no reply.'

'Yes, that is odd,' agreed the king. 'Well, keep trying. See if you can find out if Attarsiyas might have something to do with this break in communications.'

'Yes, your majesty.' The officer sensed the interview was over and backed away.

Famemnon lifted his right hand, and with a flick of the wrist, called the next one waiting for an audience in the queue to approach. It happened to be the chief priest of the Temple of Atana Potnia. 'Your Holiness, you should have come to me without waiting. I apologise on behalf of my servants. Next time I will give orders for you to have priority.'

The old priest had waited patiently in the queue, since he still was unsure of this new young king. The story of the treatment of Diwo's *maenads* at the old king's deathbed had shocked the priestly cast. They feared that the new king might not be as amenable as the old king was to the ancient religion. Caution was always wiser than making demands in these unsettled conditions.

'Your majesty, I have come to offer my services in this time of ordeal for our city, and for Ahhiyawa. May I suggest we perform a public sacrifice in the Western Agora in front of the assembled citizens as an act of propitiation, followed by an augury to ascertain the outcome of the coming struggle?' The priest lowered his voice, 'I assure you it will be favourable to you.'

A silent chuckle attempted to rise inside Famemnon at this offer, but he suppressed it and instead looked down kindly at the old priest for his attempt to fix the augury. *He's only trying to help me*, he thought. *And help himself in the process, no doubt.* 'You know, you might just have something there. An official confirmation that the gods are on our side would undeniably help our cause. You arrange it and inform me of the time.' Famemnon put his right hand on the old priest's left arm and gently squeezed to show his appreciation. The royal touch should close the bond between them.

Startled, but pleased that the king had laid his hand on him; the priest smiled and said, 'Your majesty, it would be wise to do this as soon as possible. From outside the city, we hear that things are not going to well. I will have my priests set up a big altar in the agora, just outside our temple, for all to see. If you could find time tomorrow, we should perform the sacrifice at noon. That will give my people time to organize the ceremony, and give the people time to attend.'

'So be it. Expect me tomorrow then.' And Famemnon bowed his head gently to show respect for the old priest, and to visibly show those present that the priest had his respect.

The old priest backed away, and went to organise his temple for the next day, pleased at how this audience had turned out.

At the entrance to the audience chamber a small commotion could be heard—then a number of high ranking officers came into view. They saluted the king, who bade them approach. The group was lead by the old general, the chief of his army.

'Your majesty, we have just received some urgent news which you need to be acquainted with.' General Palossos looked grave and his face was a little red, as if he'd been running. His big frame seemed to give a gentle shudder as he attempted to calm himself. 'If I may speak in quiet with your majesty.'

Famemnon grew worried at this unusual behaviour from someone he always expected to be calm and controlled. He took the general's arm and walked him into a corner out of hearing of the others. 'Well, what's happened?' he asked, fearing the worst.

'The fleet, your majesty. It's gone over to Attarsiyas. All of it! We still don't know the reason, but a number of small boats are arriving in the Lion Harbour carrying many wounded and injured; those that refused to change sides are telling stories of executions and mutilations by the renegades. They claim all the officers went over to Attarsiyas first, and then ordered their men to swear loyalty to him. When some refused, that's when the executions began. I've just rushed up from the harbour to inform you.' The general lowered his voice even more, 'It's a disaster, your majesty. They'll set up a blockade of Millawanda, and that will be the end of our trade with the outside world.' The general finished, and looked expectantly at the young king.

Famemnon stood motionless, frowning for a while, seemingly deep in thought, then said, 'So, general, this makes it vital that we make an extra effort to conclude this conflict as soon as possible. How are our respective forces positioned? Can we bring this to one major battle? Or do you suggest trying to wipe out Attarsiyas' groups with calculated raids. Any ideas?'

'Sire, I'm of the opinion that it's too late for raids. It would take too long. We don't have the time. Attarsiyas is getting stronger by the moment,' replied the general. 'At the same time....' he didn't manage to finish. A courier rushed into the audience chamber waving in their direction in a most undisciplined manner. The general was facing in that direction and stopped mid sentence in fury. '*Over here, you scoundrel*! How *dare* you burst in like that…?'

The young soldier rushed over to where they stood, and fell on his knees. 'I beg the general's pardon…but this news is *really* urgent.'

'Alright! Get up, let's hear it. It had better be important.' The general had softened, seeing it may be pertinent to what he was discussing with the king.

'Sire, general, troops in ships are on the way from the Wanax of Mycenae…to support the rebels. They've been sent from the garrison on Keftiu. My captain thought you should know right away. This came in just now via a pigeon message from someone we trust.' The poor young fellow looked troubled; he seemed to holding back a question. It was a question which he didn't voice, but it was written on his face. What now?

The general's features dropped, in despair. 'First the fleet and now Mycenae has abandoned us. How could this be?' He motioned for the courier to depart and turned back to the king.

The king's expression looked angry but determined.

'Sire,' the general continued, 'we know where Attarsiyas is.' The old general was getting angry as well. 'As I was about to suggest before we were interrupted. He's holed up in Phadhiya, near the Lukkan border. That's our latest intelligence. We have to send everyone we have, every soldier we can muster, and engage him as quickly as we can. In open battle we may yet be able to rescue this situation. If we wait, we will loose everything. Events are now so finely balanced, that in a short time, even a day, it will all turn in the rebel's favour. Give the order, and I will get the army on the move at daybreak tomorrow. We'll need to send out riders to all the scattered units to converge on Phadhiya. The rest we'll summon by pigeon post. We must hurry.' The general stood waiting for the king's decision.

Famemnon nodded. 'By the lord Diwo, you're right. Get the army mobilised. We go at dusk tomorrow. But I do have a suggestion. Bring as many of the garrison as is safe to the West Agora for daybreak. The king lowered his voice to a whisper, 'Then send a message to the high priest that it must be at dawn. He'll understand. The high priest is to perform a sacrifice, and an augury that he promises will be beneficial to our cause.'

The general raised his eyebrows and nodded. 'It will be done, your majesty. Till tomorrow!'

*     *     *

Daybreak found the garrison assemble in the large west agora waiting for the priests to do the auguries. The sacrifice had gone down well, and the aura of the gathering seemed pensive but positive. The king stood by the priest's side with the sacrificed calf laying on the altar, its jugular spouting blood into bowl.

The high priest quickly sliced open the calf's abdomen lengthwise, then laying aside the knife, thrust both his hands inside. Blood drenched the white tablecloth. He felt around inside the calf's abdomen and stopped for a moment, then went on as if he were calculating something. 'Ah!' Sighed the priest. He felt around some more, before extracting the liver, holding it up for all to see. 'The auspices are favourable,' he intoned solemnly but loudly. 'The entrails were of a good length and the colour of the liver is deep, as all here can see,' and he held the liver higher in his blood soaked hands. 'The time is propitious,' he continued, 'and the outcome of the coming battle favourable to you.' He motioned the liver in their direction.

The crowd of soldiers seemed pleased to hear this. A bit of friendly jostling went through the ranks as they became impatient to be off and succeed, as predicted by the high priest of the temple of Atana Potnia. An abrupt roar of

45

approval burst from the gathering, followed by them calling out the king's name, '*Famemnon, Famemnon, Famemnon ...Hurrah!*'

*   *   *

'Sire, we've received a message from the Wanax in Mycenae.' The courier was at the door, bursting with enthusiasm.

Attarsiyas sat comfortably on a couch, and he raised his hand for the man to approach.

The courier hurried over and wouldn't contain himself. 'Sire, the Wanax of Mycenae is sending a force to support us, all the way from the garrison on Keftiu.' He looked pleased, and seemed very young.

'Take a deep breath and tell me again,' Attarsiyas ordered.

The courier did as he was bid, breathed deeply, and composed himself. 'The message just arrived by another courier, from the coast, sire. He's almost dead with fatigue; otherwise he would be here himself. So the officer sent me to tell your majesty.'

'Is that it?' Attarsiyas was pleased. 'Any idea how many and when they'll arrive?' he inquired.

'That's all I have, sire.' The courier was a bit surprised that the king wasn't more joyful at the news.

'Thank you, you can go.'

The courier backed away and left. Attarsiyas had managed to occupy the small town of Phadhiya, to the southeast of Millawanda, not far from the Lukkan border, and was using the biggest villa of the town as his personal quarters and HQ. Naturally, the owner wasn't consulted for permission. He'd thought of inviting Madduwatta over for a talk, but wasn't sure if it was a good idea. He didn't trust him, and others had advised him to wait, until he was undisputed king before talking to him. Now this news from

Keftiu was just what he needed to hear. It was all looking good. He congratulated himself for the planning he'd put into his scheming beforehand. He'd started when he'd realised that he wouldn't naturally inherit the throne on the death of their father, although he thought he was the more deserving of the two, the cleverer one. It was then that he began cultivating various factions of the army, bribing various officers with promises. Arranging plans for after his father's demise, plans that were now coming into fruition.

An aide came through the door, past the sentries, and waited to be called to attend the king. Attarsiyas noticed him and motioned him to step forward.

'Sire,' bowed the aide, 'we have emissary from Arzawa who has just arrived from Apasa, and wishes an audience with you. Would you like to see him?'

Well now, that's interesting, thought the king. I wonder what our neighbour to the north wants from me. 'Yes, show him in, but station two guards at his back, just in case he's feeling in any way belligerent.

The emissary came in and marched forward towards Attarsiyas, bowing his head as he approached. 'Sire, I bring greetings from King Kupanta-Kurunta of Arzawa, and he sends his condolences on the death of your beloved father. He also sends his felicitations on your elevation to the throne of Ahhiyawa. He entreats me to inquire whether he can render any service to you in your struggle with the rebels in Millawanda? Anything that may put a speedy end to their mutiny.' It was said with not a hint of irony.

Attarsiyas struggled to keep a straight face. 'We thank our neighbour to the north, for his felicitations, and ask what he had in mind?'

'I am commanded to offer you arms, horses, and even troops if you so desire. My king wishes to be a friendly neighbour to you, and has a deep respect for your majesty.' The emissary clearly was serious.

'That is most welcome news,' Attarsiyas responded, 'but I believe we have enough troops to be going on with. The offer of horses and arms, however, I do believe I will accept. How much of this can you provide?'

'As of the moment, I am to offer to provide equipment for a thousand men, and more should you require it later.' The emissary stood waiting, completely serious with this offer.

Although Attarsiyas had not asked for any aid, it would be a foolish king that spurned such an offer. Was there a catch to it? What did he want in return? 'Tell your king that we will gladly accept the offer. But tell me, did king Kupanta-Kurunta ask for anything in return?'

'No sire,' the emissary looked surprised. 'He simply asks that you be a good friend to him when your troubles are over.'

'Well, you may return to your king, and assure him that we note his well wishes, and as of today, we will be a staunch friend to him.' Attarsiyas implied that the audience was over, at which the emissary bowed deeply, and backed away.

# Chapter Six

'**W**hat's that smoke, there...., in the distance,' Madduwatta demanded of his counsellor while they were standing on a balcony. He pointed at the distant thin black trail of smoke snaking skywards. 'Looks like its coming from somewhere near the town square.'

'My lord, we've just had a report that some malcontents are burning an effigy of you—out in the open. They are protesting at the taxes you've imposed, my lord.' The counsellor looked apprehensively at Madduwatta, knowing his violent temper.

'And what are *you* doing about it?' the Governor glared at his minion with contempt.

'I....I...came to report this to you, my lord.' The counsellor began to cower in front of his tormentor.

'*You imbecile!* Send some soldiers down there. Arrest the lot of them, and throw them in the deepest dungeons. Do I have to tell you everything? Show some initiative.' Madduwatta was beginning to get into a rage.

'Ye-e-s, my lord,' the counsellor stammered, backing out rapidly, almost falling over. He turned and rushed out of sight to carry out his masters bidding.

*That's a nice start to the day,* fumed Madduwatta to himself. *That bunch of miserable whiners didn't come up with that idea by themselves. Why can't they just pay the damn taxes as I ordered them to? The bloody pirates put them up to it—stirring up trouble again.*

The pirate faction still held great sway in parts of Lukka and had trouble makers throughout the port city of Ura. They were ensconced further down the coast after the battles with the two brothers, Famemnon and Attarsiyas, but resented being ousted from Ura, resented Madduwatta cutting off all supplies to the pirates. They were trying their utmost to make life difficult for the new Governor—and it helped them that this upstart of a Governor had made peoples lives insufferable by tripling the taxes. The general population hated him and were actively plotting to get rid of him. The pirates were only too willing to help stir them up.

Earlier, Madduwatta had sent for his Chief of Staff, Vasanitti, who now approached him as requested. 'Well general,' Madduwatta said gruffly as the big man faced him. 'How goes the preparations? Are we ready for the campaign?'

'Almost, my lord,' replied the general, standing stiffly. 'Just a few snags to straighten out. Too many raw recruits and not enough time to train them properly. Otherwise we're ready to go the moment you give the word.'

'How is the fresh contingent integrating? Any problems?'

'All goes well, my lord. They are well supplied and eager to go. A bit of rivalry, as you might expect, but nothing that's out of hand.'

'What's the intelligence? Do the Arzawans suspect anything?' Madduwatta was hoping for complete surprise. He had cooked up some spurious bit of Arzawan incursion on Lukka as a pretext for this attack on Kupanta-Kurunta's kingdom, and it was now time to carry the underhand plot to its violent conclusion. All was ready—at least Madduwatta hoped it was.

General Visanitti was confident but cautious. 'As far as we can tell,' the general continued, 'the Arzawans are focussed on Ahhiyawa and the burgeoning civil war there. We'll be coming through Zapislla, from the east, while they are concentrating their forces on the south. We will have a small gap of opportunity, before they realise what's happening. Then all hell will break loose.'

'And general, are you prepared for that hell?' Madduwatta smiled, and began to relax after the anger. It helped that he liked his general. His general was tall, broad shouldered, and of a dark complexion. He was intelligent and above all, at least Madduwatta thought so, loyal to his lord and master. He had been with Madduwatta for nigh on ten years, and in all that time, it was largely due to General Visanitti that Madduwatta was where he was today. 'Right, general, wait for my order. We start in a week; that should give you time to straighten the recruits out. It will take us about three days to get into position before the full assault. Let's pray that King Kupanta-Kurunta stays distracted by the Ahhiyawan civil war.'

The general stiffened some more, if that were possible. 'Yes, my lord. The week will give me time to get everything in trim. May the god of war look kindly upon this venture! I will lead the troops out and send back courier reports as and when we make progress. Thank you, my lord.' He snapped round, and marched off to make hell on earth.

Madduwatta watched him go, then turned and sauntered off in the direction of the harem.

\*     \*     \*

'My lord!' called a voice from behind the hurrying Governor.

Madduwatta turned in vexation, intent on bawling out the upstart who interrupted his fantasies. He stopped, and smiled instead. It was his chief spy; someone even nastier than himself. 'Yes, Daubum! What can I do for you?'

'I have disquieting news. Tudhaliyas has sent two agents to Millawanda to look for Satipilli. They're on their way now. We don't know who they are yet, but we're working on it. I have one of my men tracking them.'

'Hmm! Yes, that could be a problem. I had word this morning via the pigeons from the Hatti king, and he commands me to help them whenever I can. He *commands* me—and you know what he can do with his commands.' Madduwatta almost spat out the last sentence. 'This is my command to you—make sure you disrupt their journey. Don't do anything obvious, but impede them at every turn. Oh, and don't get caught. If by some bad luck, they actually get here, we may have to help them, or the Hatti king could turn nasty. You have my orders.' Madduwatta was about to turn and continue on his previous route, when Daubum called him again.

'One more item for you, my lord. Parmodius, the old king is dead and Famemnon is now on the throne.'

Madduwatta couldn't contain himself and interrupted, 'Well...well. That may be bad new for us because....' he didn't manage to finish because of the look of exasperation on his spies face.

'If you would allow me to finish, my lord, I was about to tell you that the younger brother, Attarsiyas, has disputed his brother's right to sit on that throne, and it look very much like a civil war has broken out. My assessment is that the young upstart is likely to win. More of the army seems to be abandoning the true king and going over to the upstart.'

'Have you finished?' Madduwatta asked.

'Yes, my lord. That's it.'

'Right, that last bit of information was most useful. If Attarsiyas wins, then there is a chance that I could do a deal with him.' Madduwatta stood in thought for a while, forgetting his spy was standing there. 'Well, what are you waiting for? Go and deal with those Hatti agents as per my instructions, and make *sure* of them, do you hear.' The last bit of news from Ahhiyawa had unsettled him.

'Yes, my lord,' came the voice of the spy. 'It will be done.'

# Chapter Seven

There had been a fresh snow fall over night bringing in a morning that was fresh and crisp. The heavy bulbous clouds had emptied and were gone bringing in calmer weather. As the two companions left through the open gates of Ullama, both riders waved a fond farewell to the officer above the gate, who on the preceding evening, had been so wary of them. The previous night, they had gently inquired of this officer if he'd seen any sign of Satipilli, and been told that he hadn't any idea of who he was. Mokhat had left it at that, not wanting to arouse any further interest.

The two Ahhiyawan soldiers, wrapped in fur cloaks, looked guardedly in all directions, trying to discern whether anybody was about that early in the morning. The sun had just risen in the east, and both sought to leave the city before the rest of the inhabitants were awake—in effect, trying to sneak out.

Palaiyas squinted into the vastness and poked Mokhat in the left arm with his fist, pointing into the distance on the left. 'Are my eyes playing tricks, or is that dark spot over there a person?'

'I'm afraid your eyes are being true, and yes, I can see the dot as well. Looks like someone is watching the gate.' Mokhat's frown was its own statement. 'Must be pressing for them to be out this early. It can only be for us, surely. The question is—is it friend or foe?'

'To be on the safe side, we must assume it's foe. What do you want to do about it?' A gritty look set onto Palaiyas' face. 'We can go along for a while, and then set an ambush for this fanatical dawn watcher—what say you?'

They rode along for a little way while Mokhat thought the proposition over. 'Let's see how this goes. If we get a chance, we should take him, but I'm for pressing on. Besides, an ambush means waiting in the cold, and I'm not that eager to sit in the snow and get frozen.'

Palaiyas was resigned to this decision, but somewhat disappointed. 'Thanks to that kindly officer, we have warm fur wraps and fur leggings. That should keep us warm. But, it's your call. I warn you now, though, if I get a chance, I'll *have* him. He's bound to make a mistake sooner of later.'

The landscape was exhilarating in its whiteness and both riders spurred on their mounts into the morning freshness. It seemed that the land was hilly and endless and without life, which was unusual for any part of the country. The winds had been fierce, bitter and icy, and the snows deep with blizzards covering the mountains, fields and roads as they climbed ever higher onto the high plateau. They had trouble discerning the road at times. Normally there were always people on the roads. Caravans plying their trade. Peasants working the fields. It was curious to see such a void, such a lack of life. This was a winter that would go down as the worst in memory. People were keeping their heads down and staying indoors, waiting for warmer weather to arrive.

Some time later into the morning as they were riding through a valley, Mokhat and Palaiyas came across a bizarre cluster by the side of the road. A group of people had gathered into a large huddle in an attempt to keep warm, but the temperatures had overwhelmed them and they had frozen to death in the snow. It was difficult to detect how many there were, but it looked like the group was ten or more. A couple of smaller outlines suggested there were children among them.

'So close to the city, as well. Another five leagues and they would have been safe. Such a shame and such a waste,' commented Mokhat.

'Such is life,' Palaiyas offered angrily. 'We have to fight with every breath we take. There are no free rides in this life. We Ahhiyawans are taught from childhood to fight hard and fight to win. Life isn't fair and nobody should be telling you otherwise.' Palaiyas was venting his anger in the only way he knew. 'When you were born, you didn't hear the midwife tell you life was fair, did you? Well, then you have to assume it isn't. Those poor individuals have learnt that the hard way.'

'Have you finished?' Mokhat said sternly. 'Look further, over there, past the bodies, on the far side. What do you see?'

'By the lord Diwo,' exclaimed Palaiyas, 'Footprints. Now that you've pointed it out, even further out, there's horses hooves.'

They rode over to have a closer look. There were clear signs of a fresh horse's hooves.

'These are recent,' Mokhat said. He looked around the white landscape, but saw no sign of any horses or other movement.

'I *will* get my hands on that son of a whore. I promise you. It can only be our shadow—but how in Hades did he get here ahead of us?' Palaiyas fumed at the unfairness of it. He dismounted and had a closer look. 'Only one horse, by the looks of it. The footprints are deep, so we're looking at a big fellow. The trail leads up ahead, so he's in front of us now.' A little flicker of respect for his adversary was creeping into his description. 'We seem to have a very slippery customer on our hands. I think we need to be doubly careful from now on, lest he takes us unawares. I know he's still around somewhere, I can feel him in the fine hairs on the back of my neck, and that's always been reliable.'

'I agree with you, my friend, about being careful. Let's continue. There's no more we can learn here.' Mokhat was still keenly surveying the hilly terrain for any signs of their follower.

They made another eight leagues without further incident before the light began to fade. In the hilly expanse, over a rise, they could see the outlines of Purushanda sitting on the edge of the plateau in the twilight; their destination. The city had a large frozen lake at its back to its north.

'Thank the lord, we'll have some hot food tonight,' Palaiyas shouted above the wind, which had risen.

They were bent forward on their horses, pushing ahead at a gentle canter, so as not to tire them. They would need fresh mounts in the morning. These poor things were all worn out. Neither was looking forward to having to explain to another suspicious officer that they were really not their enemies. As they approached the city gates, the sentries seemed not to be readying to challenge them. There was a frown on Palaiyas' face and he looked at Mokhat with a silent question at these puzzling non-actions.

As they approached, there was the expected officer at the gate, but he had a smile on his face, and the gate stood open, as if ready to receive them. 'We were expecting you,' was his first comment. Followed by, 'Do come this way. If you follow me, we'll get you warm.'

'And may I ask how it is that you're expecting us?' asked Mokhat.

'We received a pigeon message from Ullama,' cast the officer over his shoulder as he led his guests through the streets to the officer's mess. 'Actually, it came from the Governor of Ullama, warning us to expect you sometime today. Amazing what a piece of cotton with some scribble on it can do nowadays. Wrap it round a pigeon's foot, and here we are, keeping the gates open, just in case you came in late.'

They were in a large hall-like room, being led to a smaller side room, out of prying eyes. A big fire was roaring in the middle, and it looked more like a mini *megaron*, than a Hittite abode.

This surprised Palaiyas whose eyes rose in astonishment. 'Well, I never! How is it that you have a Mycenaean room in this Hittite city?'

The officer waved them to a table as he explained. 'When the city was being built, the first Governor was from Ahhiyawa; at least he was brought up there. He got the architect to install this small reminder of his upbringing. Now I'm afraid we're stuck with it.'

Food was being brought in by the servants, and the hot meat dishes were making the two newcomers dizzy with hunger.

'Please, help yourselves,' the officer gestured.

Palaiyas needed no further urging and got stuck in, just ahead of Mokhat. Their mouths full, they chewed with gusto, downing hot wine, and then moving onto pancakes with honey.

'You are aware that our mission must be kept quiet,' Mokhat told the seated Purushandan officer, in between mouthfuls. 'I assume that's why you've secreted us in this smaller room away from the rest of the officers.'

The officer nodded. 'Yes, the pigeon message made that quite clear. If I may, could I just have peek at the royal seal, just so I can tell my superiors that I've seen it. Later I will take you to see the Governor of the city. He wants a small word with you.'

Mokhat put the piece of meat down and wiped his hands on a cloth. He dug inside his tunic for the pouch and opened his hand for the officer to see. 'Take it. Have a closer look. I know you need to do this.'

'Thank you, sir,' said the officer as he handed the item back to Mokhat. 'I can now tell the Governor I've seen it close up. So...,' the officer continued, now more visibly relaxed. 'You've come all the way from the capital, from his majesty? And how is dear old Hattusas? I'm originally from there myself, you know.'

'Are you?' asked Palaiyas, out of politeness. 'How long have you been away?'

'More than ten years. It's not been all bad, but I do miss my home town. My parents are still there. My wife and kids are all here, and they consider this their home—but Hattusas still calls to me from time to time.' He acquired a faraway listless look to his face. 'I've got another five years here, and then I intend to up stakes and take the family back to where I feel more at home myself.'

After the two companions had eaten their fill, they were invited to follow the officer to the Governors quarters, through lengthy corridors, to the other side of the building. They found the diminutive Governor of Purushanda seated in front of a fire, warming himself.

As they entered, the elderly Governor rose and made a small bow to the two, seemingly lowly Ahhiyawan soldiers. 'Please be seated, your highnesses.'

Mokhat looked around to see if any others were in the room. 'So you are aware of who we are?'

'Yes. More pigeons have been flying. I have been ordered to tell you that a large contingent of Hittite soldiers is enroute to the Ahhiyawan border. This is confidential material. General Kishnapili is leading the expeditionary force and has orders to help you, should you need it.'

'Our biggest problem to date has been the shadow that has dogged our footsteps all the way from Hattusas,' replied Mokhat. 'In fact, if you could give orders to your soldiers to be on the lookout for any incoming shifty types following our arrival, and detaining them, we would be much obliged.'

'That I can do immediately,' said the city chief. He gave a shout, and an officer entered. The Governor called him over and whispered into his ear, then the officer left. 'There, that should do it,' he said to them. The grey haired Governor sat silent in thought for a while, and then said,

'Look, we have a trading wagon convoy leaving in the morning for the west, heading for Ivalanda. That's right in your direction. Why don't you join it? You could hide in one of the wagons, unseen. It might throw whoever this shadow is..., off the scent. What do you think? From Ivalanda it's only two to three days ride to Millawanda.'

Mokhat looked at Palaiyas, who nodded his agreement, and Mokhat said, 'That sounds like it might work. How big is the convoy?' he asked.

'Twenty or so wagons, with a sizable escort. The escort could help you, if needed,' the Governor replied.

'I'd rather they didn't know who we were. The fewer that have that information the safer I feel,' Mokhat confided. 'But we gladly accept your invitation for the convoy. Now I would like to ask you, since you're aware of who we are, if you've seen any sign of the king's chief spy, Satipilli? We're searching for him.'

'He was here about a month ago. All hush, hush! Then he left and that was the last I heard of him. Sorry I couldn't be of more help.'

'Well, thank you for that. It would seem we're on the right trail. And now, with your permission, I think we should turn in.' Mokhat had noticed Palaiyas stifle a yawn.

'I'll have my servants show you to your beds. If you need anything, don't hesitate to ask.' The Governor got up, and called for his servant, who appeared out of nowhere. 'I'll say goodnight to you both. The wagons leave early in the morning; too early for me. I wish you good fortune and a safe journey.'

The Governor gave another short bow and let the servant lead the two Ahhiyawan soldiers to their beds.

*   *   *

After a good breakfast, the following morning saw Mokhat and Palaiyas concealed in the middle of the convoy of twenty wagons heading out of Purushanda due southwest along a bumpy road across the high plateau. Nobody had been held on suspicion by the guards, from the previous night's instructions to detain all strangers. So the shadow was still loose somewhere. They, on the other hand, were sitting on some bundles of fur hides, listening for anything unusual that might alert them to what the shadow might be up to. It was really clutching at straw, especially with all the wagon noises.

After some leagues of travel, the officer in charge of the escort appeared, pocking his head through the heavy cotton cover. 'Hallo there, I'm Narmus,' he informed them. 'If anybody is following you, I haven't been able to spot them. If you want, you can ride your mounts out in the fresh air. It's cold, but otherwise, quite pleasant this morning.'

Mokhat nodded at the captain. The story he'd been told was that these two Ahhiyawan soldiers had been on a mission to Ullama, and were now returning to Millawanda. Unfortunately one of them, Palaiyas no less, had got a girl into trouble, and the family had sent their kinsmen to extract revenge for soiling their name. How could the inventor of this tale know that it was closer to the truth than he realised. Palaiyas had been crestfallen when he was told of the cover story, but he kept quiet, while feeling the burden inside of having left Hattusas without seeing Mahera and his child. He promised himself, on his mothers life, that he would return to them, and see them right.

'Thank you, captain,' Mokhat told him. 'We will ride for a little while. The jolts and bumps of this wagon is making me nauseous.'

The captain disappeared, and after trying to brush himself down, Mokhat stuck his head out of the back, and saw two fresh mounts being held for them by a soldier of the escort. He jumped down from the wagon, closely followed by Palaiyas. They ran alongside their mounts and then jumped on their horses, gently cantering off to the front of the convoy to talk to the captain.

'There you are,' yelled the captain as they were riding up. 'Well, how do you feel? A bit stiff, I should imagine.' He lowered his voice as they came abreast. 'A little exercise will loosen up the joints, heh!' he laughed easily. 'You'll need to stay alert if you're to avoid the angry uncles.' He winked at them knowingly.

Palaiyas cringed at this jibe, but it was in keeping with the cover story. 'Seems a bit of a large escort for a small trading convoy?' queried Palaiyas in return.

'We've heard stories from travellers, coming in from the west, of a large band of wild men on horses, looting and pillaging, and making a general nuisance of themselves. So the Governor thought it would be only sensible to beef up the protection for the convoy. I'm heading a small squadron of sixty cavalry. That should be enough to put most raiders off.' The captain didn't seem worried as he told them this. 'I'm sure it's just a bunch of ruffians out for a bit of fun. When they see the size of our force, they'll avoid us.'

'Let's hope you're right,' Mokhat told him. 'I'd hate to get into a fight over nothing.'

By midday, they had made good progress with no threat of any kind in sight. The meal they were offered was cold, but welcome, and was eaten on the move. Cold mutton wrapped in pancakes, washed down with wine. They went through a countryside deprived of all hope. After a while, the pervasive white scenery began to hurt Mokhat's eyes, and he squinted a lot, which was unpleasant.

By evening they were just entering the shelter of a forest, one that looked very sorry for itself, shorn of all foliage. There were signs of wolf tracks, indicating that a sizable pack had been in the vicinity. The snow had kept off, but the frost was determined to cling to the soil. The temperature had dropped as the meagre sun left the land, and all the travellers pulled their wraps closer round them.

Captain Narmus had stopped on the side, and looked around him, then abruptly came to a decision. 'It's time to make night camp,' he shouted. 'Over there,' he pointed at a large clearing to the left. 'Bring the wagons round into a circle and let's get some fires going. Melinar, get some of your men to get firewood. I want some hot food as soon as you can manage it. Get those lazy cooks busy. They've been sitting on their arses all day; it's time they did some work. Latrines close by, but downwind. We'll keep the animals inside the enclosure, again downwind. Make sure they're fed right now, before we eat. Oh! And organise a sentry rota; let's not take any chances. Wild men, or no wild men, I don't want us to be caught napping. Move to it.'

Melinar, his second in command, set to, ordering his non-coms to do his bidding—they in turn were shouting and verbally abusing their underlings. The soldiers ran to and fro, carrying out their given assignments, and before long, two large fires roared in the new encampment. The animals were happily chomping on the hay offloaded from the wagons. The circle of vehicles kept off some of the wind, and the whole area began to feel quite pleasant, especially when the smell of cooking began to drift on the air. Logs were placed round the fires for people to sit on. The drivers were all traders, except for the provisioning wagons, and they organised the seating. A couple of large cauldrons were heating above the two fires, held in place by solid A frames. That's where the food smell was coming from.

'What's cooking?' The captain demanded of the cooks.

'We've got mutton in the cauldrons, barley, and some root vegetables, sir. It'll be a substantial broth, I assure you. There's enough for everybody, sir.'

'Good man! Well, dish it out. Let's get to it.' The captain looked eagerly at the nearest cauldron.

'Just a little more time, sir. Not long now. I'll holler when it's ready.' The senior cook looked uneasily at his commanding officer.

'Alright, but some time soon. Don't look so worried, I'm not going to eat *you*.'

The cooks smiled and went to stir their pots, feeling a little easier, since their captain had finally come out with a joke. True it was at their expense, but it was still a first.

* * *

They were sitting by the roaring fire and Mokhat, finally satiated, pulled out the Ahhiyawan sword from his scabbard, and began to examine the blade. 'I wanted to satisfy myself that it was sharp enough to do its work,' he said to Palaiyas, who was sitting next to him. 'It's one of yours, isn't it? What's all this stuff on the blade? It looks like it's been engraved with running horses.'

Palaiyas pulled out his own sword and pointed to his blade. 'Yes, by Diwo, you're right. Mine's got flying griffins on the blade. It's almost a shame to use such fine workmanship, just in case it gets damaged,' he smiled. 'Look, the hilt's gold plated and the pommel is of ivory. I wonder where in Hades they got these fine specimens? Let me have a closer look at your running horses.'

Mokhat passed his sword to Palaiyas, who peered closely at the blade for a while.

'You know,' he finally said, 'I think I know where these came from. I think my father sent these as gifts with his query concerning myself. Remember Queen Nikal said he'd been asking about me. They certainly look like our stuff. I could probably even guess at the name of the craftsman in Tiryns who put these together. Strange I didn't notice this before. It felt so natural that I didn't question it.'

'Well, their magnificent pieces of workmanship,' offered Mokhat, taking his sword back and replacing it in his tasselled scabbard. 'Let's hope we don't have to use them. And now, I think it may be a good idea if we turned in. We're sleeping in that wagon with all the fur. We should be warm enough.'

Both got to their feet and strolled over to where the captain stood by the provisions wagons. He was giving more advice to the cooks.

'We're turning in,' Mokhat told him. 'See you in the morning.'

'Well, good night then. Sleep well.'

# Chapter Eight

'**W**ell? Is our guest talking yet?' Madduwatta asked the chief warder of his dungeon.

'No, my lord! He refuses to say a word.' The warder didn't tell Madduwatta that Satipilli had spoken, but only to curse the Governor for his treachery.

'Come on man, get on with it. I need to know what the scoundrel has found out. I want details. Get the torturer to put more pressure on him. I want results not excuses—or I'll find someone else who can get the information. Do I make myself clear?' Madduwatta had worked himself up into a temper.

The poor man in front of him knew well enough what the governor's temper could mean. 'Yes, my lord,' the warder muttered, and he seemed to shrink, as he backed away to do his masters bidding.

\*     \*     \*

Down below in Madduwatta's dungeon, Satipilli was suspended from a wall by chains, barely allowing his feet to touch the stone floor. He was a wiry man of medium height, now balding, but tough as they came. In contradiction, he was something of a nondescript as befits a top spy. People wouldn't give him a second glance if they saw him in the streets. He had carefully cultivated this visual deception, and it had served him well in the many scrapes he'd been through. He could do with speed, what others needed muscle power to accomplish, and his opponents had a great deal of respect for his prowess and cunning, and were suitably wary of him.

However, his downfall came from a man he'd trusted, and he'd cursed himself for not noticing the subtle changes in the man's behaviour prior to his betrayal. He had been in too much of a hurry, and didn't spot the trap. It later transpired that this turncoat had been bought with promises and gold of such quantities, that whoever had paid him intended serious nasty business with him—and now it was too late.

It had landed him in this god-forsaken hellhole, at the mercy of a sadistic tormentor who was asking him questions that he was unable, and unwilling, to answer. Deep down in his guts, he knew that if he couldn't get out of this dungeon soon, that this would be his last resting place on earth. One of the main problems he faced was that nobody knew his whereabouts—not even his subordinates. That was his usual practice, and how he normally operated. Now it worked tragically against him.

His tormentor returned and began stoking up the brazier in the middle of the room, getting his instruments white hot. This imbecile of a persecutor was a huge bald fat oaf who went about his business with a malign pleasure of inflicting pain for his own amusement. That he was paid to do this was of no consequence to him—he would have done it for free.

'You ready to talk yet,' the oaf demanded gruffly. He was hoping that his prisoner was still going to hold out. That way he could have some more fun.

Satipilli looked up at the dark ceiling, and with difficulty, tried to muster up contempt on his face.

'Good man! I knew you wouldn't let me down.' He pulled a poker out of the fire and walked over to his prisoner. 'Now we can have some more fun, hey?' He ran the poker gently, slowly across Satipilli's bare chest.

Satipilli's skin sizzled and he clenched his teeth hard, yet wanting to scream as loud as he could.

'There, there, you can let it out,' smirked the big oaf. 'No need to hold it in. I like a bit of music while I'm working.' The poker was now transferred downwards, and moved slowly up the inside of Satipilli's left leg.

That was too much for the chief spy, and he screamed out his agony at the top of his lungs.

Then the oaf moved the poker up the inside of his right leg, just as slowly, only stopping below his exposed genitals.

Again Satipilli screamed out his agonising pain.

The implication was clear, that his genitalia were next in line for the poker treatment. 'This is your last chance to save your manhood. Are you going to answer the questions, or are you going to allow me to turn you into a gelding?'

Just at that moment Satipilli's body crumpled, and he dangled unconsciously before his sadistic tormentor. The pain had been too much for his conscious mind, and it had blanked it out the only way it could.

'*A plague on you and all your family*,' ranted the fat inquisitor loudly, now deprived of his entertainment. He turned on his heels fuming and went to find someone to take his frustration out on, calling over his shoulder, 'I'll be back soon enough, you *weak* bastard.'

\* \* \*

Up in the governor's mansion, Madduwatta was pondering on how he could get his hands on Arzawa. Clearly, he couldn't just openly invade Arzawa, mainly because Tudhaliyas had prohibited him from expanding his territory. But Madduwatta fancied Arzawa's crown and was in the process of plotting how to grab it. His army was ready —and in one week....he was to attack, but he'd actually called a halt to Visanitti's departure. Lukka and Arzawa were relatively evenly matched, and he needed an advantage before he was going to challenge King Kupanta-Kurunta. He wanted overwhelming odds.

Madduwatta was utterly unhappy at only being a Governor, and spent long periods scheming on how to elevate himself to a king. Now the itching for expansion was at its worse, and so he finally made his mind up. *I'm going to have to visit that young upstart next door.* Madduwatta, having come to this conclusion, called for his chief aide.

'You called, my lord?' asked the aide, as he rushed in to attend to his master's yelling.

'Yes! Is that young pretender to Ahhiyawa's throne still near my border at Phadhiya?'

'As far as I know, my lord. He's gathering his forces there for his next move,' replied the aide.

'Good! Now I want you to arrange a visit to our would-be king, Attarsiyas. Send a messenger to Phadhiya; see if he'll accept a visit from his friendly neighbour. He's so close at the moment that it would be a shame to miss this opportunity to consolidate our friendly relations.'

Madduwatta had that conspiratorial look on his face which invariably caused the aide concern, but the downtrodden counsellor had little choice but to carry out his master's will. 'At once, my lord! As you command!' And the aide backed away, head lowered out of fear, not respect.

*    *    *

Early in the morning, a day later, Madduwatta had his chariot brought round for the lengthy journey to Phadhiya. The previous night, a messenger had returned with greetings from the would-be king and with the reply that he did not mind if the Governor of Lukka wished to visit him. He wanted to hear what he had to say.

Madduwatta read that as an invitation, and was preparing himself for the journey, when his favourite wife began wailing and making a fuss just as he was about to

69

leave. 'Be reasonable my pet, it's only for a couple of days. Then I'll be back and we can continue where we left off.'

Lawaiya had spent the night with him and was fully aware of his impending departure, but now petulantly decided to complain. In reality, she just wanted to be noticed, to ensure she stayed his favourite wife. The only way she knew how to achieve that was to make a commotion over his removal from her. 'Please don't go— I'll be so lonely without you,' she complained tearfully. 'The children will miss you, don't go, we need you here,' she wailed.

'Now, *that's enough*!' Madduwatta shouted at her, and at the tone of his voice, Lawaiya stopped, as abruptly as she had started. She recognised that she might have over done it, and she didn't want to jeopardise what she had, so she sat on the low couch trying to look meek and demure.

His personal aide chose that time to appear at the door, and coughed to announce his arrival.

Madduwatta waved him in. 'Yes, what is it?'

'My lord, some news has just come in by courier. We've just heard this morning that some ships have been sighted off the coast near Phadhiya, with a mass of fresh troops for the rebels. We're told the ships are Mycenaean. This is from our pirate "friends," who seem to worried they may be used against them. They asked us if we knew anything. As per your instructions, we did not confirm, or deny their rumours.'

'Good work,' replied Madduwatta. 'We must always stay ahead with the latest news. This information might swing the war in the upstarts favour. Anyhow, it's time to go.'

Madduwatta went down to his chariot and gave the order for the journey to proceed. He peered closely at the back of his small cavalcade to see if his horses were included in the entourage. He was bringing with him a hundred white stallions as a gift. He wanted to observe if the gift was appreciated—and if the young would-be king was as corrupt as himself. If the eyes glinted at the gift, then he was, but if he was indifferent, then he might have to try another tack.

Madduwatta endured the bumpy journey in his chariot from Ura to Phadhiya, sitting wrapped in furs on a mass of cushions throughout the whole cold day of hard driving, and even harder riding by his tired entourage. The chariot's horses had to be changed twice during the journey, before the governor's company finally managed to arrive at his destination. By then it was late into the night and the Lukkan assemblage were informed by the king's military adviser that his majesty was busy and that they would be presented to him after breakfast the next day. A large house was made available to them for the night, and after a hearty meal, eventually the bedraggled retinue bedded down.

Madduwatta rose early, finding it difficult to sleep in his strange surroundings. He found the day was bright and sunny and the house busy with preparations for the early morning meal. He dressed and went into the garden to breathe the fresh air and get a feel of his new surroundings. He spent his time thus until it was time for him to be presented to Attarsiyas.

The military adviser, the one from the previous night, came and informed Madduwatta that, 'His majesty will receive you now. Please come this way.'

'I am at his majesties pleasure,' said Madduwatta, and then told his accompanying aide to go and fetch the horses and bring them to where he was being led. He then followed the military adviser to the large mansion in the middle of the town.

The mansion was a large two storey building with a sizable forecourt. The courtyard contained a number of chariots, with various military personnel bustling about as if everything they were about was a matter of urgency—and maybe it actually was. In any event, the hubbub of

71

preparations for war seemed to impress Madduwatta, and it wetted his appetite for his own ambitions. *I could certainly use this fellow if only I could get him on my side,* was the thought running through his head as he ascended the stairs of the mansion.

The room that was being used as an audience chamber was the main living room in the left wing on the ground floor. The adviser leading him, paused at the doorway, waited a few moments, before passing him on to another of the king's aides.

'His majesty will see you now. Please come this way,' he said, leading Madduwatta into the would-be king's presence.

Madduwatta stood before Attarsiyas; head bowed down and waited for the king to speak, as protocol required him to do.

'Well, now! What can I do for the *Hittite* Governor of Lukka?' Attarsiyas asked.

Madduwatta noted that this king had reminded him of his vassal status to Hatti. 'Your majesty, I am your neighbour, and as a good neighbour, I have come to offer you my assistance in your time of strife. And also as a good neighbour, I offer you a gift of a hundred of my finest white horses to show my friendship. If you would kindly look out of your window over there, your majesty, you will see them waiting for you in the courtyard below.'

Attarsiyas, a little puzzled at this gift, went over to the window, followed discreetly by Madduwatta, and looked out. Below he indeed observed a whole herd of horses creating something of a commotion, and impeding the military from continuing with their war preparations. 'Thank you, but kindly ask your men to move them out of the courtyard to the stables round the back. We need to get on with our activities,' ordered the king. 'Oh, and thank you for your gift! They will come into handy in the coming battle.' Attarsiyas led Madduwatta back to the large chair he was using as his pseudo throne.

Madduwatta was crestfallen at the king's reaction to his gift. Such a dismissal was intolerable. "Handy in the coming battle," indeed. These horses were worth a fortune and this king had treated them as mere ornaments. *This is going to be harder than I thought,* went through Madduwatta's mind. 'Was there any way that I could be of service to you, your majesty—maybe offer some of my own troops to add to your forces?'

'Somehow I don't think that your king in Hattusas would appreciate such a move, do you?' It was said with a hint of irony. A twinkle had leapt into Attarsiyas' eyes.

'I'm sure that the Hatti king needn't know of this. It could be just between us both, neighbour to neighbour. Also there are other ways I could be of assistance. Financially, for instance. I have some influential friends who would be prepared to support you and provide various supplies you may be short of.' Madduwatta was thinking that his chance was slipping, and becoming desperate. He noted the twinkle in the king's eyes and mistook it for encouragement to bare his real intent. 'When you win,' Madduwatta continue, now unable to stop, 'we could become firm allies, and I could help you to expand your territory. I have some powerful friends in the east, with deep pockets.' There, he had said it. The implication was clear. The only territory they could both expand into is Arzawa. Surely this would-be king would want that?

'Give me some time to think about all this. In the mean time, excuse me, but I have a war to win.' Attarsiyas called to his aide to show Madduwatta out.

Madduwatta kept a firm grip on himself, but he was shocked at having just been dismissed as some common underling. He backed out, as did the king's aide.

\*   \*   \*

73

When Attarsiyas had got rid of the crackpot but treacherous governor, he called for his master spy.

The spy arrived shortly and stood before his sovereign, waiting for the inevitable questions.

'You're aware that we have a visitor from the south,' Attarsiyas asked of the spy.

'Yes your majesty. Governor Madduwatta of Lukka.'

'So, tell me, what do you know of this Lukkan?' he asked of the man who had information on everyone.

'He's not to be trusted, that's one thing I do know. Why only yesterday, I received information from a courier pigeon which informed us that it was Madduwatta whose been sending scurrilous reports to the Wanax in Mycenae of Famemnon's treachery against him. That's why the Mycenaean Wanax no longer supports Famemnon. I didn't mention it until now, because it's been good for us, but if he does it against your brother, for whatever reason, he would just as easily do the same against you—should he so decide.' The spy now waited for a response.

'Well, well, well. The rotten scoundrel! What made him do it? He's got another agenda, and I think he just hinted at it in our little chat. He wants Kupanta-Kurunta's throne. Well I never!' Attarsiyas was getting angry at this devious rapacious governor. 'I have a feeling it might be best if I got rid of him right now, while we have him in our grasp. I really shouldn't allow such unpleasant loose ends to roam around causing potential trouble for me. Look! Leave it till tonight, then get some of your troops, surround the residence and put an end to him. Understood? We can always tell the Hatti king that he got tangled up with bandits while he was inspecting his border posts. Make arrangements to make it look like that will you?'

The spy nodded and bowed his way out of the room, preparing to do his sovereign wishes.

*   *   *

Shortly after Madduwatta returned to his residence, his own spy ran into the room breathing heavily. 'My lord,' he gasped, 'we have to leave now. Hurry! We've got to go. They'll be here any minute. If we hurry, we might just make it.' The spy was beside himself, his face twisted with fear. The previous night, he'd infiltrated one of his female spies into the king's household prior to Madduwatta's arrival. That woman had been close to the audience room and had overheard parts of the king's order to "get rid of him right now," and had then hurried away to report it to her boss. The same boss had hastily rushed over to warn his master of his impending doom.

'Pull yourself together, man. Why do we have to leave right now? Talk sense, will you,' he demanded of the man.

'My lord, one of my spies has just overheard the king, after you had left, giving orders to have this place surrounded and you and all of us to be killed. Now will you make ready to leave?' The spy had finally got out what he wanted to say.

Madduwatta just stood staring at the man, stunned. He refused to believe it, but then fear set in, and he began shouting orders to his people to get the chariots and horses ready, and have his stuff quickly packed. Within a short time, the entourage were moving quietly, trying to sneak out, back along the route that had brought them there; out of the cursed town. As they moved further away, they picked up their speed—until they were out on the open road, when it turned into a full gallop, and they were running for their lives.

# Chapter Nine

Attarsiyas was standing with his senior officers, round a table with a map laying open on it, in the largest room of the villa. It was the crack of dawn and the uncrowned king was eager to get on with the briefing. This was to be the first council of war with all his commanders present. 'Where's admiral Lamatiya,' he enquired of his chief of staff. 'I was led to believe he would be present at this council.'

'He's been delayed by the tides,' his chief told him. 'We expect him shortly.'

Just then the admiral walked through the entrance, and marched swiftly over to the table. 'My apologies sire,' said the burly middle aged man. 'I have the fleet at your disposal but the tides are not yet yours to command.' He stood waiting for the briefing to commence.

Attarsiyas smiled at the admiral's tidal joke, and made it clear to all those present, that he was in a good humour. 'Now you're here, my dear admiral, we can get going. Gentlemen, may I present to you General Ioncratis, here,' and he nodded in the direction of the general at his left side. 'He's the commander of the Keftiu contingent that landed the fifteen ships on our shores yesterday.'

At that moment the commander of the Keftiu contingent leaned over and whispered in the king's ear.

'Yes, general, thank you,' Attarsiyas said, trying to maintain his good humour. 'I'm aware that I'm the Mycenaean king's vassal. Now we need to continue with this briefing. He,' pointing at the Keftiu commander, 'brings with him two thousand men. That is a substantial addition to our forces. If my advisers are correct, we should have some twenty thousand to put up against my brother's fifteen. It has swung the numbers nicely to our benefit, and I believe the outcome of the coming clash is firmly in our favour. We're here to finalise the order of battle, and to ensure that we *do* come out on top. That is the only solution I am willing to entertain. Let me now allow General Karisiyas to explain what he has in mind for his strategy and the tactics. General...' Attarsiyas turned to his master tactician.

The tall dark figure of the general seemed to grow taller. 'I'm sure I don't need to remind you all of the fundamentals. An advantage of height over the enemy if we can get it, so we must choose where we are engage most carefully. The sun should be behind us, so as to dazzle the enemy. If there is a strong wind, it should blow away from us, giving advantage to our missiles, and blinding the enemy with dust. We'll use the normal arrangement of placing the infantry in the centre and the cavalry on the wings. I want us to try the wedge formation for our centre front line. We need to try and break their front as soon as possible. We'll send in the chariots against their front line, and then follow that up with the wedge. This will need heavy infantry, and I'm proposing to give this honour to our friends from Keftiu.' Karisiyas looked at his colleague, Ioncratis, who nodded his assent. 'Good! We've been promised a thousand horses from Arzawa, but if they don't arrive in time, we'll be a little weak as far as the cavalry goes, and we'll have to stiffen it with lightly armed foot soldiers.

'We'll need to hold an adequate reserve at the back to prevent the enemy from trying to envelope our own forces. A couple of thousand should be sufficient. At the same time, we may need them to fend off the enemy cavalry attacking the rear of our infantry, if they attempt to do so. If all goes well, in the initial phase of the battle, and their front line folds under the wedge, then we'll move the reserves to the sides and use them to perform an enveloping manoeuvre against our opponents. Frankly, I hope things don't go that far.' That last comment had the officers glancing at each other, wondering what their commander had in mind. Karisiyas went on, 'I shall be on the right wing with his majesty, and I expect all commanders to watch for my signals.

'Now for the terrain! From what I can see on this map,' he pointed to the large calves hide map on the table, 'I deduce that we would have the best advantage if we engaged the enemy here.' He stuck his finger on the calves hide map some six leagues from Phadhiya. The place was a wide valley a league in length, running from east to west with shallow slopes covered with forest on either side. 'Look here, we have to come from Phadhiya, so we're entering the valley from the east, and if we time our appearance right, the enemy will be entering the valley from the west. Early tomorrow morning, this puts the sun in their eyes. The cold blast of wind is currently from the east, and that will help our slings and arrows to travel further.

'We must now determine where Famemnon's army is. It is careful planning and accurate information about the enemy that are the keys to victory. My intelligence, gentlemen, tells me that they will be just entering that valley by tomorrow daybreak.

'What should clinch it for us are the forests on either side. We'll hide some four thousand men in those forests, a couple of thousand on either side.' The general assigned a couple of senior officers for that task by pointing at them. 'You two take charge of the ambush and secrete your men before we camp for the night. I don't want the enemy scouts aware of them, is that clear?'

The two senior officers both gave their assent.

'When the two sides meet on the field of battle,' the general continued his briefing, 'it will give the impression we have roughly the same forces as the enemy—but in effect this is going to be an ambush. We'll openly display our forces in the valley, while keeping four thousand set aside up in the hills. When the battle begins, there will be an almighty shock for the enemy when those four thousand come charging down on them. I'm relying on the shock effect to finish the battle without too many casualties. I'm hoping the enemy will panic and retreat. And I don't want an orgy of killings, is that understood.' He looked around the gathered officers, to emphasise the point. Now the officers understood what the old fox had meant when he told them that he hoped "things don't go that far."

'In reality, I don't want to kill too many Ahhiyawan soldiers, because we will need them for later on. I'm relying on General Palossos to be himself. We all know the general, having served with him, and while I have a great respect for his capabilities, his ways are stolid and set. I don't think he'll be expecting an ambush. Finally, since both sides of this conflict all wear the same yellow tunic, I'm going to suggest our side have a broad red cloth tied round their helmets and each wrist, to distinguish us from the foe. It should be simple to do, since the men are now camped just outside the town walls, and the bands will be easy to remove after the battle. Also I want everyone checked for warm cloaks, woollen hats, and warm leggings, and if they haven't got them, then they're to be issued to those men against this winter cold. Get the cloth from the merchants in the town. Freezing soldiers are almost useless in a battle. That should be put into effect immediately. Now sire, I recommend you give the order for the army to march to the eastern entrance of that valley,' he pointed again at the place on the map, 'and camp just out of sight of the western entrance. If we start now, we should be there by late tonight. There we will camp overnight and wait for the foe.' General Karisiyas had finished his briefing and waited for the king's comments.

'Excellent general, most excellent,' enthused the uncrowned king. 'I do so give the order to march to this valley, immediately,' he added. 'Oh! And I do like the idea of the red head and wrist bands for our side.' He looked pleased with himself for having selected this general for his army commander. Attarsiyas fancied himself a good judge of men, and this general had vindicated his judgement. 'If there's nothing else,' he looked round at the gathered officers, 'then I suggest we all get to it. I want the army to be on the road by noon at the latest.'

# Chapter Ten

**F**amemnon' army had been on the march for the whole day without a break, from near dawn to dusk, and had made eight leagues by the evening, which was about normal for a column to do in a day. Now the twilight was encroaching and the order to make camp for the night was given. Leather skin tents were set up on the plain they were on, and large fires were started, so the troops could warm themselves from the bitter cold, which was still all pervasive in the landscape, and have hot food for their evening meal.

Provisions were unpacked, mostly barley gruel, and the cooks set to preparing the food. There was a general bustle as fifteen thousand soldiers went to create a small temporary township. All the cavalry horses were settled downwind of the camp after being fed, latrines were built, and the king's tent erected.

Famemnon asked that all his officers join him for the evening meal. He wanted to bond with them, to boost their morale, and also to ascertain their mood. Were they eager or reluctant? He had to know, since it would make a huge difference to the coming struggle. He thought all was in order with his officers, but his now departed father had always insisted, and taught him to do the same, to take the mood of his soldiers at every opportunity possible, since that could change abruptly, and disastrously affect the outcome of a campaign. If they weren't as enthusiastic as they should be, he could try and bolster their moral by various means, also recommended by his late father.

In the centre of the king's tent, there were a number of low tables containing various foods, and low couches were placed in a circle around the food tables. On one of the couches reclined the king. To his right, reclined General Palossos, commander of the army, and then in order of seniority, reclined the other officers. Braziers were lit around the tent to provide the warmth. The whole atmosphere in the tent was one of warmth, refinement, and contentment. Baggage train servants stood ready to poor wine into the owner's goblets, when it was called for. Such was the life of the higher echelon of Ahhiyawan military society.

Outside, in the cold, wrapped in their heavy warm woollen cloaks, the rest of the soldiers were lining up with their wooden bowls. They were waiting to be dished out barley gruel by the camp cooks from large cauldrons, and were extremely anxious to get the hot food inside them, to satiate their hunger, and to benefit from the warmth it would give. Some of the soldiers were grumbling about the persistent cold, about the unrelenting marching they were forced to do that day, and of the senseless fighting they were heading for. They wanted to know why the two brothers couldn't settle their differences without descending into this fratricidal civil war—but the again, soldiers always found something to grumble about.

It had been instilled into Famemnon that strong morale was everything, if he wanted to succeed in his battle tactics. His army needed to terrify Attarsiyas' troops by focusing on small sections of the enemy army, and in doing so, obliterate them utterly, then close in for the final decisive blow that would sweep away any remaining resistance with terrifying shouts of victory. The minutiae of the actual manoeuvres he was content to leave to general Palossos, but he had emphasised that he wanted to terrify Attarsiyas and his army.

Famemnon intended to display his personal bravery in the coming battle, by leading a column, with his bodyguards in the front, in a cavalry charge on the left flank of the enemy, thus heightening his army's morale by example, stiffening their resolve. And as he turned his enemy's flank, in his mind's eye, he hoped this would cause panic and terrify the foe. It might even be decisive in their triumph.

*       *       *

The following morning, while the morning meal was being prepared, a courier rode into the camp seeking the king's tent. He shouldn't have been able to miss it because of its size; however, the courier was too tired and cold to notice anything. He's been riding most of the night from near the enemy's territory and his horse was almost finished. The sentries brought the courier to the commander of the night watch, who passed him onto his senior officer; who in turn took him to general Palossos. The general read the tablet and went to inform Famemnon.

'Sire, I have some disturbing news,' said the general as he stood in the king's tent, while servants dressed the king for the coming days march.

'Yes? What is it?' demanded the king, somewhat irritated at this early interruption.

'A courier has just arrived with news that a large force of Mycenaeans have landed further down the coast...,' he was about to continue, but the king interrupted.

'And about time,' he shouted.

The general put in quickly, 'No sire, not to help us, but they're here to support Attarsiyas.'

The shock was like a body blow with an axe—the king stood there gaping with disbelief. 'That can't be right!' he burst out finally. 'There must be some mistake. The Mycenaean Wanax would not go against my father's wishes like that. No! I'm not accepting that. Send some people to check this out. It must be a mistake.' He was shaking his head in amazement.

'There's *no* mistake, sire,' said the general sadly. 'The source is impeccable. I, myself, would vouch for the writer of the dispatch. I've been half expecting this, and also dreading this news. When we didn't manage to get an answer from Mycenae, with all our message sending attempts, I guessed that something was wrong. How this has happened, we will discover eventually, but for now, we must live with it and factor it into our battle plans. I will spend the day working on what needs to be done, if anything.' The general's features seemed resigned but determined in the face of this catastrophe. 'I will, of course, let you know by this evening, what I've come up with.' He bowed and backed out of the tent.

\* \* \*

The army's march resumed, snaking out over a league in length, and it would have been longer but for the fact that it proceeded in two columns of seven thousand each. That way it provided more protection from both hostiles and the cold wind. Half way through the day, the columns changed sides, so the inner side of one column switched to be the outer side for the second half of the day's march. As both columns proceeded, rumours of the landings spread throughout the troops and they began to grumble with a vengeance—insisting they were not too keen to fight their own countrymen. Others added to the moaning with regard to the bitter cold.

By the evening, they were in sight of a long broad valley up ahead, and scouts returned to report that a large enemy force had been sighted approaching the other end of the valley. At this news, General Polossos decided to halt his columns at the western end of the valley's entrance, and gave the orders for the night's camp to be established there.

Once the tents had gone up and the fires were burning, the general went to see the king. 'Your majesty, we've had a number of desertions by foraging troops that we sent out during the day, and haven't returned. At least I assume they're desertions, but I suppose they might've come across parts of that larger force ahead, and been wiped out. That's a worrying aspect of our situation. The numbers are not large, but their inclination to disappear is disquieting. It's bad for morale.'

The king looked closely at the general, and perceived his deep concern. 'Yes, I can see you're troubled. What have you in mind?'

'Sire, I've been thinking during the day, and for tonight, I have a proposal. We, the senior officers, should abandon our cosy meal in your tent and go and mix with the troops. Eat with them what they eat. Talk with them about their worries. I'm going to suggest that you, sire, join us in this undertaking. We need to shore up their morale. I implore you to consent to this. It is our last chance to strengthen our men before battle.'

'Excellent idea, general! I've been thinking along similar lines. I've also been wondering how to put some more backbone into the men.' The king was smiling encouragingly at Palossos.

'From the scout's reports,' continued the general, 'it's clear that the battle will be joined for tomorrow. It would seem we are at one end of this long broad valley, and the enemy is camped at the other end. Like it or not, sire, we will be forced to come to conflict when we meet in the middle sometime after dawn tomorrow. We'll need to set up an extra vigilant watch tonight in case the enemy attempts to probe us in the dark.'

# Chapter Eleven

$P$alaiyas' eyes sprung wide open. He was listening hard. There it was again. *Crunch...crunch.* Somebody was by their wagon. More *crunches*, as if someone was now running off. 'Is that you,' he called out softly, thinking it might be the sentry. No answer. He tugged at his sword, and then shook Mokhat's shoulder.

'W-what's up?' Mokhat yawned, struggling to come awake.

'*Shh*!' Palaiyas pointed outside, and put his finger to his lips. From one side of the wagon, the light of the fires, which were still burning bright, allowed them to just see each other in the dark. Palaiyas got to his knees and crept to the exit, sword in hand. He pocked his head out....and saw nothing. There was a full moon that night and what with the white snow, he could clearly see the footprints leading away from their wagon into the forest. The rest of the camp in the forest clearing was fast asleep and quiet. 'Get dressed,' he hissed at Mokhat. 'We've had visitors.'

Once outside, swords drawn, fur cloaks around them, they crept off in pursuit. The sentry was nowhere to be seen. They bent low and began running, deep into the forest, following the clearly visible footsteps. A short while later, they heard someone shrieking with pain, off in the far distance.

Palaiyas, who was out in front shouted, '*Hurry*!' He no longer cared if they heard him or not. 'Someone's being murdered.'

They rushed down a frozen hill and Mokhat lost his footing, tumbling, sliding, down the incline. At the bottom he got up just as Palaiyas reached him. Mokhat brushed himself down and both continued in the direction from where the awful sound was coming from. They raced up the other side of the hill trying not to slip on the frosty surface. The shrieking had stopped. They reached the crest of the hill and saw that half way down; there lay a body silhouetted against the snow. Palaiyas reached him first just ahead of Mokhat. The poor wretch had been badly tortured—that was plain to their eyes.

'Look, over there,' yelled Palaiyas. 'There's another one.'

This time the fellow was bare breasted and badly wounded with marks all over his chest. He was unconscious, and barely breathing. Mokhat lifted his shoulders off the ground and sat him up, taking off his own fur wrap, putting it round the man to try and give him some warmth. Palaiyas searched the area and found another fellow behind another tree; this one had been spread and tied between two trees. He was still warm, had only just died. He must have been the one shrieking. Of the culprits, there was no sign. They heard people running from where they'd come from.

The first from the camp to arrive was Captain Narmus. 'What's been going on here?' he demanded. He looked around and the anger was visible. 'I have to assume this isn't your work. I can see you're trying to help. Who are these people?'

More of the escort soldiers began to arrive and the captain ordered them to carry the surviving wounded man back to the camp as gently as they could. Meanwhile, Narmus sent soldiers in pursuit of the perpetrators of this horror.

\* \* \*

Back at the camp, the two dead bodies were laid out in the snow. Narmus stood with Mokhat, silently looking down at the corpses.

'Well, what do you make of this? You say one of the criminals came to our camp; to your wagon. Why? Something isn't right here.' The captain was still upset.

Mokhat put his hand inside his tunic and pulled out the royal seal. 'I must ask you to swear on oath, that what I'm about to show you, will stay only between us two.'

The captain still incensed, began to show signs of curiosity. 'Hmm! This had better be good, or there will be trouble—for the both of you.' The captain put his hand in his pouch and pulled out a golden image of a woman's face, holding it between his thumb and two fingers. 'Right, I swear by this sacred sign of Ishtar that what I'm about to see will not go any further and if I offend, may the *waters* get me. There! Is that good enough? Now what have you got there?'

Mokhat handed the royal seal to the captain. 'Take a close look at that,' he suggested.

'Where did you get this?' the captain said cautiously.

'From his majesty the king, in Hattusas. The story you were told concerning us, was false. You were supposed to stay ignorant of the real purpose of our journey with you. This business,' Mokhat waved his hand at the corpses, 'has forced my hand. In fact, we are on a mission for his majesty, and this seal commands his subjects to help and assist us in any way they can. Are you convinced?'

The captain's caution was beginning to show signs of weakening. He handed the seal back to Mokhat, and nodded. 'It begins to make sense. 'I felt there was something not quite right with the story I was told about you. Why would the Governor's aide help some Ahhiyawan soldiers? That didn't stack up. Your not Ahhiyawans are you?'

'You don't really need to know that, but since you ask, I'm not, but my friend is.' Mokhat grinned at the captain. 'These deaths are likely to do with our work.' Mokhat thought that having gone this far, he might as well tell the captain the rest. 'The reason we sneaked out of

Purushanda was because we were being followed. It was the Governor's attempt at throwing them off our trail. From what we have before us, it clearly didn't work. Whoever it is, they are far more determined than we supposed. I'm sorry for these three, but it can't be helped. What I haven't told you yet is that, when we got to the scene of this butchery, we found signs suggesting that at least one of this band had escaped. My friend found bloodied prints in the snow going off in a completely different direction than any of the others. So, there must have been four of these men. That puts the torturers to at least double this number—and there may be more.'

The captain was listening intently. From his features, Mokhat saw that he had a believer.

'I'm going to assume you are, who you say you are, not that you've actually told me who you are. But let's say that these people were after you—what now?' The captain appeared serious. 'I should tell you that a mark on one of the two corpses there, indicate they were working for his majesties spy network. That means they were on our side. The mark is on the instep of the sole of the left foot—and it's a burn mark which would probably go unnoticed. Not somewhere one would normally look. Only if you know the mark, does it mean something. This was not always my job —if you get my meaning. This nasty business does mean that you are completely compromised.'

It was now Mokhat's turn to be astonished. 'Well captain, you *are* full of surprises. It seems fate may have thrown us together. As for the next move. Our aim is to get to Millawanda; we have business there on his majesties behalf.' Mokhat was still pondering whether to confide the real purpose of their journey to this new acquaintance. 'If we may, we'd like to continue with your convoy. I would venture it's a lot safer than us being on our own—especially after last night's affair.'

'I see no alternative for you. You're more than welcome to travel with us, in fact the Governor of Purushanda insisted that you did. Those were my orders.' Captain Narmus put out his hand to seal his invitation, which Mokhat shook. 'Now I have a question for you.' Narmus walked over to a log and sat on it, inviting Mokhat to join him. 'Well now, who do you think these people are who are chasing you?' He motioned the wide forest with the sweep of his right hand. 'It's important to know your enemy, so that you're able to put yourself into their shoes.'

'Hm...' Mokhat said, gently scratching his short beard. 'We've been pondering on that problem throughout our journey, as soon as we realised we had a shadow. Our short briefing in Hattusas suggested that Ahhiyawa might be involved. Hence our journey to Millawanda! This new king they have may turn out to be benign to Hatti, but our instructors in Hattusas made it clear they thought he might not last, and his younger brother could oust him.' Mokhat now settled down to think this through out aloud. It might pin down their enemy. 'Then again, even Mycenae was mentioned, but my companion is dead set against that notion. I suspect he finds it hard to be chased by people controlled by his uncle, even though they're in dispute. But I put that down to simple bias. Then there's Madduwatta. He's outrageously ambitious; at least the king's advisors implied that to be the case. Arzawa is a strong suspect, mainly for eyeing Hatti territory. Even Alasiya has been mentioned. Then finally, there are the Mittani, who were on the loosing side with Muwas, in Hatti's civil conflict. They've never forgiven Tudhaliyas for winning. They would sorely like to rub his nose into something.' He ceased his monologue and began stroking his beard thoughtfully.

The captain put his right hand on Mokhat's left knee and said quietly, 'If I were in your place, I'd rule out Arzawa.' He then rubbed his hands to warm them at the fire, and continued, 'They may be pushy, but they haven't the spy network to accomplish something like this. Take my word for that. Alasiya is really a non starter, mostly for the same reason, unless they're working with Madduwatta, who is a strong contender for this. Now *he has* got the network and the determination to carry out something like this. But I ask myself, what would he achieve by putting this much effort into disrupting your journey. I really can't see it. It's not some small private vendetta; so it has to be a country chasing you. Mycenae might be a player, but it would all come through their vassal, Ahhiyawa. And that's in chaos. Mittani vengeance and spite would be another *strong* candidate. But they're a long-long way from home. This operation would be extremely difficult for them. Anyway, they're busy with Khemet and trying to fend off the Pharaoh. What about the Kaska? Last I heard, they might want to upset the king in Hattusas.' Narmus stopped, and sat silently, waiting for Mokhat to respond.

'Are you sure you've changed jobs? Apart from the last item, you could almost be paraphrasing our briefing in Hattusas. I can assure you that the Kaska are *not* involved, unless my brother has turned on me. Ah…!' Mokhat just realised he'd blundered, and given out more than he'd intended.

Narmus turned and was staring closely into Mokhat's face. 'I thought I recognised you earlier, but I just couldn't be sure until now.' He resumed staring into the fire. More logs had been put on, and dawn was fast approaching. In the distance they could hear Melinar shouting orders at subordinates, organising the morning's food. 'You won't remember me but I was at the Battle of the Wide Plateau. I was in the front line when you and your friend pulled the king out of the line. We all thought you were part of the Golden Spear bodyguard. Later, after the fighting I took the trouble to find out who the two of you were. It was just such a weird thing to do. I was told a Kaska priest and an Ahhiyawan. That stuck in my memory. What was a Kaska priest doing in uniform, in the middle of a Hittite battle? I'd completely forgotten the incident, until Kaska was mentioned just now.'

'Yes, I'm sorry. I could have bitten my tongue off as I said that. Well, you might as well know, since I've told you so much already. I'm brother to the Kaska king, and I helped him before, as you rightly remembered, so that's why King Tudhaliyas asked me and my friend to help him this time. Anyhow, that's why I know for certain that the Kaska are not involved in this business. Take my word for it.'

'I'm sorry, your highness, for any familiarity. I was unaware.' Narmus seemed to be embarrassed. He didn't know whether to get up, or stay seated.

Mokhat tried to placate the captain. 'That's alright. You were *not* to know, and I'd appreciate it if you would *continue* to behave towards us as you have been doing. Anything else would blow our deeper cover.'

At that the captain relaxed. 'Thank you. I hope I've not been too forward.'

Mokhat made a snap decision—he would tell this captain who they were really looking for. 'I've decided to confide in you, just in case you have some information for us. We've been sent by his majesty to look for Satipilli, his chief spy. It seems he's not been reporting in to his majesty. Do you know of this fellow or his whereabouts?'

'I'm sorry, I've no idea who you're talking about,' replied the captain, looking sideways.

Mokhat had his answer but somehow he didn't believe the captain. He was hiding something.

The cooks began bustling round the fires with their cauldrons, preparing barley porridge for the morning meal. It was at this point that the captain and Mokhat decided to retire to another spot to let the cooks get on with their chores. Their little chat was more revealing than Mokhat intended.

# Chapter Twelve

Melinar, Narmus' second in command, came to report to the captain. 'Sir, unfortunately the wounded man we brought back during the night never regained consciousness and died just now. We now have four bodies. Shall I have holes dug for them?'

'Four bodies?' the captain queried.

'We found one of our sentries with his throat cut. I've reprimanded the other ones for sloppy sentry keeping.'

'Right! Yes, have the holes dug. We don't want the wolves feasting on them. Tonight, when we stop, I want to double the guard. We've another four days to go. I don't want to loose anymore people, understood? After breakfast, we move out. I want to make some headway today.

Mokhat had joined Palaiyas and told him what had transpired with their captain. Throughout the tale, Palaiyas' face grew broader with a grin, until he burst out at the end, 'Well…well. Who'd have thought it? He's a sly one and no mistake.'

'My impression,' continued Mokhat, 'is that he may still be part of Satipilli's spy network, but if so, he's not saying. And at this point I've already told him more than I wanted to. So, I'm happy to trust his discretion, but let's still be vigilant. What do you think?'

'I'll have to go along with that.' Palaiyas nodded. 'At least we now know what to look for in one of Satipilli's spies, and how to recognise one. I'd like to take Narmus' shoe off and have a look at the instep of the sole of *his* left foot. They should have told us this type of stuff in Hattusas.'

Mokhat tried to excuse them. 'They should have told us many things in Hattusas, but they were short of time. We'll have to make do with what we've got. Now, let's grab some food before it's all gone.' They went off to find a couple of bowls.

*   *   *

They travelled through the leafless forest for some five leagues before the trees dwindle out and they were back in the open barren landscape. All around them the wind howled like a bunch of demented *maenads*. The animals plodded ever onwards, pulling the laden wagons across the plateau with much effort.

About midmorning the captain informed them, 'We'll have to turn north just up ahead, and go along the gorge for some ten leagues. There's a bridge up there that will take the wagons.'

'Is there nothing closer?' asked Palaiyas.

'Well, yes there is, but it won't take the wagons,' replied the captain.

'What are we talking of,' Palaiyas persisted.

'It's a rope bridge, not far ahead, but it won't take the wagons,' insisted the captain.

'Will it take our horses?' Palaiyas asked.

'Well, yes it will, if you blindfold them. But it's slippery and with this wind..., I wouldn't recommend it, really I wouldn't. You're not thinking of trying it, surely?'

Mokhat was listening to the exchange and wondering what Palaiyas was up to—but he kept quiet.

'I think we might.' Palaiyas' face was set on this action. 'It would save us a considerable amount of time. My friend must have told you how urgent our mission is. It would seem to be only sense to try the bridge, if we could save some twenty leagues. I mean you'll have to go *up* to the bridge, and then come back *down* along the other side, won't you?'

'Well, yes, but sticking with the convoy is far safer than branching out by yourselves. Surely you see that.' The captain was getting worried that his charges would get themselves into some kind of mess, and he would get the blame. For goodness sake, these two weren't just any ordinary soldiers; there was a Kaska prince involved. Once he'd realised that, he'd been determined to really look after them.

'I'm sorry, but I appreciate your concern. However, we have a job to do, and the sooner we accomplish that, the safer Hatti will be.' Palaiyas stared in the direction he wanted to go. 'And I'm afraid my mind is set on the rope bridge.'

Mokhat motioned Palaiyas aside to have a word with him. 'Excuse us for a moment, will you captain.' They rode ahead until they were out of ear shot.

'What's got into you?' Mokhat wanted to know.

'I want us to get away from this convoy.' Palaiyas was adamant. 'It sticks out like a sore thumb in this setting. We might as well advertise our arrival and be done with it. Remember we're looking for Hatti's chief spy—and I can assure you we'll need a lower profile than this.'

Mokhat thought about this, and said, 'Well if you're sure. Right, I'll go along with you, mainly because you're making sense.'

They rode back and rejoined the captain.

'I'm afraid; I'll have to go along with my friend here.' Mokhat told him. 'Could you sort out some provisions for us, and an extra horse to carry them? Is that possible?'

'Remember, I advised strongly against this course of action.' The captain looked resigned to loosing his charges. 'The time saved is as nothing, to the safety you abandoning. But it's your choice. I'll have Melinar dig out some grub, and some hay for your horses. It'll be packed on a horse as

95

you request. I'll add a couple of extra fur cloaks for blankets at night. But, I'll be sorry to see you go. I hope we meet again in warmer climes. One last word of warning. I'm assuming that the wild men I mentioned earlier may be somewhere ahead. Keep your eyes peeled for them. You don't want to get into their company. I'll say goodbye now, and good fortune.' And with that, the captain rode off along the length of the convoy. Mokhat and Palaiyas understood that he had some difficulty with their parting. Within a short interval, Melinar brought them a packhorse laden with provisions. Both Ahhiyawan soldiers waved goodbye to the twenty wagon convoy and departed.

*   *   *

The two companions were approaching the gorge, and both turned their mounts to watch the lengthy convoy disappear into the distance. They felt quite alone, with the wind still blowing freezing blasts from the east.

In a short while they came to the gorge itself. Both riders gaped at the sight that hung across the gorge. Suspended before them was a substantial deck bridge. There were four very thick tension cables attached to a massive stone megalith frame embedded in the ground at their end. The same was true on the other side. This was to withstand the vertical load of the bridge. The two higher and lower cables were attached all along the side of the bridge making a solid guardrail, with the horizontal lower two cables carrying the planking. It looked more like a tunnel without a roof. This made the tensioned bridge easy to walk across in normal conditions. The tall solid guardrails almost made it look safe, but in this weather, they were taking a huge risk. The planking looked substantial enough for the horses, but there was ice on those planks, and the gentle swaying would make the crossing impossible.

They dismounted and Mokhat stood there scratching his beard. 'It's far too slippery to take the horses,' he said, stating the obvious. He didn't really want to cross this gorge.

'The gorge isn't that wide, only about five wagons in length,' observed Palaiyas. 'The real problem is its depth. I would not want to tumble into that.' He looked bemused.

'I have an idea,' offered Mokhat reluctantly. 'We'll obviously have to cover the horse's eyes, but to make their hooves less slippery, why don't we cover the hooves with cloth as well. Then we'll take them across one at a time. What do you think?'

'You think the cloth on the hooves will stop them slipping?' Asked Palaiyas, somewhat pensive.

If the truth be told, both were thinking of rejoining the convoy. It wasn't that far ahead, and with a little hard riding....

Palaiyas took out his knife and began to cut strips of cloth off the back part of his saddle. 'Five pieces should do it.'

Watching Palaiyas, Mokhat began doing the same. Palaiyas finished tying the cloths on his horses hooves, then tied another cloth round the horses eyes and gently but firmly, talking quietly to the horse all the time, led him to the beginning of the rope bridge.

'Wait till the wind dies down a bit,' Mokhat advised. 'And then you'll have to move quickly. There's no other solution.'

Palaiyas waited patiently for the wind to subside, and then, still talking to the horse, moved him onto the planking. Leading his horse, he tried to go as quickly and as safely as he could. Half way, he slowed as the bridge swayed, but then he made a rush over to the other side, removing the horse's blindfold in a flourish as he got there. The horse had slipped slightly a couple of times, but quickly recovered. His was a sure footed animal.

Mokhat was next. He tied the pack horse to a stump nearby and then waited for the wind to calm. When there was a lull, he took his own animal over in one cautious rush, thinking that if this was his last day on earth, he really didn't want to be seen as showing reluctance. He wanted Palaiyas to see his friend was bolder than he felt.

'Thanks be to Illuyankas, that's over,' exclaimed Mokhat, as he removed the blindfold from his own horse. He stood by his friend's side. 'Shall we toss a shekel to see which one goes back and brings the packhorse over?' he asked Palaiyas.

'No need. It was my loony idea to go this route. I'll do it. You stay here and hold the horses.' Palaiyas removed the cloths from the hooves and took them with him for the packhorse.

He again waited for calm, and steadily led the animal across the planking. Somewhere in the middle the wind picked up and the packhorse panicked. It refused to go any further and was pulling back on the reins. Then it slipped and its feet went sideways through the guardrail. It lay there struggling, making matters worse. Mokhat stood rooted in horror as the scene unfolded. Palaiyas was tugging on the reins trying to get the horse to stand up but it was a hopeless task, and the more the horse struggled, the more the bridge swayed with the planking showing signs of breaking under the horse. With reluctance, Palaiyas let go of the reins and backed away to where Mokhat was, all the time shaking his head. His own safety was at stake. They watched the doomed animal desperately struggle as the planks gave, and it plunged into the chasm.

'I'm...I'm shocked...' Palaiyas was trying to say something, but for a change, he was lost for words.

'That's all of our provisions gone,' lamented Mokhat. 'Oh, and don't take offence. I'm not blaming you. It's just one of those things. Thank the lord Illuyankas, that you're safe. It could easily have taken you with it.'

'Don't remind me. Phew, that was close....' Palaiyas had regained his power of speech. 'You saw...there was nothing I could do. It got spooked and refused to move. Look there...the bridge is a bit of a mess. There's no going back.'

'We're both alive, and that's the main thing,' Mokhat insisted. 'As for the provisions; we can always scrounge something with this seal I'm carrying. We'll make out, never worry,' Mokhat was beginning to look ahead.

'Well, let's make a move. We can't stay here.' Palaiyas said.

Both mounted their steeds and wrapped their cloaks around them tight, then began to canter to the west, still heading for Ivalanda.

After about a league further on, the road took them through a small broad valley with shallow slopes, which cut them off from the howling wind for a while. All seemed peaceful on both sides of the valley until they heard a howling from high up on the slope to the right. They pulled up and peered upwards to discover what animal had made the sound. All of a sudden an arrow landed near Palaiyas. Then another one, followed by a third, which embedded itself in Mokhat horse, in the hind right flank.

'*Quick!*' shouted Palaiyas, '*turn back!* We need to go back the way we came.' He swung his horse around, just as Mokhat's animal collapsed onto its right side. Now they could see horses coming at them from above, at least twenty riders. Arrows were still falling around them everywhere, and it was by sheer luck that none had struck them more than the one which had felled Mokhat's horse. The whooping and racket coming from the wild men was distracting. Palaiyas wanted to stop and help, but Mokhat's horse had trapped his right leg by falling on him. The wild men were almost on them, and Palaiyas knew both would be caught if he stopped to help Mokhat.

With a last effort, Mokhat threw something with all his might at Palaiyas, who caught it with some fancy acrobatics. *'I'll be back,'* he yelled at Mokhat over his shoulder, who was frantically waving him away. Palaiyas looked at the pouch Mokhat had thrown and understood, then he kicked his horse into a full gallop and sped off the way he'd come, leaving Mokhat to his fate.

# Chapter Thirteen

Famemnon sat broodingly on his charger, working himself up, intent on displaying his personal bravery as he had promised himself at the first night's camp. He noted the sun was against them, shining directly into his army's faces, but there was nothing he could do about it—and to make things worse, the cold wind was against them.

He had placed himself on the right flank of his army, as was customary, waiting at the head of his royal bodyguards, in a column of horse that was five hundred strong, eager to lead them in a cavalry charge against the enemy's left flank. This display of bravery was intended to be an example to heighten his army's morale, and to stiffen their resolve. It was to complement the previous night's pep talks, when he and his senior officers had wandered round the campfires talking to the ordinary soldiers, resolving their disquiet, trying to stifle the grumblings, calming their pre battle nerves.

He badly needed to cause panic and terrify the foe that was lined up in battle formation only a quarter of a league in front of them. To this end, he first sent a hundred chariots against their frontline. The chariots with their three occupants would run parallel to the enemy's front line and discharge their arrows and javelins at those troops, then head back to their own right flank and support the cavalry during the battle.

He again hoped his own charge at their left flank might break it, and even be decisive in giving them their triumph. Peering diagonally across, he could just make out Attarsiyas on his horse, surrounded by his senior officers. Both forces were drawn up in battle order and appeared to be well matched. The dawn start had turned into mid morning, and both sides were now ready, confronting each other, eager to engage. The previous night's pep talks seem to have worked and turned the tide against the grumblers. Any moment now, he intended to give the command to charge, and then his battle would begin.

\*   \*   \*

Attarsiyas, diagonally on the other side of the field, spied his sibling at a distance, staring at him. He watched dispassionately the mass of chariots harassing his front line. They were irrelevant pin pricks, and he ignored them. He felt no remorse at what he was about to do to him. So far the ambush had not been detected, and he grinned at the shock they would provoke in the foe opposing him. He gave the order for his troops to bang their shields with their swords; this was the signal for those up in the forests to emerge and begin their descent.

\*   \*   \*

Famemnon raised his right sword arm, and pointed forward with it, yelling at the top of his voice, '*CHARGE!*' With him in the lead, the five hundred strong column burst into a strong canter before turning into a full gallop, fanning out as it went headlong forward into the wind. The enemy seemed not to react, and simply stood there, banging their shields with their swords, waiting for the charge to reach them, which puzzled the king. When the charge had gone about three quarters of the field towards its foe, Famemnon spied movements up in the hills to his left. With the sun in his eyes, he was forced to squint up the hill and to his utter amazement, and shock, he saw a large force descending down on him, running down the hill, firing slings and arrows as they came, threatening his flanking manoeuvre.

He came to a quick decision and changed his angle of charge, swinging left, heading uphill towards the descending horde that threatened to upset his victory. He was determined to stop them.

Missiles came raining down on the cavalry column, unseating riders from their horses, toppling some of the horses to the ground, and still the two sides were a good distance apart. Then suddenly a roar came from behind catching Famemnon's attention by its sheer volume. He made out the tail of his chariots just rounding his right flank, having completed their work. Yet there was a great scream of panic that emanated from the soldiers on his front line. It forced Famemnon to look hard at what they were staring at, while an arrow just missed him, flying close to his left cheek. His frontline soldiers were pointing at the other side of the valley, at the hill opposite, to the right. They had just begun advancing against the enemy and now they had come to an abrupt halt. This outrageous action of his front line forced the king to call his column to a standstill, despite the barrage of missiles still coming down on his own column. He saw that other side of the valley was teeming with enemy soldiers charging down against his right flank.

Swiftly, he swung his horse round to the right and led the remainder of his column back down the hill of the valley towards his front line, abandoning his doomed attempt at engaging those before him. It had been a desperate attempt to save his diminishing vision of a victory. Famemnon's column rode past the senior officers of his army, still sitting on their horses on the left flank, all watching their commander, General Palossos. Famemnon glanced furiously at his commander, noting a sad look on his face, but he rode on, intent on getting his frontline moving forward again, to engage the enemy.

As he rode on furiously towards them, Famemnon was dismayed to see his frontline throw down their weapons and began a headlong disorderly retreat. Faced with the massive enemy forces coming down both sides of the valley, their own flanks clearly being unsustainable, only the foolhardy or deluded would have waited there to be annihilated. Yet some of the line had stopped and were amazed that they weren't being pursued. The enemy front line hadn't moved. It emboldened some of soldiers to ludicrously presume that they yet may save the day, somehow, and maybe get back into the fight and rescue their plight, but as they were pondering this, the enemy wedge began to advance, to come at them with swords hammering on their shields, as did those on the sides of the hills. This produced more panic and they all turned on their heels and ran for their lives as swiftly as their feet could carry them.

Famemnon, in frustration, yelled at the top of his voice for them to stop, to turn and fight, but in their panic, they were beyond his control. Distressed at his soldier's cowardice, and at his inability to reverse their flight, he turned the remainder of his column, some eighty remaining members of his elite bodyguard, and about a hundred and fifty of the rest of the cavalry column, towards the enemy's army, intending to face the enemy alone if need be.

However, just as he swung his horse into the wind, readying to charge his foe again, he spied Attarsiyas in the distance, coming towards him with four of his horsemen. Famemnon watched as Attarsiyas left three of his horsemen behind, and approached Famemnon with one man, who now carried a white flag tied to the tip of a spear.

Famemnon immediately assumed, in his now self-absorbed and deluded way, that Attarsiyas had come to his senses and was now offering to surrender his forces, and to recognise him as the rightful king of Ahhiyawa.

Famemnon kicked his horse forward to meet his rival, not noticing that his column had turned, and was riding quietly away, abandoning him to his fate. When he, the rightful king, was within shouting range, Famemnon yelled at his sibling above the wind, 'So, little brother, at last you've come to your senses, and I presume you're offering to surrender your forces to me.'

On hearing this, Attarsiyas stopped, and muttered under his breath, 'Still as mad as ever.' Attarsiyas then raised his right hand, turned to face the group of three he'd left behind on their horses a short distance back, pointed at them, then swung his hand over his head and pointed at Famemnon. Famemnon, now absorbed by his own fantasy, ignored this gesture by his little brother, and kept coming towards his foe to accept his sibling's surrender. A short moment later he felt a jolt, looked down at his chest, and saw an arrow sticking out of his chest, and a patch of blood spreading on his yellow tunic. As he fell sideways off his horse, he glanced at his brother, and the last thing Famemnon saw in this life, was a grim grin on his rivals face.

\*   \*   \*

While the final part of the sibling tragedy was being played out, the whole of Famemnon's army was in full flight. Only Famemnon's senior officers remained on the field of battle. At length, General Palossos and his senior officers made a great show of drawing their swords, then turning those swords towards themselves, holding them with the handles facing their enemy. Thus General Palossos, commander of Famemnon's defeated forces, kicked his horse forward, and led his senior officers towards his opposite number, to Gen Karisiyas, to offer his unconditional surrender. As they met, General Karisiyas dismounted and accepted the old general's sword, and then embraced his old opponent, in a sign of clemency and former friendship. To those nearby on that cold field of battle, witnessing the end of the civil war, old Palossos seemed to have aged immensely, and they were moved to watch a few small tears flow gently down the old general's cheeks.

At Attarsiyas' insistence, Famemnon's body was removed from the field of battle and placed on a wagon for royal burial later.

\*    \*    \*

A few days later Attarsiyas rode past the Kalabak Hill outside Millawanda, entering the city gates with his large entourage, to universal acclaim as the rightful king of Ahhiyawa. He was given the keys to the gates of Millawanda by the commander of the garrison. He was also informed that the High Priest of Atana Potnia was waiting in the western agora to anoint him king and offer him the crown of Ahhiyawa.

Thus it was that Attarsiyas became the only legitimate king of Ahhiyawa, and his first official act was to hold a public royal burial for his poor dead brother. And so, later that day, a procession wound its way down the sacred way outside of Millawanda's walls, lined with soldiers and citizens, heading the short distance eastwards to the cemetery, where the royal tomb was to be found. After a few simple words from the new king over the tomb, it was sealed.

Famemnon had begun his reign as the rightful king in succession to his father, and maybe he would have ruled well and benignly, but under the pressure of battle, he turned into a deluded fantasist. Although that was not the epitaph Attarsiyas had put on the tomb. On the other hand, Attarsiyas had begun his rebellion as a young upstart, but had then grown over the period of tribulation into maturity and adulthood, with a large measure of flare and commonsense. His reign could turn out to be of significance for the future of the kingdom.

# Chapter Fourteen

Madduwatta arrived back in Ura exhausted, upset, and afraid. He had made a terrible enemy of the very person he needed as an ally, and the consequences might be dire for his whole future, if he had any. It had taken him two whole days using evasive routes to get back home and he wasn't sure as to what to do next. It was clear a disaster had befallen him, but who to blame. To think that it might have been his fault was absurd. It had been a misunderstanding, that's all. The would-be king was too young to understand how the world worked, and had been naively disposed to misrepresent Madduwatta's offer.

But to be on the safe side, he sent for the general commanding his army, and General Visanitti came quickly, eager to hear how his trip had gone.

'General, I want you to double the garrisons on our border with Ahhiyawa. Make sure our borders are sealed tight, especially as the Ahhiyawan are at war with each other. I don't want to get pulled into their conflict for any reason or pretext. Is that clear?' Madduwatta was agitated and distracted. 'Oh, and general…we will postpone the trip to Arzawa as of now—until the climate improves on our Ahhiyawan border. Stand the army down from that and concentrate on securing our border.'

The general answered in clipped tones, 'Yes, my lord. It shall be done.' He turned and marched out of the room. Now the general knew how the trip had gone. It had gone badly. He needed to know how badly? For that he'd have to have a talk with the master spy. If it was a complete disaster, as it seemed from his governor's behaviour, then he would have to prepare for war—but not with Arzawa. That's if it was likely to go that far.

Next Madduwatta sent for his chief spy. The spy had been debriefing those spies who had just returned, so he knew exactly what had happened, and was already in the governor's mansion waiting to be summoned.

'There you are Daubum!' Madduwatta pulled himself together for his chief spy. He didn't want the spy to know how worried he was. 'Listen carefully. I want you to send as many men as you can spare to Millawanda, and other parts of Ahhiyawa, to warn us of any impending attacks.' He stopped and looked carefully at the spy's self composure, and he guessed that he knew everything. 'I see you've been talking to your friends who came with me to Millawanda. Then you know what's happened. We may yet have to turn to our protector, the Hatti king, but I'll try to postpone that as long as I can. How's Satipilli holding out?'

'I'm afraid he isn't,' replied the spy. 'he's too damaged to be of any use to us, and he knows who we are, so we can't let him go. I'm afraid there's only one thing for him. I was just waiting for you to come back and give the order to terminate him. He's barely alive right now.'

'Yes, a pity. Well, let's see if we can make good use of him one last time.' Here Madduwatta began to look crafty. 'I want you to take him as he is to Ivalanda, and wait for those *two* who you're following to turn up. You told me they were heading in that direction. If that's still the case, then I want you to finish him, and dump the body just as those *two* arrive. See if we can dissuade them from going any further. Can you do that?'

'I'm not sure that'll work, my lord. They're a stubborn pair. Why not kill those *two*, and have done with them. It's more practical.'

'They've been sent to look for Satipilli—and if they find him, their job's done. So they might just turn round and go back and report what they've found. It's worth a try. If it doesn't work, we'll have plenty of time to terminate them, but if it works, we'll have got rid of them without throwing any suspicion on ourselves. Do I make myself clear?'

The chief spy, from bitter experience, found it pointless to argue with his master. 'Yes, my lord. I'll see to it at once.'

After the spy master had made his exit, Madduwatta fell into gloom and began to regret having plotted rebellion against the Hittite king. He even regretted having gone after Satipilli, but that was all too late. His major problem was that he may be forced to seek help and protection from Tudhaliyas if things turned nasty. He had absolutely no illusions about Ahhiyawa's ability to crush him if it so desired. He now began to hope that the civil war would continue as long as possible—so that it kept them too busy to think of him.

Then he began to conjure up ideas as to how he could help and extend that conflict, and soon he was back at his plotting ways and a look of contentment rose within him. He felt at his most agreeable when he was plotting someone's downfall.

\* \* \*

Several days later Daubum asked for an audience with the Governor, and was duly escorted into the audience chamber. He found Madduwatta in a good mood, humming to himself, staring towards the balcony.

'Well, and what can I do for my chief spy, on this glorious day?' Madduwatta had spent the night with a new addition to his harem and was full of the joys of life.

'My lord, it is with some regret that I have to inform you that the Ahhiyawan civil war has come to an end. We couldn't do anything to prolong it. I've just received word that yesterday Attarsiyas won a decisive battle against his brother and Famemnon was killed on the battle field.

109

Attarsiyas is the new legitimate king in Millawanda. A bigger problem is that four of your garrisons were attacked on our border with Ahhiyawa. Whereas one managed to repel the attack, another three did not and succumbed to the aggressor. I fear, my lord, that Attarsiyas is sending you a message, and it isn't a good one. I believe we may have a lot more to come from that direction.'

This is not what Madduwatta wanted to hear, not on a pleasant day like this. It spoiled his mood and he frowned at the news. 'I had a foreboding that something like this might happen when we got back from Phadhiya. It really isn't good enough. I really wish that things had turned out differently. Now what am I to do?' He began pacing up and down. 'Any suggestion, Daubum?'

'I'm afraid, my lord, that this is now out of our hands. We can only hope that Attarsiyas remembers that we have a guardian in Hatti, and that he should not press us too hard. It might be an idea to remind him of that.' The spy shrugged, as if to say, that was the limit of his ideas.

'That's a splendid idea. I'll get my scribe to deliver a protest note to the Ahhiyawan king, reminding him of the Hittite power to the east and that I am his vassal.' Madduwatta's disposition lifted, and he smiled at the spy. 'Good! Thank you, you may go.'

Just then, an aide announced the arrival of a courier from the east. Madduwatta jerked at the news, fearing the king in Hattusas had somehow got wind of what was happening, and had decided to send for him. 'Where's he from,' Madduwatta inquired of the aide.

'My lord, he wouldn't say. He just said from the distant east.' The aide fidgeted uncomfortably.

'All right, send him to me. I'll have to find out for myself. Do I have to do everything around here?' He demanded of the retreating aide.

The courier appeared, and Madduwatta immediately relaxed. He was indeed from the far east. Further east than even Hattusas. 'Well? What have you got for me?' He barked at the courier. Then realised his mistake, took the man by the elbows and walked him quietly out onto the balcony. He said in a whisper, 'Well?'

The courier understood and whispered back, 'My lord, his majesty in Wassukkani sends his greetings. He wishes me to remind you of your promise to help your benefactors. I brought no written message for the sake of security, and so I'm to speak to you on behalf of his majesty. There is the matter of the large sum of gold his majesty has advanced you. Although you were promised more, there seems to be a distinct lack of activity regarding your promised rebellion. Are you ready yet? When is this rebellion to occur? His majesty needs to know that his time and money are not being wasted.'

Madduwatta stood and listened in utter dismay. Things had changed. He might be attacked any moment now by his neighbour, and here he was, being berated by a courier for not rebelling against his only possible saviour. The dismay turned to anger, but he kept it hidden down deep. He'd taken the payment and now he would have to prevaricate.

He said to the courier with as much sincerity he could muster, 'We're about ready. Any day now! I just need to tie up a few loose ends. Tell his majesty that we're almost ready. By the time you return to Wassukkani you will surly have heard of my defiance to the king in Hattusas. Tell your majesty that I have strong allies in my neighbour Ahhiyawa. This rebellion will succeed, I promise you. You may take my assurances to your majesty in good faith. Now, can I get my people to feed you? You must have had a long journey? Maybe a little relaxation and some fun later on, eh? I can send a good female to you; we have some very fine women that will give you what you want.'

The courier looked a little surprised by all these tempting offers and said, 'I could do with some food, certainly. I also need four fresh horses for the return journey. As for the rest; maybe some other time. Thank you all the same.' The courier had been warned not to dawdle in Ura. He'd been warned that the governor might try to delay him. It was all tempting, but he was duty bound to refuse the offers.

Madduwatta feigned disappointment and then told his aide to take this fellow and give him some food, but also to make sure that the horses he got would go lame sometime on the journey, but be sure not to make it too obvious.

# Chapter Fifteen

**M**okhat lay with his right leg pinned under his injured horse, watching Palaiyas ride away to safety. He struggled to get free but to no avail, his horse was far too heavy. The horse thrashed about in an attempt to get up, but this simply made matters worse for him. While Mokhat made these strenuous exertions in what he considered to be a life and death struggle, all the time the onrushing wild men got nearer and would soon be close enough to finish him off. It was at the realisation that he could do little or nothing to free himself that he finally gave up the effort.

Mokhat could now see the large group of horsemen descending on him and he began to fear for his life. They'd made their intentions quite clear by firing off their weapons at him, so it seemed commonsense that they would finish him off when they reached him. Soon the yelling ceased from the descending horde and the wild men, all with drooping moustaches, were all around him, sitting on their ponies, looking down at him, pointing, and laughing. One man barked an incomprehensible order, and another man jumped down from his pony, came round to Mokhat's struggling horse, took a knife from his boot, and cut the poor horse's jugular, putting it out of its misery. Another shout of more incomprehensible commands from the leader, and some ten men dismounted, surrounded Mokhat's horse, and began rolling the dead horse off of him.

*Why don't they just finish me of now, instead of wasting energy removing my horse*, the morbid thought fluttered through Mokhat's mind.

An ugly brute with a scar down the left side of his face, and a long drooping flaxen-haired moustache, came over to

Mokhat, pulled him up from the ground, forcing him to stand on the one good leg, snarled something incomprehensible at him, poked him with his left hand, then raised his right hand across his chest with a whip in it, and struck him so hard across the right temple, that he knocked him unconscious.

*　　*　　*

Mokhat woke with a thundering headache. It was night time and he was tied over the wheel of some cart, unable to move. His right leg felt numb and his hands were frozen. Some ten cubits in front of him blazed a large campfire with a number of the wild men sitting round it, cutting off pieces of meat, and eating what looked like the remnants of a goat that was roasting over the fire. Further away there were ten or more campfires, and the noise of human activity suggested this was a large group. Near his fire there was much loud talk and lots of laughter, which accompanied the delicious smelling food. It was then that Mokhat realised he'd not eaten since the previous day, and as a result, his stomach made a lot of rumbling noises in complaint. What he couldn't understand is why they were keeping him alive.

The movement of his head had caught the attention of one of the men sitting facing him round the fire near to him. He pointed and shouted something; got up and came over to check Mokhat's bindings. Mokhat noticed twisted ropes of yellow hair hanging from his waist and snake shaped gold bands on both bare biceps. He checked the bindings and then out of spite, kicked Mokhat's right leg and laughed, shouting something at his pals. They joined in the laughter, and he then rejoined them at the fire.

For Mokhat, he spent the worst night of his entire life tied to that wheel, enduring the cold, popping in and out of consciousness. Sometime during the night, someone came and put his fur cloak around him. Although he didn't see who it was, it saved his life until the morning. At dawn, he could see more of the camp, and he could just make out the shapes of about ten more carts like the one he was tied to. Men were beginning to stir and fires were being stoked up that had somehow managed to be kept lit throughout the night.

One big fellow, long red hair tied backwards, sporting a drooping moustache, came over to him, untied him, and led him to the back of the cart and pointed inside. He was dressed in fur trousers and wore a fur coat tied with a belt round the middle. He seemed to have what looked like scalps hanging from his belt. Mokhat looked at him puzzled, but the big fellow pointed again inside the cart, so Mokhat parted the flaps, making as if to go inside. The big man smiled and nodded. With flaps parted, Mokhat was surprised to see that the cart had a door behind those flaps. He climbed onto the back of the cart, pushed the door, and went inside. The oblong room was empty, but it was warm with the overpowering smell of human occupation. He guessed this was where the wild men had slept last night— out of the cold and off the ground. It was a portable dwelling the like he'd never seen before.

Who were these people, he asked himself for the umpteenth time? From what he'd seen of their apparel, they were dressed in strange outfits, all wearing those strange drooping moustaches, and they didn't resemble anything he'd ever come across before. They were mounted on weird small ponies rather than the usual larger horses he was accustomed to. They were wild in more ways than their shouting and yelling. All were clad in dark furs, wearing trousers, carrying spears and round shields, or bows and arrows, while on their heads they wore pointed bearskin hats.

The warm atmosphere inside the portable room began to make him drowsy, and he lay down on one of the furs spread over the floor. No sooner had his head touched the floor, than he fell asleep. He woke from a fitful sleep when he felt an excruciatingly sharp kick in his back and the fellow with the scar down the left side of his face, was shouting down at him in his own incomprehensible tongue. He was pointing at the door and kicked him again.

It was patently clear he wanted him out of this room. At this command, Mokhat hurried to crawl to the door with his bad leg, and jumped down from the cart, falling onto the ground. Scarface had followed him, and on landing on the ground, kicked him again for good measure. Mokhat tried to move further out of reach, but Scarface picked him up and walk-limped him over to where he'd been tied before, and retied him to the wheel. He was really tied to the sides of the cart, but across the wheel, since the wheel was made of solid wood. He spent the whole morning like that, tied to the wheel, being ignored for the most part. About noon, the red haired man came over to him, when Scarface wasn't looking, and pushed a small piece of black bread into Mokhat's mouth and poured some fermented milk down his throat. It sustained and warmed him somewhat, but he still hadn't eaten a proper meal in three days.

In the afternoon the wind changed direction and the weather became a little warmer; as a result, Mokhat felt a glimmer of hope. That was soon dashed when Scarface reappeared to check his bonds. The ugly wild man then went over to talk to some of his cronies, which prompted them to jump on their ponies and gather some fifty cubits in front of where Mokhat was tied. Suddenly, whooping and yelling they rode at Mokhat, and when they were only thirty cubits from him, they fired their arrows at him from their strange bows. He clamped his eyes shut, heard thud after thud of arrows striking the wheel; he opened his eyes only when he felt they had finished. All the arrows missed him but imbedded all around him in the solid side of the wheel. Some of the arrows were to his left side, some to his right, and some near his head, but their marksmanship was extraordinary. Eight arrows in all! He was sure if they had intended to hit him they could have chosen any part of him and struck their target. On the one hand Mokhat was astonished at the wild men's marksmanship, and on the other, he was petrified with fear. The eight wild men returned to their starting position, laughing and joking, treating his suffering as an amusing diversion. It was surely only a matter of moments before they would aim directly at him, and put him out of his misery.

Scarface came over to the wheel, crookedly grinned at Mokhat, pulled the spent arrows out from the wheel, and walked over to the side. Then the group of horsemen came at him again, and again loosened eight arrows into the wheel all around him—and with each thud, Mokhat thought that it might be his last moment on this earth. The impact on his mind was shattering. Every arrow strike into the wheel was like a death knell, every thud of an arrow might be his last moment. It was tearing his mind apart. He was shaking with fear and sweat, and it was clearly to Scarface's liking.

Again this sadistic persecutor came over to the wheel and removed the arrows, then yelled something at his eight cronies, and moved away from the wheel. Yet again they charged, but with a difference; this time they were throwing spears. This time one of the spears took a small part of his earlobe off Mokhat's left ear. He felt the heavy thud of the spear and then the tremendous pain in his left ear. It almost came as a relief that he'd been hit, for more than once he'd expected one of the missiles to strike him. Yet surprisingly, all the other spears had missed him, and protruded from the wheel like some obscene giant hedgehog. Mokhat's right leg was paining him, and his knees finally gave way. He hung there limp with terror spread over his face. He'd wet himself, and began to sob.

Scarface's reaction was to laugh himself into a fit at their prisoner's pathetic state. He called over his companions, who rode over on their ponies, and roared with laughter at Mokhat's incontinence. They seemed to think it was exceptionally hilarious that their captive had broken down and begun to cry while they were having such fun.

Then abruptly the merriment ceased, and Mokhat pulled himself together. He looked at what had caused the silence and saw that another of the wild men with the drooping moustache had appeared from round a cart. He seemed to be even bigger than Scarface, had flaxen-hair and gold earrings in his earlobes, and the group appeared to defer to him. On his head he wore a helmet encrusted with golden animals. He shouted at Scarface, and Scarface began to fidget uncomfortably. His cronies were also acting awkwardly in front of what Mokhat took to be their leader. Then the ginger haired man joined the leader and spoke quietly in his ear, with the leader nodding his agreement. The leader then shouted something at Scarface, which induced him to fetch his pony, mount it with a jump, then both he and his companions galloped out of the camp.

The ginger haired man came over to Mokhat and undid his bonds, and helped him to the nearby campfire. Mokhat squeezed the man's arm in gratitude, while he dried himself in the heat. The ginger haired fellow with his drooping ginger moustache, brought him some more black bread and a jug of fermented mare's milk, and sat by Mokhat while he wolfed this meal down with gratitude. When Mokhat had finished the food, and had dried himself sufficiently, his saviour took him by the arm and led him to the room in the cart to rest. Why this ginger haired fellow was helping him out, Mokhat had no idea, but he was extremely indebted for his intervention. He had probably saved his life for the second time. Now, back in the warmth of the cosy room, lying on the furs, he nodded off in exhaustion. But his dreams were full of arrow thuds and nightmares.

Mokhat woke with a start when he felt a hand round his neck. It was Scarface. The brute jerked him by his throat, up off the fur he was lying on, and threw him at the door. His archenemy was back from wherever he'd been sent to, and wasn't happy to find his captive lying in the warmth. Scarface dragged Mokhat back to the wheel and tied him to it once again. Mokhat noticed another shadow standing a little way back, watching the proceedings.

The shadow came slowly forward and said quietly, 'Well now, how's my friend here treating you?'

To hear a recognisable language stunned Mokhat and he looked closely at this large figure before him. A dawning of recognition came over him. This was the same dark haired bearded shepherd he and Palaiyas had seen when they crossed the Marassantiya River some days back; breaking up a fist fight between the two wagon drivers with his crook. Mokhat began to understand what was happening to him, and why. This all had to do with their search for Satipilli, and this fellow was attempting to prevent them carrying out that task. 'My friend was right to be suspicious of you,' Mokhat spat out. 'A shepherd with no flock giving the both of us deadly glares. Who are you working for?' he asked, not really expecting an answer.

'Tut, tut,' said the shepherd, almost whispering. 'Even though I don't presume you'll survive this ordeal, I'm too cautious a man to give out information for free. At least we have one of you. It's a pity your friend managed to get away.' He then turned to Scarface and began talking to him in his own language.

Again Mokhat was astounded by the turn of events. How did this false shepherd know this strange tongue? 'You are full of surprises!' Mokhat exclaimed, interrupting their little chat.

'*Enough* from you!' hissed the shepherd with pure menace, and he reached out his right hand and grabbed Mokhat by the throat in a powerful grip. He must have felt the chain round Mokhat's throat, and in a malevolent moment, he grabbed it, and yanked it off. On it was Mokhat's black dragon pendant of Illuyankas. 'I'll have this as a souvenir of our little meeting. Now be *still*, or I'll have my

119

friend here deal with you right now. By the way, I've talked to the leader of these people and he assures me you will get no more help. Astonishing what a little gold can do. He's now happy to let my friend here, do as he pleases with you. I will say *goodbye* to you now. I don't imagine I'll see you again.' With that threatening inference, he went and sat by the fire.

Scarface joined him, laughing, and joking with this false shepherd. He then poked something in the fire, pulled it out and came over to Mokhat. Scarface held a red hot branding iron in his right hand and he pushed it at Mokhat's chest, burning through his heavy tunic and scorching his skin. Mokhat yelled out loud with agony of it, screaming his anguish into the still night. Scarface thought that was very funny and he laughed all the way back to the campfire, reinserting the iron back into the fire.

Mokhat couldn't believe what had just happened. The pain was a lingering trauma driving him to the brink of despair. He looked at the vile creature who'd done this to him and realised he would be back with the iron to continue his torture. He wasn't sure he could remain sane the next time Scarface came at him. The night was cold but he was sweating. Just at that moment, to Mokhat's surprise, both of his antagonists got up from the fire and walked away into the night, leaving him to face his demons in the cold and the dark. The throbbing from his chest was pounding its way all along his sinews to his brain, giving him a splitting headache. How much more of this could he take—he simply could not tell, but there was a limit to human endurance.

# Chapter Sixteen

In spite of the night's chill, Mokhat eventually managed to doze off, even with the pain in his chest; he was just too exhausted. As dawn broke, he was in the middle of a nightmare when he was awoken by a hand clasped over his mouth. *Not Scarface again*, thought a terrified Mokhat with a start. Couldn't he leave him alone just for a bit? He opened his eyes to see Palaiyas' face staring into his own. His eyes widened, and his whole being lit up with joy. His friend removed his hand and put a finger to his lips indicating he should be quiet. Then he cut the bonds tying him to the wheel and helped him away round the wagon towards the dark side. Mokhat had noticed a couple of bodies by the fire, indicating what Palaiyas had been up to.

'We're about to hit this camp,' whispered Palaiyas. 'I thought I'd better get you out before we did that, otherwise you might end up as one of the casualties. By the way, I'm returning the royal seals to you right now.' He pushed the pouch back into Mokhat's hand, the one he'd thrown at the retreating Palaiyas as he left him under his horse.

With his freedom, Mokhat's wits returned, and the blood rose in him to find Scarface. He tied the pouch back round his neck, rubbed his hands to get the circulation going, and then gently rubbed his chest. 'Who's going to hit the camp? Who've you got with you?' he whispered at Palaiyas.

'I have a large Hittite squadron hiding in the gully over there, some five hundred men,' Palaiyas pointed beyond the line of carts to a dip in the landscape. 'They're just waiting for my signal. Well? Are you ready for some revenge?' Palaiyas grinned mischievously. He gave a wave in the direction of the gullies to whoever was watching for that signal, and a multitude of horses began to ride towards them, fanning out into a broad line of gallop. Palaiyas bent down and picked up a sack from which he handed Mokhat, a sword, a couple of daggers, and a warm fur cloak. 'Right, let's go and find your tormentor.'

Mokhat fastened the cloak around his shoulders, stuck one of the daggers in his belt, and adorned his face with a grimace of anger and revenge. He'd been waiting three long days for this moment; a moment he thought would never be his. Mokhat, sword in one hand and a dagger in the other, still limping on his right leg, throbbing pain in his chest, followed Palaiyas back to the cart and waited for the doors to come crashing open.

After a moment, those inside the cart heard the thunder of the horse's hooves descending on them, and the doors burst open with wild men trying to rush out, only to be met with sword thrusts, from Palaiyas and Mokhat. Just then, the five hundred strong Hittite squadron arrived and joined the two lone combatants in the slaughter. About thirty Hittites on their horses arrived at their cart door to give Palaiyas and Mokhat a hand.

Mokhat and Palaiyas were standing on the ground hacking at the wild men's legs, crippling the first three before caution prevailed on those within the cart. But the newly arrived soldiers were able to slice and gash downwards from their horses at the wild men. One of the wild men made a mad dash and rushed through the door, flinging himself headlong onto Palaiyas, who jumped aside and stabbed him in the underbelly with his dagger. Almost simultaneously, another did the same but was cut down by a soldier on horseback. A third flung himself at Mokhat, and received exactly the same treatment as Palaiyas had given his man.

A few moments of silence descended on those in the cart as caution asserted itself, while those outside waited and listened to the whispering inside and the cries and fighting around the other carts in the first light of dawn. Then all of the wild men in the wagon came rushing out of the cart in a bunch, hoping that their numbers might overwhelm those waiting outside. They had no idea that the numbers favoured those waiting in the daybreak. The sun had risen into the chilly morning sky and promised a fine day for the battle.

No sooner had the wild bunch of men leapt from the tail of the cart, then they were fighting for their lives as they hit the ground. The wild men didn't stand much of a chance but they gave an excellent account of themselves in the vicious fighting. The predicament for them was they were overwhelmed by the odds against them and had simply not been prepared for battle at that point of sun-up.

Mokhat went at his foes ferociously and fought like a demon, maiming and slashing as if he was working out his whole anger for what they had done to him. The gentle thoughtful priest of former times had been replaced by a fierce vengeful warrior bent on killing as many of the wild men he could lay his hands on. In the melee, Mokhat tried to find Scarface, but he couldn't take his attention away from the man in front of him, who was trying to kill him. His blood was up and he ignored the pain in his chest and right leg. In the turmoil all around him, he was unable to discover Scarface's whereabouts, although he imagined each opponent was his vile tormentor.

As the fighting died down, Mokhat noticed Palaiyas had gone missing. He looked for him on the ground, and when he didn't see his corpse, he went to look for him in those still standing. Some of the Hittite squadron were still chasing down some of the wild men; those who had made a run for it.

Mokhat found Palaiyas beyond the last cart, standing over the body of...Scarface, of all people. He was furious. 'Damn you! May Lelwani take you! Why couldn't you let *me* finish him off?' His face was tense and enraged; then just as suddenly, he became dejected, all in a matter of seconds. Looking down at the body of Scarface, he realised he felt out of control. His anger returned. He so badly *needed* to have killed this thug that....that he stood there speechless. Palaiyas had taken *this* away from him, and he felt anger at Palaiyas.

Palaiyas partly understood why Mokhat was in such a state, having been in many battles, and having seen how the combatants behaved afterwards. Many were simply traumatised after all the killing, laughing and crying at the same time. From a hiding place a distance away, Palaiyas had witnessed the arrows being fired at his friend, and frankly thought that his friend had been killed by them. When the wild men went back and fired the arrows again, and again, he realised they were playing a sadistic game at Mokhat's expense.

Palaiyas had been looking for Scarface so that Mokhat could deal with him, but the ugly brute had engaged him in mortal combat, and then he had to fight for his life. Scarface had been a tough customer to kill, and he couldn't afford to fool around with him. He'd had to fight with all the skill he could muster, and slay him the first chance he got. Now all he could do was stand and stare at his friend's helpless frustration—and his fury at having missed his quarry.

'I'm sorry my friend,' Palaiyas said sincerely. 'I had no choice but to kill him. I know you *needed* to do that but there's no way I could have saved him for you. He just wouldn't let me do that.'

Hearing his friends words, Mokhat realised he'd have to live with what had happened to him—*and* would have to try and get over it somehow. His anger abated. He threw down his sword, grasped Palaiyas by both shoulders, and hugged him, saying, 'Thank you, my friend. Thank you for rescuing me—and....thank you for killing this scum. I'm eternally in your debt. I hope I can return the favour some day.'

'I hope I never get into the same kind of fix where you have to,' Palaiyas said with relief and a smile. The little joke broke the emotional tension and they went to see the commander of the Hittite squadron to thank him for his help.

The commander was talking with a few of his officers near the first cart in the line, when Palaiyas approached. 'Excuse me General Kishnapili, may I introduce the reason we're all here. This is Prince Mokhat, brother to the Kaska King.'

'Your highness, I'm glad you're in one piece. It is most fortunate we were in the vicinity when your friend found us yesterday. Otherwise this would have ended.....' he left the rest unsaid. The general raised his eyebrows as if that were the completion of his sentence. 'Anyway, my men have found five of these ruffians still alive, hiding in the undergrowth, and one of them keeps pointing at you and shouting something. He's a wild red haired brute and we're having some trouble keeping him quiet.'

'Where is he?' Mokhat interrupted, alarmed that they might execute him. 'Don't hurt him. He's the one that saved my life yesterday.'

The general walked around the carts, leading Palaiyas and Mokhat to a group of his soldiers standing with their swords aimed at the five captive wild men. As Mokhat appeared, the red haired man began to shout incomprehensible words at him, smiling and pointing to himself, then making chewing motions with his mouth. Next to him stood the leader of the wild men, fingering his right gold earring, wearing his gold encrusted pointed helmet. He'd somehow survived the battle. He also tried to smile at Mokhat, but Mokhat remembered what the shepherd had told him about the gold, and how he'd thrown his weight behind Scarface. Mokhat totally ignored the leader and instead pulled the red haired fellow out of the group and clasped his hands, trying to imply his gratitude for his help. At Mokhat's reaction, the leader stopped pretending to smile, and understood that his duplicity had been uncovered.

'May I ask a favour of you, general?' asked Mokhat, holding the smiling red haired man by the shoulder.

'Indeed you may, your highness. If it's in my power, it shall be done. Then afterwards we can go and eat something. I'll wager you could do with a bite.'

'I don't care what you do with those four,' Mokhat nodded at the surrounded wild men, 'but this one,' he clasped the red haired man's shoulder to him; 'I'd like you to give him provisions and let him go. Can you do that for me? Then we can go and eat.'

'*That* certainly is within my powers,' the general answered. 'Consider it done. Now, we've found some of their roast meat and I have one of my men roasting a duck over there,' he pointed with his head at one of the wild men's fires that had been stoked up. The general gave orders to one of his officers for the ginger fellow to be provisioned and sent on his way. Then he led the way to the fire, and Mokhat followed gratefully, impelled by his hunger. A little while later, sitting on a log, Mokhat devoured the duck in a most un-princely manner, and smeared some of the duck fat on the developing scar on his chest. Palaiyas joined him in the duck feast munching on some of the wild men's roast meat, replenishing himself after all the fighting.

A little later, the general strode over, smiling, said, 'One of my men tells me there's someone not far away who's anxious to meet with you. A soldier from Purushanda at the head of a wagon convoy. Do you know anything about this?'

Mokhat had finished eating for the moment, and beamed at the news. 'Indeed I do. We were with that convoy until we separated from them near a gorge. We thought we'd move faster by crossing the rope bridge over the gorge, while the convoy was forced to go north to a bridge. The fellow who's asking for me must be Captain Narmus, is that right?'

'I'm not aware of his name,' replied the general, 'but you seem to know each other, so it must be the same Narmus fellow. He says he's waiting for you about a league further on, if you wish to rejoin him? And while we're at it; I think I might join you myself. After all, we're all going to Ivalanda.'

'The more the merrier—and the safer,' Palaiyas quipped in.

\*　　\*　　\*

A while later, the squadron was on its way towards where Narmus had bivouacked his convoy while waiting for them.

Mokhat was riding between the general and Palaiyas. 'General,' asked Mokhat, 'do you have any idea where those wild men came from? I couldn't understand a word of their language, and their outfits didn't fit in with anybody I've ever come across. I almost got killed by a gang of total strangers, and I need to know a little more about them.'

'This is what I managed to gather from their leader, whose name by the way is Genger, and he speaks passable Luwian, so we managed to converse. He tells me they're a *Gimirri* raiding party; they call themselves Gimirri, from across the waters, north of Wilusa. They paid the Wilusans a sum of gold to be shipped over the water from the north lands to here, to see if they could help themselves to some of our bounty. It seems they were doing quite well until now. That red haired fellow you got me to let go is called Airyaman.'

Mokhat couldn't help but interrupt, 'You don't happen to know the name of the fellow who tortured me, a big fellow with a large scar down the left side of his face, do you?' He looked intently at the general's face.

'Yes, I did manage to find out his name. Prince Palaiyas asked me to. He thought you might want to know. The leader tells me his name was Savanghi. I gather he's dead. Well anyway, as a result of all this mayhem, I've brought those four along with me to stick in the Ivalanda dungeons, to see if we can get some more information out of them. Oh! And their carts look interesting as well. I need to find out more about these people, so we can prepare a better welcome for any more that decide to venture this way. I've told the leader that if he cooperates, I might let him live. He seemed only too willing to talk. '

'There was a shepherd fellow here last night, talking to Savanghi, in his own language.' Mokhat thought he might have a chance at more information. 'I think he was the reason these wild men went after us. Any idea who he is? We really badly need that information for our mission.'

The general called for his officer to bring the leader, Genger, to him on a horse. He was not to be given the reins of the horse at any cost. The officer was to hold the reins. The leader duly arrived and the general began to question him. At first Genger was reluctant to speak of the shepherd, but after a severe talking to by the general, he opened up. All this was carried out in Luwian.

'He tells me that he knows the shepherd as Napat. This fellow turned up one day in their camp and spoke to them in a dialect that is recognisable to the Gimirri. He spoke to Genger in Saka. Gave him a large pouch of gold and asked them to catch you two. Genger says the Saka are a small tribe to the very far east of the Gimirri, in the open plains north of the Black Sea. Napat told Genger that he had fallen foul of a large family back in his lands, having ruined their daughter and then refused to marry her. The family went after him and he escaped over the mountains between the two seas, north east of Hatti. He made his way down to the Mittani and then came over here. That's all he knows. I'm of the opinion he's telling the truth.'

Palaiyas smiled at the story he'd just heard. It was almost identical to their cover story given to Narmus when they joined his wagon convoy.

Mokhat then asked the general, 'Can you ask him if he knows who this Napat is working for; that's the most important answer we need. Who's put him up to this? Who's got him following us?'

The general spoke to the leader, but Mokhat could see from the body language that Genger didn't know the most essential answer.

'I'm afraid he's no idea who he's working for. All he knows is it must be someone rich, because the sum of gold wasn't small.'

# Chapter Seventeen

Throughout the journey to join Narmus' convoy, Mokhat had been quiet and introspective. He hadn't said much to Palaiyas about his ordeal, and the latter had not pressed him on the subject. Palaiyas assumed that when his friend was good and ready, he'd broach the subject himself, but only if he wanted to get some of it off his mind. Nevertheless, Palaiyas could see his friend had been deeply affected by the traumatic experience.

They rode on like that, with the wind blowing and the clouds threatening more snow, through to noontime. Then the squadron climbed a dip in the frozen mountainous landscape and crested the hill in front. Before them, formed into a large circle, was their destination; Narmus' twenty wagon convoy. He had Mules and horses tethered downwind inside the wagon circle and in the middle were a couple of large campfires. People were sitting around it, warming themselves as the squadron neared. Some forty or so people around each fire. From a distance, Palaiyas saw quite a few sentries on duty; one man in particular was seated facing their way on a wagon, doing his watch. Palaiyas pointed him out to Mokhat —and as the sentry saw them, he jumped down and hurried to another man seated at the fire. Both then hurried back over to the wagon and climbed on the seat to get a better view of the oncoming squadron.

As they neared hailing distance, Palaiyas rode forward and shouted at the figure on the wagon seat, '*Narmus, is that you?*'

'Who *else* do you think it might be? We've been waiting for you since yesterday evening.' As Palaiyas came closer, he continued, 'I thought we'd never see you again after the gorge. Where've you been all this time? I thought you'd reached Ivalanda by now.'

Palaiyas got off his horse and Narmus jumped down from the wagon. They met and shook each other's forearms. 'Good to see you again, captain. Got anything hot for us to drink?'

'Over there, there's a hot brew waiting for you at the fire.' Narmus waited until the rest of the squadron rode up. He'd been so pleased to see Palaiyas that he'd only just then noticed Kishnapili, and he sprang to attention. 'Sir, Captain Narmus reporting. Everything is ready should you wish to inspect the wagons.'

'Stand easy, captain. I'd be more interested in a hot drink. It's been cold out here today.' The general turned to his officers and said, 'Get your men to see to the horses then they can join us at the fire.' He then spoke to his deputy, 'Captain Haliya, please go and tell Colonel Tipali, to bring the rest of the men here.'

Captain Haliya saluted, climbed on his horse, and was off at a gallop away from the wagons.

Mokhat mentally noted in passing, *what other men?*

'And you,' the general motioned to another officer, 'park the Gimirri carts against the wind in a row by those wagons over there.'

The officer went back down the line to the cart drivers and relayed the general's orders.

Captain Narmus said, 'Please come this way,' and he led the way through the gap in the wagon convoy towards the fire. '*Cook!*' Narmus shouted at the fellow by the cauldron, 'pour the General a hot drink, then pour us some hot drinks, then get some food for the new arrivals. Hurry man!'

A log was cleared for the general to sit on, and those by the fires made room for the newly arrived soldiers. Mokhat and Palaiyas sat near the general on one side, and Narmus on the other.

After some hot wine, the general turned to Mokhat and confided, 'Your highness, I have a small confession to make to you.' He tried to look contrite, but failed. 'It's not entirely by accident that Prince Palaiyas found us the other day. Before I left Hattusas, I was given strict instructions by his majesty to keep an eye out for the pair of you. Were I to come across you, I was ordered to render you all the assistance you required. The fact is, the other day I had scouts out looking for you both. I estimated that at you normal rate of travel, you should have been somewhere around here. Furthermore, considering what has happened to you, I feel duty bound to escort you as far as Ivalanda. What have you to say to that? Any objections?' He cocked his eye in anticipation of an objection.

Both Mokhat and Palaiyas raised their eyebrows at the news that this general had been searching for them. They looked at each other and smiled.

Mokhat spoke first, 'Interesting! It would seem we have little choice but to accept graciously. We were trying to keep a low profile, but look where that got me. Yes, I think I would be only too happy to have you and your men escort us to Ivalanda. By the way, how many men have you got with you?'

'His majesty sent me to bolster up the garrison on the Ahhiyawan border, and I have two thousand horse, chariots, and supply wagons. I have just now sent one of my men to bring the rest of the regiment here. They should be here by sunset. Then tomorrow,' the general turned to face Narmus, 'I'm going to suggest we get back on the road by about mid morning, if that's alright with you captain. It's your wagon convoy, after all.'

'Yes sir. Mid morning it is, sir,' Narmus responded.

A couple of the wagon drivers brought a small table from one of the wagons and placed it near the fire. 'This is for you and the two princes, sir,' Narmus said, pleased at his initiative.

The general shook his head, 'No captain. On a march, I and my officers eat with the men. I find it more rewarding. It reminds me of my youth, and it strengthens the bonds between us. If your highnesses wish to eat at the table, I'll find that acceptable, but I'm staying here if you don't mind.'

Narmus was surprised at this unusual behaviour. He'd always assumed officers would want to eat separately, and he assumed the general would want to do the same. Partly dismayed at the refusal, but impressed by the reasoning, he said, 'I'm happy for you to stay here. I know that their highnesses will want to stay here with you,' he looked to the two princes for confirmation.

The two princes both nodded their agreement. Narmus waved for the table to be removed, and packed back to where it came from.

More fires were lit outside the wagon circle for the five hundred strong contingent of newcomers. Areas were cleared for those yet to come, and the vicinity began to look like a large scale military encampment. Cooks got busy unpacking all the rations they had with them, in the promise from the general that they would be replenished when his own supply wagons arrived.

After what seemed a long wait, hot mutton broth was dished out in bowls, and those that could, dug in to the warming meal. Others waited; bowl in hand near the fires, for the cooks to make more broth. Then they ate their fill.

\*　\*　\*

A while later, when the sun began to set in the wintry sky far below the western horizon, and the camp was settled, a deep thunder of many horses was heard and the rest of the general's regiment arrived; another one and a half thousand men to be fed and settled in. For the next couple of hours there was banging and shouting as the non-coms ordered tents to be set up, latrines built, and horses fed and bedded in.

Then there followed a lengthy period of silence as the newly arrived soldiers ate their evening meals. Later that was followed by a number of songs coming from the soldiers round their campfires—one group trying to out-sing another faction round their individual campfires.

*   *   *

At dawn the next day, over two thousand individuals were prodded into life by the shouting non-coms, yelling at cooks to prepare the morning's food, yelling at reluctant rousers, shouting at sentries to report. Both Mokhat and Palaiyas were used to the various camp noises, having served in their respective armed forces, even so, they were both reluctant to get up and face the new day. Mokhat in particular could have done with more rest, having spent the night fitfully suffering reoccurring nightmares from his recent ordeal. He woke in a sweat; his face was full of misery, before he quickly composed himself. Palaiyas had been woken a number of times during the night by Mokhat's ramblings, but he hadn't had the heart to wake him. Neither of them mentioned anything to each other, and they dressed themselves in a strained silence, each one mulling over their own thoughts.

After the morning meal, the tents were packed and reloaded on the wagons, the campsite was tidied up and by midmorning as promised, the entire regiment was lined up in two columns, ready to continue its journey to Ivalanda. Each column was led by two hundred and fifty cavalry, followed by ten of Narmus' wagons, followed by five of the Gimirri carts, which in turn were followed by five hundred cavalry; then came fifteen regimental supply wagons, and finally bringing up the rear were two hundred and fifty cavalry. Just in front, in between the two columns rode the general and his deputy with Mokhat and Palaiyas, then came his staff officers, those not leading detachments.

'Well what say you, shall we be off?' the general asked Mokhat. He raised his hand not waiting for a reply and motioned the two columns forward. The weather had turned milder and less chilly, and everybody was hoping the cold weather spell was over.

As the regiment made its somewhat weighty move towards Ivalanda, Palaiyas asked the general, 'Where are your prisoners?'

The general told him, 'Locked in their own cart, the leading one. I have ten men detailed to guard them night and day. I shall flail them alive if they loose them. Why do you ask?'

'Out of pure tidiness. I haven't seen them since the fight and was just wondering. We've another two days before we get to Ivalanda and I've decided to keep an weary eye on them. No offence to your men, you understand.' Palaiyas was being diplomatic.

'Well, if you wish to do so, your highness, I've no objections.' But the general was a little curious as to why this prince of Tiryns was still interested in those brigands.

By mid afternoon the wind had picked up and the sky looked ominous with dark heavy clouds looming overhead. The general looked at them, then turned to Mokhat, 'What do you think you highness? I have a feeling we're in for a storm, and possibly a bad one at that.'

'I agree, general. Might be an idea to halt until it's over,' Mokhat replied.

The general raised his hand and stopped the convoy. He turned to his deputy, Colonel Tipali, 'Right, I want all the wagons in a large tight circle over there,' he pointed at some flat ground to the right. 'All the animals inside and everything tied down tight. When this storm hits, I want us all under cover. Those not able to get into wagons should take shelter underneath them. If we do this right, we should come out of this will little or no damage. Please see to it!'

The deputy sent the officers down the line to transmit the instructions, and soon the wagons had been brought into a double circle. Before the last one was in place, tiny ice crystals were falling. The animals behaved a little restlessly, sensing the storm to come. The trickle turned from ice to snow to ice a few times, and then it really started coming down hard. It couldn't make up its mind whether to rain ice or snow, so it did both. Soon the wind was blowing, with swirling clouds of wet snow obscuring much of the surrounding landscape. With the increasing wind the temperature dropped and the wet snow turned to ice. Visibility fell to an arm's length in front of the face for anyone unlucky to be still out there. The iced snow stuck to the wagons, the animals, and to the landscape turning it a glazed white.

*   *   *

The storm lasted until late afternoon when the sky began to clear and the sun managed to break through. Then people started to poke their heads out into the fresh air, and were treated to an illuminated ice-capped countryside with the light reflecting sharply off the icy white exhibition, the penetrating glare hurting their eyes. The beauty of it took their breaths away. But all too soon the light began to fade from the sky, all down to the shortness of the winters day. It was then that the general decided that they might as well make where they were, the night camp.

The general climbed out of the wagon he'd been holed up in to stretch his legs, followed by Colonel Tipali, Mokhat and Palaiyas. He got Tipali to check that everybody was alright.

As his deputy went to check on the wagons, an officer came running up to him, looking embarrassed and whispered in the general's ear. The young officer handed the general something in a surreptitious manner, which raised Mokhat's and Palaiyas' eyebrows.

'What?' exploded the general. 'What do you mean they're gone? And what's this?' he opened his hand. In it lay a broken chain attached to a black dragon pendant. 'Where did you find this?'

'Sir, it was on the rugs inside the cart. Do you want to speak with the individual soldiers who were guarding the prisoners?' The officer was shamefaced.

'One moment general, may I see that,' Mokhat asked.

The general handed over the pendant to Mokhat, and on recognising it, he snarled at the officer, 'How in the lord's name could you let this happen. This is mine. It's my pendant of Illuyankas which hung round my neck until that fake shepherd wrenched it from my neck. The one calling himself Napat. Are you telling us this Napat has managed to get past your guards and release the prisoners?'

The misery on the officer's face redoubled. He nodded and said, 'It must have happened during the storm.'

The general's scowl turned into a smile, 'Well this is one for the scribes. That rascal is taunting us—well mocking you two, really. He's managed to sneak in under cover of the storm and steal our captives from under the noses of two thousand men. That *is* a neat trick. I can't help but admire his cheek.'

Palaiyas was also smiling at the audacity of this Napat. 'He's been so persistent in dogging our footsteps,' he said to Mokhat, 'that we really must find out who's employing him.'

Only Mokhat looked unhappy. He fingered his pendant and scowled at it. 'Yes we must! May I also remind you,' he said to Palaiyas and the general, 'this is not a game. I was almost killed as a result of his persistence, and I frankly would like to get *my* hands on him and to show *him* how much I admire *his* cheek.'

The sarcasm wasn't lost on the general, and the general felt suitably chastened. Then the general said to the officer still standing and waiting, 'Fetch me the man in charge of the prisoner's guards. I'd like a small chat with him.'

The officer stood there looking even more uncomfortable, if that were possible. 'I'm sorry sir, but that would be me.'

'*Well?* What have you to tell me regarding this escape?' The general's face darkened. Mokhat's admonishment had spurred the general to be more serious in this matter, and the officer now bore the brunt of it. Also the general didn't like it that the officer hadn't told him immediately that it was he who was in charge of the prisoners.

'Sir, as per your orders, we got under cover when the storm hit. Me and my men went under the cart, and I can assure you, no one came near us. We were watching out for that. We couldn't see much due to the snow and low visibility but we listened very hard.' As the officer told this, he began to see how flimsy it now sounded.

'And in all your listening, you didn't hear this man sneak up and release your prisoners. How is that? Were you all asleep?'

'No sir, we....I'm sorry sir.' Now the officer stood at attention. He knew what was coming.

'Consider yourself demoted to non-com,' thundered the general. Now get out of my sight.' The general turned his back on the now demoted disgraced man.

The former officer saluted, then slinked away, head bent, and as he went, began removing his officer's insignia.

# Chapter Eighteen

**D**aubum, Madduwatta's chief spy, went to see the Governor's aide with a request to see Madduwatta. The aide didn't bother to see if the governor was free, knowing he would want to see him right away.

Daubum was shown into the audience chamber, and the aide withdrew backwards making his obeisance.

'What can I do for you?' Madduwatta asked in a distracted tone. He had a lot on his mind, what with the Ahhiyawa incursions, and now that damn courier appearing out of nowhere, demanding he fulfil his promises. The plotting and the promises were made at a more propitious time when everything was going the governor's way. Now it had disintegrated with a vengeance.

'My lord,' Daubum began, 'letting the courier go was *not* such a wise decision. I would be of little use to you if I didn't know everything that happened in Ura, especially here in the governor's mansion. When the courier gets back to Wassukkani and there is *no* rebellion to report, the king there is going to be extremely angry that you lied to him, via the courier. You already have one powerful enemy on your northern doorstep and you will have added another real nasty enemy in Wassukkani. Is that what you want, my lord?' Daubum waited for Madduwatta's response to his analysis.

The grim expression on the governor's face said it all. 'Well then, what do you suggest? I assume you have a suggestion or you wouldn't be here?'

'I suggest, with all deference, that you get your scribe to write a tablet to the king in Wassukkani informing him with regret, that his courier has been kidnapped by the pirates. Inform him that before you sent the courier on his way with your reply, with four horses and provisions, you offered to have him escorted to your eastern border, but the courier declined your offer. How the pirates got hold of him so far inland, is something that you're looking into. The rest you can leave to me. Is that acceptable to you, my lord?'

Madduwatta's face changed from gloom to cautious hope. 'You're a demon, Daubum. Where do you get these ideas from? You know the courier left early this morning? Well of course you do! Silly me! Yes, do what you need to do and let's hope it works. When you've done what you're going to do, come and report to me, so that if need be, I can deny everything. Carry on!'

Daubum, having foreseen the governor's acquiescence to his plan, had four of his men waiting with horses so that they could catch up with the courier. They rode out of Ura as speedily as they could manage on the road leading eastwards. It was mid-morning when Daubum's party left Ura and by mid-afternoon they had their quarry in sight. Daubum swung south and sought to parallel the courier for a short while before attempting to race ahead and ambush him, but to Daubum's amazement, the courier also swung south. *Now where's the fiend heading off to,* thought the spy?

The pursuers had to hide to avoid this peculiar courier, who seemed to be going towards the sea. He was still leading the three spare horses he'd been given and that was slowing him just a little. Again, Daubum moved ahead of the courier to set an ambush, and this time he wasn't disappointed. The ambush party waited on the other side of a bridge straddling a river, with four of Daubum's henchmen secreted out of sight beneath the planking so they could then leap over the bridge rails when the time came. The courier was almost over the bridge leading to Bastiniya but had to go slowly due to it still being a little slippery from residual frost. As the courier reached the other side of the wooden bridge, Daubum pretended to pass him, but then at the last moment brought his horse into a diagonal to block the horse the courier was riding. Sensing a trap, the courier made an effort to swing his stallion around just as those hidden behind him pounced, swinging over the bridge rails and blocking his retreat. They ignored the extra horses and swarmed around his mount, one grabbing the reins and the others pulling him off the horse. It was all over in a matter of seconds.

'Now my fine fellow, where on earth are you heading for? You're a bit off your route to Wassukkani.' The courier was being held by Daubum's cronies, squirming and pulling, trying to get free. 'No point in struggling, my dear fellow. Only answers are going to set you free,' chided Daubum falsely.

Seeing there was no way out, the prisoner ceased his exertions and relaxed. 'Your governor shall hear of this,' he threatened. 'I'm on official business; you have no right to detain me. You would do well to let me go on my way for your own safety.'

'I'm sorry you feel like this. I'm also on official business—and the governor already knows of this. It is *he* who sent us.' Daubum stared at the courier, who seemed startled, then it dawned on the courier that he would never reach Wassukkani if he kept silent.

It was with that hope, which springs eternal in the human breast, that the courier told Daubum all; he fervently hoped that he might be allowed to live. It seems that the courier had wished to avoid the long landward route and had arranged with the pirates in Bastiniya to have himself shipped to Ugarit, from where it was a shorter journey to Wassukkani. He had arranged this on the way to Ura. Now he was heading towards the port of Bastiniya when they'd apprehended him.

Daubum listened attentively and knew the man was telling him the truth. Daubum nodded to one of his henchmen, and he promptly stuck a knife in the courier's back. The courier slumped to the ground and the four henchmen stripped the deceased of his attire and dragged the naked body to the river, pushing the corpse into it. It would float downriver to the very port he was heading towards.

'That should help him on his way,' Daubum said in macabre jest to his henchmen. 'Now let's collect all these things,' he pointed at the courier's clothes and satchels, 'and put them on his horse. I want to examine them when we get back.'

The ambush party set off back to Ura, arriving there by nightfall. Daubum went to see the governor immediately.

'My lord,' said Madduwatta's chief spy when he was standing in front of the governor, 'I have determined the whereabouts of our missing courier,' which was said loudly with a crooked smile, indicating he was speaking publicly, should anybody be listening, 'and located him in Bastiniya, a port controlled by the pirates. The latter was probably the truth, for by the time they returned to Ura, the courier's corpse would indeed have floated down to the port. 'The last time I saw him,' continued the spy, 'he was begging for his life. I fear, my lord, that he may have been killed by them. I suggest you wait another day and then have the scribe send another shorter tablet saying that you fear the king's courier may have met with his death at the hands of the pirates. You will be very sorry and apologetic, but the courier should have let you give him an escort to our eastern borders, as you had proposed. You feel it might be unwise to rely too much on unreliable couriers; however, you await the *next* courier.'

'Hmm!' said Madduwatta, taking the spy by the elbow into a corner to speak with him more confidentially. 'I'm not sure this is going to work,' he whispered. 'All it's done is give us a bit of breathing space. See if you can think of something else. In the mean time, you need to deal with

Satipilli. Take him to Ivalanda tomorrow and do what needs to be done. Clear?'

'Yes my lord,' Daubum replied, and they parted.

Daubum made his way down to the dungeon where Satipilli was kept and asked the jailer how his prisoner was keeping.

'I don't know how he's lasted this long,' said the jailer. 'He's one tough fellow and the hardest nut we've ever had to crack. He still refuses to talk, and unfortunately there's not enough left of him to torture. Even that fat oaf of a torturer has lost interest in him—and that's never happened in the whole time I've been here. I keep expecting him to die, but each morning I check, and he's still breathing.'

Daubum looked meaningfully at the jailer. 'Well you can stop worrying. Tomorrow I'm going to take him off your hands. Patch him up as best you can and have him ready to travel at first light tomorrow. Tie his hands with rope so I can cut it easily when I need to.'

'He's made a mess of his water works, the torturer, I mean,' the jailer told Daubum. 'He'll be leaking all the way to wherever you're taking him. Best use a cart to transport him, otherwise he'll leak all over the horse.'

'Right! I'll deal with that, don't you worry. Just have him ready to travel for tomorrow.'

*    *    *

Early the next morning, waiting behind the mansion, there was a cart for Satipilli with straw and a blanket for covering. Daubum had ten of his henchmen as escort while another drove the covered cart. Out on the road northwards, this little party of Madduwatta's thugs had settled down to a long journey that would take them the whole day. The wind was benign, coming as it did from the south. It felt as if the weather was changing for the better and a thaw might set in.

143

What little frost remained was melting making for heavier going with so much slush on the road.

Mid afternoon Daubum met a party coming towards him, but from a distance he didn't recognise them. Only when they neared did he recognise his most trusted employee, Napat.

In a while as they met and their horses stood abreast in the road, Daubum asked him, 'Hallo Napat! Long time no see. Who've you got there with you? Friends of yours?'

'It's a long story,' said Napat wearily. 'Do you want me to come along with you or shall I go to Ura and wait for you there? I could do with a rest.'

Daubum wasn't apologetic when he said, 'Sorry Napat. I need you with me. We're heading to Ivalanda to deposit a friend of yours. Oh! And I see you've been borrowing horses again.'

'The locals just seem to leave them; some cavalry this time, so I help myself.'

'As long as it doesn't come back to bite me.' Just on cue, there was a moan from the cart.

'Who's in there?' Napat asked.

'That's our cargo. The Hatti spy you snared for me. We're taking him back to where you found him. He's a bit messed up but that won't matter; not to him at least.'

'In that case, I'd better introduce you to my friends here. He pointed at the massive companion sitting on a horse next to him, 'That's Genger, and the other three are his men. Their Gimirri, or what's left of them. I managed to rescue them from the Hittites while those lazy cowards lay hiding under a cart from a little storm.'

'I'm sure what you've just said means something to you, but *I* can't make head or tail of it. You can explain it to me as we go along. We'll stop in a while and have some food, then you can tell me what's been happening to you.' Daubum kicked his horse into motion once again and Napat followed with the Gimirri in tow.

Napat was chattering to Genger in their own tongue, to Daubum's irritation, explaining who Daubum was, and that they should go along with him and be nice to him, if they wanted to survive in this land.

A while later the little group stopped and the food was extracted from the cart and handed out, mostly dried meat and unleavened bread washed down with wine. While they ate Napat made a full report of what had transpired since they last met.

'So that's what's left of the whole Gimirri raiding party, eh!' Daubum commented contemptuously. 'A bit clumsy allowing yourself to get wiped out like that, if I may say so.'

Napat shrugged his shoulders as if to say, not my problem.

'Well, maybe I can use them. After all, you came to me like that. You'll have to teach them our language before they can be of any use. Tell them what I said. They can work for me if they want to, but be careful to explain the rules to them. No freelancing!'

They continued the journey well into dark, slept for a short period, and were back on the road before dawn. As the sun came up, they broke camp and were back on the road. They had breakfast on the move and by mid morning, they could see in the distance the city of Ivalanda outlined against the horizon.

Daubum stopped the group and pointed. 'That's our destination, but it's crucial to my plan that no one sees us. I want us to get close but we must stay well out of sight. Napat, I want you to go east and keep an eye out for that regiment you spoke of. As soon as you spot them, come back and we'll settle with Satipilli here. Then we dump him on the road just outside of Ivalanda, so those two can find him. The governor wants it that way. Then you, Napat, can stay behind and let me know what happens. Take your pals with you. If those two turn back east, come and tell me at once, otherwise, if they continue west, follow them, and get rid of them. Can you do that for me?'

'Sure boss! If they go east I come and tell you, if they go west, I kill them. No problem!' Napat smiled roguishly.

'Tell your pals here to follow my hand signals. Now you go and look out for the regiment, and hurry back when you catch sight of them. Off you go!'

Napat told Genger to watch for Daubum's hand communications and then rode off to the east to lookout for the coming of the regiment. Daubum took the rest of his party closer to Ivalanda using gullies, trees and any other camouflage he could find. In a winter landscape, it was difficult due to all the white background. Nevertheless, he eventually secreted his group in a shallow gully behind a small hill, in a spot where he could not be seen from the city walls. He had his people cut branches and build a sort of shelter, not against the elements, but against prying eyes. There they sat and waited as the day wore on. Luckily the milder climate on the back of the southerly wind alleviated some of the hardship. They ate and Daubum talked to his henchmen, while Genger and his three pals listened and made comments in their tongue, trying to get to grips with this strange language.

As the sun began to set, Napat came hurrying back, trying to be inconspicuous—he rode the horse while hanging onto its sides, striving to eliminate his silhouette. This stunt riding impressed Daubum but was second nature to the Gimirri.

'They're just coming,' Napat said as he jumped of his horse. Whatever you're gong to do, you need to do it now. Where's the cart? The one with Satipilli in it?' Napat asked.

'We had to abandon that some way back. It was too conspicuous. Satipilli's lying over there, still moaning,' Daubum said dismissively.

'Shall I finish him?' Napat offered.

'Yes, do that, but use this,' said Daubum, pulling out a Mycenaean dagger from his robe and giving it to Napat. 'That will implicate Ahhiyawa in his murder. After he's dead, make sure you stick it in his chest so it's nice and visible. Get your pals to give you a hand to carry him over to that road to the right over there, the one leading to the city gates. Make sure you're not seen. It's getting darker, so that will help. Then come back and report. Good luck!'

Napat did his foul deed quietly, hand over Satipilli's mouth, then got two of the Gimirri to give him a hand carrying the corpse to where Daubum had indicated he wanted it left. When he came back he told Daubum that everything had gone as he wished it.

'Good,' Daubum smiled. 'I'll leave you the rest of the supplies. Now I'm going back to Ura and you stay here with those four and do as I asked you. Can you do that?'

Napat smiled back and nodded.

# Chapter Nineteen

The night had been relatively quiet, and dawn found the regimental encampment awake and bustling with activity.

'Another dawn, another day,' Palaiyas commented inanely over his shoulder, as he stood outside their wagon.

'Stating the obvious is hardly news,' returned Mokhat, still in the wagon.

'Maybe not, but the weather's changing with the wind coming in from the south, and its bringing in more benign temperatures; for me that *is* news. You ready yet?' Palaiyas said cajolingly.

Mokhat still felt aggrieved that their prisoners had escaped. It sat on his mind like a heavy weight. What really sat on his mind was the ordeal he went through, and the prisoner's escape was a displaced surrogate anger for that ordeal. As a member of the Kaska royal family, he wasn't accustomed to such treatment. Nearly put to death, scorched with branding irons, being abused. He personally had never been subjected to such behaviour in his whole life, and was outraged that someone could do that to *him*.

Even prior to the wild men outrage, Mokhat had decided to abandon his priestly garb forever. Now he reaffirmed it to himself. That was what was going through his mind in the wagon while he was dressing, and while Palaiyas was chitchatting with him standing outside the wagon. Mokhat intended to emerge from his ordeal as simply Prince Mokhat of the Kaska—no longer a priest. He'd lost his belief in Illuyankas, and consequently abandoned him forever.

Where was Illuyankas when he was being tortured? How could the great dragon god allow his priests to be so terribly abused? That nasty brute even stole his pendant of the god himself. Outrageous! These thoughts had been going round and round in his head ever since the ordeal. These unanswered questions had brought him to his final resolution. When they had finished in Ivalanda and were back on the road to Millawanda, Mokhat promised himself to tell his friend of his momentous decision.

'Right,' Mokhat said as he climbed out of the wagon, 'lead me to the food.' He made an effort to put on a less surly face.

\*　　\*　　\*

Breakfast was a swift affair, gulped down hurriedly because the non-coms were scolding everybody to get finished quickly. They had orders to get the regiment back onto the road as quickly as possible. The general wanted to make it to Ivalanda by nightfall.

The general was out front leading the two columns with his deputy and officers, while making small talk with Mokhat. The latter took a chance and sneaked in the escaped convicts into the conversation.

'I'm still a bit disgusted, general, that the prisoners managed to escape with so many soldiers guarding them. What were the soldiers doing *under* the carts hiding from that storm. Those Gimirri carts have flaps in front of the doors, why couldn't the guards hide behind the flaps? Then they would have been sheltered from the storm and still doing their duty of guarding their prisoners.' Mokhat seemed pleased at his analysis and looked at the general for approval of his conclusion.

The general sighed and said, 'Your highness is right. What can I say? But the fact is that they are gone and all this scrutiny won't bring them back. I'm sorry my men failed in their duty, but I've demoted the commander responsible and frankly I feel the matter is now closed. It may not have turned out satisfactorily but few things in real life do.'

It was a clear rebuke for Mokhat and he felt somewhat embarrassed for having mentioned the matter. It was just that he simply couldn't leave it alone. It was nagging at him. A clear displacement of anger and frustration. 'I'm sorry general; you're right. I won't mention it again. Mokhat excused himself and went back down the line to have a chat with Narmus, who was staying close to his twenty wagons. Soldiers being what they are, and Narmus well understood their minds, would pilfer given half the chance, and he wasn't going to give them that chance.

By the afternoon Mokhat had rejoined the general at the head of the column and brought Narmus with him. They were travelling along when a scout came back and informed the general that there were wolf tracks crossing the road ahead; a sizable pack.

The general turned to Narmus and said, 'You're the expert for this area. Should we have a hunt or leave them to it. What do you think?'

'My guess is that they're probably heading for Lake Anisaniya for the water, about a league in that direction,' replied Narmus pointing to the right. 'I don't think they'll stick around for us to have sport with. Best leave them to it.'

A little while later they spotted the large wolf pack paralleling them on the right, keeping pace with them. There must have been at least fifteen of the hungry looking animals; all had their muzzles turned towards the column, eyeing them. They were keeping a distance but clearly showing a strong interest in the long procession of soldiers.

'Well, how about that?' said Palaiyas bemused. 'What was that about us hunting them? They seem to have turned the tables and are hunting us. How do these demons think they can take us on?'

Mokhat told him, 'Wolves normally hunt big herds, singling out the weakest of prey, separating their chosen victim from the large herd, and then killing it. Usually a calf or such like. As far as this pack is concerned, we're just another large herd. They're trying to search out our weakest prey; a stray horse, or a lone man popping into the field further from the side of the road to do his toilet. Just before you ask, we have a lot of wolves where I come from and I've studied them some.'

The wolves continued to parallel the column for some time before they vanished as suddenly as they had appeared.

Narmus told them, 'They've abandoned us and probably decided to head for the water. There's prey around the water with animals drinking. It's a better option than taking on a large *herd* like ours.' He rode up to the general and suggested, 'General sir, it's a good sizable lake over there and I thought you might want to take on some fresh water. Give the men a chance for a short rest.' In reality Narmus was a keen fisherman and wanted the opportunity to catch some fish; make a hole in the ice and pull out some nice fish to roast over a fire.

'I'm sorry captain, if we're to make Ivalanda by nightfall we can't stop. Some other time maybe.'

Disappointed at not being able to get at his fish, Narmus thought, *what's so blasted important about getting to Ivalanda by nightfall?* As Narmus was silently fuming, he could see in the far distance to the right, the sharp white light coming off of a large flat body of frozen water, which made him more dejected and he went back to rejoin his wagons, waving a goodbye to Mokhat and Palaiyas.

After a number of leagues further, climbing hills and going round mountains, the light began to fade. Then four scouts came back and informed the general that they had sighted Ivalanda in the distance. It was only a short ride away and that they would be at the gates in a while. The general told them to go ahead to the city gates and inform the sentries there that a Hittite regiment was approaching with two thousand men. That they should not be alarmed and that they should inform the garrison commander and the governor of the city of their imminent arrival.

The scouts had not been gone long before two of them came back in a hurry and reported to the general that they had come across a corpse by the side of the road, just ahead.

'Well, good! We'll have a look when we're passing,' the general told the scouts. 'Better still, would you mind, your highness, going with them and seeing if there's anything worth investigating in this dead man.'

Mokhat had been a little bored and welcomed the opportunity to do something different. He looked at Palaiyas, who nodded, and they both rode off with the two scouts to see what all the fuss was about. A little further, just as the scouts had indicated, they came across an old man with a dagger sticking out of his chest. They dismounted and had a closer look.

'Look at the state of him,' Mokhat commented. 'He's been in the wars. All those scars, and if I'm not mistaken, he's been mutilated. Poor bastard! I wonder who he was?'

'You're right,' agreed Palaiyas. 'He has been in a nasty battle and lost badly. I think he's been tortured.' He bent down and touched the body. 'Hm! The body isn't entirely cold. He seems to have been killed recently.' He told the two waiting scouts to go ahead and rejoin the companions, which they did.

Just then Narmus appeared. 'Hallo there!' He greeted them. 'What have you got there?'

'What are you doing here?' Mokhat asked in return.

'The general asked me to go ahead and introduce myself to the city sentries to pacify any qualms they may have of seeing a large contingent of soldiers approaching. You know how it is. The general doesn't want them firing on us.' He looked closer at the corpse lying on the side of the road. It prompted him to dismount and come closer, leading his horse. When he was standing by Palaiyas, Narmus suddenly became quiet and seemed to go ashen in the face, although it was difficult to tell in the fading light. He bent over the body and gasped; he felt the neck and sat back on his haunches, finally he pulled the dagger out and stood up.

Mokhat and Palaiyas had watched this curious behaviour with interest. 'I gather you know him,' commented Palaiyas,' staring into Narmus' face for confirmation.

A deep sadness overcame Narmus and he lowered his voice. 'And so should you,' said the captain. 'Aren't you supposed to be looking for him? It seems you don't recognise the master spy of the Hittites. That's Satipilli, the man you were sent to search out. Well, now you've found him.'

Both Mokhat and Palaiyas stood rooted to the spot in shock. 'We…we were expecting to find him alive,' burst out Mokhat. 'Neither of us has ever seen him and the little picture we were shown in Hattusas wasn't drawn to well. But how is it that you recognised him, Narmus? I remember you telling me earlier that you didn't know who Satipilli was.'

'He was my *real* boss. I couldn't tell you before, but I still work for him…worked for him,' he corrected himself. 'I was supposed to meet him in Ivalanda and then go with him to Millawanda.' Narmus stood there looking lost, yet with a glimmer of anger rising.

They stood there in silence for what was a moment, but felt like a long time, and then at that point the column came into sight. The general waved to his deputy for the column to continue, but halted himself and dismounted. 'What's happened here?' he asked, joining the other three.

'This is the dead man your scouts found,' Mokhat told him. He looked around to make sure no others were in earshot then said quietly, 'He's also the reason why *we're* here. The king sent us to look for him—and as you can see, we've finally found him—but not how we expected to find him.'

'Must be someone important. Who is he?' The general inclined his head at the body.

'Yes, he is...was...important. He was the chief spy for his majesty. His majesty hadn't heard from Satipilli in a while and he sent us to find out what had happened.'

'Ah! So that's the famous Satipilli,' exclaimed the general. We've all heard the name, but of course we've never been privileged enough to put a face to the name. The general turned to Narmus, 'Did you know the man?' Then he noticed the dagger in Narmus' hand. 'What's that?' He motioned at the dagger.

'Yes sir, I knew him,' and Narmus didn't elaborate. 'This sir, is the dagger I pulled from his chest. My guess is it's supposed to implicate the Ahhiyawans in his killing. It's so childishly obvious, that it is clearly an attempt to mislead us. I must inform you sir, that I in fact worked for Satipilli, and now I intend to find out who killed him. I was only the commander of the escort for those twenty wagons, and now we're at Ivalanda, I ask to be relived of that command, sir. You could incorporate all my men into your regiment. I work best alone.' Narmus had regained his composure, and a look of determination had replaced the previous one of dejection.

'If that is your wish, then I'm authorised to do that. I formally relieve you of your command, captain. You're now a free agent.' The column was still passing and the general waved one of his officers over. 'Get some men to collect this body over here, and put it in a wagon, carefully.'

The officer called over a small detachment to carry out the order. A wagon was seconded from the convoy and it stopped while Satipilli was carefully placed inside the vehicle, then it continued on with the rest of the convoy.

The general turned back to Narmus and said, 'We'll take him into Ivalanda and have our medical man take a closer look at him to see if we can't learn something about his killers. If that's all, let us continue. We can discuss this while we're riding.'

The four mounted their horses and resumed the journey in a subdued atmosphere, with hardly a word spoken. Each pondering the implications of finding Satipilli's corpse. Mokhat wondered what to do next. Palaiyas was thinking on the same lines. Narmus was silently fuming and promising himself to discover who Satipilli's killers were, while the general was working out the logistics of accommodating two thousand soldiers in Ivalanda.

The general, followed by the two princes riding with Narmus, reached the city gates and were met at the gates to the city by the garrison commander. The two generals had a small chat and then both men led the way through the gates. The right wing section of the column led the way inside first, followed by the left wing section, bearing straight for the city's military barracks. The garrison commander detached himself and motioned for Mokhat and Palaiyas to follow him, which they did. They waved goodbye to Narmus and suggested they meet later on. The garrison commander led them through the narrow streets into a building in the middle of the city, up some stairs into the Governor's presence. The general of the garrison whispered for a while in the governor's ear and then introduced Mokhat and Palaiyas to him.

The governor was a portly man with dark features, and he looked kindly at them. 'Your highnesses, may I welcome you to our humble city. My commander informs me that General Kishnapili will join us shortly. May I offer you some refreshment? I'm sure you could use a hot drink of wine.' He waved his servant over and instructed them to fetch food and drink. The group of four retired to the couches to continue their chat while the food was laid out on the low tables in front of them.

'Now what's all this about a body? Kishnapili said something about it to my general here, but I can't make any sense of it.' The governor feigned this interest.

Mokhat replied looking closely at the governor, 'Let me ask you first; do you know Satipilli?'

The governor's eyes shot up, 'But of course I know him. He was here about four weeks ago, and we had arranged an evening meet, but he never showed up. I assumed he'd gone about his usual business. You know, of course, what his business was?'

'We were sent by his majesty to discover his whereabouts. He's actually been out of contact for those four weeks, and that's not usual. Yes we *do* know what his business was, that's *why* it was so crucial to discover where he'd got to,' replied Mokhat. 'Now he's turns up *here*? Well, the body in question was none other than Satipilli, recently killed outside your gates and dumped for *us* to find.'

The governor's face drained of blood and for a moment Mokhat thought he was going to faint.

'I'm convinced it was no accident that *we* found him and not some other people,' Mokhat continued. 'I even suspect I know who did this—at least who carried the act out, not the people behind the act.' At the latter statement, Palaiyas thought he knew what Mokhat had in mind. Having been together for a while, they almost thought in tandem.

The governor pulled himself together somewhat, but the shock was clear all over the governor's face at the identity of the body. '*Satipilli?* Are you *sure*? He was always so careful.'

'No question of who it is,' Palaiyas told the governor, adding his voice to the conversation. 'Captain Narmus recognised him at once. Narmus worked for the man. We found Satipilli with a Mycenaean dagger sticking out of his chest. The Mycenaean dagger was a cheap stunt, and I for one resent it on behalf of Mycenae.'

That got a second glance from the governor and his general. 'I thought those uniforms were a disguise. Are you saying your from Mycenae?' the governor asked.

'Yes I am,' replied Palaiyas firmly, then added, 'From its port city, Tiryns. That makes me Mycenaean.'

The governor and general turned their attention to Mokhat. 'May I ask where your from?'

'It must seem we're a curious pair. What my friend refrained from telling you is, he's the son of the king of Tiryns, while I'm the brother of the Kaska king. However, what is crucial for you to understand is, we're here representing the king in Hattusas.' Having said this, Mokhat then removed the royal seal from his pouch and handed it to the governor to inspect.

'I do not question his majesties choice of representatives. If I seemed startled at who you were, I humbly ask for your pardon. Apart from my hospitality, what can I do for your highnesses?' The governor recovered his jolly deportment.

'We'll need tonight to discuss the new developments,' Mokhat told him, 'to decide what to do next. In the mean time, in your next communication with Hattusas, could you inform his majesty as to what's happened to Satipilli. We may have something to add to that message tomorrow when we've decided our next move. Is that alright with you?'

The governor beamed at them, 'Why certainly! Now eat and drink your fill. I'm sure the journey took it out of you. You'll have comfortable bed for tonight, I assure you. Oh! May I make a suggestion? Change your uniforms. I can let you have a couple of Hittite army uniforms. You'll be a lot safer in them while you're on Hittite territory.'

After the meal, Mokhat and Palaiyas thanked their host, bade him goodnight, and told him they would see him in the morning, and then they went in search of Narmus. They took heed of the governor's advice and asked the officer, assigned by the governor to show them around, to show them where to get the Hittite army uniforms. He took them to the quartermaster who issued them with two Hittite captain's uniforms, and they changed into them.

They found the real captain in the officer's mess in the military barracks. He was sitting in front of a plate of meat, poking at it in a disinterested aimless manner. He seemed more involved with a flagon of wine and was gently sipping from a goblet.

'There you are,' Mokhat said in a loud jolly voice, hoping to break through the din surrounding him. 'We've been looking all over for you. We need to talk.'

Both the princess sat down at his table without waiting for an invitation. Palaiyas continued, 'Has the medical man looked at the body yet?'

Narmus acknowledged them, and then opened his eyes wide at their new dress. 'Well that's more like it. Every time I see you in those Ahhiyawan uniforms I check where my dagger is. In Hatti its wiser to wear those, and a lot safer. As for the body; yes he has. He's certain that Satipilli was badly tortured before he was killed. He suffered enormously before dying—and when I get my hands on whoever it was, I will return the favour with interest.' His voice had turned cold, detached, and frightening.

'Narmus, we do know how you feel, and we sympathise. But getting your hands on whoever killed him is only half the solution,' said Mokhat with passion. 'Finding out *why* he was killed would be the real response. He was killed to prevent the king from finding something out. If we can find out what that was, it would be the best revenge for Satipilli, don't you think? Why not finish the job he started; it would be the best legacy in his memory?'

Narmus came out of his angry introspection and looked at the two princes for the first time since they sat down. The coldness began to leave him and he gave them a half smile. '*You're right!* Of course you're right. I've been stewing in my lust for revenge. That's not what Satipilli taught me. He would want me to finish his work for him. Thank you for pointing out my little stupidity. Are you both going to continue what he started—and if so count me in.'

'Good man! I knew we could rely on you,' Palaiyas said. 'You have a slight advantage over us, which is why we need you with us. You know how Satipilli thought, his methods, how he went about doing things. You know the spy business, we don't.'

Narmus sighed. 'If only I had an inkling of what he was after, what he'd found, it would make uncovering whatever he'd started, much easier. We were supposed to meet here in Ivalanda, and he was going to fill me in on what he was doing.'

Mokhat said, 'I'll ask the governor tomorrow if Satipilli told him anything at all before he vanished. He was expected to meet with the governor but didn't turn up, again all this just before he disappeared. Palaiyas, tomorrow can you ask the general commanding this garrison if Satipilli talked to him. If so, about what? Did he talk to anyone else? What did he show an interest in? Ask him that. See if we can get a clue on anything he did.'

Narmus, now more himself said, 'Now that you've made me realise the vengeance I've been stewing in isn't enough, I feel much better. And since we three are now going after the culprits together, I suddenly feel very tired. It's been a long day. I'll see you tomorrow at breakfast, but now I've got to find a pillow. I'm all done in!' With that, Narmus drained his drink and went off to his bed, wherever that was, leaving Mokhat and Palaiyas sitting there.

Abruptly Palaiyas turned to look at Mokhat and said, 'When we were with the governor you said, "you had a suspicion you knew who killed Satipilli." What did you mean by that?'

'I think you know well what I meant, but if you want me to voice it out loud, then here it is for what its worth. Who's been *following* us all the way from Hattusas? I even met the cursed man when they held me prisoner. That damn false shepherd, Napat. I'll swear he had a hand in Satipilli's murder. What we don't know is, who he's working for. More to the point—why did Satipilli need killing? Satisfied now?'

'Yes, sorry. I just needed to hear that.' Palaiyas seemed satisfied. 'It's the same thing that's been running around in my brain. I wanted to hear it so that we weren't at cross purposes. I'll warrant he's still outside these city walls right now, waiting for us to come out. Anyway, we'll cross that bridge when we come to it. For now, I'm for bed. Let's go find the governor's aide and see what's been allocated to us for the night.'

# Chapter Twenty

The next day at dawn Mokhat found the governor deep in conversation with his garrison commander, General Kishnapili, and his deputy Colonel Tipali. They had a calves hide map laid out and all four were pouring over it. The governor's aide announced that Mokhat was waiting in the anteroom and the governor came out to talk to him.

Removing his serious face and lightening his demeanour he said, 'Good morning, your highness. I hope you slept well.'

Mokhat replied, 'Yes, thank you. Now if you wouldn't mind, I have a small question for you. When did you last see Satipilli?'

The governor thought for a second, but seemed a bit uneasy, then said, 'I believe it was about four weeks ago. He was here in Ivalanda. Why?'

'Did he say anything to you about what he was up to? Anything all? Even the slightest suggestion he made, could be vital. Please try to remember,' Mokhat beseeched.

The governor rubbed his plump chin, fidgeted, and thought for a while, then shook his head, 'No! He always kept everything close to his chest. He asked me that subsequent to the evening meeting I should have horses and provisions ready for him the following morning. He would give me all the reasons when we met that evening. He also asked me to keep his presence quiet, not to mention to people he was here. I did what he asked. That's all, sorry.'

'Thank you for that. I'll think on it.' Then Mokhat changed the subject, 'I've also come to ask you to add the following to the message to Hattusas. *Myself and my companion have enlisted Captain Narmus, someone familiar with Satipilli, and we're going to find out why his majesties chief spy was killed. We'll keep them posted when we can.* You may have to shorten it, but that's the gist. Can you send that for me? Thank you.' He left the governor to his briefing and went to find Palaiyas.

Mokhat met up with Palaiyas in the officer's mess. Narmus and Palaiyas were sitting together, eating barley porridge for breakfast. 'Here,' Palaiyas motioned to a covered bowl, 'I kept this for you. Where we're going you may need it,' he said in between mouthfuls. 'I've just been to see our erstwhile garrison commander. The garrison general told me that Satipilli was interested in Ahhiyawa just before he went missing. He wanted to talk to someone who'd been to Millawanda; find out the layout of the city. He was seeking information about the Ahhiyawan chief spy. That's all the general could tell me. I don't know why, but I didn't entirely believe him.'

'Well its still a lot more than we had yesterday. That's it then. We continue to Millawanda—and find their chief spy. Let's ask him what he knows. All agreed?' Mokhat looked for confirmation from his friends.

'I'm in,' said Narmus.

'Let's finish this,' Palaiyas motioned to the food, 'then we'll need fresh horses and provisions. We should be ready to leave as early as we can.'

\* \* \*

Outside the city, the winter had relaxed its grip on the morning countryside and the wind from the south had brought in some milder temperatures. The ground frost was fading from the hilly landscape and the going was relatively benign. A few black vultures circled overhead, searching for carrion that wolves or foxes might have left behind. A number of bustards were roaming the terrain, pecking at what they could find in the thawing ground.

'You know, I used to complain about the summer heat we normally have here,' Narmus voiced to his fellow riders, 'but now I'd welcome the heat back with open arms. I'm not a great fan of all this frost and snow.'

'Where I come from up in the mountains, we normally have frost *and* snow,' Mokhat told him.

Both Narmus and Mokhat looked to Palaiyas for him to offer his thought on the subject. He merely shrugged and said, 'Snow...snow? I think we banned it from Mycenae. It's certainly not allowed to fall on Tiryns. Winter there is humid but compassionate, much like we Tirynians.'

At this both members of his audience chuckled quietly and raised their eyebrows as if to say, likely story.

Then Palaiyas abruptly kicked his horse and was off, making a wide circle and backtracking to look for Napat. From time to time all three riders had gone to great lengths to try and determine if they were being followed. Palaiyas made it a habit to double back a number of times checking for pursuers, but invariably he came back without finding anyone. A little while later after his latest reconnoitre, he came back and shook his head, indicating that he hadn't found anyone.

Palaiyas said to Mokhat, 'Remember that the only time we ever saw him was when we were crossing the Marassantiya River the second day out of Hattusas. We also know he followed us at least as far as those wild men who ambushed us. You saw him and talked to him. His intentions are clearly hostile, and we have to assume, deadly. So we have to assume he's out there somewhere, watching. We need to be on the guard for an ambush; he's sneaky and its how his mind must work, I would say.'

'I think you're right,' agreed Mokhat.

Narmus added, 'He's seen us do the doubling-back, so how about changing tactics? We press ahead at double speed and see if he can keep up. It might not work, but at least we'll be moving a lot faster than we are.'

They all settled on this line of action, and picked up their pace to a full gallop, putting some pressure on the three pack horses they had in tow. Needless to say, they couldn't keep this tempo up for very long without exhausting their mounts, but they made good headway for a respectable distance before being forced to stop for a rest.

They climbed off their horses and tethered them to some leafless bushes just below a ridge. Then they sat on the ridge giving a splendid view of where they'd come from, and began digging in to some biscuits and dried meat, washed down with wine.

Narmus noticed a rock-thrush pecking at the sparse grass on a small hillock a small distance away, and he got engrossed in its activities. The pale blue head and neck contrasted magnificently with its orange underbelly as it hopped around the ground looking for insects. It must've been finding something because it kept on doggedly pecking away at the hillock; Narmus realised all of a sudden, it must be having a go at an ant's nest that had minimal guards during this season.

'Well time to go. We've been here long enough,' declared Palaiyas.

It was only then that Narmus realised how long he'd lost himself in the thrush's performance. He shook his head gently and chided himself. He clearly hadn't come to terms with the death of his mentor yet. He needed to mourn Satipilli properly if he was to clear his emotions for the coming encounter with their enemies.

The three companions mounted their horses and began a good canter down the other side of the ridge. A little distance on when they had reached the bottom of the hill and were riding on the flat again, Mokhat noticed small movements in the distance ahead and pointed at it. They could barely see them, but it looked like a large group of people had spread themselves in a long line, and Mokhat wondered what they were up to. They were now about seven leagues out of Ivalanda. As they neared the long line, it began to dawn on the three riders that those ahead were clearly trying to block their passage. It seemed bizarre that people on foot would try to take on three riders, but the closer they rode to the stretched line, the more they began noticing various kinds of farm implements in their hands pointed at them. Scythes, wooden forks, staves and all sorts of improbable items were being brandished that could be used to cudgel someone into submission.

\* \* \*

When they got to hailing distance they stopped and Narmus shouted to them, '*What is your intention with us?*' as loudly as he could.

One burly fellow with a stout pole in his hand, stood out in front of the stretched line, and he shouted back, 'We're looking for a donation for our children's food. Times have been very hard this winter and we've nothing left to give them. Anything you can spare would be most welcome.' He looked behind him for support from his band of followers, then turned and stared at the three horses carrying provisions.

'I'm sorry for you, but this is no way to treat peaceful travellers journeying through his majesty's lands,' Narmus responded. 'Make way or we will be forced to use our swords on your skulls. As you can see, we're all soldiers and many of you will surely die if you continue to block our path.'

This brought a commotion within the ranks of the starving, for it was obvious to the three riders that some of them were indeed badly malnourishment. One or two left the line and made to get out of the way of these soldiers. Others remained in the line and showed their defiance by shaking their implements at those on the horses.

'Can't we just go round them?' Mokhat asked Narmus.

'I'm afraid if we go round, it will take us away from our road, and what if we meet another lot like this? Do we go round again...., and again? And what about the next lot of travellers who come this way? They may not be so well armed as us, and this offensive crowd will rob them of everything they have. We can't allow this to continue. Surely you can see that. If they succeed with this banditry then this area becomes lawless for all the others. I'm still a soldier of his majesty and his law rules here, not theirs. I can see they're hungry, but highway robbery is not the solution. What if others hear of this lots success? His majesty will have a full-scale civil disobedience on his hands. No! This stops here!' The vehemence in Narmus' voice brooked no contradiction. He had found a release for his emotional frustration and was intent on dealing with these people as only a captain and soldier could.

'Put like that, I see that we have little option but to go along with you, and through them,' Mokhat agreed.

Palaiyas had already drawn his sword.

Narmus shouted at the crowd in front, '*As a captain in his majesty's army, I order you to disperse or face the consequences.*'

More shuffling went on but the line held and showed no sign of dissolving.

Narmus said more quietly, 'I'm sorry to have to do this, but you leave me no choice.'

With that final statement Narmus and Mokhat also drew their swords and made ready to break through the line. The ragged crowd began to shuffle towards them, shaking their makeshift weapons at the riders. In return, the three horsemen made ready to charge at the hungry bandits, swords raised and shields protecting them from any flying missiles. They charged at the burly leader of this motley band, hoping to discourage his boldness. If he fled, then

Narmus felt, the rest would also follow him and the unrest would be over.

A group of tougher ruffians stepped out from behind the burly leader ready to give him support, suggesting this outrage was no spontaneous affair. More likely to be local bandits out looking for easy pickings, using these hungry simpletons as camouflage. The latter thought went through Narmus' mind as he descended on the leader. His cronies attempted to trip the horses with their poles, but failed. With one downward slice, Narmus cleaved the leader's head, while Palaiyas took out two of his cronies. Mokhat furiously thrust and sliced into those he could as if in a state of frenzy. He was once again working out his own frustration at the ordeal he'd gone through with the wild men.

As the trio wrecked havoc amongst the bandits, those that could began to run. Few of the rabble stood their ground and fought back with their pathetic weapons, preferring to make a run for it, all except for those around their deceased leader. They fought desperately but were no match for the trained soldiers they were facing. One by one they were cut down from above. Finally, the trio were left alone, with only dead bodies scattered about them. They dismounted and took stock of their situation.

'That's put paid to their little game,' Narmus said assertively, still on a high from the fight.

'Is everyone alright? Anyone hurt?' Mokhat asked, concerned at his companions welfare.

Only Palaiyas seemed undaunted; he took fighting as part of a normal days living. He'd been fighting ever since his childhood and found a battle just as normal as getting up in the morning. He looked at the carnage all around him and shrugged his shoulders. 'Yes I'm alright, why wouldn't I be? They didn't stand much of a chance did they? Stupid people!'

'Check the horses, make sure they're alright. Then we need to continue. Still, a pity these poor beggars had to resort to highway robbery.' Narmus almost sounded compassionate compared to his previous tone.

They checked the horses and each other, and the gods seem to have been on their side that morning. They had come out of the fight with some minor scratches but no serious wounds. They left the scene of the fighting behind them as quickly as they could, almost in indecent haste, because of the futile nature of what had happened.

Half a league down the road the trio came upon a small group of travellers, trying to stay out of their way, all bedraggled, hungry and miserable.

'I think these are some of the people who ran for it, when the fighting began,' said Palaiyas.

Narmus rode to them and barred their way.

'Please, no more!' they pleaded. 'We're sorry, but we had no choice. It was those Aknezi thugs that forced us to block the road for them.' They backed away from Palaiyas' horse, as he arrived to support Narmus, rightly fearing what its rider might do to them.

'Who's Aknezi?' Palaiyas inquired forcefully.

'The big fellow who was talking with you before the fight,' replied an emaciated looking fellow.

Mokhat joined in by asking, 'What I want to know is how come your in such a state? How is it you have no food. Most people put aside enough to get them through winter, yet here you are trying to rob people on the highway.'

One woman was bold enough to shout, 'Ask the governor why we're so poor.' Then she thought better of the outburst and tried to hide behind another woman.

Narmus asked, 'Who administers this region? Who's in charge here?'

The people could see that they weren't going to be attacked so they began to talk. The woman who'd hid, now came out from behind her companion and said, 'It's the governor in Ivalanda, he's the robber, not us. He taxes us out of our homes, out of our food, until we end up on the road at the mercy of thugs like that Aknezi.'

At this information, Narmus scowled and said to Mokhat, 'I knew I didn't like that fat governor. I didn't talk to him but from a distance he looked like a greedy over fed administrator who was up to no good.'

Mokhat said, 'As you say, he may be no good, but I'm sorry to say, its not our business. We have work to do, and this governor is Hattusas' problem. So let's get on our way if you've satisfied your curiosity.'

Narmus turned and got to his pack horse, and removed one of the bags of barley flour, and then to everyone's surprise, he gave it to the bold woman. 'Make sure everyone gets an even share,' he warned her.

After the admonition, the trio waved at them and left to continue their journey to Millawanda. By this time it was early afternoon, when a while later after a couple of leagues more, they saw a group of horsemen accompanying a cart, coming towards them. As the party came closer they saw it was a troop of cavalry guarding the cart.

'Wonder who this lot are. Must be heading towards Ivalanda,' suggested Palaiyas.

'We'll soon know,' replied Narmus.

As the small column came abreast both sides halted with the officer leading the troop halting by Narmus' horse. 'Hail and greetings,' he said. 'Are you just coming out of Ivalanda?' asked the troop captain.

'Indeed we are,' replied Narmus. 'Left there early this morning heading for the frontier. Where are you coming from?'

'We're just returning from a tax collecting expedition for the governor. Hence the guards,' he swept his hand at his men.

'You may find your passage a little easier,' Narmus told him, 'Now that we've just cleared the highway up ahead of a group of bandits trying to hold us up.'

At this information the captain raised his eyebrows. 'You don't say. Well thank you. That is good news. I'm sure our tax collector will want to thank you in person. Why don't we stop and share a goblet together?'

Narmus looked at his companions, and they nodded their agreement.

'We'd love to,' responded Narmus.

All three dismounted, as did the troop captain, and he led them to the cart. From inside the cart a head popped out. 'Why have we stopped?' said the disembodied head.

'We have guests.' The captain indicated the three Hittite officers standing next to him. 'I thought we'd be hospitable to these three fellow officers. What do you think? Got any of that wine left, you're so fond of?'

The three could see that this tax collector wasn't too keen on sharing his wine with these strangers, but he really didn't have much choice. He was only in charge of the tax collecting, while the troop captain was in overall charge of the expedition.

'Why of course. Do come inside my cosy little den,' and the disembodied head disappeared back inside.

The troop captain led the way round the back of the cart and climbed inside, followed by the three companions. They sat on sacks of barley flour round a makeshift table while the tax collector reached for a flagon of wine and added four more goblets onto the crude table. He poured wine into the goblets and lifted his to his lips a little too eagerly for politeness. The troop captain sneered at the collector and shrugged his shoulders at his three fellow officers.

Mokhat had a thought, 'Tell me, when did you leave Ivalanda?' he asked the tax collector.

The man put his goblet down and said, 'Some four weeks ago, why?'

'We three are on an errand for his majesty and I need to ask you, do you know of a man called Satipilli?'

The tax collector smiled, 'Well yes, I know *of* him. I saw him with the governor the previous evening before I left for this tax collecting trip. I remember because I wanted to talk with the governor, but he said he was busy with this fellow he had standing with him. I mean I know it was Satipilli because he'd come to me earlier and asked me some questions about Arzawa and Lukka. He wanted to know if I had any information regarding these two places. I do a lot of travelling you see, so I pick up a lot of rumours.'

The surprise on the three companion's faces was evident. 'That scoundrel lied to us!' exclaimed Mokhat.

'Now I want you to be absolutely sure,' Mokhat said to the tax collector. 'You say the governor met Satipilli in the *evening* before you left, is that right? This is very important.'

'I'm certain. He was standing as close as you are to me right now. It was definitely Satipilli he met.' His eyes screwed up into a query as to why he was being asked this.

'You don't know how helpful you've been and I appreciate it greatly,' Mokhat told him. 'Now I would request that you didn't talk about this. Can you do that?' Then he turned to the troop captain and asked him to keep this amongst just those present. 'It's a matter of utter importance and I speak for his majesty in Hattusas.'

The tax collector seemed pleased that he'd been able to help in such a matter of importance and it inflated his self esteem. The troop captain agreed but looked wary of Mokhat's claim to speak for the king.

Mokhat noticed this mistrust and was forced to show him the royal seal, whereupon the captain almost sprang to attention in the cart.

'It is now essential we three have a confidential talk amongst ourselves, so if you'll excuse us, we'll say goodbye and leave you. I would venture that you will see us again quite soon.' With this all three companions climbed out of the cart and made for their horses. They mounted and rode off some  distance to have their talk.

'Now we know!' Mokhat burst out when they had stopped. 'That damned governor lied to me about Satipilli.'

Narmus was adamant, 'We must return to Ivalanda and confront this fat governor. The problem will be, if he denies what that tax collector told us, then its his word against his underlings. Who is Hattusas going to believe?'

# Chapter Twenty One

The three fellow travellers had decided they couldn't go on to Millawanda without confronting the lying governor, so they raced back to Ivalanda to do just that. They had to reach the city before the tax collector's party, just in case the troop captain decided to warn the governor of what had occurred. They couldn't take any chances. Things were a little out of control, what with the governor's lies, and then they had to ask themselves, who else was involved in this intrigue. How far did it reach in that city?

They made good headway galloping back when the sun began to show signs of fading from the sky. They needed to be inside the city gates before nightfall. It was only down to Palaiyas' sharp eyes that allowed him to spot the column in the fading light. They were way off in the far distance, a long column moving in the opposite direction, away from Ivalanda.

Narmus shouted loudly so both could hear, '*Kishnapili!*' and pointed frantically in that direction. The trio changed course to intercept the general's column, and a little while later they rode up to the general having exhausted both riders and mounts.

Narmus began by greeting the general excitedly, 'Sir, we are incredibly glad to have caught you like this. This couldn't be more auspicious. We have some outrageous news and we badly need your help.'

'Slow down lad. Be more concise. What would you like from me? I told you before you left Ivalanda that if I could assist you in any way, I have orders from his majesty to do so. So, start at the beginning and tell me what's happened.'

Mokhat decided to take the lead. 'First, general, this is important; could you please stop the column. You'll see why as I explain.'

The general was surprised at this request but agreed. He nodded at Colonel Tipali, who raised his hand and called the column to a halt.

Mokhat then continued, 'The governor lied to us about Satipilli, about not meeting him in the evening he was supposed to. We came across a tax collector returning to Ivalanda from a four week absence and we got to sharing his hospitality; I asked him on an off-chance whether he had come across Satipilli. I was desperate, having no real leads to follow, so I tried this long-shot and it seems to have paid off.

'He told us, he clearly remembered Satipilli standing with the governor *in the evening,* when the governor told us Satipilli had missed *that* particular meeting. I asked him how *sure* he was it was Satipilli? He told me that Satipilli had come to him earlier and in the course of a chat, told him his name, then had asked him some questions regarding Arzawa and Lukka. As a result of the governor's lies, I now have to suspect the governor had something to do with our quarries disappearance. Our problem is, how to confront this lying governor? If you were present, he might think twice about using force on us. I can't think of any other way he's going to wriggle out of this.'

'So you want me to come back to Ivalanda with you to confront the governor,' summed up the general.

'That's it exactly sir,' interposed Narmus.

The general looked at all three men and they all nodded, that this is what they wanted.

The general shrugged and said, 'So be it. I was given explicit order to help you and I intend to do that.' He gave the order for the column to turn back to Ivalanda, bringing on many surreptitious moans and groans from his troops.

174

On the return journey they had to make their way in the early dark of the evening with scouts picking out the best route. Luckily there was a full moon that night and it lit up the landscape with an eerie light. It made the return trip just a little easier.

As they were travelling the general made an announcement. 'I've been giving this problem of out return a small amount of thought. As you can imagine, my return is going to cause some suspicion, and if the governor smells a rat, then we won't get through the front gates. So I've devised a plan. It's not the first time I've had to take a city, so I have some experience. Bear with me gentlemen,' he told the trio. 'I'm going to call a travelling briefing of my officers, which should explain all. He had Colonel Tipali send for his staff officers and they joined him riding in parallel to him on either side.

'Now listen up,' he raised his voice so all could hear. 'We've got a change of plans. We're returning to Ivalanda to arrest the governor of the city.' This got some sharp looks from his staff. 'And in order not to arouse suspicion, I'm going to tell them at the gates that our water has been deliberately contaminated by someone in the city, and we need to replace it before continuing our journey. That should allow us to get into the city itself. Once inside, I want six of my best officers with me at all times. We are going to take charge of the garrison commander and question him with regards to the governor.

'I want all the garrison officers under arrest until we find out how deep this goes. That's a job for you, your highnesses. The story will be that there is a force coming from the west and we need to have all the garrison officers in a room for a briefing to defend the city. When their inside the room, you captain,' he pointed at one officer, 'will seal it and nobody leaves until I say so. Is that clear? I want five hundred soldiers to create a perimeter surrounding the place where the officers are to be kept. I'm going to impose military rule on Ivalanda in his majesties name. As you know, I have the authority to do so. I want you, Colonel Tipali, to take two hundred men,' and he motioned at his deputy, 'and arrest the governor. If you have to use force in order to do so, you have my permission to use all the force necessary to carry out that order. The cover story for any of the garrison who question what's going on, is that we are preparing to defend the city from a large force approaching from the west. I want a few of our senior officers to go to the garrison barracks and order the garrison to stay in their quarters until further notice. They're to be confined to barracks for the whole of the next day.

'Any questions so far.' The general looked around at his staff and waited. Nobody responded, so he went on, 'Good! If we do this right, there will be the minimum of bloodshed, and by a miracle, maybe no one will get hurt except the governor. The way this is unfolding I don't think the governor is going to be in charge for very long. I want you Colonel Tipali to take two senior officers to ride ahead to Ivalanda right now. Take fifty men with you. The gates will have been closed for the night. Tell them to expect us and tell them why. I want the garrison commander to meet me at the gates.'

The deputy sent the officers in question to collect the fifty escort and then all of them went on to Ivalanda.

'When we get to the city, the six officers I mentioned earlier, will accompany me while I take the garrison general for a quiet chat in a room somewhere in the guardhouse. Make sure you allocate fifty men to discretely support you in guarding the room I'm in. We don't want to be disturbed. If the general is clean, he will be the new city commander and I'll leave him to deal with the governor, otherwise it will be his deputy, and so on down the line until we clean out this nest of traitors.

'Questions? No! Right. Go brief your men, and tell them we have uncovered a plot by Arzawa and Ahhiyawa to take over the city with the help of some traitors in the garrison. We're returning to sort it out. That should give them a reason as to why all this is happening.'

The trio listened to this briefing with some admiration for its thorough planning, especially given the short time he'd had to organise it.

'Well my friends, have you anything to add to what I've just done?' The general knew he'd done a good job and looked calmly at the three companions.

'Excellent and thorough, as far as I can see,' Mokhat commended.

'Contaminated water! Brilliant idea!' added Palaiyas.

Narmus just sat in admiration at the abilities of this general.

The general continued organising small details until they got within sight of the city. By then it was around midnight. The two officer and their fifty men reported back that the city gates were open for them and the commanding general was waiting there for their return.

As the column approached the gates, Kishnapili dismounted, as did his six appointed officer guards, and both generals shook hands.

'What's all this about contaminated water?' asked the garrison commander.

'Someone in this city has sabotaged our water containers,' Kishnapili told him quietly, then took his colleague general's elbow and walked him to the gate guardhouse. 'Can we talk alone?' he asked the garrison commander. Thus implying there were things he didn't want others to hear. Unnoticed, silently the six officers stationed themselves on either side of the door leading to the guardroom keeping just behind the two men.

'Well if you think it necessary,' answered the commander, and led the way into the guardroom. He motioned the eight guards inside to leave, and at that point the six officers joined the two generals inside the room.

177

This didn't worry the city commander as it was normal for officers to accompany their general.

Through the gates, the column proper was entering the city itself, and officers leading their men were moving swiftly to carry out the general's prearranged plan. Colonel Tipali took his two hundred soldiers towards the governor's mansion. Mokhat and Palaiyas assigned to take charge of rounding up the garrison officers went to work with gusto. Kishnapili didn't want them present when he interrogated this garrison commander. He wanted it to be just senior officer to senior officer. It had something to do with Hittite military pride.

Inside the guardroom four of Kishnapili's officers circled quietly round the back of the indigenous general as if looking for something.

'Now my esteemed colleague, I have a problem I would like your help with,' Kishnapili began. 'It has come to my attention that your overweight governor has not been as forthcoming with the truth as he should have been to his highness Prince Mokhat. The prince holds the royal seal of his majesty and when he asks about the whereabouts of Satipilli, it is as if his majesty were here asking that same question.'

The garrison commander began to look worried and glanced at the officers now standing on either side of him. 'What has that to do with me?' he asked but with less certainty. 'You should go and take the matter up with the governor. He's the one that was dealing with Satipilli.'

Kishnapili came close to his opposite number and stared him in the face. 'Believe me general, that is already well in hand. At this moment I'm looking for traitors.'

At those words, the garrison commander became alarmed and tried to push past Kishnapili intent on heading for the door. The four officers grabbed him and sat him forcefully in a chair. The commander tried to shout but a gag was quickly stuffed in his mouth and he was then tied to the chair.

'I'm sorry you did that,' Kishnapili told him. 'It implies you have something to hide. Now I want the truth. What happened to Satipilli? Mark my words; I will have the truth of the matter.' The general then turned to one of the officers near him and said, 'Draw your sword, and on my command, I want you to cleave off this traitors head. That is a direct order. Are you ready?'

The officer drew his sword and nodded that he understood.

'Now I'm giving you one chance to come clean. Try to spin me a tale and I will not hesitate to give the order to this officer here to finish you off. Understand this, your general days are over; whether you stay alive is the only question for you to consider. And no self pity. You knew what you were doing. So, speak now or go meet your demons.'

The garrison commander looked as if he were going to get angry at his treatment—then he looked at the raised sword and the seriousness in the officers eyes, and switched to dejection. 'I..I'm sorry, I was a fool. I suppose I got greedy. Stupid really! That damned governor has a silky tongue when he wants to. But yes…, he did lie to you…, to his highness I mean, when he said he didn't know what happened to Satipilli.'

'Now that's better,' Kishnapili told him. 'Right, start from the beginning. What happened and when. I have my men arresting the governor right now, so don't worry about him. He's for the chop. But first, tell me, who else is in this dirty plot. What about your deputy? Is he in it with you?'

'No! I swear it. I didn't think I could trust him. He's far too loyal to the crown.' Having realised what he'd just said, he hung his head. 'Yes I am a traitor. I should not have done what I did. Mostly I turned a blind eye to what the governor did, and that was wrong of me.'

'Right,' Kishnapili said. He motioned to one of his officers, 'Go fetch his deputy. I'm appointing him the new commander of this garrison. Also try to find out what the situation is. Have we got full control and have we detained the governor? Go!'

'Now,' he turned back to the former general, 'Tell me all. What has been happening here?'

The weary general began, 'Some four weeks ago, we had a number of merchants come into the city. Nothing unusual in that, but one of them, a burly bearded man wearing fine merchants robes asked to see the governor and that's when all this underhand business was set in motion. I took him to see the governor and he asked me to stay and witness what transpired. The merchant offered the governor ten thousand shekels to detain Satipilli. When the merchant said that, the governor looked at me, as if to say are you in or out. That moment was my downfall. I nodded to him that I was in, and in doing so I made a mistake. Satipilli trusted the governor as part of the Hittite administration; that was *his* downfall.'

'His *downfall* was trusting a couple of *traitors*. So far I'm inclined to let his majesty deal with you. What would make your sentence easier would be if you could tell me who this burly merchant worked for? Who was behind him? Do you know?' Kishnapili demanded fiercely of his prisoner.

'That I don't know. If I knew I would tell you, but I don't.'

There was a series of knocks on the door, which was in accordance with a prearranged signal. One of the officers answered it, and then brought into the room the deputy commander of the garrison. He'd been told why his own commander was no longer in charge and what his crime was. The deputy came in and looked in disgust at his former commander, then turned his back on him.

Kishnapili told him, 'If you wish it, I'm in a position to appoint you, on behalf of his majesty King Tudhaliyas, as the new garrison commander. Do you so wish it?'

The man arched his back and accepted the appointment.

'As of now, I'm giving you a field promotion to the rank of full general. It'll be confirmed later by Hattusas on my recommendation. I'm afraid your first act will be to deal with this traitor here.' Kishnapili motioned with his head at the former general. 'Your second act must be to go talk to your garrison officers who we're holding in the great hall of your barracks on the pretext of a briefing. They'll need reassurance and to be told of the change in command. I will personally deal with the governor.' Kishnapili now turned his attention to the officer who'd fetched the deputy. 'Well, what did you find out? Have we taken the governor?'

'Yes sir. Colonel Tipali found him in his bedroom abusing a young boy.' The officer told him. 'We have him locked in his cellar with some of our men. He's shouting and ranting that we will regret what we've done. Would you like to see him?'

'Yes I would. Now go and take the new commanding general to his officers and bring me back the two highnesses; bring them to the cellar. I want them to witness the governor's demise.' To the rest of the officers present he said, 'Right lads, we're going to visit the soon-to-be-gone governor. Oh! And bring that one there with us,' pointing at the tied ex-general, 'just in case this fat governor keeps denying everything. Now then let's find this cellar. You there, bring some lights and lead the way.'

One of his officers talked with the one who knew where the cellar was and then led the way through the dark to the centre of the city to the governor's house which was standing in a square. This was the middle of the night and all should have been quiet, but word must have got around and some of the population were awake, because there were a number of windows open watching all the military goings on.

They reached the destination where a large group of Kishnapili's men stood outside guarding the house. They all jumped to attention at the general's approach. The party went inside where there were a number of officers talking to Colonel Tipali in the hallway. Everyone there stood to attention.

Colonel Tipali came and reported, 'He's in the cellar sir. All's quiet and we had little trouble.' He led the way through to the back and down into the cellar. Down a flight of stairs they came out into a large room with ten burly men guarding the seated governor.

Immediately the fat governor saw Kishnapili, he tried to rise and say something but was pushed back down into his seat by a tough looking non-com. 'I must protest,' said the governor now back in his seat. As soon as he saw the tied hands of the commander of his garrison, he closed his mouth, realising this was more serious than mere bluster would relieve.

Kishnapili stood in front of the governor with a look of contempt on his face. 'You greedy treacherous maggot! Did you really think you could get away with doing away with his majesties chief spy?' The general was really angry. 'Are so insolent in your self delusion that you thought nobody would find out? All for a miserly ten thousand shekels.'

Listening to the general, the governor realised there was no use bluffing and blustering anymore. His general was a prisoner, and he was surrounded by guards. He hung his head out of self pity not shame. If he got out alive he'd be lucky.

Steps were heard coming down the stairs and then Mokhat and Palaiyas were followed by Narmus and some other officers.

'I'm glad you could join us your highnesses,' said the general. 'I've just been telling the governor where he stands. Would you like to add a few words to my castigation?' The general stood aside to make way for Mokhat.

Mokhat stood there shaking his head. Finally he said, 'You are a bare faced liar and now I want to know the truth. No more of your nonsense. What happened to Satipilli?' He stood there waiting.

After some moments to collect his thoughts the governor said, 'Since you know the sum of money and have my general prisoner there, then you know that I sold Satipilli to a merchant. The price seemed to be right.' He said that as if it was simply a business transaction.

Mokhat was shocked at his callousness. Again he shook his head in disbelief and turned his back on the fat lump sitting there almost smug in his own fantasy.

Kishnapili took over again. 'I'm told you taxed the district to destruction with your greed, but that wasn't enough—you then sold your country for money. To some burly bearded merchant, no less. You are an utter disgrace to your profession. Have no delusions; first light tomorrow morning you are to be executed by having your head removed. Also I hereby confiscate all your property and chattels. All the money will go back to the people you robbed with your tax fiddles. As of now, this city is under military rule until further notice. Take this one to the dungeons,' the general indicated the former commander of the garrison, who was standing between two officers with his head bowed, witnessing the final act of this scandalous drama.

The former governor seemed not to have heard his sentence being pronounced and sat smiling to himself, now oblivious of those around him.

Narmus said to Mokhat as they were leaving the cellar, 'We now know how Satipilli was taken, and what finally happened to him, but not the why. That needs to be uncovered.'

Palaiyas added, 'And we all know who we think the burly bearded merchant is, the one the general mentioned.'

'It must have been Napat,' voiced Mokhat. 'He fits the description. What is frustrating is not knowing *who* he works for. Why did they want Satipilli out of the way so badly? What was our master spy up to?'

'There, the three of you have your work cut out for you,' said the general who was just behind them. 'Now I suggest we get some sleep in what's left of the night. Tomorrow I feel might be a busy day. May I also suggest we sleep here in the former governor's residence? I'm declaring it my new HQ. It all seems to be a most fitting conclusion to our business.'

They all agreed and went upstairs to find their beds.

# Chapter Twenty Two

'Yeh? Hmmmm..! What?' Grumbled Palaiyas as Mokhat shook him awake. He opened his eyes and looked at his friend. 'Oh! Sorry. Yes, I know. Is it really dawn already? I only closed my eyes a moment ago, and it's time to get up. What a wretched life we lead!'

'It is wretched, but we all share the same misery so stop complaining and get dressed. We promised to witness the governor's execution and it was scheduled for dawn. Hurry, I'll see you downstairs in the entrance hallway. I'm going to find somebody to see if they've started yet.' With that parting shot Mokhat disappeared through the doorway.

In the hallway he found a couple of officers already on duty. He asked Colonel Tipali, 'Has the governor's execution got under way yet?'

'No your highness! General Kishnapili wants the new commander present since it's his garrison now. We're searching for him as we speak.' The colonel kept glancing at the entrance, expecting to see someone come through it.

'Isn't he in his quarters in the barracks?' Mokhat persisted.

'No! We haven't seen him since last night.'

Just then another officer walked quickly through the entrance saying, 'No sign of him anywhere sir. And there's worse to come...the old commander has gone missing. The dungeon's been opened; the jailer's dead as well as a sentry, and horses have been taken from the stable.'

Palaiyas came down the stairs and joined Mokhat.

Colonel Tipali asked the newly arrived officer, 'What on earth's going on?' Not waiting for a reply, he turned to his companion and asked, 'Is the old governor still safely in our custody?'

'Yes sir, I checked just now. We still have him downstairs in the cellar. There are twenty men guarding him,' replied his companion.

General Kishnapili was heard shouting at someone outside with his distinct and recognisable voice, and then he walked in through the entrance and saw Mokhat. He came to him and said, 'A complete shambles! I'm sorry your highness. It looks like the deputy was in cahoots with the old commander. Both of them lied to us to save their scrawny necks. I've only just heard.

'A sentry reports that two officers arrived at the western postern gate during the late hour of darkness before dawn, and requested the gate be opened for a reconnaissance mission. They said they were chasing a group of bandits who've been robbing the communities around Ivalanda. Both had horses and knew the password for the night. They wore some camouflage as is usual for reconnaissance and the sentry saw no reason to stop them. I would think they're heading for Arzawa as fast as their horses can carry them. I've dispatched one of my officers leading a hundred men, troops from the garrison. I won't hold my breath for their recapture. As I said, a complete shambles. Right, lets waste no more time. Colonel, go fetch the governor. Let's at least do one job properly.'

The governor appeared after a small wait, being half carried, half dragged between two burly soldiers. He was trying to wriggle free of his escort with little success. The general led the way outside, into the city square, followed by Mokhat and Palaiyas with Narmus joining them, having just come down the stairs.

'Nice of you to join us,' remarked Palaiyas over his shoulder.

'Sorry, overslept.' Narmus yawned and rubbed his eyes. 'I'm still not sure I'm awake. So are we going to watch that fat lump get his just deserts?'

Now the governor's legs gave way completely and he had to be carried into the middle of the square. He was blubbering something about being so sorry…but nobody took any notice.

A small crowd had gathered, even at that early hour in the morning. Colonel Tipali dispatched an unnecessarily large group of soldiers to hold them back. A few priests had come out of the temple to Taru opposite the governor's mansion and were watching the ensuing spectacle intently. The governor was led still squirming to a block in the middle of the square and pushed onto his knees, and then one soldier held him roughly by his hair making sure his head was flat on the wooden block. Two other soldiers were needed to hold his arms extended because the governor continued to struggle, trying to get free.

The city executioner had been found and he was waiting with his long bronze axe. Kishnapili didn't tell the governor why his sentence was being carried out as was usual, simply because the governor would not have heard him in his state. The executioner looked at the general, and Kishnapili nodded at him, then the axe man swung his axe and the governor's head rolled along the ground a short way spurting blood, as did his neck stump.

'Good riddance to bad rubbish,' Narmus commented. 'Pity his cronies got away.'

Kishnapili nodded, 'There I must agree with you. I can't stand corrupt administrators, but worse than them is a traitorous soldier.'

'I must say I didn't expect this turn of events,' added Mokhat. 'The whole city seems to reek with corruption at the top. Before you leave general, you're going to have to do something about it. Those closest to the commander and his deputy must be removed.'

Kishnapili looked grim. 'I'm not leaving. I'm staying here to sort things out. I'm going to send my deputy, Colonel Tipali, to continue to the Ahhiyawan border with three thousand from this garrison. I'm keeping my men with me. That will mean I'll have two thousand from the garrison and my two thousand—that will even up the numbers. My men will decontaminate the others; I trust them to do that. I'll send for another governor from Hattusas with the proviso he be squeaky clean. Until then, this city is under military rule and I'm going to root out every corrupt civil servant and military man I can find, so help me Taru.'

'General, sir, there's a tax collector who should be arriving anytime today who you might want to question,' Narmus told Kishnapili. 'He's been doing the former governors dirty work for him and he should be a mine of information on corruption here in the city. He probably knows where all the loot is hidden and much more.'

'Hm! Thank you captain. That's most helpful. I look forward to meeting this tax collector. Some time today you say. I'll have the gate inform me when they arrive. But look here, its about time I thanked you properly. I can't do much for the two highnesses, but I can certainly do something for a captain in the Hittite army. I hereby promote you to full colonel. Is that acceptable to you, colonel?'

Narmus sprang to attention and said, 'Yes *sir*.'

Mokhat turned to Narmus and said, 'Congratulations. You deserve it.' Then he suddenly remembered something and said to the general, 'We sent a message off to Hattusas via the old governor. I have to assume he never sent it. You reminded me when you mentioned Hattusas earlier. General, would you mind sending the same message to his majesty on my behalf. I'll give you the full message before we leave.' He looked at Palaiyas and Narmus and said, 'I think we'll leave early tomorrow morning. We need a good nights sleep after last nights mayhem. If I could ask you general to see that we have fresh horses and provisions ready for the morning, I'd be much obliged.'

Palaiyas clapped Narmus on the back and added his best wishes for his promotion.

'You know this is entirely your fault,' smiled the general at Mokhat, sweeping his arm in an arc around him. 'If you hadn't met me yesterday, I wouldn't be standing here today and that treacherous governor would still be in charge. So the least I can do is let you have what you ask for.' Then completely out of character, he winked at Mokhat and chuckled.

Palaiyas said, 'General, we're going to go and celebrate the colonel's promotion; find a tavern somewhere for a drink, have some breakfast, and see what the local life is like. We'll see you later.'

'Good! If you see anything I should know about, tell me over dinner tonight.' His invitation clearly brooked no argument and he gave the trio a wave as they left.

\*    \*    \*

The three companions walked past the temple of Taru and into the nearby streets at the back of the imposing temple, heading in the general direction of the barracks. At the end of the street on the left, they came across a dead body lying in the gutter. On the other side of the intersection, there was another body seemingly dumped against a wall.

'What the demons is going on?' asked Narmus. He went closer to the body near the wall and turned it over, watched by his companions. 'They've been beaten to death by the looks of it,' he observed. 'This city is rougher than I thought.'

Palaiyas noted the movement of a shutter across the street at one of the windows above him. '*Hey you there!*' he shouted up to whoever it was. '*Show yourself. I just want to ask you a question.*'

An old crone showed herself and yelled at him, '*What'd ye want soldier?*'

'What happened here,' Palaiyas asked her in a conversational tone, pointing at the nearest body.

'Oh, nothing! Some of the local lads where cleaning out the governor's spies, that's all,' she replied. 'Just a bit of harmless fun; nothing for you to worry about.'

'Harmless fun?' Mokhat was appalled by the callousness. 'I wonder what that withered old woman would call hurtful fun?'

The hag vanished from the window slamming the shutter closed and the trio continued their walk. A little further on, they found the local vigilantes had been busy again clearing out the old governor's undercover agents. They discovered quite a few more bodies and all of them had been beaten to death. Closer to the barracks the same retribution had occurred to some of the soldiers. They asked a couple of soldiers returning to their quarters why a soldier was lying dead in the gutter and were told the same story as the old woman had given them. Vigilante justice for stool pigeons.

There and then Palaiyas decided to complain, 'All this walking is making me hungry and I haven't had any breakfast yet.'

'I can see a hostelry over there,' suggested Narmus, leading the way to the tavern. 'Let's see if he's open?'

Through the open door they could smell the odour of roast meat, barley porridge, and pancakes, mingling with the smell of human sweat, even at this time of a morning. It was a couple of hours after sunrise and the day was in full swing. The place was crowded with people eating and slurping barley ale, with a muffled but audible sound of grumbling, which stopped as soon as three senor officers came in.

The proprietor, a broad muscular man, came over and said, 'Welcome good sirs, what can I do for the army?'

'We'd like a table somewhere quiet, and some wine, if you can manage it,' Mokhat told the man. 'We'd also like some food if you can spare some.'

'Of course sirs, please come this way. I'll get the wife to serve you. There's a quiet table over here in the corner where you won't be disturbed.'

'Are you always so busy at this time of a morning? Seems like the whole city's in here.' Narmus laughed as he said this.

'Don't mind them, sir. I think some of them are celebrating the demise of the greedy old governor. They're fairly harmless,' retorted the tavern keeper.

'Now where've I just heard that?' said Palaiyas amused. 'Harmless heh?'

When they had seated themselves, Palaiyas noted quietly, 'I've an idea that this *harmless* lot in here may have had something to do with all the bodies littering the streets.

They sat waiting and no wife appeared so Narmus got up and went to find the tavern keeper. He was bypassing a table where a lout sat laughing out loudly with three other men, and just as he came abreast of the lout, the drunk swung his arm back and hit Narmus a backhand blow on his belt. Narmus reacted instinctively by thumping the drunk on the head with his clenched fist as hard as he could, which stunned the drunk for a moment. Then Narmus continued on his way.

The drunk shook his head, rose and threw his jug at Narmus' back, swaying and shouting, 'Come back and try that again!'

Narmus turned and retraced his steps carefully. He raised his eyebrows as if to say, *did you say something?* Then hit the large drunk hard in the stomach, and the drunk sank to his knees, gasping for breath. 'Watch your mouth you drunken windbag.'

The drunk's friends were staring daggers at Narmus but stayed in their seats. All four seemed to have been downing a lot of ale. Narmus turned and went on his way to find the tavern keeper. He returned to his companion's table leading the proprietor's wife.

'Sorry about the wait,' said the proprietor's wife. 'It's mayhem in here at the moment. Now what can I get you sirs?' she said with a broad smile.

'Bring us a large flagon of wine, a huge plate of pancakes and a plate of roast mutton.' Palaiyas ordered for them all. 'The wine first, if you wouldn't mind.'

'Right you are sirs. I'll be as quick as I can.' And she was off to see to their order.

The proprietor's wife was as good as her word. The wine arrived almost immediately, shortly followed by the food. They toasted Narmus' promotion a number of times, then the three companions drank and ate their fill.

'Goodness, I needed that. We didn't really have a proper meal all day yesterday, what with all the fighting and chasing after Kishnapili,' declared Palaiyas.

Narmus sat there satiated and patted his stomach. Mokhat leaned back and sighed with contentment. They finished the wine, called for the proprietor and paid the bill, then they made their way to the exit through the crowded tavern.

Standing on the street outside the tavern was the drunk and his pals. He'd managed to gather a few more of his cronies, making around nine thugs in total. They stood there bellicose with a variety of cudgels; three even had swords at the ready.

Palaiyas was out first and immediately got angry. 'Go home and sleep it off before you get hurt,' he snarled at them, then drew his sword and dagger.

Narmus was next and drew his sword to face the drunk he'd hit in the Tavern. 'You just couldn't leave well alone, could you? This time I will teach you a proper lesson you won't forget.'

Mokhat was standing shaking his head in disbelief that a simple breakfast had turned into a life threatening affair. Still shaking his head he drew his sword and dagger in a resigned manner. Some things in life just could not be avoided.

Narmus went after his man with a thrust, but had to take on another two to get at him. These thugs were street brawlers and as such no match for professional soldiers. Narmus sliced and stabbed through the two who were acting as if they were there to protect the drunk who had started all this. Both lay wounded on the street while the drunk ended up being pinned against the wall of a house, drooling and begging for his life.

Palaiyas had four of the thugs to contend with, but he simply and efficiently dispatched all four leaving them with sword and dagger wounds; three were dead and the other was dying. For the thugs it was a whirlwind encounter with seasoned soldiers who thought little of killing the ruffians. They were half befuddled by too much ale and paid for their obduracy with their lives.

Mokhat was still hacking away at three of the thugs, two of whom had swords, but his heart wasn't really in the fight. He saw the encounter as something that should have been avoided, rather than ending in a life or death struggle. Narmus and Palaiyas cradling their swords in their arms, ended up as smiling spectators watching Mokhat dally with his two assailants; the one without a sword lay dead. Finally Mokhat managed to find an opening in the opponent to his right and thrust his sword in his stomach, just as the other man was readying to thrust his sword into Mokhat. Mokhat readied to parry with his dagger but Palaiyas intervened by whacking this fellow on the neck with his own sword putting an end to the threat.

Standing amongst the carnage they looked bemused at the unnecessary loss of life. Mokhat was still shaking his head at the idiocy of it all.

'What can you say? Stupid, stupid people!' Blurted out Narmus. 'What was the point of all that?'

A cart pulled by four soldiers rounded the corner coming from the direction of the barracks. They pointed at the bodies and drew up the cart next to them. From behind the cart the non-com in charge came up to the senior ranking officer, Narmus, and said, 'May we take these away sir,' pointing at the bodies.

'Why nothing would make me happier. Yes, take them. We saw more bodies over towards the back of the main temple.'

'Yes sir, we've orders to collect those as well. There are more squads clearing the entire city sir. General's orders, sir.'

Palaiyas called to them, 'Let's head back to the mansion. I've had enough exercise for today,' and wondered off in the direction of the square followed by his two companions.

# Chapter Twenty Three

**T**hey heard a lot of commotion coming from the direction of the square, with people running from it and soldiers running towards it. As the trio came past the temple to Taru, into the square proper, soldiers were holding back a crowd straining to see what had happened on the far side of the square near the military governor's mansion.

Palaiyas grabbed one soldier forcing him to stop, then asked him, 'What's going on?'

The man was in a state of disbelief. 'The governor's been killed. Over there,' he pointed in the direction of the mansion.

Narmus annoyed, said to the lad, 'Talk sense man. The execution was at dawn. That's all over and done with.'

'No sir, the new governor was killed just now. Some assassin got to him and stabbed him,' said the soldier becoming more distressed. 'He was inspecting all the corpses that have been brought to the square when one of his officers stabbed him.'

Hearing this, Narmus was off running towards the mansion entrance, followed by Palaiyas and Mokhat. As he neared, there was a multitude of officers blocking his view of the scene, and he began pushing his way through them.

'Excuse me, *let me through please…*' Narmus finally spotted Kishnapili's deputy, Tipali, and made his way through towards him, again closely followed by Palaiyas and Mokhat. 'Sir, Colonel Tipali, sir, what's happened?' But by then it had dawned on him that the soldier had meant the new military governor, and that could only mean Kishnapili.

On the ground, covered by a blanket, lay a body with a trickle of blood just creeping out from under it.

'Hallo Narmus,' said Kishnapili's deputy hovering between sadness and anger. 'Yes, it's true...., he's dead...' The utterance came like a leaden weight from his lips.

'But *how*?' asked Narmus trying to be as quiet as he could in a sudden attack of deference. 'How *did it* happen?'

Colonel Tipali sighed and said, 'We've caught the shite...the rotten assassin. He tried to take his own life after he did *that*,' he motioned at the inert body, 'but one of my men was too quick for him and disarmed him. A lot of people jumped on him and bundled him off to the cellar.' He jerked his head in the direction of the mansion.

'I *can't* believe he's dead.' Narmus was having trouble holding back his tears. 'Any idea *why* the bastard did it?'

'He's *not* one of *our* officers,' Tipali said. 'He's from the garrison, and another garrison officer thinks he might be an Ahhiyawan infiltrator. If that's true, then I'd have to conclude that's it's all about the job we were sent out here to do.'

Mokhat then intervened, 'You mean reinforcing and strengthening the border?'

'Yes, that's it. But we need to get a confession out of the assassin.' Tipali said. 'Only then can we confront Ahhiyawa with the evidence. Even then, they're bound to deny it.'

Palaiyas moved forward and placed a hand on Tipali's arm. 'Look here colonel, let me have a go at him. With all due respect, he's more likely to talk to me than a Hittite. I was very fond of Kishnapili and this assassination thing is no way to wage war. I feel the need for a little vengeance.' Palaiyas looked at Mokhat meaningfully when he mentioned assassination.

Mokhat looked aside and knew what Palaiyas was referring to. Before they'd met, three years ago, he'd been the spiritual advisor to the Kaska Assassin's Guild and had been revolted at all their antics, so much so that when he discovered they'd killed Queen Walanni as well as

Muwatallis, he'd assassinated the assassins and disbanded the guild.

Colonel Tipali looked at Palaiyas and replied, 'Well, if you think you can get him to confess, he's all yours, but I need a couple of my officers present at this. Is that alright with you? They won't interfere, I promise, but I need them there.' Tipali whispered into the ear of one of his officers and he rushed away to carry out whatever order he'd been given.

'That's fine by me,' Palaiyas told Tipali, 'only I warn you, they won't understand a word of what's going on. I'll be talking to the assassin in Mycenaean, that's if he *is* Ahhiyawan. Better warn your officers,' Palaiyas told him. Palaiyas then faced his companions and told them, 'I must do this alone,' referring to his interrogation of the assassin. 'I may have to do things that you may find offensive, and I don't want you to think any less of me for doing that. If you were present, I might restrain myself for your sake, and then this assassin would benefit.' He turned to Tipali and asked to be taken to the cellar by the two witnesses the new commander insisted he needed.

Two fresh officers arrived on the scene led by the officer sent to fetch them, and these fresh arrivals led the way into the mansion, out to the back and down to the cellar.

'Right! Now I'd better go and assert my authority before someone else does,' said acting General Tipali to those officers nearest him.

\*   \*   \*

The new general called an emergency meeting of all the regiment's officers and told them what had happened—although most of them had already heard. As Kishnapili's nominated deputy, he then told them he was assuming command in the dead general's place. All top senior officer ranks in the regiment were to step up a notch, these to be confirmed by Hattusas when the time was right.

197

All the plans made by Kishnapili were still valid, only Tipali's deputy, Mekiner, was being promoted to brigadier, and he would lead the three thousand of the garrison to the border in his stead. Military rule was to stay in place and a night curfew was to be put into effect for the next three days. The garrison was to stay in lockdown until they could determine how many other infiltrators were still there. Tipali gave these instructions to his officers in his majesty's name, and asked them all to carry out their patriotic duty.

* * *

In the cellar, Palaiyas found the assassin tied firmly to a column supporting the cellar ceiling. He came and stood in front of the man and simply stared into his face for a long time. The assassin stared back, almost insolently, clearly hostile.

As he was doing this, the two officers allocated to watch him, scrutinised his every move. They found a couple of chairs and sat at such a distance as not to crowd Palaiyas.

Finally Palaiyas asked the assassin, in Mycenaean, 'So who are you? I've been looking at you carefully, and I can tell you're a fellow Mycenaean. No doubt of that. There's no point in keeping quiet now. Your jobs finished. You did what you were sent to do—the only question for me is, who actually sent you? I know it wasn't the new king. I've met him. He's a bit of a young hothead but I don't think he's into assassinations. It's not the Mycenaean style. So who in Millawanda would be into such a thing....? I wonder....?'

Palaiyas stopped and continued to stare at this nasty piece of work that was tied up in front of him. He could see this fellow was fanatical, just by the way he returned Palaiyas' gaze. There was bitter hatred in his eyes. 'You know, I've met people like you on Keftiu, people that oozed hatred from the very pores of their skin. I've also seen how they acquired that hatred. *We* instilled it in them; *we*

Mycenaeans did things to them that shouldn't be done to dogs or cattle. We seized their culture, a culture a thousand years older than ours, and poured scorn on it. We mocked their religion and stole their writing system. Then we pretended we were superior. Yes, I've seen hatred. So now, I wonder what your story is?' Palaiyas stood there staring at this assassin for some time, thinking, then walked away and sat with the two officers assigned to watch him.

'Nice little speech you gave there, your highness,' said the larger of the two officers in Mycenaean.

Palaiyas was taken aback at hearing his own tongue when he wasn't expecting it. 'So that's why Tipali chose you to watch me! I might have guessed it. Him as well?' He motioned to the other officer sitting next to him.

The other officer nodded and told him, 'I'm afraid both of us speak Ahhiyawan. That's why we've been given this detail.'

The big fellow took over again, 'My name is Onasiyas, and this here is Feliyas. Ever since you joined our column we've been meaning to have a chat with you but the time was never right. Nice to finally have a natter, with all due respect of course.'

'Of course! So what's your story? How come two Ahhiyawans are serving as officers in the Hittite army?'

Just at that moment the prisoner gave an anguished howl while desperately trying to break free of his bonds; he struggled for a few moments and then gave up.

The three sitting there looked in the assassin's direction, then continued with their conversation.

'You asked what our story was. Well we're both from the western border regions, only we ended on the Hittite side of the border. We're from the same village and both of us chose to join the army. Since we speak Ahhiyawan, and come from respectable families, we chose to buy our way into the officer class, that's assuming they would have us. Tipali was only a captain then and took a liking to us, so here we are.

Actually, when the regiment was sent to the western border region, Tipali remembered us and insisted we join him and Kishnapili, may Taru rest his spirit. We know the border area, and it would have been foolish not to use us.'

'Yes, and of course Tipali's right,' agreed Palaiyas. 'Well, there's another Ahhiyawan tied up there. Any suggestions? What would you do to get a confession out of him? You heard him just now. He's getting restless.'

'Have you thought of sticking his head in water a few times. We've found that to be most effective on occasions,' suggested Captain Onasiyas.

Palaiyas slowly shook his head, 'No, I'm afraid it wouldn't work this time, not on him. When you do that to someone, they usually want to stay alive, so they hold their breath while their head's under water, but this son of a bitch here would breath in the water as fast as he could to get out of this life. Remember he tried to do away with himself earlier. No, that's not going to work. And it's pointless calling for the cities torturer. This one's a fanatic and would die rather than talk, and would welcome the pain. It would justify the hatred that I saw in his eyes. No, we need something a little bit more cunning than that.'

The officer's curiosity had been aroused. Feliyas asked, 'What had your highness in mind?' he asked on behalf of both them.

Palaiyas rubbed his chin, 'First, could you, Faliyas, go blindfold and gag the prisoner, and put some cloth in his ears so he can't hear us. Then I'll fill you in.'

Faliyas did as he was asked and then returned to his seat.

Palaiyas continued, 'Have either of you come across a mushroom called *immortality*? It's got a red cap with white spots on it.'

Both the captains smiled at the question. Onasiyas replied first, 'I'm beginning to have a glimmer of where you're going with this, but still the *how* escapes me.

*Immortality* is one of those mushrooms that drive people imprudent enough to take it, into a fantasy world. Or if you're a priest, into claiming to be able to speak directly with the gods.'

'Tut..tut..,' said Palaiyas. 'Another sceptic! You should always believe what the priests claim, otherwise you'll undermine their trade. But yes, that's the mushroom I'm referring to. Do you know where I can get a couple, here in the city?'

'I'll go and find out for you, your highness,' offered Feliyas.

'Yes you do that, will you. If you find it, bring some back with you. Find a herbalist and then commandeer the mushrooms if you have to. Better still, pay him double what he asks for them, and I'll reimburse you when you return. Oh, and bring a pestle and mortar from the kitchens while your at it.'

'So where *are* you going with this?' inquired Onasiyas.

'I've a job for you as well,' Palaiyas told him. 'Can you go and find Prince Mokhat and ask him to let you have the Ahhiyawan uniforms. He'll know the ones I mean. Bring them back with you. I promise not to go near the prisoner until you return. In any case, it would be a waste of time without the items I've asked the both of you to get for me. Then we're going to play a little game with this assassin and see if we can't get him to give up the name of the person who sent him to kill Kishnapili.'

Palaiyas sat on the chair, working out the details of his little plan, and watching the prisoner, until the two officers returned.

Faliyas was flushed with exertion and came to show Palaiyas the pouch of mushrooms he'd brought with him. 'Are these any good to you?' He knew the answer to the question because the pouch contained four of the mushrooms they called *immortality*. He'd also brought the mortar and pestle.

Palaiyas beamed, 'Good man, I knew I could count on you.'

Footsteps could be heard coming down the stairs and Onasiyas walked in holding a bundle in his hands. 'Prince Mokhat's compliments and could you be careful with them as they are the only ones we have. That's what he told me to tell you.' He placed the bundle by the chairs.

'Now then, let me tell you what I want you two to do. That,' Palaiyas pointed at the bundle, 'contains two Ahhiyawan uniforms. I want you to go and put them on. In the mean time I'm going to prepare these mushrooms, then we're going to force feed them to the prisoner—and then the fun begins in earnest.'

The two officer's curiosity by now was at bursting point, and they went over to the other side of the cellar and got into the Ahhiyawan uniforms. While they were doing that, Palaiyas crushed two mushrooms into the mortar with the pestle and poured some water on them, mixing them until he had a respectable paste. The officers returned and he eyed them as if he were inspecting them on a parade ground. He adjusted a few minor items and then pronounced himself satisfied.

'We're going to remove the gag only and I'm going to force this down his throat. You Onasiyas, hold his nose when I do that, otherwise he'll spit it out.'

They went to the prisoner and removed his gag. '*Fuck you*! *You bunch of bastards.*' Was what came streaming out of the assassins mouth, just as Palaiyas rammed a stick crosswise into his teeth so as to keep his mouth open. Feliyas pulled his head back and Onasiyas held his nose, while Palaiyas scooped the paste into his mouth in between the stick with his fingers. When all the paste was in, he jerked the stick out and closed the man's mouth with both hands. The assassin struggled but to no avail, and was finally forced to gulp the paste down his food pipe. The three let go of the prisoner long enough for him to cough and spit. Palaiyas brought his water pouch out, uncorked it and then rammed the spout in the coughing mouth, pouring some liquid down the man's throat. The assassin swallowed the liquid automatically to get rid of the bad taste of the paste. The three let go of the prisoner and stood back. Then their prisoner spluttered and spat, even trying to vomit to eject the stuff they'd forced him to take, but all in vain.

'Now let's take his blindfold off and take the cloth out of his ears,' suggested Palaiyas. 'We'll need to wait a lengthy while for this to take effect. Let's go sit down and watch.'

They removed the blindfold and ear plugs, then went back to their chairs and sat down.

After a moment, Palaiyas got up and said, 'Now, I'm going upstairs to change. I'll be back shortly. When I come back I'll fill you in on what I want to happen.'

He was gone for a time and then he returned dressed in a dark robe and looking somewhat sinister. The two officers were clearly puzzled.

'Right gentlemen. I'm going to play the role of his jailer,' Palaiyas motioned at the assassin, 'and I want you two to stand on either side of me and act as guards. Don't say anything. You're just here as props. We're going to pretend we're in a dungeon in Millawanda. You'll see where I'm leading to as the plot unfolds.'

By now some time had gone by and the prisoner was sagging in his bonds and sweating profusely, dry retching a few times. After a while, he abruptly stood rigid with his back against the pillar and began to twitch, followed by a series of convulsions. Suddenly his heavily dilated eyes sprang open and he looked around in a confused manner. He shook his head, stared around him, and shook his head some more; only then did he notice he was tied up. The flickering of the light caught his attention and he stared at it for some time. Again he shook his head a number of times and then demanded in slurred Ahhiyawan, 'Where am I?' Then he jerked his hands and again demanded, 'Why am I tied up?'

Palaiyas came forward and faced him, 'You're tied up you scoundrel, because you killed a fellow officer,' he said in Mycenaean. 'You're a disgrace to the Ahhiyawan army. Don't you remember? You were in a brawl and you stabbed him to death. Now the king's decided to make an example of you. You're for the chop.'

'I...I...don't remember...I don't remember anything.' He moaned and looked around the cellar in confusion.

Palaiyas told him, 'Your in the Millawanda dungeon. I'm here to get you to recognise your guilt. These are friends of the officer you killed,' Palaiyas motioned at the two Ahhiyawan officers standing on either side of him.

'But... but...I don't remember,' he almost pleaded. 'I'd remember if I killed someone, wouldn't I?'

Palaiyas waited for what seemed a long time before he continued. 'King Attarsiyas has ordered me to give you one last chance to save yourself,' he said forcefully. 'That's if you want it.' Then he changed his demeanour and tried to look disinterested. He waited for the reply. This was a crucial moment in this plot. Would the assassin take the bait?

'I don't remember,' he kept saying over and over. Then he stopped, looked at Palaiyas for a while and said, 'What last chance? What do you want from me?' Again with a pleading voice.

Palaiyas smiled inside, but his face was set into a serious frown, 'I want you to go across the border to Ivalanda and kill a certain general. You'll have to infiltrate the garrison and get close to this general, then you're to kill him. Can you do that for me?' Palaiyas closely scrutinised his victim's face. Would it work?

The *immortality* paste was making the prisoner screw his face up into a twist as if he was trying to work something out. He kept shaking his head, as though he was clearing it. His face began to twitch with the contradiction that had been initiated in his head and he seemed to have no way of untangling the problem. Finally he blurted out with a forceful shout, '*But your not Sflokos!*' Then he added, 'I'm not taking any orders from you!'

At the sound of this name, Palaiyas grinned. '*You're quite right..!*' He shouted at the assassin. Then more calmly, 'You're quite right. I'm not Sflokos—and you're already finished. Thank you for your help.' Palaiyas turned and motioned for the two officers to follow him.

Behind him, the assassin was going into a serious convulsion and he was thrashing about as much as his bonds would allow. His eyes turned up until only the whites showed and his was dribbling saliva and sweating badly.

'Frankly when I started this,' Palaiyas announced, 'I wasn't certain it would work. But as you can see, we do have a name. Now all I need to do is change back into my uniform and find out is who this Sflokos is.'

'Now there I might be able to help you,' offered Onasiyas. 'I think this fellow might be the Ahhiyawan spymaster. I may not know the king of Ahhiyawa as you seem to do, your highness, but we were briefed in Hattusas on the major characters in Ahhiyawa's high command, and that included a certain Sflokos. We were told he was a devious, nasty piece of work. As soon as I heard him shout, Sflokos, I realised he was probably the one who'd sent this assassin to kill Kishnapili. If you'll excuse me your highness, I'd like to go and take this uniform off and put my own on instead. I think Feliyas would like to do the same, and then I'll need to go and report what we discovered to General Tipali. I'd like you to join me in doing so, since it was your brilliant plot to steal the information from the assassin's unwilling lips.'

# Chapter Twenty Four

As Palaiyas came out of the cellar into the main hall, he found Mokhat and Narmus pacing about in the hallway of the mansion. He waved Onasiyas and Feliyas to keep going and report to Tipali; he said he'd be along shortly.

As soon as Mokhat saw Palaiyas, he hurried to him and grabbed him by the arm saying, 'Well? How did it go? Did you get what you were after? Come on, don't keep me in suspense.'

Narmus was just as eager to know what had gone on in the cellar. He crowded Palaiyas on the other side of Mokhat.

'Will you slow down and let me tell you,' Palaiyas told the both of them in a tired voice. 'Yes, I've broken the bastard. He gave up what he would have taken to his funeral pyre. We think we have the man who sent him to kill Kishnapili. He's someone called Sflokos. Apparently he's the Ahhiyawan spymaster. What with the fight earlier outside the tavern, and now this lengthy grilling, I'm suddenly feeling very tired.'

'Sflokos, eh? I've heard of him,' muttered Narmus. 'He's Satipilli's counterpart in Ahhiyawa. By all accounts, quite a nasty piece of work. Satipilli was very wary of him. He's supposed to be very cunning and devious. Just the type to send assassins to do his dirty work for him.' Narmus stopped and saw the other two were watching him. 'Now what? We have the real assassin's name, but what can we do about it?'

'Tomorrow we continue to Millawanda. We'll see what happens when we get there,' Mokhat declared. 'The whole situation from the time we left Hattusas, reminds me of an overflowing river, one that makes its own channel and causes havoc and chaos. We have no control over what's occurring here right now, but if we're vigilant, we might be able to make use of some of the chaos. I suppose we're still intent on finding out who was behind Satipilli's murder, and why? Am I right?' Mokhat looked at his companions for confirmation.

'His majesty in Hattusas is relaying on us,' confirmed Palaiyas.

'Even if you were intent on stopping your search for his murderer, I would have to go on by myself,' declared Narmus. 'I can't let this go unavenged. I simply can't.'

'Now Narmus, we're all in this together. We're not stopping. I just wanted to hear you say it out loud—to reaffirm your commitment. We'll continue until we have the culprit, I promise you,' assured Mokhat.

'Now, my friends, I must go and report to Tipali. See you later.' Palaiyas bounded up the stairs two at a time to where he thought Tipali might be found.

\* \* \*

Mokhat took Narmus by the arm and led him towards where he thought the kitchen would be. 'It's been a long time since breakfast and I'm starving. What say we find someone to feed us?'

'I don't need my arm twisting for that,' smiled Narmus. 'Anyway, it's getting dark outside, which suggests to me that it's about dinner time. Amazing how quickly the day has gone, what with nature shortening it in winter. That reminds me, have I told you recently how much I hate winter,' he added.

'No, not recently, but I take note. I'll see what I can do about it for you. I used to have connections up there.' Now coming from Mokhat, that last jest was tantamount to blasphemy, which gave an indication of how much he'd changed of lately as a result of his ordeal with the wild men.

*    *    *

Tipali was having a quiet word with Onasiyas and Feliyas when Palaiyas found him.

'Ah, there you are, your highness,' Tipali noted as Palaiyas arrived. 'I'm told by my officers here that you came away with a good result. I had an instinct you would find a way of cajoling the information from the assassin. Firstly, the question is how convinced are you that the information is real, and secondly, do you really believe that this Sfokos sent this assassin to kill General Kishnapili?'

'Sflokos, general, Sflokos, with an *l*, and yes I do.' Palaiyas was adamant. 'There was simply no possibility he could lie, not with what he had in him. I presume Onasiyas told you what I put down his throat. His mind was so befuddled with what he had, that it had no room for lies or deviousness.'

'Well if you're sure, then my report to Hattusas will say that it was he who was the assassin.' Tipali seemed please with the outcome and beamed at Palaiyas.

'Yes general, I'm convinced that Sflokos was responsible for Kishnapili's death. I'm also fairly convinced that the Ahhiyawan king had no knowledge of the deed. I'm sufficiently convinced of that to broach the matter with the new king when I reach Millawanda. I will have to report to *him* to free myself of an obligation, as it was his father who sent me to Hattusas on that errand for him in the first place.'

As Palaiyas told him this, Tipali raised his eyebrows in wonder. 'So you're still leaving us? I thought I might persuade you to join the column to the border.'

'Sorry General, Prince Mokhat, Colonel Narmus, and I are off early tomorrow morning heading for Millawanda. I want to see if I can find this Sflokos, and since Satipilli was so interested in Millawanda's layout, I want to know why. It seems if we're to find Satipilli's killer then that is the next logical destination. We may not find anything, but we have to

208

exhaust all dead ends. As for the border, general, I'm sure Onasiyas and Feliyas will serve you much better than I would. They know the area much better than I do.'

'Well, if you really must continue your travels, so be it.' Tipali tried to sound disappointed. 'You know you can always count on my future support, just as if I were Kishnapili. But now that I've mentioned him, there is something you must do tonight; you *and* your two friends. We're having a wake-dinner for our dear departed general, and I insist you join us. It'll be a regimental do with all the officers present. He would have wanted you to be there. I'll send Onasiyas here, to fetch you.'

Palaiyas thanked him and went off to find his friends again.

*     *     *

Later that evening Onasiyas found the three companions sitting in the mansion's lounging area, sprawled out on some couches, sipping wine from goblets.

'The general and the regiment request the pleasure of your presence. If you'd be so kind as to follow me back to the barracks.' As it was an official wake-dinner, Onasiyas was being very formal.

'And hallo to you, Captain Onasiyas,' Narmus responded. He looked to Palaiyas for confirmation that this was indeed Onasiyas. He'd only glanced him when they passed by each other in the hallway.

Mokhat stood up, as did the other two, and followed Onasiyas out into the square. There was a six man honour escort to conduct them to the function and Onasiyas led the way.

The officer's mess in the garrison barracks had two long tables joined to the top table in a u shaped arrangement. Tipali sat in the middle as commanding general of the regiment while Mokhat was placed on his right with Palaiyas on his left. Narmus sat next to Mokhat. The dinner began in a sombre mood with a eulogy by Tipali extolling the virtues of their dear departed Kishnapili. Tipali's deputy, Mekiner, followed by recalling some incidents in Kishnapili's career as commander of the regiment. He dwelt on the ruse Kishnapili used recently to re-enter Ivalanda with his contaminated water story. Officers were nodding in admiration at his cunning.

Toast were made and drunk to, followed by more toasts. First came the sombre music from a group of musicians and as time and wine loosened the atmosphere, more lively music was demanded. Some of the officers joined together on the dance floor and performed the national Hittite dance, arms around each others shoulders, doing fancy footwork to the tune being played.

'The general would have liked this,' Tipali told Mokhat loudly over the music. 'He had a liking for the ordinary soldier and always enjoyed watching them have fun. On a different subject, your highness, we're finding more bodies, but this time here in the barracks. It looks like the ordinary soldiers are having a good clear out of Ahhiyawan infiltrators. We found five today and there may be more to come. Not a pleasant business. If they're suspicious of anyone, they won't wait for proof; they'll just act.'

Mokhat shook his head in regret and asked, 'How the blazes did it get so bad here?'

Tipali shrugged, 'My guess, it's all down to the greedy governor they had in Ivalanda. He was so busy lining his own purse that he ignored his duty of protecting normal Hittite interests. This is the result.'

Just then two officers were performing a sword dance and it became too noisy to continue any kind of conversation. Encouragements were being shouted and the tempo of the music speeded up. The officers were wielding their swords in mock combat to the music and how they missed injuring each other was down to their skill with their weapons.

Mokhat was captivated by the sword dance and was annoyed when Narmus gently pocked him in the ribs with his elbow. Mokhat looked at Narmus only to have Narmus draw his attention to Tipali who just had had a visitor whispering in his ear and then he seemed to smile as if he'd been told something funny. Mokhat asked the general, trying to raise his voice above the music, 'I see that you're enjoying yourself.'

'Now more so than ever,' Tipali replied. 'I've had word that Kishnapili's assassin has just left this world and they think it was probably due to the paste he was forced to consume. I must thank Prince Palaiyas for ridding me of the need to execute him.' The smile spread on his face and he gently placed his hand on Palaiyas wrist and whispered in his ear. Palaiyas smiled and nodded.

Now a group of officers placed swords on the floor in two star patterns and began to dance amongst them to some lively music. Wine was flowing and the genial atmosphere bolstered everyone's mood. By the end of the evening there were quite a few people drunk, and so finally, Tipali called a halt to the proceeding, thanking all those present for getting pleasure from the wake—he was sure Kishnapili would have been pleased that his staff had celebrated his demise in such an agreeable fashion.

\*   \*   \*

The next day brought problems for those who had imbibed in excess, with many a hangover at breakfast time. Daylight had just shown itself and all three companions were busily gulping down the hot barley porridge, which was a staple in the army canteen.

'Did you check the horses?' Mokhat asked Palaiyas between mouthfuls.

'First thing I did when I got up; went to see to them even before breakfast. Three fresh horses are waiting for us at the stables, and three pack animals with provisions to last us for a week.'

'Narmus, can I ask you to see the general and thank him on our behalf, and give him the messages for Hattusas which I'm about to give you.' Mokhat was penitent for avoiding Tipali but intent on getting underway. 'If I go and see him, I fear we won't leave till late in the morning. We really need to get an early start if we want to make good headway. Give him my apologies and these messages, and remind him to talk to the ex-governor's tax collector whom I mentioned to Kishnapili. He'll find it useful to sort out the corruption in Ivalanda.' Mokhat handed Narmus a clay tablet, 'Then come straight to the stables. We'll wait for you there.'

\*     \*     \*

Ivalanda began to recede in the east as the trio retraced their earlier route towards Millawanda, with Palaiyas casting wary eyes over his shoulder in case Napat or his henchmen were following them. The wind had changed and was coming from the northeast, and the temperature had dropped again.

Once more they broke their journey on the ridge they had sat on two days ago, tethering their horses on the same leafless bushes just below the ridge. The ridge still gave them a splendid view of the route they'd come down, and Palaiyas kept searching for Napat while he ate the biscuits and dried meat. Narmus looked around for the rock-thrush which had so engrossed him earlier but it was nowhere to be seen. The sparse grass on a small hillock was looking empty without the bird but the ants must have surely appreciated its absence.

After they finished their meal, they rode down the other side of the ridge, and a little further on, looked for the place where they'd battled with the line of hungry people. As they passed the spot of the combat, they saw many half eaten human carcasses, scavenged by wolves and other carrion.

212

'That reminds me,' Narmus said to Mokhat, motioning at the half eaten cadavers they were passing, 'Just as I was leaving, General Tipali ordered a mass cremation outside the city walls, also asking people if they would come and collect their dead before they got thrown on the fire. Those killed as spies for the governor and those that the soldiers thought were Ahhiyawan infiltrators. I think he wants to catch some more infiltrators, if they're stupid enough to collect those bodies.'

'That's good,' answered Mokhat, half listening. He was still appalled by the awful sight of those mutilated human carcasses and was glad to be leaving them behind.

'Tipali's also sent for reinforcements from Purushanda and Hattusas,' continued Narmus, who was voicing a train of thought out loud, using Mokhat as a sounding board. 'He's asked them to send a new general to take over in Ivalanda. He told me that the assassin made a previous attempt on Kishnapili when we *first* arrived in Ivalanda, but it was so badly bungled that the officer who noticed another officer coming at the general with a knife, thought he was going to offer the knife to the general as a gift, until the knife carrying officer tripped and fell over. He picked himself up and ran away, which made this fellow suspicious. Only later did he realise it was the assassin when he saw him again, and told Tipali. He's been demoted for incompetence. If he'd mentioned it earlier they might have apprehended the fellow *before* he'd done the deed *and* saved Kishnapili's life.'

By this time it was the middle of the afternoon and the wind had switched again to coming in from the southwest. It felt a lot warmer than it did when they'd set out from the city earlier. The surrounding landscape was hilly and strewn with rocks and boulders, and in winter it looked even more barren than it otherwise would have been in summer.

Palaiyas had stopped and was staring behind them into the far distance, prompting them also to stop. He raised his hand and said, 'Have a look over there,' he pointed in the direction they'd come from. 'I think I saw a glint, a flash, from that direction on the horizon. It might have been the sun hitting something metal.' He asked the both of them, 'Can you see anything?'

All three stared for a while where Palaiyas pointed.

'Can't see a thing!' Declared Narmus, peering into the far distance.

'Neither can I,' added Mokhat, straining to sit higher on his horse.

'Ah well, might have been the sun hitting a puddle of water, although I doubt it. We still need to be on our guard. I just have this feeling we're being followed again,' Palaiyas explained, but not convinced by his water speculation. He'd been sure he'd seen a glint of metal.

'We probably are, but playing cat and mouse with them is too time consuming and I'm all for making speed towards our destination,' Mokhat insisted this was the only course open to them if they wanted to throw off any pursuers. 'So instead of stopping and looking behind us, what say we make some speed until nightfall?'

They all agreed to this course of action and proceeded to kick their horses into a gallop. It was a steady gallop and by dusk they had managed to put some twelve leagues behind them before the horses began to falter, as did the light. They rode over the crest of a hill and down into a small narrow valley running from north to south. There was a small stream running through the centre of the little valley and Palaiyas suggested it might be a good place to camp for the night. Bare bushes and a few leafless trees squatted on the banks of the stream making the place look somewhat forlorn.

'I can just picture this place in springtime,' mused Narmus after dismounting and leading his horse to the water for a drink.

'Here, it's just as good now, than in your fantasy springtime,' Palaiyas told him, leading his own mount to the water. 'We have shelter and lots of firewood and even running water. What more could you want?'

'Well, since you ask, maybe a little feminine company wouldn't come amiss,' Narmus responded, still thinking of spring and warm weather.

'Now that's different,' Palaiyas joked. 'We could all do with a little of that, but what woman in her right mind would be out here with three old soldiers like us, I ask you?'

Mokhat listened to this banter and shook his head. 'Isn't anyone going to make a fire? Forget about your fantasies and come back to cold reality. We need to get some hot food going before we can settle down to more jokes.'

'Sorry, you're right. I'll go gather the wood,' Narmus told him.

For their first night's meal, they were having a couple of rabbits that the person who packed their provisions had included. These roasted on two spits while Mokhat turned the spits with both his hands. 'Almost ready,' he shouted at his companions.

Narmus sat poking at a burning log in a distracted manner. He looked interested when Mokhat shouted that the food was ready.

After the meal and some hot wine, they relaxed sitting on the log and felt more at ease than they had done the whole day.

'Ivalanda turned into a bit of a sordid mess, don't you think?' Narmus asked Mokhat, trying to get a perspective on what had occurred in the last three days.

'Who would have thought such a rotten governor would stay in power without being overseen by the higher authorities,' added Palaiyas. He had got fond of Kishnapili and was still sad at how his life had been ended by a lone assassin.

Mokhat, who was distracted by thoughts of Satipilli and Millawanda, got up. 'I'm just going to check the horses.

Make sure they've eaten and that their nicely hobbled and settled for the night.'

All three continued to discuss for a while longer the events in Ivalanda, and what they might to find in Millawanda, and then turned into their blankets that were spread close around the fire.

# Chapter Twenty Five

'*Hey you!*' Palaiyas shouted as he sprang to his feet from under his blankets, sword at the ready in his hand. They had all gone to sleep with their swords unsheathed, cradling them, on Palaiyas' recommendation, just in case they needed them quickly during the night.

Narmus and Mokhat followed Palaiyas jumping to their feet, armed and ready. They saw the outlines of five men in the moonlight, attempting to lead all their horses away from the camp. Any further attempts by the thieves at carrying out their theft by stealth was immediately abandoned and they slapped the horses rumps to send them galloping away into the night. Then the five outlines came at the trio, swords drawn, and a fight to the death ensued.

Palaiyas met his large opponent, wielding his own sword at him, only to be countered in a clash from his enemy's sword, the sound of metal against metal ringing out loudly in the stillness of the night. He was close enough to his foe to see the tell-tale drooping moustache of the Gimirri. Palaiyas was up against Genger, the big chief of that hoodlum tribe, who was trying to hammer him into the ground with his sword in a series of over arm blows, which Palaiyas successfully parried. He tried to push his dagger into Genger's guts but was kicked away. Palaiyas did however manage to catch Genger's calf with that dagger and draw blood. Genger cursed loudly in his own tongue and renewed the attack, but he was now limping.

There were three trying to put a quick end to Narmus, but when Genger shouted for help, one of his men came to assist him in fighting Palaiyas, giving Narmus a better fighting chance.

Mokhat was up against Napat and the fight was fierce, Napat relying on his height and strength, while Mokhat relied on his superior fighting skills, a proficiency which he'd tried to improve ever since his previous ordeal with this same opponent. Mokhat had a score to settle with Napat and this time he wasn't tied to a wheel but could lash out at his tormentor with a sturdy sword in his hand. He made the most of his opportunity to avenge himself for Napat's foul misuse of him, by cutting Napat when he could, without doing too much damage. He wanted to draw the fight out, to make Napat suffer, as Napat had made him suffer with the branding iron.

Something demonic had been aroused in Mokhat, giving him a fluency with the sword that otherwise he'd never had before. More cuts on Napat's arms, some on the legs, some on the sides, and Napat, this false shepherd, began to feel a fear that was normally alien to him. He unexpectedly felt that he might actually loose this battle to the death. In one last desperate move, he lunged at Mokhat, and then abruptly pulled back, throwing his sword, blade first, at Mokhat; he then tuned tail and ran for it as fast as his long legs would carry him.

Mokhat couldn't believe his quarry had abandoned the fight. He stared, panting, at Napat's back as the blackguard raced out of the valley and up the far side of the hill. Mokhat gazed around in frustration looking for another fight but only saw Genger lying on the ground, as was his crony who had come to help him, both struck down by Palaiyas.

Narmus was still struggling, and seemed to have been wounded by his two opponents, prompting Palaiyas to rush to his aid. He was there in a few strides and helped him finish off one man, while the other adversary was following Napat as fast as he possibly could.

All of a sudden Narmus dropped his sword, then his dagger, and sank to his knees clutching his left side. Palaiyas came to him and knelt with him, holding him up by the shoulders. 'Is it bad? *Mokhat, give us a hand over here,*' he shouted to his friend. '*Narmus is hurt.* We must have a look and see how bad it is.'

Mokhat came quickly and took him by the other shoulder, 'Bring him over to the fire. We need to get him on his blanket and have a closer look.'

'I'm alright, really,' exclaimed Narmus, it's only a flesh wound.' He winced as he said it. 'There were three of them at me. One of the blackguards caught me with a thrust, then rushed away to help his chum have a go at Palaiyas.'

Narmus tried walking but had to be carried underarm to his blanket by his friends, still clutching his side. When they'd laid him down they could see that he'd lost a lot of blood. His entire left side down to his ankles was soaked in red. When they'd cut open his tunic and exposed the wound, they could see a deep gash.

'Press hard where the wound is,' Mokhat told him. 'It will stop some of the bleeding.'

'I'm sorry my lad, but you're not going to like what comes next,' Palaiyas told Narmus. Palaiyas thrust his sword into the fire and poked it around to get it into the hottest embers. 'Mokhat, can you put some more wood on the fire please. Oh, and get me some wine and water. Also get me his extra tunic from the bags. I'll need to tear it up to make a bandage. Luckily the horses weren't loaded when they drove them away.'

When Mokhat returned, he noticed Narmus staring anxiously at the sword heating in the fire. Mokhat poured out a good goblet of wine and offered it to Narmus. 'Drink this down. You'll need the liquid. You know if Palaiyas doesn't cauterise the wound, you'll bleed to death.'

Narmus took the drink and gulped it down, then just nodded and settled on his side still holding the wound tight, but offering up his wounded side for Palaiyas to do his worst. Palaiyas waited till the sword was hot, and then removed it from the fire, and almost simultaneously, Narmus removed his bloodied hand. Mokhat poured water quickly on the wound to clean it a little, and without hesitation, Palaiyas carefully applied the hot sword to the wound so as to burn it closed. Narmus gritted his teeth, clenched his fists, and didn't make another sound. With the sizzling sound and the smell of burning flesh the flow of blood ceased. Mokhat poured some more water on the wound, giving Narmus much relief from the burning heat. Palaiyas put down the sword and began to tear up Narmus' spare tunic, using it to bind it around his wounded waist.

'I'm afraid that's the best I can do. Now you must rest and try to get some sleep in what's left of this night,' advised Palaiyas. 'Here, have some more wine; it'll help you to sleep.'

Narmus settled down into his blankets after another goblet of wine, and tried to relax, closing his eyes, but his teeth were still clenched from the pain. This was Narmus' most uncomfortable night he could remember, and given time, he would hope to forget it.

Mokhat put his finger to his lips and motioned Palaiyas over to the other side of the fire, then sat on a log and patted the place next to him for Palaiyas to join him. 'Damn and blast!' he whispered to his friend in mock exasperation, 'After all the warnings we gave ourselves yesterday, about guarding against an ambush, and reminding ourselves how sneaky Napat was, and all that; here we are, sitting *without* horses. How did he do that? I never heard a thing, and believe me; I had one ear open listening out for him.'

'It was sheer luck on my part that I woke up,' sighed Palaiyas. 'Some instinct snapped my eyes open. Maybe I heard them somehow, and thank my *manes* that I did. They could have murdered us in our sleep, only they chose to go after the horses first. But you're right, here we sit without horses. If I thought we could catch the horses I'd be out there looking for them right now, but those mounts are from Ivalanda and that's where they're headed right now at a frightened gallop. What I'm more worried about is Narmus. He's lost a lot of blood there and if that wound gets infected, he and we are in big trouble. As it is we'll probably have to carry him somehow.'

'One good thing came out of this,' whispered Mokhat. 'I don't think Napat will bother us anymore. I think I frightened him off. He actually gave up the fight with me and ran for his life; and believe me, I would have killed him had he stayed. Then of course, there are those bodies over there. I notice you put paid to Genger and his pal. Congratulations! It's a pity two of them got away.'

'So, what *are* we going to do in the morning; any ideas?' Palaiyas was fishing for Mokhat's thoughts on what might be done next.

'My best idea is for us to try and get some rest, even if we don't sleep,' Mokhat advised. 'I'm going to sit near Narmus and make sure he's alright. You've done us proud tonight but, please Palaiyas, I really would like you to climb back into your blankets and stay there till dawn. Even if you don't sleep, the rest will be a great help for what's to come tomorrow.'

Palaiyas sighed deeply, indicating his reluctance, but did as his friend asked of him. He went quietly and lay in his blankets until dawn.

*     *     *

Narmus awoke with a start, after finally falling into a fitful sleep close to dawn. He found Mokhat sitting nearby poking the fire with a tree branch, looking at him.

'I noticed earlier, you finally managed to nod off. I was hoping you'd sleep a little longer.' The concern was etched into Mokhat's face. 'So how do you feel?'

'Sore and stiff after all the fun we had, but otherwise alright. The side is still throbbing, but that's a good thing, isn't it?' Narmus said this trying to smile, but it turned into a grimace when he made a move to get up.

'Please stay in your blankets,' Mokhat implored him. 'I want to have a look at that wound before you try to get to your feet.'

Narmus turned onto his right side and the bandage seemed to be a little wet with seeping blood, but on the whole, much better than Mokhat expected.

'That extra bit of sword work last night by Palaiyas seems to have worked. The main flow is stopped. That wound may have cut some muscle so you'll have to use your spear to lean on. Then you can have a go at getting up.'

Palaiyas was on his feet and looking to get some barley porridge going. 'We've got all those provisions and no way of transporting them,' he complained to Mokhat. 'And how's our wounded colonel this morning?' He asked Narmus.

'Much better, thank you,' Narmus forced himself to smile. 'I forgot to be grateful last night when you cauterized my side. I know I would have bled to death if you hadn't done that. I'm in your debt, your highness.'

Palaiyas waved his response, as if to say, it was nothing, and went to the stream to get some water for the porridge.

Breakfast was a sombre affair with Narmus wincing with pain at his every spoonful, and Mokhat continually glancing at him, in between mouthfuls, to see if he was coping.

Palaiyas on the other hand seemed unconcerned and ate his meal with enthusiasm. 'I've been thinking,' he announced to his companions as he shovelled more porridge into his mouth. 'We have all our provisions, and I know we can't take most of it with us, but we could take more than one man can carry if we made a small square frame from branches and tied the frame onto two trailing poles. I've seen this done in some of the poorer villages. We could use both our spears as the trailing poles. We tie only those provisions we consider urgent onto the frame, a sack of porridge, two skins of water and a couple of pans should do it. It's a sort of wheel-less chariot, if you can imagine that. If we find it too hard to pull, we could stop and simply eat what we can manage, and then abandon the rest. That's *instead* of abandoning the stuff right now before we start. What do you think? That assumes that Narmus can manage to walk on his own.' Palaiyas looked at Narmus for confirmation that he could manage to walk on his own.

Mokhat looked at Narmus, and was just about to reject the idea because they'd need all their strength to help Narmus, when Narmus cut in and said with determination in his voice, '*Yes*, I *can* manage by myself. This expedition isn't going to fail because of me. Whatever your objections, I insist on walking alone; with the help of my trusty spear here of course,' he patted the spear lying on the log beside him.

'I'll get started on the platform then,' was all Palaiyas said and wandered off to find some branches to cut with his sword.

When Palaiyas came back with the wood, Mokhat voiced his anxiety for their future, 'You know, we need to set out with a purpose,' he declared. 'We have to try and find a farmhouse or some other habitation if we're going to get horses again. Even an ass would be of use; we could carry Narmus on it. We can't walk to Millawanda. What about trying to get to a river? We could use it to get downriver to the sea.'

'Now there you might have hit on an idea,' replied Palaiyas. 'If my reckoning is right, one of the southern tributaries of the Meandros River isn't too far from here. Remember I came this way last year when I was going *to* Hattusas. The river downstream comes out into the bay opposite Millawanda. If we were in a boat we could sail right into the Lion Harbour. That would be one in the eye for Napat, after all the effort he's made to try to stop us getting there. The alternative is, we could go around looking for habitation for weeks in this wilderness but the river is right over there,' he pointed northwards as if it was just out of sight over the ridge. 'What say you? Shall we head for the river? It's a known location and we're bound to find a boat we can use.'

Mokhat scratched his beard and then shrugged, 'You've managed to convince me. Let's do it. It stops any aimless wanderings on our part. As you say; it comes out near Millawanda, and that's good enough for me. Narmus, agreed?'

Narmus tried to look positive and gave his wholehearted support for the journey to the river.

They got their belongings together and Mokhat shouldered his shield and grabbed his spear while Palaiyas did the same and they set off dragging the frame with the food on it. They'd reinforced the spears with some other poles for ware and tear. Narmus carried a light sack over his right shoulder, containing their spare tunics and other personal items; this was covered by his shield, holding this with his left hand, propping himself up with his spear in his right hand. Palaiyas had wound around his own waist all the rope or twine they had with them. Thus it was that the little expedition set out on foot to make their trek to the distant river.

Mokhat took one last look at the items from the packhorses they were leaving behind. 'It breaks my heart to have to leave all that stuff—but there's no choice, is there?' He was talking to himself because the other two were already moving off.

Narmus hobbled along as best as he could and didn't complain at all. Dragging the two spears with the square frame tied across it was no easy matter when the ground was rough or there was a hill to climb, but they managed to make progress during the rest of the morning. By noon they had travelled a league in the direction of the river. At least in the direction Palaiyas believed the river to lie in.

'My guess is we'll reach the tributary sometime today,' Palaiyas speculated as they plodded onwards. 'Sometime late in the afternoon, probably. We could camp on the bank overnight and make a move downriver tomorrow, if we can find a boat. If not, I'm prepared to try and build a raft.' Palaiyas seemed to have been energised by some urgent desire to get to Millawanda and nothing was going to stop him. He even picked up his pace, but had to slow back down when Narmus wasn't able to keep up.

# Chapter Twenty Six

**P**alaiyas was spot on when he predicted they'd reach the river by late afternoon. They heard it before they could see it, the loud roar of the tributary. When they crested the hill obscuring its view, it wasn't as wide as Mokhat had expected and so he seemed disappointed that it wasn't a bigger river. He had to remind himself it was only a tributary of the Meandros proper.

'Well, you were right all along. I'm sorry if I ever doubted you,' Mokhat apologised to Palaiyas. There were moments on the journey when Mokhat had questioned the wisdom of looking for a river *somewhere* in a possible direction, although he'd kept his scepticism to himself. Now he was a little embarrassed at his lack of faith in his friend and so felt the need to make an apology.

'I have an instinct for finding my way,' Palaiyas replied in response to the apology.

Narmus stood there and for the first time since being wounded, he felt a glimmer of hope. He saw them reaching the river as a sign from the gods, that all would turn out well for their expedition. He sighed with relief, and the other two heard his sigh. They glanced at him and saw him smiling at the river.

'How do you feel, Narmus?' Mokhat asked, concerned at his sighs.

'Never better,' Narmus answered truthfully. 'We're going to make it; I mean, reach Millawanda that is. A little boat ride and we're there; that's right isn't it?' he asked Palaiyas.

'Absolutely,' Palaiyas reassured him. 'Simply a small boat ride and then you'll get a lot of rest so you can recuperate. We need you with us. You're our motivating force. Without you we'd lack the backbone needed for such a venture.' As he said this he looked at Mokhat to back him up.

'Quite right! Now let's get down to the shore and see what's what,' Mokhat encouraged them both.

The light was beginning to fade as they reached the shoreline. The river wasn't very wide but it was swift flowing at this time of year. They made a fire and Palaiyas cooked them each a generous portion of the porridge they had sweated so hard to pull all the way to this spot.

'With a full stomach, can you really say it wasn't worth hauling the sack of barley flour all the way down here?' he joked.

Mokhat's response was to pat his belly and sigh in contentment, while Narmus simply smiled and nodded his agreement.

\* \* \*

The night was uneventful, except for the noise of the furious flowing river roaring on its way next to them. The three companions slept in fits and starts until the first light of dawn put a stop to their restless dozing. Breakfast was speedy and brief, while Palaiyas laid plans for their raft. They had a good look around and hadn't seen the slightest signs of other people, so they had to assume they were utterly alone. Palaiyas found a few untrimmed logs stuck in some rocks further up the shoreline. He and Mokhat manoeuvred them down to the pebbly beach close to where they had camped.

'No boat I'm afraid,' Palaiyas motioned at the logs, 'but the raft I promised you is about to become a reality.'

'Have we enough rope for this thing,' Mokhat wasn't so sure he wanted to trust his life to a flimsy contraption that Palaiyas might have in mind.

'I should think so. I'm sure it'll be enough. Better still; let me ask you what the alternative is? Do we stop and abandon our voyage because we don't have a full fledged boat to go down the river in?' Palaiyas looked boldly at his friend, daring him to contradict him.

'No, of course not, it's just that.....' and he let the rest trail off as he saw Palaiyas' scowl.

They got busy with chopping down more logs, while they allowed Narmus to do some of the lighter trimming of the branches from the logs they supplied. He simply wouldn't sit quietly as they'd asked him to; and the good news was that his wound wasn't leaking.

Later, Palaiyas sat resting with the others, staring at their hoard of logs. 'Eight logs across and one at each end holding them together. That should do it. What do you think Mokhat, Narmus? One rudder at the back and we're ready. All we have to do now is tie them together. The biggest problem is going to be the rudder. On a river like this, we have to be able to manoeuvre the raft around rocks and boulders if we're to stay alive. I'm thinking of putting a deep U cut into the back and putting a stout branch across the end to hold the rudder firmly in place. If you've got a better idea I'd like to hear it? I and Mokhat will have stout poles to push away from obstacles. When the water is not too rough, maybe you Narmus, could take the rudder, but when it gets rough I reserve the privilege of taking it myself.' He looked at them both to see if they had anything to add to what he'd just said.

'So let's start tying the logs together,' Mokhat suggested.

It took them well into afternoon to make a raft that satisfied Palaiyas. It appeared sturdy enough, but all afternoon, Mokhat had been looking at the speed of the water flowing past them. He didn't like what he saw.

'I know we don't have a choice, but that water seems treacherous to me,' Mokhat commented to Narmus when they'd tied the rudder into place and stood back to admire their handiwork.

Palaiyas had heard, although Mokhat hadn't meant him to. 'So let's walk to Millawanda, shall we? It's only another fifty leagues.' The sarcasm in his voice made any other comment redundant.

Mokhat broke the atmosphere with a practical suggestion. 'The afternoon is almost finished and I don't think we want to launch this raft in the dark. So let's secure it and make a fire. Let's get some food going and we'll spend another night on this shore, then we can start early next morning. What do you think Palaiyas?'

'I agree. It's only sense. We can't run this river in the dark. I'll go gets some wood and start a fire.' They found a small clearing and moved their camp a little inland to lessen the sound of the river. 'Narmus, please sit and have a rest; you too Mokhat. I feel energetic. I'll make the food in a minute.' With that Palaiyas busied himself while they sat and watched.

Fully fed, they climbed into their blankets exhausted after all their work and fell immediately into a deep sleep.

In the morning after breakfast they readied the raft for launch.

'Where do you want me to sit when we start,' Narmus asked Palaiyas, whom he saw as the self appointed captain of the raft.

'Let me take the rudder to start with,' Palaiyas said. 'Then you can take over when we have the raft going nice and steady. Start with sitting in the middle. Mokhat, can you give me a hand to launch this, and then take the outside with your pole. Right, are we ready….?'

Narmus sat with what was left of the barley flour, holding onto the sack with their personal items in it with one hand and hanging on to their shields and weapons with the other.

Mokhat and Palaiyas gave an almighty heave and then quickly ran through the shallows to jump onto the raft as it left the shore. Mokhat took the outside station with his pole, looking for obstacles in the water, and Palaiyas grabbed the rudder to try and imbue the raft with some control on where they were going. He didn't want to take the raft into the middle of the water where the current was the fastest, so he steered it to stay closer to the left bank from which they'd launched.

The raft bobbed up and down in the fast flowing water and made it all but impossible to control as it sped on its way. Palaiyas was exhilarated by the excitement of it all, and by finally moving rapidly in the direction they'd intended to go in. For him, Millawanda was just round the corner.

Mokhat was concentrating on staying on the raft and not falling overboard. The up and down motion was making his stomach churn, and until he got control, he almost lost his breakfast. There was a bit of a wind and this finally forced Mokhat onto his knees if he were to stay on the raft.

After heading down the tributary towards the Meandros for some time, they reached calmer waters and a lot of the buffeting stopped. At this point Palaiyas insisted they retrieve their swords from the sack and sheath them in their scabbards.

The wind dropped and the trip began to take on some aspects of a gentle cruise. Palaiyas managed to steer the raft close to the left bank and so stay out of the middle current, much to Mokhat's appreciation, and they made good headway on their journey.

By early afternoon, up ahead, they spotted the confluence where their tributary met the Meandros proper. They approached the confluence with some trepidation, and as the raft swung into the Meandros, the current seized the raft and drew it into the middle of the river, into the fastest part of the flow.

When the raft lurched deep into a hollow dip between waves, Palaiyas yelled at them, '*Hang onto something!*' His mouth kept moving but they couldn't hear the rest above the noise of the turbulence.

Mokhat was already on his knees and sank further onto his stomach, lowering his centre of gravity. He held the edges of the raft with both hands in a fierce grip, determined not to be thrown into the water.

Narmus was looking lost in the buffeting, holding onto all their possessions, and grimacing from the jolting his injured side was receiving. As the raft lifted out of the deep hollow, it tossed and flipped him to the right, upwards and sideways into the water. Mokhat stretched out his hand in a desperate gesture, but to no avail. Palaiyas was hanging onto the rudder as if his life depended on it, and it probably did. Neither of them could do anything but watch in shock as Narmus disappeared beneath the turbulent waters. One moment his head was bobbing up and down, the next he sank out of sight beneath the waves. The two horrified spectators didn't even see him struggle, for he seemed to sense that there was little use against such a force of nature as this raging restless river.

The raft carried the drenched stunned survivors ever onwards, down for a long while till late afternoon, and as the river widened the waters calmed, but by then Mokhat had tears in his eyes and neither of them spoke. The raft had settled down in the calm water and was now back under Palaiyas' rudder control, so he aimed the craft into the left shore as best he could, and after a bit of a struggle, managed to beach it onto the shingles. Both climbed from the raft in a depressed mood.

Palaiyas stood and watched the calm waters, and kept shaking his head. 'We only met him a week ago, yet I feel like I've known him all my life.' He then began tugging the raft further up the beach with unnecessary violence.

Mokhat gave him a hand but his thoughts were elsewhere. 'He was a generous man and I'm pleased to have been able to know him, even if it was only for a short while. A true friend who will be sorely missed.'

Both were eulogising for someone they had befriended in this hostile world, and someone who had returned their friendship with an open heart.

'I hereby vow in his memory, to find Satipilli's killer and put an end to his miserable existence.' Palaiyas said this with vehemence in his voice that would have made a listener shudder with fear. He looked at Mokhat expecting him to join him in this oath.

Mokhat simply said, 'I so vow,' but he said it emphatically. He was still too sad to be angry. His thoughts were on the first time they had met Narmus, while secreted in his convoy of twenty wagons coming out of Purushanda. The tough faced officer in charge of the convoy pocking his head through the heavy cotton cover of their wagon to introduce himself. Mokhat's eyes got moist again at the memory.

'It's too late to go on,' Palaiyas declared. 'I need to sit around a fire and reflect; and I have a feeling you need to do the same. We'll stop here for the night and go on tomorrow; agreed?'

'Agreed!' Mokhat was also in no mood to continue. Palaiyas was right, he did need to stop and reflect on their loss. It didn't seem right that they should just continue as if nothing had happened.

They secured the raft by dragging it even further up the shore, then they moved away from the shoreline and Palaiyas lit a fire. By this time it had become quite dark. He made the food from what was left of the barley flour, although the flour was somewhat damp, and they both ate the hot gruel in silence, both staring into the burning embers.

'There are a few things that I want to do before we continue with our journey tomorrow,' Palaiyas told Mokhat after they had eaten and were sitting on a log round the fire. 'Firstly, we're going to empty the water skins and fill them with air.'

Mokhat raised his eyebrows in a puzzled expression at this line of talk. He was expecting some gentle reminders from Palaiyas of Narmus' kind nature and his friendship towards them, but instead Palaiyas was talking of emptying water skins.... had he flipped?

'I'm going to tie the water skins to your waist with a length of rope that I have left,' Palaiyas continued, ignoring the puzzled frown on Mokhat's face, 'so that should you get tossed into the water for some unforeseen reason, all you have to do is pull on the rope and reach the inflated water skins. They will keep you afloat no matter what happens. As for me, I'm going to cut myself a small log and tie myself to it. I'm a very strong swimmer, coming from a town by the sea, so that even in that river, I should be able to take care of myself. It's only a damnable pity I didn't think of the water skins for Narmus before this—he might still be with us if I had.'

As Mokhat listened and understood what Palaiyas was trying to do, he felt a rush of warmth towards his companion. Palaiyas hadn't flipped; he was making plans so that both of them would survive another catastrophe, such as the one that had overtaken Narmus. This time there would be no tragedies, at least not if Palaiyas could avoid it. And yes, Palaiyas had assessed the situation correctly. Mokhat wasn't a strong swimmer and the inflated water skins would probably be indispensable if he were to live through being hurled into those cantankerous waters.

'Yes, I could see from your face that you thought my brains had seized up, but now you know they haven't.' Palaiyas sat there with a benevolent smile. 'If you were to join Narmus, I don't think I could take it. We've been

233

through thick and thin together and I've got rather too fond of your ugly mug being around. It would be too much for the fates to grab you just when I need you the most. Who would help me fulfil the oath to Satipilli?'

'Palaiyas, I appreciate your concern. And I've got fond of you too, and for the same reason.' Mokhat was somewhat embarrassed by the sentiments being expressed. 'Anyway, I promised the king I would look after you, but here you are turning the tables on me. But you're right; there's the oath and there's my swimming to account for. If I were to be thrown in the river, I've already assumed I wouldn't survive, simply because my swimming isn't good enough. Now you seem to have taken care of that. That then allows me to fulfil my oath to Satipilli. Very neat!'

'I try to be.' Palaiyas beamed with pleasure that his plan had met with approval. 'There's one other item I want to mention before we turn in. Whatever happens, if we do end up in the water, make sure your sword is firmly attached to your waist. When we're on land again, that is the only item that will distinguish you from the local farmers and will show you are a Hittite soldier. I'm sure I don't need to tell you that safeguarding the royal seals is even more important. I'm pleased to notice they're in a pouch round your neck. Now enough of my advice, and I suggest we both turn in. Ah, one more thing before we do, I ought to mention it that we've only enough food for breakfast tomorrow, and then another meal after that; then we'll have to forage. Just thought I'd let you know.'

'I'm sure something will come up.' Mokhat climbed into his blanket thinking of Narmus, and then lay there gazing above him at a deep dark sky, dusted with myriads of twinkling stars.

\*   \*   \*

The next morning they cast off early, after eating breakfast, into a placid flowing river that hid its tempestuous nature with such an innocent countenance that Palaiyas spat into it for presenting such a deceitful image.

They had travelled maybe a league before the waters became choppy once more. The river had entered a narrow canyon and the raft was almost impossible to steer with any degree of control. It clipped along a rock wall and nearly swamped them in a swell, forcing them to hang on for dear life. They were drenched once again and lucky to be still afloat. The raft took a tremendous pounding against the sides of the chasm and Palaiyas feared that it would break apart at any moment. Mokhat was helping Palaiyas in trying to control the rudder, but all the while he kept his eyes on the inflated skins just in case the raft lost its battle with the granite gorge.

Palaiyas pointed ahead and Mokhat saw that he was pointing at what looked like the end of the gorge looming up ahead of them. Talking was impossible because of the noise and so Mokhat smiled at Palaiyas in response to his pointing, indicating he understood what he was referring to.

The raft lurched out of the canyon into an open landscape with low banks on either sides of the shore leaving the high walls behind them. The waters calmed after a short run and went back to being a deceitfully calm river once more.

They drifted downriver for what seemed quite a long time, according to Palaiyas' estimate, going some three leagues before they saw the rapids in front of them. First came the increasing number of boulders sticking out of the water with their accompanying eddies and micro eddies near the shore, and then the waves increased in size and became distinctly choppy. They went over a number of pourover drops with the water washing over the raft each time, drenching them and soaking what was left of their barley flour. Palaiyas left Mokhat at the rudder while he crawled forward to try and use his pole to push away from any boulders, if he could. At the speed they were going there wasn't much chance of avoiding the rocks sticking out of the water. Each time they hit one; the raft lurched and shuddered so that Palaiyas indicated with gestures that Mokhat should make sure he was holding the inflated water skins. Palaiyas was tied to his log with a rope.

When the final moments came they were both almost resigned to what would happen next. The raft smashed into a large rock and broke apart, hurling Palaiyas and his log into the middle of the river, while Mokhat grabbed his inflatable skins and gave way to the inevitable by leaning over backwards into the water. That way he had some control over where he went. He pushed the water skins under each of his arms and then tried swimming away from the spot where the raft had been. He tried crawling his way towards the closest shore. His overwhelming worry was that he had no idea where Palaiyas had disappeared to, and he hoped he was right about being a strong swimmer.

# Chapter Twenty Seven

**I**t was the controlled entry into the water that prevented Mokhat from falling into the fastest part of the flow and so allowed him to come up against the first boulder that he hit. His water skins kept his head up and they also cushioned his bounce off of that large boulder, to the extent that he even managed to push closer to shore. With a lot more crawling and an almighty effort, his feet hit the river bottom and he desperately scrambled ashore, tugging his inflatable skins with him as he left the water, dropping exhaustedly onto the shore. He only stayed like that for a short moment while he caught his breath. His mind was racing with the fear of loosing Palaiyas. He jumped up and immediately fell over his own sword, dangling from his belt. He began frantically searching the river for signs of him, but couldn't see over the surface because he was too low on the shoreline; so he climbed the bank until he was able to see the far side of the river.

He walked along the shoreline with the water skins over his shoulder, looking into the river for his companion until he finally found him in an eddy, clinging to the downriver side of a rock close to the far shore of the river, but without his log. Palaiyas was staring away from him, searching the shore closest to him, looking for a likely spot to head for and hadn't seen Mokhat watching him from the other bank. He seemed alright and that was a big relief for Mokhat, but he wasn't going to stop worrying until he'd seen Palaiyas standing safely on the other shore, on dry land.

Palaiyas pushed off from the rock and with powerful strokes, swam to the far shore after struggling with the fast current, finally walking out of the water as if he'd gone for a simple energetic swim. He turned and saw Mokhat standing, waving at him, and he waved back. He stuck his thumb up to indicate he was okay, and Mokhat returned the signal, saying he was also alright.

Palaiyas motioned to Mokhat that he should walk along the shore downriver, and he began to do the same. This was the middle of the afternoon and the sun was warming and drying them as they travelled on opposite sides of the river. They had noticed that the further they went downriver, the milder the weather became. Here, the grass was growing on the banks and the bushes had all their leaves on them. The closer they got to the sea the warmer the climate. And so for a league both of them walked down along the banks of the river that had sought to claim them for its own, until finally they came to a right bend in the river.

Mokhat saw it first; the little village round the corner of the bend and he frantically gestured that Palaiyas should take care approaching it. Palaiyas either didn't care or hadn't understood Mokhat's gestures, because he walked into the village, albeit hand on sword, but with his head held high. Mokhat could only stand on the other side of the river and watch at what would transpire. There were a number of boats heaved up onto the village shoreline, clearly indicating this was a fishing village.

First Palaiyas met an old man on the outskirts of the village; he talked to him and the old man led him into the village proper. The old man took him to the village headman and Palaiyas spent some time inside his mud hut, before eventually coming out with the headman and going down to the shore. The headman called to some of the villagers and they came running to help him launch one of the fishing boats.

The six boat paddlers had to go up the river against the current to land on the opposite bank. Mokhat was waiting for Palaiyas as the fishing boat beached on his side of the river. Mokhat came to Palaiyas as he stepped ashore and embraced him. 'I'm so glad you're alright. At first when I couldn't find you, I began thinking the worst had happened.'

'You can't get rid of me that easily,' Palaiyas joked returning the embrace. He then turned and introduced the village headman. 'This is Faleri, the man in charge of the fishing village. He's kindly offered to put us up in his hut for the night.'

Mokhat shook forearms with the small man in a formal manner as befits a first meeting. 'I'm grateful to you for coming to get me. You will be well rewarded for your kindness.'

'He knows that,' Palaiyas said in an aside to Mokhat. 'I've explained to him that we are soldiers on an errand for his majesty the king in Hattusas, and that if he provides all what we need, his majesty will give him whatever he desires. It seems he wants a large flock of sheep. They'll provide meat and wool for the whole village. I told him that this was not a problem. A flock of a hundred sheep is what sealed the bargain.'

The fishing boat took both of them back across river to the village and to the headman's hut. The headman's wife served them a fish stew and they mopped it up with unleavened bread. They all went outside and sat on benches in the warming sunshine in front of the headman's hut. The wife then brought them a much needed hot drink of chamomile tea.

'There's something else in this tea. What is it?' Mokhat asked the headman's wife, tasting something bitter.

She brushed her hair out of her eyes and said in a low voice, 'It's just a local herb, your excellency, which will pick you up. We use it when we need to go out on long trips. It won't do you any harm I promise you. I thought you could do with it after your experience in the water. I know I shouldn't of listened in on your conversation with my man, but I couldn't help it.'

'Hmm! Interesting,' Mokhat told her. 'Yes, I do feel a little more vigorous, now that you've explained why. What about you Palaiyas?'

'I'm always vigorous,' Palaiyas replied, smiling with excess energy. He caught the headman's attention and asked, 'Tell me, how far are we from the Ahhiyawan border?'

'It's just down there, your excellency. Just past that curve in the river. There's a small Ahhiyawan army outpost there with about fifty soldiers. They know us and don't bother us none. We supply them with fish from time to time. They supply us with metal for our fish knives in return,' replied the headman.

'And how far is Millawanda from here?' Palaiyas persisted.

'If you start from here in a boat in the morning, you'll reach Millawanda by evening. It's about five leagues downriver. You come out into a bay and then swing left and there's Millawanda on an outcrop above you on the other side of the bay.' The headman was looking puzzled at Palaiyas, at all these questions.

'Yes, we are, is the answer to your question, although you haven't asked it yet. We are going to Millawanda. It's on the king's errand, as I explained before. Now if you want to be paid, you'll have to send some of your lads to Ivalanda to collect the sheep. I'll give you a message for the military commander, who's a good friend of mine. He'll make sure you get your sheep. Be sure to send enough of your men to guard the flock or you'll loose them to hungry bandits. Better still, I'll ask the commander in Ivalanda to provide you with an escort to bring the flock safely back here. Bring me an animal hide and mix some soot into a bowl of water, not too thin mind.' Palaiyas turned to Mokhat and spoke quietly. 'I can't write your wedge shaped lettering so you're going to have to write the message to Tipali for me. I'll whittle a wedge maker for you from wood, and you can use the animal hide and the soot water to write the message. Just tell him we're alright and that he owes the bearer of this message one hundred sheep and no questions asked. He should provide an escort back to the bearer's village. You can add the mark of your royal seal to tell him it came from you and his majesty, so he won't think these fellows are trying it on. That should do it. Any comments?'

'No! You seem to have covered everything.'

'Hallo, what's this?' Palaiyas asked, as a large group of the villagers began to gather in a space before the headman's hut even though the light was beginning to fade.

The headman nodded and rose to his feet. 'I see news is travelling as fast as ever in our small community,' he said loudly to the gathering. 'Yes, it's true. These two soldiers are here to help us grow and prosper. They have promised to supply this village with a hundred head of sheep if we help them to get to Millawanda.' He looked at Palaiyas to confirm what he'd just said. Palaiyas nodded first to the headman, then to the crowd in general. 'They want us to supply them with one boat and enough food for two days. I know that since it's the winter season we're low on food, but the exchange is so generous that we must find a way to help them. In return, I promise you, every one of you will have a share in the benefits from the flock of sheep.'

A cheer arose from those gathered and they began to dance on the spot. One thing led to another, and before anyone could stop them, there was a blaze roaring in the village clearing and people were dancing to flute music and some fish were being roasted to celebrate the arrival of the new visitors. The women sang a number of folk songs in unison, followed by a couple of folk dances from the men. Palaiyas and Mokhat stayed for a short time but then made their excuses and turned in, being exhausted from their escapades in the river.

The headman then asked everyone to go to their homes and be less noisy so the visitors could get some rest.

* * *

The following morning saw the two companions wolfing down more fish stew with bread. Then Mokhat wrote the brief message to general Tipali in Ivalanda regarding the sheep. Palaiyas shook the headman's forearms, and both of them were taken down to the shore where the boat that had been allocated to them awaited them. It was a solid flat bottomed craft easily sufficient to carry the two of them to wherever they wanted to go down the river. Good sturdy oars and a rudder at the rear made manoeuvring less haphazard than it had been on their flimsy raft. There was a small sack of barley flour carefully wrapped inside a leather pouch, and the inflatable skins had returned to being used for their original purpose; to transport drinking water.

Mokhat sat at the back with the rudder and Palaiyas grabbed the oars, while many of the villagers shoved them off from the shore back into the river from whence they came. The whole village had turned out to shout their farewells, wishing them a safe journey.

The waters were placid and they soon came to the Ahhiyawan army encampment mentioned by the village headman. Palaiyas swung the boat towards them and rowed contentedly until he beached it by the waiting soldiers. 'Leave this to me,' he told Mokhat.

As Palaiyas stepped out of the boat, a young officious officer said in Hittite, 'And where do you think your going?'

To which Palaiyas replied in Ahhiyawan, 'And who do you think you're addressing young man. Stand to attention when you address a prince of Tiryns.' Palaiyas and

Mokhat were both in Hittite uniforms, which is why the officer was being so aggressive.

It stopped the arrogance in its tracks. The young captain was no longer certain who was in command. 'I'm sorry sir, but until I can be certain of who you are, then I'm afraid I will continue to do my duty and guard the border.'

'So let's start again. I am Prince Palaiyas on a secret errand for his late majesty, King Parmodius, sent to Hattusas to see the Hittite king; now returning to report to his new majesty, King Attarsiyas, on the outcome of that mission. Am I making myself clear so far, captain?'

'Yes sir.' The young captain listened to Palaiyas' Tirynian accent and was beginning to believe that a prince was indeed standing before him. 'I'm sorry your highness. It's that I wouldn't have expected to see you rowing yourself while he,' and the captain pointed at Mokhat, 'sat there doing nothing.'

'Young man, that is Prince Mokhat of the Kaska on an errand for the Hittite king escorting me back through Hittite country.'

Now the captain was really put out. Two highborn princes in a miserly fishing boat. How was he expected to behave in such circumstances?

'Yes sir, I mean, I see sir.' He was starting to get flustered.

Palaiyas pulled at a small chain round his neck concealed inside his tunic, and extracted a small ring, showing it to the captain. The captain's eyes shot wide open in astonishment and he sprang to attention. 'Sorry sir. I never doubted you, your highness. How can I assist you sir?'

Mokhat was observing all this and was curious as to what Palaiyas had shown the captain. He never mentioned it, but it must be some kind of royal seal that the old king had entrusted to him.

The four soldiers standing a couple of paces behind their captain looked on, ready to assist him in any rough stuff, but when they saw their captain jump to attention, they took their cue from him, and also sprang to attention.

'Relax lads,' Palaiyas said quietly to the captain and soldiers. 'Stand easy. Now we're all friends, maybe I could invite myself and my friend here, to have a little wine with you. Won't you lead on?'

The captain told one of the soldiers to stay with the boat and see it was secured. Then he about turned and marched back up the shoreline, followed by the rest of his men, until the little party reached the small encampment. It was a small fortification and had a wooden palisade round it with a gate. The captain called out to the sentry and the gate swung open. Two soldiers stood on either side of the gate as the little group marched through it. They all headed for a wooden hut where the captain had his normal HQ. He yelled for his orderly to bring the best wine and the bronze goblets were filled.

After a few sips, Palaiyas told the man, 'Look captain, we stopped here more out of politeness. If we'd simply sailed past, you would have had to come after us, especially not knowing who we were. However, now you know, and if we're to reach Millawanda by evening then we really must make a move.'

'As you wish your highness. I'm entirely at your disposal. Of course you can stay as long as you desire, but if you must go; so be it. I can let you have horses to continue to Millawanda, if you so wish?'

'Thank you for that kind thought, but frankly I like rowing, so we'll continues as we are. Goodbye!' This was said in Ahhiyawan and Mokhat hadn't understood a word. He would definitely have opted for the horses.

The captain was genuinely sorry to see his high profile guests depart so soon.

Back in the boat Palaiyas took the oars again, impelling the vessel down the river, making good headway towards their goal. He had insisted on rowing saying, 'All this time on land, I've missed this type of exercise. Back home I used to go swimming almost every day, and I did at least a league of rowing before the midday meal.'

'Well, I've offered to row,' Mokhat told him. 'But if you must, then you must. I'm glad the business at the border went so smoothly. For a moment I thought the captain was going to give us trouble, but you seem to know your own people. By the way, what was it you showed him that so impressed and convinced him to believe you? I have the two royal seals you know about; the Hittite and the Khemet one.'

'As you've rightly guessed, I have the royal signet ring of the old king. This was supposed to ease my passage through Ahhiyawan territory. I never needed to use it until now.' Palaiyas shrugged as if it were no matter of importance.

Switching to another subject, 'We have some unleavened bread in that leather pouch the old headman gave us. Do you want some?' Mokhat asked Palaiyas. 'It's about time we had a bit of food.' He found the pouch and rummaged inside, pulling out some bread and an onion.

Palaiyas laid down his oars and took the bread and onion, pealing it slowly with his dagger. They were running in deep water in the middle of the channel which had a zigzag run with big eddies. The river snaked around a bit down here and he kept a weary eye on where they were being taken. It had become a little rougher but there was no sign of any rapids. The eddies meant there were underwater boulders below them, which is why Palaiyas had contrived to ease the boat further into the middle of the channel, into the deep water.

Mokhat munched on his bread in a contemplative mood now that they were in a proper boat. The raft had made him nervous, but in this boat he managed to relax, pealing his onion calmly. 'I'm fond of onions,' he confided to Palaiyas. 'I could eat them all day, boiled, fried in fat, or raw as now.' He munched away contentedly.

It was early afternoon and the sun became quite hot. The sky was clear and the day felt almost like early spring.

Mokhat sighed and said, 'Remember the cold weather we had earlier. The icy conditions in that gorge where we lost the horse with all those provisions. It hardly seems ten days have past yet the weather suggests another time altogether. Then there was that snowstorm when Napat released the Gimirri captives. I can't believe we're in the same country.'

'We're not!' Palaiyas declared, still chewing on a piece of bread. 'We're in Ahhiyawa, and the climate has always been nicer here. Our gods are kinder to us than the Hittite ones.' He smiled when he said this to indicate he was teasing Mokhat. With Mokhat's recent aversion to religion, Palaiyas thought he should tread gently when mentioning the gods.

Mokhat laughed out loud, 'Why of course, your right. We crossed the border back there and so we are in a different country. Let's hope your Ahhiyawan climate continues to stay as favourable as this. So now, how are we going to go about finding out what happened to Satipilli when we get to Millawanda?'

They came to a fork in the river and Palaiyas asked Mokhat to guide the rudder so that the boat took the left branch, which Mokhat did. The water was flowing fast and steady at this time and Palaiyas decided to switch seats with Mokhat, taking charge of the rudder.

'First things first. Most pressing thing I need to do when we get to Millawanda is to report in to the new king,' Palaiyas informed him. 'From there we should get accommodation from friends of mine, assuming they are still alive. Remember it's been more than a year since I was last there. What I want to do more than anything is have a hot Mycenaean bath and get clean again. Then we can go about the business of Satipilli. I suspect we need to find the whereabouts of this Sflokos. I'll ask around, discreetly of course, see if my friends know where we can find him.'

The boat was making good speed and the river was beginning to widen, suggesting that they could be reaching the delta area. By late afternoon they came out into the delta of the river itself, and the open sea lay not too far ahead them.

# Chapter Twenty Eight

'**F**inally,' exclaimed Palaiyas. '*Look! Over there!* I think I can see a dolphin…there! There's another one.' He pointed eagerly to the right, into the distance. As they got closer they could see a small school of dolphins cavorting about just off shore. Jumping out of the water, and splashing back in again. 'Mokhat, I've just realised something. I'm homesick. I'd like to greet my father once more before he passes away. He's getting old you know.'

Mokhat watched his friend, and saw he was happy and sad at the same time. 'Maybe you could find the time to go across to your city. Let's see how our business goes here. If we could find the answers to who killed Satipilli, and why, we could then tie this up and you could catch a ship.' Mokhat wasn't sure this line of thinking was all that helpful to him. The way this conversation was developing, he would end up having to say goodbye to his friend.

They were now well out into the bay fed by the Meandros River and Palaiyas urged the boat to the left with his right oar. Mokhat was back at the rudder and because they were now in the bay, Palaiyas had gone back to rowing. Before them in the far distance, both he and Mokhat could see the large peninsula jutting out into the sea, and high on a promontory they could just make out the outlines of the imposing city itself. They still had a long way to go to get to Millawanda, but they now had it in their sights.

Palaiyas kept up a punishing pace on the oars and they travelled a couple of leagues in no time. They soon passed the offshore island situated off the cliffs to the north east of Millawanda. As the light was beginning to dwindle, they rounded the headland and made for the Lion Harbour. The sun was disappearing beyond the western horizon just as they entered the harbour mouth. This was all down to Palaiyas' local knowledge of the place. He was still insisting on doing all the rowing and almost regally, he rowed them past the harbour guard towers, who didn't bother challenging such a small vessel, and it was too dark to make out the Hittite uniforms. Palaiyas rowed all the way to the starboard dockside and landed the boat at a quayside.

'You down there, what's your business here, and why are you coming in so late? Lucky for you we hadn't put the chain across the harbour just yet.' Another officer stood above them on the dock with officious questions for them.

Only Palaiyas understood what he was saying. For Mokhat this was a strange language and he kept quiet, letting Palaiyas deal with the shouting from above.

'Give me a chance to catch my breath,' answered Palaiyas. 'Hang on, we're coming up and I'll explain everything.' To Mokhat he said, 'Just let me deal with this fellow and then I'll take you up to the palace—get you some proper food after all that peripatetic travelling. I'm teasing you again.' He stood in the boat and climbed up a wooden ladder leading to the top of the dock, followed by Mokhat.

'What kind of uniform are you wearing?' The officer was screwing up his nose at the garb. 'Is that Hittite stuff your wearing?'

'Just calm down will you,' Palaiyas raised his voice. 'Yes its Hittite. Now get that man behind you with the light to bring it over here. You'll want to see this.' Palaiyas pulled on the chain round his neck and extracted the signet ring.

The officer called the soldier bearing the torch to shine it on what Palaiyas was holding, and then raised his face in astonishment. 'I don't understand. Where did you get that?'

'Captain, are you all there between the ears? Do you know what this is, or are you just acting dumb? This is the royal signet ring and the bearer is to be treated with respect, do you understand me?' Palaiyas was angry at the delay caused by this thick officer.

The officer was beginning to understand that this matter was beyond him, and probably above him as well. 'Sorry sir, it was just that I wasn't expecting this,' he indicated the ring. 'So, how can I help you?'

'I'm leaving this boat in your charge.' Palaiyas was being facetious but the officer hadn't caught on yet. 'My friend and I are going up to the palace and I want that fellow with the torch to accompany us. I don't want to take *you* away from your duties on the dockside. Do you think you could get this fellow to come with us?'

'Yes sir.' He motioned with a nod of his head, for the soldier with the torch next to him, to escort Palaiyas and his friend.

They went across the harbour agora, led by the torch bearer, up the winding path leading to the city on top; through the lion gate in the city walls, alongside the Northern agora and down the Sacred Way. The palace was situated next to the south agora and Palaiyas sauntered through the palace gate as if he owned the place, leaving his torch bearer behind, standing with the sentry at the gate. He wasn't challenged until he went into the palace entrance, and even then, he seemed to be affronted that someone should have the temerity to question the nature of his business.

'Would you be so kind as to tell his majesty that Prince Palaiyas of Tiryns has returned from Hattusas and would like an audience with him at his earliest convenience,' he told the officer who'd stopped this wandering Hittite officer.

The officer looked closely at this prince of Tiryns and his companion, and marched smartly away to inform his majesty of the request.

The same officer returned a while later, smiling apologetically, 'His majesty is eating with some of his courtiers and wonders if you would like to join him.'

'We'd love to, wouldn't we *Prince* Mokhat?' answered Palaiyas, making sure the officer caught the title. 'Lead on.'

The officer led them through the palace, into a large room on the ground floor, filled with people on couches, eating and listening to a trio of lyres playing some largo music. At the far end of the room reclined King Attarsiyas, munching on something that may once have been a bird. The officer led them to the king's couch and backed away.

The king motioned Palaiyas to sit next to him and Mokhat sat next to Palaiyas, on the far side from the king. 'Well Prince Palaiyas, it's about time you showed up. We've been looking all over for you.' He was staring disapprovingly at the Hittite uniforms they both wore.

Palaiyas was startled at this news. He was expecting to have to go into a full explanation of his trip and why it took so long, and all that, but here they were, actually looking for him. Why on earth would they be looking for him? He raised his eyebrows to query the situation, 'Why, may I ask, with respect, would you be looking for me?'

'There isn't a ship that comes in from Tiryns that doesn't have a message from your father asking for your whereabouts. For a year now he has deluged our envoys with questions as to your situation and your location, and unfortunately we were unable to give him a satisfactory answer—until now, of course. Where ever have you been?' The king smiled benignly to show it was a polite enquiry. 'Please help yourself to the food, while you tell us.'

Palaiyas did as he was bidden. He ate and explained where he'd been and why. The fact that the old king had sent him to Hattusas had been forgotten, what with the regime change, and his appearance right now was a surprise to the new king. Time had made the reason for his errand irrelevant. Palaiyas removed the royal signet ring from the chain around his neck and handed it to the king, who looked at it with fondness.

'You know, when they were cremating my father, I wondered what had happened to this ring. I thought my brother had appropriated it, but when he was killed and I still couldn't find it, I assumed I would never see it again. I'm grateful you've returned it. I have fond memories of this ring on my father. So now, who is your companion?'

Palaiyas turned to Mokhat and introduced him to the king. 'This is Prince Mokhat of the Kaska. A good friend and a steadfast companion. He's saved my life on at least one occasion.'

All this was being conducted in Mycenaean and Mokhat couldn't understand a word of it. He was hungry and busied himself on chomping away on some roast chicken. He understood that he was being introduced to the king by the body language, so he swallowed and said in Hittite, 'I am honoured to be here and thank you for the food.'

Attarsiyas responded in Hittite, 'Your welcome, your highness. You're a Kaska I'm told? I've heard quite a bit about your people. They seem to have been a thorn in the side of the Hittites for a long time. You must tell me, after you've eaten of course, how it is that you came to befriend our prince from Tiryns. You must admit it is a bit strange.'

Mokhat was stunned that the king had responded to him in Hittite. 'I'd be most pleased to tell you the story, your majesty.'

Over a lengthy meal Mokhat told the king how he'd prevented a backstabber putting a knife into Palaiyas in a bar brawl in Hattusas three years ago. How they'd become firm friends as a result of that event, even to the point of going into battle together in the Hittite civil war. How he now accompanied Palaiyas, as a companion, to conclude Palaiyas' obligation to the former king and return his ring.

At the mention of the ring, Attarsiyas looked at it in wonder that he'd actually got it back.

'Well, I must say, that is a fine story you've just narrated.' Attarsiyas was impressed at this Kaskan Prince having saved a Mycenaean's life. 'Should you need anything that is within my powers to grant, then you have only to ask. Will you be accompanying Prince Palaiyas back home to see his father?'

Mokhat was startled at the question. 'If he wants me to, I will, but I don't think he's made a firm decision in that direction.'

The lengthy meal came to a close and Palaiyas assured the king he would visit him in the morning. They took their leave and went in search of a bed for the night with those friends Palaiyas had mentioned. From them he discovered that Sflokos was known to the top echelon of the city and had a nasty reputation. Someone not to be trifled with. He was also known to frequent the docks in search of information coming in on the ships. In the morning, they should try the market place first, and then the three docks that fed the city.

In the morning they dressed in civilian clothes and took a stroll through the city, ostensibly to do a bit of sightseeing, but in fact they were searching for the Ahhiyawan spymaster. Palaiyas had a description of Sflokos from captain Onasiyas but matching the description to a face was not as easy as it may have seemed. Then there was the description of Sflokos from Palaiyas' friends. Medium height, thin in build and thin on top. Palaiyas' friends laughed and said that if they saw a snake on two legs, then they'd found their quarry.

They tried the Temple Harbour first as it was the largest of the three ports. It was utterly unprotected, open to the sea, and entirely lacked the presence of Sflokos. It was unwise and therefore impossible to ask if anyone had seen him. Then there was the Theatre Harbour, more secluded but still without proper defences on the shoreline, but at its back the massive fortifications were there up on the hill. Again no Sflokos! However, Palaiyas found a couple of skippers to talk to, although Mokhat couldn't understand a word of what was being said.

They had to go up from the Temple Harbour, through the south agora, and as they crossed that square, they became aware of men following them. Palaiyas spotted them as they went through the Lion Gate down to the Lion Harbour, the harbour they'd landed at the previous night. It had towers on either side half way down the harbour entrance and a heavy chain across between the towers barring entry to any wishing to attack Millawanda.

As they reached the docks Palaiyas pointed and said, 'Look, there's that officious captain from last night. I'd like to avoid him if at all possible. Let's hide behind this wool bale over here. Hopefully that will get rid of our followers and this nosy captain.'

Mokhat followed him behind the stack of bales and they crouched there till the captain had gone.

'Hmm! What are you two doing?' said a gruff voice. 'Clearly up to no good, I would say.'

They turned and saw they were being observed by an elderly gent of medium height, thin in build and a balding head. Palaiyas shook his head in disbelief. Captain Onasiyas' description fitted the appearance of this fellow.

'Are you by any chance Sflokos?' Palaiyas asked.

The elderly gent raised his eyebrows, 'Who wants to know?'

'Well I do. I've been looking for you.'

'Let me see. Now you seem familiar. Oh yes, I remember you. You were sent by our late king to Hattusas with a message. Pal...Palaiyas isn't it? So, what can I do for you?'

'I was wondering if you know what happened to a certain fellow by the name of Satipilli.'

'Why are you interested in him?'

'A friend of a friend asked me to look him up when I got back to Millawanda.'

Sflokos looked cagily around him and motioned for them to come further behind the stack of wool bales out of prying eyes. 'You know he was a Hittite spy, do you?'

'Are you sure? By the way—what do you mean by "was"?'

'Is, then. Yes, I'm sure. He was indicated to me by the governor about a year ago when I was with a trade delegation visiting Ivalanda. I thought it strange the governor exposed him like that, but hey, I take what comes. He seemed to vanish as soon as I took an interest in him.'

'Know where he went?'

The thin shoulders shrugged and his demeanour slipped into outright hostility. 'Your better off leaving that alone. It's not at all healthy to ask these types of questions.'

Palaiyas withdrew the Mycenaean dagger from his belt pouch and showed it to the spymaster. 'Ever seen this before?'

Mokhat was surprised to see *that* dagger, but kept silent mainly because he couldn't understand what was being said.

'Where did you get it? Yes I've seen it—it belongs to me. Where did you find it?'

'It was found sticking out of Satipilli's chest outside of Ivalanda.'

'Really? So? Are you accusing me of killing him?'

'If the shoe fits, wear it.' Palaiyas had ceased being polite and was now just as hostile as Sflokos.

'That Satipilli had no idea what he was up against. He thought it was us who were stirring up the trouble between Arzawa and Hatti, but he should have looked closer to home.' Sflokos almost spat out the statement in contempt.

'What do you mean?' Palaiyas asked quietly but with an unmistakable sinister undertone.

'When we recently had our unfortunate civil war, we were offered the services of the Governor of Lukka, if we would in turn help him deal with Arzawa. The greedy blighter wants to be king of Arzawa. Being Governor of Lukka isn't enough for him. You want to know what happened to Satipilli, go to Ura. The answer lies there. Ask Daubum if you want these answers; do yourself a favour, don't bother me anymore.' Sflokos said this with derision, and then turned his back on Palaiyas.

Palaiyas in an impulsive gesture pulled Sflokos' right shoulder with his left hand, spinning the elderly Ahhiyawan spymaster around and then returned Sflokos' dagger to him by sticking it into *his* chest with his right hand. 'That's for Kishnapili,' he spat out in anger. The dagger went into the place where his heart should have been. Palaiyas shook his head, watching Sflokos buckle at the knees and crash to the ground with shock on his face. 'Maybe I shouldn't have done that, but I did that on the spur of the moment. I liked Kishnapili—and I didn't like this one.'

'We'd better hide him, *quick*.' Mokhat advised. 'Stick him further in, behind this bale, there, in between those two.' They pummelled the body until it almost disappeared in the crack between the two wool bales. 'Now let's get away from here. They'll be looking for whoever killed this scum,' Mokhat told his friend.

'Yes, you're right! That, I can tell you, was the first spur of the moment decision, and now I've just made a second spur of the moment decision. I want to go home to Tiryns. I was wondering if you would like to come with me. We started this together, and I feel we should finish this together. We'll only stay there a week and then come back in this direction. What do you say?' Palaiyas looked determined to carry out his intention of going home.

Mokhat stroked his beard and finally said, 'Fine, I don't think we can ever come back here again. So we'll go to Tiryns. Then it's straight back to Lukka. Remember this

Sflokos fellow,' he flicked his wrist at Sflokos, lying there hidden in the bales of wool, 'mentioned Ura and this other fellow called Daubum. It looks like we might have to go to Ura if we want to resolve Satipilli's murder,' Mokhat commented.

'It's noon now. We'll separate here.' Palaiyas was now animated. 'I want you to go up to the city and then down to the Theatre Harbour. There's a ship with an eye painted on its prow. Wait for me by that ship, and try to keep out of sight. I'm off to see my friends. We need some money to buy passages on the ship. I was talking to the skipper of that boat earlier. He's out of Ugarit bound for Tiryns.' And with that, he was gone.

Mokhat made his way up to the city and on down to the Theatre Harbour to find the ship with the painted eye on the bow. More bales of wool stood on the dockside which he used to hide behind. He didn't have to wait too long before Palaiyas showed up.

'Psst! Let's go!' Palaiyas motioned to Mokhat. He led the way onto the ship and made his way forward to where a dark red haired man sat munching on some dates.

'Hallo skipper! Remember me? I said I might be back.' Palaiyas was as friendly as he could be.

'Hi, yes I remember you. You wanted to know how long it would take to get to Tiryns. It's still the same. I told you before. Three to four days.' The captain waited, knowing what was coming next.

'Well, I and my friend here would like to purchase passages on your beautiful tub, back to my home town.' Palaiyas smiled and jingled a bag of coins to let the captain know he had money.

'You're *from* Tiryns then?' said the tall red haired captain eyeing the bag of coins.

'I have ten talents of silver here, more than twice the price of a passage for two. Interested?' Palaiyas was taking a chance offering him more than the normal fare, but he knew those from Ugarit were always amenable to being bought.

This captain laughed out loud. 'We sail on the high tide, which is mid afternoon, today; after we propitiate and make the usual offerings and prayers to Baal Zaphon in expectation of a safe and profitable journey. In other words that means shortly. Are you on or not?'

Palaiyas tossed the bag with the coins to the muscular captain, who caught it deftly; then he went back to picking at his dates, motioning for the two of them to join him. Mokhat sat and selected a few choice ripe dates, popping them in his mouth with loving care. He'd heard more unintelligible speech in the last two days than he had in his whole lifetime. Palaiyas watched him munching contentedly, and then turned his attention onto the sea and the forthcoming journey.

# Chapter Twenty Nine

They had been out at sea for some time and Mokhat had still not found his sea legs. He was leaning over the side, retching; less now than before, but that was because his stomach was entirely empty. Palaiyas was lolling about in the middle of the ship resting on some canvas on the cargo hatch cover, seemingly asleep.

Mokhat lifted his head and breathed in deeply. He pulled back his shoulders and tried to regain some semblance of dignity. More deep breathing followed. This made him a bit dizzy so he zigzagged over to Palaiyas and sat down, head between his legs.

'Still feeling groggy, eh?' Palaiyas was watching him sympathetically propped up on his elbow.

'We might not be on this boat if you hadn't stuck that knife into that snake.' Mokhat was grumpy and uncomfortable, so he was being unpleasant to the cause of his misery, as he saw it.

'Are you trying to tell me that I shouldn't have avenged Kishnapili? I know it was impulsive of me, but did he or didn't he deserve his fate?' Palaiyas sounded affronted at the implied criticism.

'No, it's not that. Oh, I don't know. I've been miserable since we set sail. I suppose I'm just taking it out on you. I suppose that cur did deserve what you served out; but why must this boat keep moving the way it does? I'm sorry; I'm not making any sense, am I?' Mokhat lifted his head and his face was white as a sheet.

'You do look terrible. The bad news is, there's nothing much that can be done. Wait…! I've just remembered something. Stay here and I'll be back soon.'

Palaiyas jumped up and ran to the stern of the boat to the skipper, who was talking to the two men holding the tiller. An animated conversation took place between the two of them, which culminated in the captain going to the bow where the cook was preparing some food. Palaiyas rejoined Mokhat, followed closely by the captain. The captain had in his hands a small beige coloured root, a piece of bread, and a goblet of wine.

'We call this root *ziggiberis,*' Palaiyas told him, taking it from the captain. 'I want you to take a bite of it, chew it and swallow it. It tastes somewhat strong, but this will cure your stomach for certain. Trust me! Take it with a small piece of bread and then have a drink of wine to clear the taste. You'll feel better in a little while.'

Mokhat looked suspiciously at the offering, but feeling the way he did, he'd take anything if it could ease his suffering. He broke off a piece of the Y shaped root and saw a stringy yellow core. Taking the bread the captain offered, he broke a small piece off and put it in his mouth unconvincingly, then put the root in on top of it, chewing it well. It had a strong sharp taste, half spicy and peppery, half lemony, slightly sweet, and as for texture, it was so fibrous it seemed he was eating fine string. Palaiyas then produced a bronze goblet of wine and Mokhat quickly poured the wine over the whole, swallowing as he went. He was just about to retch up, but then stopped himself. He sat down on the canvas that was draped over the cargo hatch, looking worse than ever.

'I'll just rest here for the moment.' He spoke as if he were in a trance. He lay his head down and shortly he was snoring.

'Well, I never! This stuff hits people in different ways,' the skipper noted. 'First time I've seen it knock someone out.'

'He was exhausted,' Palaiyas excused his friend. 'What with all that heaving over the side, it must have taken more out of him than just the contents of his stomach.'

Sometime late in the afternoon, Mokhat awoke, stretched himself leisurely and sat up. Palaiyas had thrown a blanket over him; he folded it, and used it now to cushion his seat.

'Well my fine friend, how are you feeling?' Palaiyas was sitting on the other side of the cargo hatch observing Mokhat. He'd been concerned that the root had such an unusual effect on his companion that he'd stayed and watched over him as he slept.

Mokhat stood, looked around, 'Strange, but I feel much better.' He breathed in deeply. 'Yes, much better. Whatever that stuff was, it seems to have worked.'

'I came across it when I was in Keftiu. Seems to come from somewhere in the east.' Palaiyas joined Mokhat and they both went and leaned over the side of the ship.

The weather was calm and held a slight breeze, enough to keep the sails full of wind, so the ship was making good progress towards the west. There were some fifteen crew on the ship which was roughly thirty five cubits in length. It had both a rounded bow and stern with a single mast and a large square sail on that mast. A typical medium sized cargo vessel out of Ugarit marked with the all seeing eye of El painted on the bow, and just now the crew were all busy at various tasks.

'You know, this is the first time since I stepped on this boat that I've felt calm and in control of my body.' Mokhat had regained enough of his composure to begin to think this might not be such a bad trip after all.

'I'm sorry I put you into this situation. If I'd controlled my impulse with Sflokos, we could have made this trip at leisure. As it is, we're fleeing for killing some vermin.' Palaiyas was trying to apologise, but didn't know exactly for what.

'I was also fond of Kishnapili, but I might have waited a little longer to exact my vengeance for his death.' Mokhat knew the awkwardness that Palaiyas felt. 'When did you decide to go back home?'

'It hit me when we came out of the Meandros River in our little boat. You know, when we saw the open sea in the bay before we reached Millawanda. I suddenly felt homesick. That, and knowing that my father was getting older by the day. I wanted to see him before he passed on; just to thank him for all his hard work with me.' Palaiyas was getting a bit gloomy and had a faraway look on his face.

'Who's this Daubum Sflokos mentioned before he died?' Mokhat decided to change the subject.

'Daubum? Oh, yes, he did mention him didn't he?' Palaiyas returned from his daydream and grinned apologetically. 'Whoever he is, we'll find him in Ura; that's if we are to believe a dying spymaster.'

'Sflokos knew Satipilli, and presumably Satipilli knew who Sflokos was.' Mokhat was stroking his beard in thought. 'It would seem logical then to assume that Daubum must be someone in their line of business, and if he's located in Ura, then he might be a Lukkan spy. If I remember his exact words, he said, "Ask Daubum if you want these answers." I'd even go so far as to speculate that this Daubum might be Madduwatta's chief spy. What do you think of that?'

The wind had picked up somewhat and the ship began to lurch a little more, but neither Palaiyas nor Mokhat noticed, so engrossed were they in their examination.

'Makes sense!' Palaiyas was beginning to get into the spirit of their analysis. 'If Madduwatta has been stirring up trouble, then he might use his chief spy as his main tool. Could it be possible that this Daubum was responsible for Satipilli's death? But if so, to what purpose? What did Satipilli find out that would sign his own death warrant? We're supposed to find out the "who" and the "why" of his death. At the moment we *might* have the "who," but the "why" escapes me entirely.'

'Me too! What if this Napat works for this Daubum? That would explain his following us and wanting us dead. How did they know we were sent to look for Satipilli?' Mokhat was feeling angry. 'There's a leak in Hattusas; there must be. Right from the moment we left the capital, this Napat has been on our tail. We first saw him on the Marassantiya River, remember? We've only shaken him since that fight in the night after we left Ivalanda, when I nearly killed him. But what has Arzawa and Madduwatta's desire to become its king, got to do with Satipilli's murder? There's a missing part to this puzzle which we have yet to find.'

Just then the captain came over to them and told them, 'You'd better find some shelter. From what I can see, we're in for some rough weather over the coming night. You might want to strap yourselves in. The light's almost gone and the wind is continuing to pick up. I fear there's a storm brewing.'

At that information Mokhat lost all his previous calm and looked at the sea in trepidation.

'It's all right,' Palaiyas reassured him. 'I've been in rougher weather than this. Just do as I do and all will be fine. Best bet is to head for the back of the boat, but stay with me.'

Mokhat followed Palaiyas to the stern of the boat and they stationed themselves mid-deck in the rear part of the vessel where Palaiyas made sure Mokhat was tied to a ships support just in case the waves began to swamp them. The thunderstorm picked up but never really showed its full power. The wind was from the south so they ran before it with their sails down; otherwise the force of the souther would have demolished the mast. They could see bolts of lighting striking the sea but none came down near their vessel.

That night was the roughest Mokhat had ever experienced on land or sea, but thanks to the root he'd had earlier, he didn't feel sick at all. The night seemed to last an eternity and the dawn saw the vessel still in one piece, with very little damage. The vessel had been pushed northwards by the storm and now the skipper corrected the course taking her back in the direction they were supposed to be on. The captain reassuringly told them it was only a little storm, more of a squall than a real storm, but Mokhat didn't want to experience anything stronger.

The following day was calm with only a slight breeze, and the two friends spent their time lolling around on the canvas covering the cargo hold. They hadn't slept at all during the night of the storm, so they made up for it during the day. They awoke around mid afternoon and were invited by the captain to join him for a meal.

'Paying those extra talents gave us a nice compliant skipper,' Palaiyas joked, 'one who's eager to please. He's been very good to us, so far.'

Mokhat listened to his banter as they made their way to where the red haired captain waited, and where the cook had laid out an Ugaritic feast; olives, figs, dates, pine nuts, almonds, bread, biscuits, cheese, grapes and other various fruits. There were even freshly baked fish wafting towards them. There was a large flagon of wine for them to wash the lot down.

All three of them sat cross-legged on the deck with a low table between them. 'Please, don't stand on ceremony, help yourselves.' The captain crammed some fish into his mouth and heaped bread on top. He held out his goblet and the cook, come servant, filled it. Then the cook filled the other two goblets for the guests. They ate and drank, and chatted about Ugarit, the vessel's home port; and where his travels had taken the captain. In turn Mokhat told him about the Kaska, and Palaiyas in his turn accounted for his trip to Hattusas, but neither gave any hint at their station in life or the real purpose of their journey. Each participant in the conversation circumnavigated candour to suite their own intention.

The routine on the vessel continued in this vain for another two days; eating, sleeping, chatting, and breathing in lots of fresh sea air. Throughout the rest of journey westward, bearing in mind this was the winter season, the weather stayed calm, if somewhat breezy. Yet the temperatures in Millawanda and on the sea had been mild, almost spring like, much more to the liking of Mokhat. Even Palaiyas seemed to unwind in the more clement ambience they were bathed in.

On the morning of the fourth day everybody on board was swept with an anticipation; the expectation of arrival at their destination. The relaxed mood had ebbed with the morning tide. The crew were busy mending sail, scrubbing the deck, making the vessel shipshape.

The two passengers stationed themselves at the bow of the boat looking for signs of land. They'd passed many an island in the preceding four days but these were always in the far distance, not really anything that concerned them. This was entirely different; for Palaiyas it was a homecoming, and for Mokhat, the sight of a land he'd heard much about from his friend.

As they rounded the island of Spetsos into the Gulf of Argolikos, Palaiyas gave Mokhat a detailed description of what he was looking at. Where the best olive orchards were to be found; who grew the finest grapes. The further they went up the gulf, the more enthusiastic Palaiyas became in his excitement. He even went to the captain to congratulate him on his navigational accuracy, to which the skipper of the boat replied that he'd done it many times, and this was no big deal.

By late afternoon they sighted Tiryns and Palaiyas suddenly became thoughtful and quiet. So much so, that

Mokhat became worried that something awful awaited them; some trouble of which Palaiyas hadn't told him.

'Why so glum? You're almost home. You should be overjoyed.' Mokhat was trying to ease information out of his friend.

'I was just reminiscing of the time I left this port. The high hopes I had of success; of coming back as a general or something. Instead, here I am, returning with my tail between my legs, in all likelihood fleeing from a city with a price on my head. It's not how I'd hoped things would turn out. What kind of welcome should I expect?' Palaiyas sat with his head in his hands, looking very morose.

'The welcome of a son returning to see his father, *and* his family.' Palaiyas' mood had swung from euphoria to misery in a short a time. Mokhat stood there thinking, helpless, watching his friend scrape the bottom. 'Are we not on an errand of vital importance? You are a friend of the King of the Hittites. If you wanted to be a Hittite general, I'm sure Tudhaliyas would arrange it; if you want, I'll ask him for you. I can even make you a Kaska General right now. I have the power you know?'

That brought a smile to Palaiyas' face. He stood up, shook off his melancholia and clasped Mokhat by the shoulders. 'You're a good friend to me, *Prince* Mokhat.'

'I try to be *Prince* Palaiyas.' He returned the shoulder clasp and they watched the port getting nearer.

'What's all this "prince" business?' asked a familiar voice from behind them.

They turned to see the skipper of the boat watching them with a wry look on his features.

'We were talking in Hittite; how is it you understood what we said?' Palaiyas asked the captain.

'I speak Hittite, Mykenian, Keftiu, and Khemetian,' replied the captain with a shrug. 'I've travelled a lot, and I have to do business with all sorts. I have about ten languages I'm fluent in; and I can swear in twenty more.' He smiled disarmingly.

Since we're almost there, you might as well be introduced,' said Mokhat. 'You have been privileged to have Prince Palaiyas of Tiryns on your vessel. The son of the king of this land you are about to dock your vessel in.'

That raised the captain's eyebrows. 'I've met your brother...., and now that you've mentioned it, there *is* a family resemblance. Your highness, I hope you've taken no offence to anything that's occurred whilst you've been aboard my ship.'

Palaiyas waved his hand in dismissal. 'I've had a most pleasant voyage, thank you captain. Have no fear; I shall recommend you to my father as someone to do business with.'

As they approached the docking berth, Palaiyas noted another officer waiting on the dockside to ask them their business on these shores. He had an escort with him of twenty men to enforce his authority. Then as suddenly, his face relaxed as he recognised who the young colonel was.

The plank was lowered and Palaiyas led his companion ashore, to be confronted by the officer—who stared at him, as if he wasn't sure of what he was seeing.

'Have I changed so much, my brother?' Palaiyas asked the officer.

'Is it really *you*, Palaiyas?' The officer's jaw had dropped and he didn't move.

'Come now, Amphitryon, give your older brother a hug.' Palaiyas grabbed the gaping officer in his arms and squeezed.

The officer recovered and hugged him back. 'Father's been looking all over for you.' He babbled. 'Mother's worried sick, wondering if your still alive. But by all the gods, it's good to have you home again.' Small tears began to run down Amphitryon's face.

The twenty soldiers he had behind him, dropped onto their knees in acknowledgment of the return of their crown prince.

'Come; let me introduce you to a friend of mine.' Palaiyas turned to Mokhat and said in Hittite, 'This is my brother Amphitryon, of whom I've mentioned.' To Amphitryon he said in Mycenaean, 'This is Prince Mokhat of the Kaska; a sound and loyal friend who saved my life. As a great favour; treat him as you would treat me.'

Amphitryon took Mokhat's forearms and bade him welcome in Mycenaean, to which Mokhat responded with a broad Kaska smile.

# Chapter Thirty

They left the port and in the fading light began the short walk uphill to the citadel while Palaiyas told Mokhat to expect a warm welcome in Tiryns. Amphitryon's twenty soldier escort trundled behind, throwing up a small cloud of dust. The moon was out enabling them to see the glittering waters of the gulf behind them as they trudged uphill, and a little further on at a Y shaped crossing, Palaiyas explained that the left fork would have taken them to Mycenae, which was three leagues further north inland, sitting across the route from the Plain of Argos to the Gulf of Korakou. Palaiyas went on to elucidate that at the outset, this was Mycenae's wealth, exacting a toll from travellers who wanted to travel from Argos to the north. From there, Mycenae perched on its mountain citadel went on to dominate the whole peninsula with its wealth, and even further, so that now all the city states gave their fealty to Mycenae.

It wasn't long before they saw equidistantly spaced lights atop of massive walls in front of them. The walls extended to the entire area of the top of the hill they were approaching. The path led them round the southern end of the city and then northward till they came to a short path branching to their left, leading up a steep ramp to the main entrance gate to the palace. Mokhat noted that the overhead key stone of the gate was in the form of two lions supporting a pillar.

'Reminds me a little of the lion gate to Hattusas,' Mokhat commented to Palaiyas.

Palaiyas was preoccupied with his homecoming and merely shrugged at this suggested similarity. 'There's another bigger gate further on up the road that leads to the lower city for the ordinary people,' he told Mokhat distractedly.

On the left of the gate there was a thick tower, and to the right was an arm of the wall, with a tower at its end, so the outer gate seemed to be well set back between them and protected, since any attackers would be forced to cross that narrow corridor, while the defenders could hit them from above and from both sides. Mokhat's military upbringing took note of all the salient defensive points as they approached the gate.

A sentry atop the wall shouted down, 'Who goes there at this time of night?'

To which Amphitryon responded with the night's password. The sentry recognised the prince's voice and ordered the gate opened. Inside the party turned left up an alley flanked by a tall containment wall to their left and high buildings to their right, leading towards the palace gate proper. Sentries were being alerted that the prince's party was returning and a sudden flurry of activity showed them standing to attention as the party went by. Through the gate and then into the outside courtyard which held stables to their left and storage rooms at the far end. To Mokhat the massive scale of the buildings was reminiscent of Hattusas.

Swinging right they went through three porticos containing two roofed reception rooms with various dolphin frescos, then into the main courtyard where at the far end, they left their escort which dispersed to their quarters, then through another room fronting the forecourt leading to the *megaron*. This forecourt had a vast beautifully tiled floor with a variety of geometric designs, and to the right in this forecourt, there was an altar with a sacrificial pit in it. The tiling impressed Mokhat with the sheer luxury of it. They went through two more porticos into reception rooms with more frescos and then into the heart of the palace, the *megaron* itself. This was the throne room, with the throne on the right-hand side on entering, with a circular hearth surrounded by four painted columns in the middle and a covered hole in the roof above the hearth.

'Wait here,' Amphitryon indicated. 'Warm yourselves by the hearth and I'll get father. He'll want to greet you himself no matter the hour. I'll order some refreshment as well.' He rushed off towards the exit near the throne, leaving them to wander over to the hearth where the embers were still glowing even this late at night.

'Well, what's your impression so far?' Palaiyas asked Mokhat, reaching out his hands to the warmth of the embers.

'My biggest problem is the language barrier,' Mokhat complained. 'Otherwise, its more or less as you've described it many times. The massive walls, the frescos are unusual and interesting, but most of all I liked the tiles on the floor of that courtyard we went through.'

'Wait, I'll take you out on a lion hunt in a couple of days when you've settled down. That'll get your blood running.' Palaiyas was himself again and his mood had improved.

Through the doorway where Amphitryon had vanished, there now appeared an old man, who approached them, wearing fine robes. '*Palaiyas, my son*! Why have I not heard from you in such a long time?' Scolded the old man as he came near.

'Father, I'm your humble servant.' Palaiyas dropped on his knees to the old man.

'Now, none of that!' His father bent down and lifted Palaiyas onto his feet. Then they embraced and stayed like that for a time, with Palaiyas' face on his father's shoulder.

'So, where have you been that I couldn't find you?' His father finally said as they separated. 'Let me look at you. You've grown older, but have you become wiser?'

'Yes, father, I've grown older.' Palaiyas left it at that. Then he turned to Mokhat to introduce him in Hittite. 'This, as you've already guessed, is my father, King Alkaeus.' Then Palaiyas faced his father again, 'And this father, is a very good friend of mine, Prince Mokhat of the Kaska.'

Mokhat bowed deeply to the old king, and said in Hittite, 'I'm deeply honoured to meet the father of my friend.'

Palaiyas translated his words and Alkaeus looked pleased at those kind words.

'Tell him, he's welcome in my house,' the old king told Palaiyas. 'Tell him; while he's in my house I will treat him as if he were one of my sons.'

When Palaiyas translated this, Mokhat became somewhat embarrassed at such an honour. 'And if he will allow it,' Mokhat asked Palaiyas to translate, 'I will honour him as my second father.'

Servants arrived and food and drink was laid out on low tables with couches being brought in for seating.

'In the morning you will see your mother,' Alkaeus told his son, 'but she's been unwell and we must let her finish her sleep.'

They stayed up chatting till near dawn before they retired to their beds. For Mokhat, to sleep in a proper bed for a change was going to be sheer luxury.

They slept through the morning until noon, finally being roused by the sounds of cheering from a large crowd gathered at the palace gates. News had gone round that the Crown Prince had returned and the populace were eager to let the prince know he was welcome back home.

A slave came to help Mokhat dress in clothing of the finest cotton. He washed quickly and put on the clothing generously supplied by his host, then was taken out to be presented to the household.

Mokhat was led into a large room with couches where the elderly king sat with his elderly wife. She looked a little frail but was beaming with happiness at the sight of her returned son. Palaiyas sat next to his mother and was holding her hand protectively. Amphitryon sat next to his father looking kindly at his brother's compassionate behaviour towards their mother.

A veritable feast of food was laid out in plentiful quantities on the low tables and the king was picking at it distractedly, popping a few grapes into his mouth as he watched Palaiyas consol his mother.

Mokhat was led in by a servant and Palaiyas rose and introduced him once again, for the benefit of his mother. Queen Astydameia, Palaiyas' mother, smiled as her son explained Mokhat's position in Kaska, while king Alkaeus continued to pop grapes, beaming benignly with pride at his family's reunion, holding Amphitryon by the wrist.

Later, Palaiyas was obliged to show his face to the crowd. They'd been loudly chanting his name outside the palace gate. Having been away for so long, he felt a little embarrassed at being paid such tribute, but as the Crown Prince he had a duty to them and he performed it to his best ability.

Afterwards in the palace forecourt Palaiyas took Mokhat by the arm and led him up some stairs to the palace roof. From there they climbed the stairs to the southwest tower. In a small building situated on the roof of the tower, he kept a falcon which was looked after by a slave. The falcon hadn't seen him for over two years but as soon as the slave opened the door, it gave a shrill whistling cry of recognition on hearing his voice, and flapped its thin pointed wings with excitement.

'She recognises you, your highness,' cried the slave, both man and bird overjoyed at their masters return.

Palaiyas put a thick leather glove on his right hand and brought the bird out into the open, removing its head cap. It was magnificent specimen with a blue-grey back, horizontal barring with thin clean bands of dark black underside, and a black colouring on top of its head.

They waited while the slave went to the edge of the tower roof and yelled down to someone they couldn't see. From a distance four or more pigeons went soaring into the air dashing away over the walls and racing into the countryside. Palaiyas threw his falcon in their direction. Thin tapered wings flapping against a cloudless sky, the hawk sped up high behind the pigeons and with sharp piercing recurring cries designed to instil fear into another bird; it swooped down at an enormous speed to pluck one of the pigeons out of the air with its powerful talons in a graceful effortless show of power. It circled once and then smoothly landed on Palaiyas' outstretched arm bearing its dead prey. Palaiyas placed the bird on the tower roof surface and it began busily dismembering the pigeon with its strong sharp hooked beak. Balanced by its long tail, the thin tapered wings flapped as it tore into the pigeon, gulping the morsels greedily.

'That's what I call a job well done,' smiled Palaiyas as he watched the falcon feed on its fresh kill. 'Tomorrow early, I promised you that we'd go out on a lion hunt. I assure you it will be a thrill of a lifetime.'

'How long have you had this falcon?' asked Mokhat. He'd watched the falcon kill with interest, since back in Nerik he had slaves performing similar tasks, but in Kaska they were trained to go after messenger pigeons, and so it was part of the military.

'About seven years. It's in its prime. Did you see the grace with which it swooped on its prey? I'm always amazed at the speed of that swoop.' Palaiyas was filled with pride at the falcon's performance.

'How do you feel now that we're here? We've spent most of the afternoon with your family. Has it satisfied your itch to come here?' Mokhat was wondering how long they were likely to stay in Tiryns. He was abstractedly looking at the city from this vantage point, noting its design.

'Yes it has, since you ask. But I still need to have a long talk with my father. I want to tell him some personal things.' Palaiyas was too preoccupied with his falcon to notice Mokhat's restless intent. Palaiyas was attempting to share some of his youth with Mokhat. 'Are you not enjoying yourself?'

Mokhat watched the falcon finish the meal. 'Yes I am, but my lack of understanding of your language makes it difficult for me.' Mokhat took the opportunity of being on the roof to look at the layout of the city below. To the north lay the lower city where all the ordinary people lived and worked. Everywhere he looked, he saw flat roofs on massive buildings. Yet he estimated that the whole of Tiryns would fit into Hattusas at least ten times. Even Nerik was larger.

The sun was beginning to lower in the west and the light was ebbing from the sky, still gleaming from the distance, sparkling over the bay of Argos. A few dark clouds were moving in from the east and a gentle wind was blowing at them suggesting they could be looking at unsettled weather conditions to come.

'I hope the weather holds for the lion hunt,' Palaiyas commented, as he noted the dark clouds Mokhat was looking at. 'As for the language problem, I don't think we'll be here long enough for you to have to worry too much about it. In the mean time, I'll be your translator.'

An evening feast was organised and many people of note were invited to rejoice at the return of the crown prince. It was a lengthy and taxing evening for both Palaiyas and Mokhat, although the king made an effort to find people who could speak Hittite so that Mokhat would not be left out.

\*　　\*　　\*

The next day Mokhat awakened at dawn to the sound of shouting coming from the main forecourt. He tried turning over and going back to sleep, covering his head with the pillow, but instead of lessening, the noise increased. Men's voices yelling, women's voices crying and screaming broke the stillness of daybreak. After a while Mokhat gave up and got dressed. As he left his room, it all suddenly became quiet, apart from the distant sound of marching feet, clearly receding and thus implying whoever they were, they were in the process of leaving.

On his way to the *megaron*, he puzzled at what could have happened, baring in mind this was the king's palace. It did occur to him that there might have been a palace insurrection and with that in mind he had his hand on his sword as he entered the *megaron*. By the hearth sat king Alkaeus on a couch with his arm round his wife, comforting her over some tragedy. The king looked angry and Amphitryon was stomping about, back and forth, cursing and shouting at the slaves and servants.

Palaiyas was nowhere to be seen, and thus he was unable to understand a word of what was being said. Some catastrophe had clearly occurred, but to whom and why, he was left guessing. Mokhat was unable to form the question or converse with Alkaeus his host and Palaiyas' father. Amphitryon came over to him and laid his hand on Mokhat's arm, and said something softly to him. From this Mokhat understood that all the commotion had something to do with Palaiyas and since he wasn't present, he feared the worst.

Try as he may, he could not get himself understood, nor could he understand anything being said to him. Finally, Amphitryon went to his father and they had a long conversation. Amphitryon then left the *megaron* and Mokhat sat on a couch not far from the king. Astydameia, Palaiyas' mother, was still inconsolable and the king kept his arm around her while she cried on his shoulder.

Amphitryon returned shortly, leading a young woman by the arm, bringing her to Mokhat. He said something to her, and she said, 'I am bid by his highness to tell you that his brother has been taken prisoner by soldiers sent by the Mycenaean Wanax.'

This was said in Hittite and Mokhat's jaw dropped open in astonishment.

The striking young woman continued, 'My name is Ulurra and I'm to be your translator for the duration of your stay. If you wish to ask them any questions, I will translate for you.'

The relief on Mokhat's face said it all. 'My goodness, you are a welcome sight. I was wondering how on earth I would make myself understood. Thank you for coming to my rescue. So now, am I to understand that my friend Palaiyas has been taken prisoner by someone from Mycenae?'

'Yes, your highness, the Wanax, the King of Mycenae is the feudal sovereign of this land and Tiryns is subject to him. Over a hundred Mycenaean soldiers descended on this palace at dawn and took prince Palaiyas away to Mycenae. I've not been told why they did this, but king Alkaeus was not able to stop them without going to war against his own brother.'

The king motioned for them to come to him and so Mokhat, followed by Ulurra, went and stood before the king.

King Alkaeus said something, and Ulurra translated the following, 'He says he's sorry but your friend Prince Palaiyas was taken to Mycenae under escort to account for his desertion from his post in Keftiu. My king tells me to tell you that it is likely that they will send him back to Keftiu to complete his tour of duty.' She stopped and listened to the next bit she was to translate, and hesitated. Finally she said, 'My lord wishes me to tell you that, he is transferring ownership of myself to you, so that you may have a tongue in this land. You are highborn and should not be silenced by a foreign language. I am now yours to do as you will with.' She bowed her head to Mokhat in resignation.

'Tell the king that I'm grateful for his kindness and that I would like to borrow your use, but I don't wish to own you. Oh! And thank him for me.' Mokhat had noted the hesitation of this woman and assumed she didn't want to be transferred to him.

Ulurra translated what he'd said and then said to Mokhat, 'The king insists that you should have me.' Then she brightened up and said, 'he said that should you decide to go back to Hatti, that I should go with you back to where I came from originally.'

The king dismissed them and continued to comfort his wife.

Mokhat nodded and walked away from the king, followed by Ulurra. 'Could you go and ask Prince Amphitryon to join me outside.'

Ulurra went over and translated this to the young prince and they all then wondered out of the *megaron* into the outside court.

'Please ask the prince what he intends to do about his brother's captivity,' Mokhat told Ulurra.

She listened to the response then said, 'The prince says that he is going up to Mycenae in a short while to plead his brother's case. What he also says is that he's engaged to the Wanax's daughter, Alkmene, and he's torn between loyalty to his brother and the desire not to upset Elektryon.'

Mokhat listened carefully. 'I presume Elektryon is the Wanax.'

'Yes you highness,' replied Ulurra.

'Ask him if he would like some company on his trip to Mycenae. I'm afraid you're invited as well.' Mokhat was intent on seeing if he could help Palaiyas in some way. For that to happen he had to get close to Palaiyas. He also

278

thought he ought to take all the money he possessed, money Palaiyas had given him, just in case a bribe might do the trick. He went to his bedchamber and grabbed the sack with his personal possessions in it and flung it over his shoulder, ready for the road.

# Chapter Thirty One

Amphitryon led the way along the long road that crossed the plain of Argos, followed by Mokhat and Ulurra. It was late morning and they'd been walking north for a while up this road leading to Mycenae, almost seemingly out for a stroll, apart from the sacks both Mokhat and Ulurra were carrying over their shoulders. As far as the eye could see, they passed fertile fields that would normally have grown wheat, barley, and flax, the main staple crops that fed and clothed all the towns in the plain. But it being the winter season, the fields stood barren. On the distant hillsides on the right of them, there were an abundance of leafless olive trees and rows of empty grapes vines. Thus they were witness to what should have been the "Mediterranean Trilogy" of grain, olives, and grapes. Come summer the abundance would thrive once again.

They'd been walking in silence for a long time and then Ulurra suddenly informed Mokhat. 'His highness wishes me to tell you that we have passed Argos to the far left of us, and in fact, it's now at the back of us. He also wishes me to tell you that we should reach Mycenae around mid afternoon.'

Mokhat wondered at the significance of the intelligence about Argos and asked Ulurra why he'd been given this information.

She asked Amphitryon, and then informed Mokhat of what he said. 'It's of no real significance right now but it's always useful to know where you are and what towns are close by.'

Mokhat thought that was a little cryptic to say the least. He decided to change the subject. 'Ask his highness if he's set a date for the wedding?'

There was a lengthy conversation and then she told Mokhat, 'His highness says that so far, they are secretly betrothed, and that he hasn't talked about it to her father yet. This is the real reason he needed to go up to Mycenae today. He was going to ask the king's permission for the hand of his daughter.'

After another half a league of plodding along the road, Mokhat once again asked Ulurra to translate for him. 'Could you ask Amphitryon if I can pose a delicate question to him?' They had walked into the afternoon and the sun shone brightly overhead.

She made the enquiry and gave his response, 'He says that as his father has made you his adopted son; that made you his adopted brother, so ask away.'

'King Alkaeus is brother to king Elektryon, is that not so?' Mokhat felt a little awkward asking this, but curiosity had got the better of him.

Ulurra did as requested and Amphitryon replied at length. 'His highness says he knows what your question is. He says he had this conversation with Palaiyas last night. And yes, we are first cousins—but he says that he will repeat to you what he told Palaiyas. That they are passionately in love and he can't live without her; nor can she without him. Fate has sealed their futures and there is little that they can do but go along the path that fate has chosen for them.'

The translated statement seemed to brook no argument. Mokhat understood that the strength of the couple's intentions would withstand all entreaties to the contrary. They had bound themselves to each other and they would fight anyone who tried to separate them.

The road skirted the Era shrine, dedicated to the wife of the great god Diwe, which was situated half a league to the left of the highway, so Amphitryon informed Mokhat. In the far distance ahead of them, Mokhat could make out a sizable cluster of villages built around a high up citadel. Within a short time they passed a number of hillside farms straggling down to the Argive Plain; all part of the outer suburbs of Mycenae.

Amphitryon told him, via Ulurra, that Elektryon and his fellow nobles and their families, together with the priests and their families lived in the citadel, while the rest, most of the artisans and workers lived outside the walls in informal settlements stretching north, northwest, and southwest. Mycenae was not a city in any sense, but a collection of villages dependent on Mycenae for protection.

To the right Mokhat could see a strikingly imposing hilly landscape, with the city constructed on uneven ground and on different levels with artificial terraces, crowned by the citadel itself. Mycenae itself stood on the crossroad between the Argolis and the Gulf of Corinth, seemingly an isolated fortification in an inhabited landscape, yet that was the source of its power. It was situated on a nodal control point leading from the Plain of Argos to the coastal Corinthian Plain, controlling access to the Valleys of Nemea and Berbati.

The party crossed a bridge running over a stream and went through one village at the bottom of the road leading up the east slope of the ridge to the citadel. It had an array of artisans hard at work out in the open carving ivory, producing pottery, carving stone, busily spinning wool and flax and textile workers on small looms weaving cloth. They heard the sonorous hammerings of bronzesmiths and goldsmiths churning out their metal ware. It was a hive of activity producing goods for trade and the enrichment of themselves and those in the citadel.

They left the Argive Plain and began the long climb upwards in a right veering arc towards the citadel. Amphitryon was becoming more animated as he neared the stronghold, in anticipation of his request for the Wanax's daughter, that he babbled on to Mokhat, explaining that in the Argive Plain flax was grown for linen clothing and sesame for its oil. Planted on the hillsides were fig trees, and large olive orchards for the production of olive oil. The olive oil was much used as body oil and in perfumery. Grapes were cultivated producing several varieties of excellent wine.

To Mokhat the citadel seemed small compared with Hattusas, but well fortified with massive walls. After a long walk up the steep road they reached the citadel flanked on either side of the gate by high walls from which the defenders could rain missiles down on any attackers. Over the entrance he noted again there was the carving of the two lions on either side supporting the pillar. Amphitryon told him it was the emblem of Perseus, the founder of Mycenae, and now the family crest of the Perseides, his successors.

As they came through the Lion Gate and under the heavy broad lintel covering the portico, the sentries on either side nodded at Amphitryon, recognising him as a prince of Tiryns, and allowing him and his guests to enter without challenge. To the right of them Mokhat glimpsed an entrance in a large ring of stonework wherein a number of soldiers were practicing their sword work. Going further up the steep ramp, veering left, they came to some even steeper steps cut into the hill. Amphitryon led them up those steps and turned left onto a ramp which would lead them all the way up to the palace.

They climbed in a long half circle, noting the magnificent cluster of building situated on the top of the acropolis, with the *megaron* being prominent, its entrance facing south. The sun was low in the sky as they proceeded on the path that climbed up to the northeast, until they came to stairs on the right leading to the uppermost part of the acropolis. Along a short path they came to the first building, the *propylon*, which were two single-columned roofed porticoes back-to-back. Amphitryon led his party through the *propylon* and upwards along the west terrace access ramp to the great west portal, then they turned left into a long narrow corridor and out into the main forecourt surrounded by double storied buildings. Amphitryon was now striding confidently, leading them to the entrance of the *megaron*. He seemed to have conquered his anxiety and was determined to make a respectable claim for the hand of the king's daughter.

Amphitryon spoke to Ulurra and she told Mokhat that he wished them to wait in the Main Forecourt, while he went inside and talked to the king.

Amphitryon, without waiting for Mokhat's response, marched into the porch of the *megaron*, paved with gypsum slabs and colourful plaster walls, and through the vestibule into the *megaron* chamber. He found the Wanax to the right in the ornate *megaron*, sitting on his throne. Coloured frescos decorated the entire *megaron*. The king was in deep conversation with one of his generals. Elektryon was pointing his finger at this army commander and raising his voice. Then as suddenly, he stopped and sat back on the throne. The general looked nonplussed, backed away from Elektryon and left the *megaron* in a hurry.

Elektryon spied Amphitryon waiting to see him and motioned him over with an imperious wave of his hand.

'Your majesty,' began Amphitryon as he faced the king, 'I come here with a heavy heart, laden with anxiety and hope. As you are no doubt aware, Alkmene and I have been friends and companions from our childhood, and over the years a bond has developed between us that has blossomed into a sincere respect and love.'

Elektryon's face began to scowl which should have warned Amphitryon that all was not well with his presentation, yet having committed to it, he had little choice but to continue.

'I come here before you, your majesty, to respectfully request her hand in marriage, and to seek your consent to this joyous union, which would make us both happy.' There, he'd done it. It was only then that Amphitryon perceived the dark cloud that had arisen on the king's face.

'*How dare you?* The brother of a *criminal* and *coward* who didn't have the guts to fulfil his duties to his sovereign and finish his tour of duty; how *dare* you ask for my daughter's hand? *Never! Never!* I suspected something like this was going on. I've locked her in her bedroom, and she stays there until she comes to her senses.' The king was in a rage as he spat these words out at Amphitryon. Elektryon rose from his throne and walked past Amphitryon as if he were not there. Over his shoulder he called out, 'You're dismissed. Oh! I'm excluding you from Mycenae for the next ten years on pain of death, should you ignore my decree.' The king continued towards the hearth.

The young prince stood rooted to the spot for a second in shock at the vehemence of the king's words. In a flash, he watched his future crumbling before his eyes and it was too much for the young prince. He turned in a suddenly fury as his temper got the better of him, rushing at Elektryon's back, giving the king a shove. Elektryon stumbled forward and collided with the heavily plastered ring of stones edging the hearth, cracking his temple on the sharp edge of the hearth. He rolled over once, a deep ugly gash visible in his forehead, and then he was still—with his eyes wide open staring into the underworld.

Amphitryon reached him and immediately saw the king was no more. Swiftly he glanced around the *megaron* and was relieved to note they were alone. Without thought, he heaved the stout body up and hoisted it into the smouldering fires of the hearth, raking some ashes over the corpse to hide it. He needed to buy some time if he were to escape; it was a desperate urgent self preservation driving him. Next, he rushed to the north end of the *megaron*, went through into a passageway leading to the small flight of stairs that climbed up to the private apartments of the palace; frantically searching for Alkmene. He hurried down the main corridor, now lit by oil lamps, trying to remember where her bedroom was situated. He tried two doors, both opened, so they were clearly not the locked one. The third door he tried was locked, he called out her name and she answered. He burst it open and grabbed her wrist and almost dragged her down the corridor to the stairs before she put her foot down and refused to go further without an explanation.

Briefly he told her what happened, but not how he had hidden the body. She agreed they should try to escape, so they carried on down the stairs and out to where Mokhat was waiting for them in the twilight, his sack over his shoulder. As Mokhat saw Amphitryon coming out of the porch from the south corridor, he began to say something, but it was in Hittite and unintelligible to the young prince. All Amphitryon understood was the name Palaiyas. Amphitryon said something to Ulurra and she interpreted this for him as, 'Quick, we've got to get out of here. It's a matter of life and death. If you value your life, follow me.'

Amphitryon led the way to the right out of the Main Forecourt, down a corridor running to the back of the *megaron* towards the back buildings. They walked calmly through a long building and out into the open, then past the house of columns on the right, almost as if they were out for a stroll. It was essential that they didn't attract any attention, so in spite of the impulse to run, Amphitryon made a heroic effort to walk, and ensured the others did the same. The fading light helped as the few people that were out were now heading for their evening meals.

They went down the path leading to the northern Postern gate, and in passing a building; they found a couple of grooms brushing down a couple of horses by the side of the road.

Amphitryon took the imperious approach and asked them if they knew who Alkmene was. They looked at her in the dark and were a little bewildered, until she came forward into the light that shone from the building entrance, then they bowed deeply giving him the answer he wanted. 'We are going to take these horses out for an evening ride, and if you wait here, we will bring them back in a short while and you can continue brushing them.

He didn't wait for them to agree but simply took the bridles from them, handed one to Mokhat, and they walked the horses downhill, turning right into the Postern gate. At the gate, Amphitryon let Alkmene do the talking, and she told the sentries that they would be back shortly after an invigorating evening ride out in the country, a short picnic, and they would be back. The picnic was to explain the sacks Mokhat and Ulurra carried. As he passed the sentry, Amphitryon winked at the senior non-com in a show of bravado. To Amphitryon's amazement the non-com winked back, in a silent message wishing him well, then saluted the princess. He opened the double wooden doors and the little party went down the ramp leading to the main road that went by Mycenae.

The four escapees halted on the main road while Amphitryon told Ulurra to tell Mokhat that he had accidentally killed the king—that is why they were having to run for it. She said that Amphitryon and Alkmene were now going to flee north to Thebes where he would seek sanctuary with his maternal uncle, king Kreon of Thebes. Mokhat was welcome to come with him if he so wished.

Mokhat had Ulurra tell Amphitryon that what he was trying to tell him in the *megaron* forecourt was that he'd seen Palaiyas. He was being escorted, in chains, by a large group of soldiers, heading down towards the Lion Gate. He was grateful for the offer to see Thebes, but he and Ulurra were going to go after Palaiyas. Mokhat gave Amphitryon the horse he was holding and hoped he would make better use of it, because he had to continue on foot back down to Tiryns. Mokhat was assuming that the soldiers were taking Palaiyas back to Keftiu and he fully intended to follow him there and help him escape. If he used the horse, he would pass the column escorting Palaiyas, and he didn't want that just in case he had the story wrong. Luckily for him there was a full moon that night and he would have them under surveillance all the way to Tiryns; he wanted to stay low against the skyline and follow them on foot throughout the night.

Amphitryon and Alkmene climbed onto their horses and galloped off to the right into the night, heading into the Berbati Valley, and then they would swing north towards Thebes. Mokhat and Ulurra heaved the sacks onto their backs and turned left down the road that led to Tiryns.

# Chapter Thirty Two

From their vantage point on the elevated road below Mycenae, looking down onto the Argos Plain in the moonlight, Mokhat could just make out in the far distance, a column of soldiers marching down the road to Tiryns. A tip of the Bay of Argos was visible in the vastness with the moonlight shimmering off it.

Mokhat told Ulurra, 'We're going to have to hurry if we want to catch up with that column.'

Even in the dark he could see that she looked tired and was probably hungry and thirsty, but just then there was little he could do about it. She sighed quietly, clutching her small sack, and followed her new master without complaint.

The two of them made good speed in spite of the long day they'd already endured, and when Ulurra stumbled a couple of times, Mokhat helped her to regain her feet and relieved her of her sack, putting it inside his own. He rested a short time before rushing on after the column.

Sometime half way along the road to Tiryns, Mokhat and Ulurra spied the marching soldiers up ahead. At that point he suggested a rest. They'd caught up to the column not because of their own efforts, but due to the officer in charge of the column giving a long rest his soldiers as they were having to march throughout the night. After that it was a matter of keeping out of sight and keeping the column within earshot. The sound of marching feet told them how close they were to the soldiers.

As they went past the turning to the Tiryns citadel, it was clear to Mokhat that the column was heading down towards the port. That meant he'd guessed right; Palaiyas was being taken back to Keftiu to complete his tour of duty there. He would probably have to complete his undertaking under close supervision, but the authorities were insistent he conclude his obligation to his sovereign; even though the sovereign was no more.

At the entrance to the port Mokhat ceased tracking the column and went directly to the quayside to look for passage to Keftiu. Although the soldiers weren't aware that Mokhat was connected to Palaiyas, Mokhat would not take the chance of getting on the same ship, even if he were able to. It was with this intent of finding a ship that Mokhat and Ulurra arrived in the port at daybreak after two days and a night of walking without food and drink, and only a modicum of rest.

The first priority for Mokhat was to find some sustenance for the both of them. It may have been dawn, but the port was already busy with dockers loading and unloading cargo. With all the dust and grime of travelling, they blended in with their surroundings as though they belonged. He found a food stall and bought them a plateful of barley pancakes and fried fish, to be washed down with a jug of wine. They sat at a bench and demolished the food; only then did the tiredness hit him. He decided he and Ulurra would have plenty of time to sleep on the ship when they were under way, so he forced himself to stay awake and went in search of a captain.

He walked along the quayside looking at the vessels moored there, trying to ascertain where the ships might be bound, but it was a hopeless task. He also needed to avoid the ship Palaiyas might be on. It was going to be tricky due to his lack of language and having to rely on Ulurra to do the talking, but then sometimes luck takes a hand and he recognised the eye of El on a ship berthed where they'd disembarked three days ago. He explained to Ulurra that they'd come to Tiryns on this ship and if he could find the captain, they *might* be able to buy passage on it out of here, depending on where the ship was going.

Mokhat noted the ship stood low in the water, fully laden with new cargo, ready to depart. If only it were heading his way, then lady luck would have a new devotee. He boarded the vessel along the gang plank and discovered the captain busily checking bills of lading on a series of clay tablets.

Mokhat dropped his sack on the deck and opened his reacquaintance with, 'Nice to see you're still busy turning a shekel.'

The captain looked up warily, and then smiled broadly, also responding in Hittite, 'Your highness! What an unexpected pleasure. Did you leave something behind?' He chuckled at his own wit.

Mokhat joined in the banter, 'Why? Did you find something that belonged to us?'

That gave the captain his moment, 'Only a couple of berths; but then you could hardly take them with you, could you? So now, what can I do for you, your highness?'

'Speaking of a couple of berths, may I ask where your next port of call is going to be?' At this point Mokhat did the fig sign behind his back with his right hand for good luck.

The captain was as cautious as ever, 'May I ask why you wish to know?'

'Depending on your answer, you may reacquire a couple of passengers. So where are you headed?'

The captain shrugged and said, 'My next port of call is Aminiso. Any good to you?'

Mokhat had no idea where this Aminiso was so he fished some more. 'If Aminiso is on Keftiu, then I'll claim those berths you spoke of.'

'It is. And you're welcome aboard. Have you eaten?' The captain was all smiles and called over one of the crew to put away his bills of lading. 'We sail on the noon tide. If I may be so bold, your highness, you look like you could do with a brush up.'

Mokhat was on the verge of being affronted at such a suggestion, but then looked down at himself, and glanced over at Ulurra, and saw the captain was understating his condition. He spread his arms to ask where.

The captain led him and Ulurra to a wooden bucket standing on a ledge which was filled with water and then showed him where a drying cloth hung. After a clean up, they were invited to have some barley porridge with the captain. At this point Mokhat paid the captain seven talents of silver for their passage, knowing it was more than needed, but it also made for fewer questions.

'We both need to have a good rest. We've been travelling all night. Where is there a quiet spot so we won't be disturbed?' Mokhat asked the captain after their second meal.

The captain took them to the bow and showed them their berths. A couple of pallets with straw mattresses and a canvas overhang. 'The voyage will last around three days and this is the best I can do for you. I'll wake you in the afternoon, if that's alright?'

'This is fine,' Mokhat assured him, extracting Ulurra's sack from his own and handing it to her, then tossing his sack into the back of the yawning. 'By the way, have you got any more of that disgusting root you gave me on the voyage here?'

The captain smiled again, 'I'll have it ready when you wake up. You'll find a blanket at the back of the mattress. Sleep well.'

*   *   *

When Mokhat awoke, the ship was heaving up and down, so he knew they'd sailed. He threw aside the blanket and climbed out from under the canvas yawning and stood up. The sun was beginning to set in the west on the starboard side and the sky was clear of clouds.

'Good morning your highness,' said a woman's voice from behind him. For a split second Mokhat became disorientated by the ships movements and didn't recognise Ulurra's voice. Then he remembered and turned to find a beautiful woman standing there, holding out in her hands a small beige coloured root, a piece of bread, and a goblet of wine. 'Thank you Ulurra.' He took the root and put it in his mouth, followed by the bread and chewed. Then he poured the wine over the lot and chewed some more. It didn't affect him the way it did the first time and he didn't feel at all tired; just invigorated.

The ship was doing well, there was a good wind in the sails and the crew were mostly relaxing on the deck of the cargo hold.

The captain arrived almost unnoticed. 'I hope you've rested sufficiently, your highness.'

'Yes, thank you; and thank you for the medicine. The little nook of a berth is surprisingly comfortable. I almost feel like my old self again. By the way, let me introduce my translator to you. This is Ulurra; a gift from the king of Tiryns.' Mokhat turned to Ulurra, and she bowed her head in submission. 'Ulurra, this is our double-time saviour, Captain Nikmed from Ugarit.'

'I have some more food for you if you're hungry.' Without waiting for an answer, the captain rushed away as he noticed a rope flapping in the wind. He tied it off and shouted for his first mate to demand the reason why his ship was being run so sloppily.

'As you can see,' Mokhat said to Ulurra, 'our captain is a hard taskmaster but he's been good to me and Palaiyas. So, are you hungry?'

'Thank you for asking but I've already eaten, but I've laid out some fruit and figs for you; together with some drink. It's at the stern, near the captain's station.' She walked away and Mokhat followed her, admiring her poise.

He ate some of the food but found he wasn't all that hungry. He went over to the starboard rail and watched the sunset. The sun was just about to disappear over the horizon and the scene, with the dark blue of the sea, the multicoloured shading of the sky from dark to light, and the deep red ball of fire sinking into the deep blue, was bursting with intense colours. Ulurra was near him, leaning over the rail and looking at the same scene; she seemed mesmerised.

Now that things had calmed down and both were rested and fed, Mokhat's curiosity got the better of him, 'So now, Ulurra, what were you doing in Tiryns? You're obviously a Hittite, yet you served the Mycenaeans. Tell me, how did this come about?'

'It's a long story your highness; are you sure you want to be concerned with it?' She was a little reluctant to go into her story. It had been a painful life and even though he was her new master now, she was disinclined to go through it all again.

'Yes Ulurra, I do want to hear your story. I like to know who I'm dealing with, and how far I can trust them. I'm on a delicate mission and you now seem to be part of it. I need to know who you are. So please tell me your entire story…in detail.'

'As you command, your highness. I'm originally from Ivalanda; that's my home town.'

On hearing this Mokhat's ears pricked up with this pleasant surprise.

'I was engaged to a young man ten years ago. His family had an estate on the border between Ahhiyawa and Hatti. One day, ten years ago, he took me there to introduce me to his family. We were having a marvellous time when suddenly out of nowhere, a squadron of Ahhiyawan cavalry went through the area killing and taking people prisoner. All of my fiancés family were butchered. I was spared because one of the officers took a fancy to me. He took me prisoner, and I went to Millawanda with him, but no matter how much he beat me I refused his advances. Finally he got fed up of my unwillingness to bow down to him, so he put me up for sale in the local slave market.

'I was standing there almost naked when the bidding started, and I knew I was in trouble. The bidders were rough types looking to fill their brothels with new slave women. What I didn't expect was that one of the bidders, an old man, kept bidding right up to the end and I became his property, to the utter disgust of the brothel owners. I was seventeen years old then and I wasn't looking forward to having an old man climbing all over me. To my amazement, my new master was a kind gentle scholarly scribe who bought me because he took pity on me, knowing what would otherwise happen if the porn predators got hold of me—I would end my days in a brothel.

'He was elderly and kind to me and we stayed in Millawanda for five years while he worked hard at court as an official scribe to the then king. I did his housework and cooked for him. Never once did he make any indecent proposals to me; I was lonely but grateful for that. About five years ago, he became home sick and he took me back to his home town of Tiryns. He died last year, and I then joined the king's household, where you found me.'

For a while Mokhat was silent, and then he told her, 'I'm grateful that you've confided your story to me. I now know why you were so hesitant; it must have been painful to remember such a tragedy. Believe it or not, I was in Ivalanda only a short time ago; me and Prince Palaiyas. Do you still have family there?'

'I had a brother in the Hittite army, an officer. I don't know what's happened to him, it's been so long now. Ten years is a long time. I would dearly like to go back to Ivalanda, but...' and she hesitated, 'I'm yours to command.'

Again Mokhat looked closely at her. 'There's been something bothering me ever since we met. I feel I've met you before, and yet that cannot be. There's something familiar about you, yet I can't put my finger on it. Tell me some more about your brother.'

'What can I say? He was a good brother to me. He's older than me by six years; his name is Narmus, and ....' She stopped, seeing the look of shock on Mokhat's face.

'*Narmus* you say. Now I know why you looked so familiar. The family resemblance is there. I don't know why I didn't see it before.' Then he remembered what happened to Narmus. He had to tell her—but how? In truth, he hadn't yet reconciled himself with Narmus' death and so he now found it difficult to speak of the circumstances that ended his friend's life. 'I have to tell you something that's very difficult for me to talk about. Come; let's sit down on the cargo hatch.'

It was dark now, but the moon had risen and it threw an eerie milky brightness on their surroundings making the sea shine by reflecting a sparkling lustre. They made themselves as comfortable as possible on the hard surface of the hatch, while Mokhat composed his thoughts.

'I and Palaiyas knew your brother. He was a good friend to us and we respected his qualities. Until a week ago he was travelling with us....' He was now having difficulty with his voice.

Ulurra noticed all this and began to prepare herself for the worst.

'We were on a raft going down the Meander River, which can be tempestuous in places, and he.....he was thrown from the raft when we hit some very rough water. We couldn't do anything to help him. He was gone so quickly that somehow, I'm still finding it difficult to come to terms with his loss. I'm so sorry to have to give you such bad news. You have my deepest sympathies.' Mokhat was having trouble holding back his tears.

Ulurra had no such inhibition and she silently wept for her now deceased sibling.

Mokhat saw the state she was in and he gently put his arm around her shoulder. She rested her left cheek on his right shoulder, and they stayed like that for some time, rocking gently to the heaving of the boat, each struggling to come to terms with their own thoughts, their own grief.

Finally she straightened up, wiped her eyes, and said, 'Thank you for telling me. I'd rather know, than not know; and I'm glad he had such good friends as you and Prince Palaiyas. For the last ten years, I've often worried over what had happened to him. Our parents died when we were young and Narmus more or less took care of me while I was young. He was a friend as well as a brother, may he rest in peace. If your able to, your highness, maybe you could tell me some more of how your knew my brother, how you met him and such like.'

'I will, Ulurra. I can tell you this; he was made a colonel just before he died. You can be proud of him. But in time I will tell you all I know,' and he left it at that. The time had run away with them, and it was now quite late. 'What with the fresh sea air and all the talking, I think it might be an idea if we got back into our beds. We should try to get back into our normal sleep routine. Now I know who you are, Ulurra, tomorrow I'll explain what Narmus, Palaiyas, and I are up to. As I said before, it's a delicate mission, and quite probably dangerous. If you're to be with me, then I feel you have a right to know what we're doing. Oh! There is a promise I'm prepared to make to you right now....I *will* get you back to Ivalanda—where you will be *free* to decide your own fate.'

His last statement astonished her, but pleasantly. She climbed onto her mattress, sad and happy all at the same time. Sad to hear the news of her brother—but happy at the promise of a future freedom.

\*　　\*　　\*

The next two days were largely uneventful with the sea being modestly rough, which was normal for the time of year, but not unmanageable for experienced sailors. The wind was blowing from the north, moderate to strong, giving them an extra burst of speed, bestowing a good disposition on the captain. However, without any warning, in mid afternoon on the second day out, they had a short cloudburst which chucked down a lot of rain in a short time, drenching everybody and everything. At the end there was a mix of hail and thunder, and it was the thunder that frightened Ulurra, prompting her to hide under her canvas yawning until it was over.

As promised, Mokhat told Ulurra the whole story of how they met Narmus and under what circumstances. He related all that had subsequently occurred in Ivalanda; finding the dead spy master, the corrupt governor, their fight in the tavern, the murder of the general. Then he related the account of their fight in the middle of the night with Napat and his cronies, and how Narmus was injured in the skirmish, making him vulnerable later on. He told her how the loss of their horses forced them in to taking the trip down the river, quickly avoiding repeating what had happened to Narmus, then their arrival and departure from Millawanda. He even told her how Palaiyas had eliminated the Ahhiyawan spy master in a fit of anger and revenge. The story took a long time to recount and passed the time on board, and before they realised how the hours had been whittled away in the telling of the tale, the captain came to them on the third day and announced that they were shortly to arrive at Aminiso.

'From what I remember of Palaiyas' account of his stay on this island, he spent most of his time in a place called Fausto,' Mokhat told Ulurra while the captain listened in.

'You mean Phaistos surely,' corrected the captain. 'It's on the other side of the island, almost on the southern coast.'

'Well, Phaistos then. Look captain, I have a serious proposition for you. First I want to show you something which might help you make your mind up.' Mokhat took out the royal seal of Khemet from his pouch and showed it to the captain. 'Do you know what this is?' he asked in all innocence.

The captain looked at the seal, then at Mokhat with surprise. 'Where did you get that?'

'From its legitimate owners. So you do recognise it?' Mokhat asked again.

'Yes, I've had occasion to be pressed into their service. It was either that, or loosing my rights to trade in Khemet. You are a man of amazement, your highness. A Kaska prince with a Khemet royal seal; this is a complex intertwined world we live in. So what can I do for you? I assume you want me to do something, not entirely above board?'

'It should be no great risk to you.' Mokhat smiled in as friendly a manner as he could manage. 'All I want, is for you to find me a boat or ship that will take us off of this island when the time comes. How long will it take me to get to Phaistos?'

'By my reckoning we should be docking about mid afternoon. If you managed to find horses and rode through the night, you should be in Phaistos around noon the next day. Stay on the road through the mountains or you'll get lost. There's a good road leading from Knossos, which is the administrative centre, to Phaistos. The Minoans were good road builders. If you want a ship, then you'll need to get from Phaistos down to the shore at Kalamaki beach. I'll try to have a boat waiting for you there three days from now; it'll be there from dawn onwards on the third day. I can't tell you where it's going or anything like that, but it will take the three of you off the island. I assume that's what you really want. When I was waiting in Tiryns, I saw them take Prince Palaiyas onto a boat in chains. Putting two and two together, I would guess you're here to rescue him and so with you two here and the prince, that makes three. Am I right?'

'I take my helmet off to you, captain. You have guessed the situation just right. Three days from now it is then. For this help, captain, I'm going to ask Khemet to pay you fifty talents of silver; but the snag is,' and Mokhat tried to look apologetic, 'that you will have to collect it from Khemet. I assume you will be going there at some point in your journey.'

'If I didn't know better,' the captain said with a wry smile, 'I'd assume you were a mind reader to add to all the other talents that you have. After Aminiso my next port of call is Djanet in Khemet.'

'When you get there,' Mokhat told him sincerely, 'get in touch with the pharaoh's palace, and tell them that Prince Mokhat of the Kaska says that they owe you fifty talents of silver for services rendered to me and Prince Palaiyas. You have my word, they *will* pay you.'

'And you have my word,' said the captain with a grin, 'I will be there to collect. Business is business. It's an old motto in Ugarit.'

As they were bantering the ship's lookout sighted Aminiso and brought the news to the captain. The captain said to Ulurra, 'With apologies to your highness,' he nodded to Mokhat, 'we're talking Hittite at the moment, but I assume you will be doing the talking on shore, and here in Keftiu the official language is Mycenaean, so I will tell you. Just on the outskirts of Aminiso, on the road to Knossos, there is a tavern called the *Food & Grapes* with a stable attached. You can't miss it. Tell the landlord that Captain Nikmed from Ugarit sends his compliments, and asks that he supply you with two horses, as a favour to me. That should get you to Phaistos—after that you're on your own. I wish you fortune and success.'

# Chapter Thirty Three

Mokhat and Ulurra said their farewells to Captain Nikmed after the ship docked and were soon on the gangplank to shore, loosing themselves in the crowd on the quayside, avoiding any soldiers, trying not to get noticed. They hurried through the narrow streets of the small port, heading for the outskirts as directed by Nikmed.

They found the *Food & Grapes* according to Nikmed's directions and went inside, looking for the landlord. It was nothing special as taverns go, but it was cleaner than most. As it was late afternoon, they expected to find the tavern full with after work drinkers, instead it was mostly empty. Mokhat heard a male voice shouting at someone in the kitchens as soon as they entered; this turned out to be the landlord. Ulurra told Mokhat that he was threatening to sack the cook for not having the evening food ready for the expected rush. When he finally came out from the kitchen, he looked furious, but then he saw them waiting and rushed over with a smile that was almost genuine.

'What can I do for you?' he asked obsequiously, then added, 'I'm sorry we're short of staff at the moment, so if its food, then you'll have to wait for a while.'

Ulurra said, 'We bring you Captain Nikmed's compliments and he asks if you would hire two horses to us for a trip to Phaistos.'

The landlord stopped being servile and looked hard at them, then grinned. 'And what does this captain look like?' He was being extra cautious.

Ulurra described the captain to him, red hair, tall and muscular. As soon as he heard the phrase "red hair" he beamed at them, but this time it was sincere.

'I'm sorry, but I had to be certain that it was *my* Captain Nikmed and not some other. We're living in trying times. So you're off to Phaistos, eh? Well look here, let me get you some food and a flagon of wine and you can sit down and relax. I assume your staying the night. I wouldn't recommend night travel; not through those mountains. By the way, doesn't he speak at all?' the landlord said to Ulurra, meaning Mokhat.

'Yes he does, but not this language. I'm his bondwoman and translator.' Ulurra felt uncomfortable relating this to a stranger.

The landlord nodded in understanding and went to get the wine. They heard him tell someone down a corridor that he wanted two horses ready for a long trip in the morning. In the mean time Mokhat and Ulurra had made themselves comfortable at a table and he'd got two talents of silver ready for the horses, covering them with his hand.

The landlord came back carrying a tray filled with pancakes, cold roast duck, olives, and a flagon of wine. He placed the tray on the table, and then poured some wine into two pottery goblets. At that point Mokhat asked Ulurra to find out how much the landlord wanted for the hire of the horse and the night's stay?

The landlord stroked his chin and then said that his standard charge for a night and such a journey was one silver talent and that he couldn't take any less.

Ulurra translated this. Mokhat uncovered his hand and said, 'But could he take more?' She told the landlord what Mokhat said.

The landlord grinned, 'That I could. For that sum, I'll even get you some food for the journey. Will bread, dried meat, some cheese, and olives, do for you? I'll put in a skin of wine as well.'

Ulurra told him that it would do nicely; then she invited him to join them.

Mokhat had emptied his goblet and held it up to have it refilled; and the landlord obliged. Then Mokhat tucked into the pancakes and duck, and told Ulurra to help herself, which she did, gladly.

The landlord pulled up a stool and sat down. He explained to Ulurra, 'All the roads are clearly marked. Can you read Mycenaean?' he asked her, and she nodded. 'On the outskirts of Phaistos you'll find a tavern called *The Upturned Turtle*; tomorrow, leave the horses with the landlord there. We have a reciprocal arrangement for this kind of business. Be careful on the mountain road; don't stop for anybody. There are bandits along that route, so tell your master to keep his sword handy; and you'd both better wrap up warm because there's still snow on that road.'

Ulurra translated all the landlord had said, between mouthfuls, and Mokhat responded with, 'Thank the landlord for his information. But to change the subject, ask him why his tavern is so empty at this time of night. Tell him I'm curious.' Ulurra did as she was asked.

The landlord sighed and said, 'Two nights ago, we had some trouble in here. A couple of soldiers began to abuse some locals and it ended in a big fight. One of the soldiers was killed as were a couple of the locals. The authorities have tried to close me down, but I have a few friends who prevented that. Now they are trying to discourage my clientele from drinking in here. They've barred their soldiers from coming in here, and are pressurising the locals not to drink here. It'll blow over. I've had this kind of trouble before from the authorities, mostly because I'm from Ugarit. What keeps me in business is my local connection. I help the Minoans as much as I can. I think they've been hard done by with these Mycenaeans. I'm telling you this because I know you're not Mycenaean. Me and Captain Nikmed come from the same place, that's why he sent you to me. My guess, from what I can hear of your language, is that you're Hittites. Am I right?'

Ulurra was mildly surprised at this information, and she translated this to Mokhat.

Mokhat smiled and nodded. 'Tell the landlord he's correct. Also tell him I'm sorry to hear of his troubles.' Mokhat was left with the impression that the landlord was mixed up with the locals in their fight against the Mycenaean occupiers of Keftiu. The problem all along had been that he didn't know where they had taken Palaiyas. Was he in Knossos or Phaistos? Maybe they'd taken him to another part of the island altogether? The problem of how to find him might have presented itself with this landlord; only if the landlord could be induced to make use of the local population to find Palaiyas. That depended on the landlord's connections with the local underground resistance. 'Ulurra, could you delicately ask the landlord if his sympathies lie with the locals, the Minoans?' Mokhat would carefully observe the answer to see how the landlord reacted to the question.

She did as he asked, and the landlord sat there looking from side to side, wondering what he should divulge to this pair of Hittites. Finally he seemed to have made his mind up. 'I must admit my sympathies are with the underdog. Why do you ask?' He was as cautious as a cat.

Ulurra translated this to Mokhat. He then told her, 'Tell him I'm going to lay my problem on the table for him. Tell him we came to Keftiu to rescue a close friend of ours, a Mycenaean held captive by this administration and forced into suppressing the locals against his will.' Ulurra kept a running translation going as Mokhat talked. 'He escaped from this island a couple of years ago because he couldn't do the killing they were asking him to do.' Mokhat stopped because the landlord's face had become a puzzle. The landlord was behaving as if Mokhat was telling him old news.

'You wouldn't be referring to the Prince of Tiryns by any chance?' The landlord asked.

Ulurra translated and it was Mokhat's turn to lift his eyebrows. 'Well, yes. Prince Palaiyas is a friend of mine. He's been dragged back here to finish his tour of duty, against his will. I want to get him out.' He'd told him so much, and as he was Nikmed's friend, he might as well go all the way. 'In three days time, Captain Nikmed has arranged for a ship to pick all of us off the beach at Kalamaki, if we can get there in time. First, I must locate where they've taken Palaiyas. Is there anyway you can use your local people to find out where he is.'

Ulurra told the landlord what Mokhat had said and waited for the reply.

'I can do better than that.' The landlord smiled. 'You're right, I am involved with the local resistance. We've been tracking your friend ever since he landed here early this morning. He is a legend on the island. The first highborn Mycenaean they could trust. He treated them like civilised people from the time he arrived, and they noticed it immediately. They actually helped him escape two years ago. We were planning to do the same again.' The landlord put his hand in his pocket and pulled out the two talents of silver and pushed it back across the table to Mokhat.

Mokhat sat there bemused, and shook his head, as Ulurra translated what he'd said. 'Tell him the money is his, and more if he helps us to find and rescue Palaiyas.'

Ulurra told the landlord, who suddenly began to look angry.

'This is *not* about money,' he said in a loud voice. 'It is about principle; the principle of freedom. It is about being treated as civilised people in your own country. I cannot accept your money for helping the man who treated my friends as they should be treated.' Then he stopped himself, and smiled diffidently. 'If however, you wish to make a contribution to our resistance fund, then that's an entirely different matter.'

When Ulurra had translated this, Mokhat put his hand in his pouch and pulled out another eight talents to add to the two on the table; he pushed this over to the landlord. 'Tell him this is my contribution to the resistance fund. Tell him I will talk to the Hittite king, when I next see him, and see if we can't do something about sending him some more funds later on.' Mokhat wanted to make certain that this kingpin in the local resistance would make an all out effort to help him rescue his friend.

The landlord having heard Ulurra, took the talents from the table and pocketed them. Then he told her, 'We know the Hittite king is all powerful; maybe he could send an army to free us? If not, then we certainly could use some more funds. Thank your friend for me on behalf of the resistance. Now, as to Prince Palaiyas; he's been taken to Phaistos, via Knossos, as you correctly surmised. They set off by horse as soon as they landed. By now they will be somewhere near Gortys; and that's where we plan to ambush them. That might be taking place as we speak.' Having dropped this meteor splash of information, the landlord sat back looking amused.

Ulurra told Mokhat what he'd just said, and watched Mokhat's face turn into astonishment. 'An ambush.....what, right *now*?' This turn of events was incredible and he found it hard to take in. He asked Ulurra to tell the landlord, 'Pass on that I'm very glad I confided my problem to him. What had the resistance in mind if they were successful in this ambush?' Mokhat wanted to know where this was going.

Ulurra did as asked and the landlord told her, 'We were looking to get him off the island, as we did the previous time. But now that you tell me that dear Captain Nikmed has arranged a ship for this enterprise, it makes our job much easier. You will go down to Gortys tomorrow and link up with your friend, and then we will help you get to Kalamaki beach to catch the boat; that's assuming nothing has gone wrong. With this type of operation, you can never tell. With luck on our side, you should see Prince Palaiyas tomorrow. Now I suggest you get some rest. It will be an early start tomorrow.

The food had all been demolished and they settled down to a few more goblets of wine before turning in for the night.

# Chapter Thirty Four

Early next morning, after a good breakfast, Mokhat told Ulurra that they had better be on their way as it was getting late.

She rose from the table and told the landlord that they were ready to go.

The landlord responded with, 'Wait a moment while I get the food for you.' He dashed off to the kitchen and they heard him shouting again, but he came back shortly carrying a sack and a wineskin. 'I've sent someone over to the stables to get the horses ready for you. I see you've got some warm clothes; you'll need them. Otherwise, good fortune! If you see Captain Nikmed before I do, say hallo to him for me.'

Mokhat and Ulurra went out back to the stables and found three grey mares, blankets over their haunches, ready to go. Mokhat noted that a dark haired fellow of slight build with a sallow complexion was mounting the third horse.

The landlord came running out and said to Ulurra, 'I'm sorry, I forgot. This is Aranare, he's going to be your guide to Gortys. He's a Kaptarian, but that's their name for what you call Minoan, and Keftiu is really called Kapadar. He's also your passport to a safe journey through the mountains. If the bandits see him, they won't touch your party. Also he knows how to get in touch with the Kapadar resistance in Gortys, so look after him.' He then helped Ulurra onto her horse.

Mokhat jumped onto his mare and they were off with a final wave to the landlord. They swung their horses out of the yard and trotted gently through the narrow streets of

Aminiso until they got to the other side of the little town and onto the road leading towards Knossos.

They rode out of Aminiso heading southwest through the countryside for a whole league, skirting a large mountain to the left of them, until they reached Knossos, a large palace ensconced on a hill. Aranare avoided the palace entirely and took them round it heading south-southwest for a lengthy three league ride that skirted a mighty range of mountains to their right. At that point, they ate some of the food while they were riding, so they didn't loose any time. Then Aranare led them west-southwest, climbing higher onto a snow covered road for just under five leagues, where they ate more of their food rations, before going downwards on the road that led to Gortys. Gortys stood in a valley which Aranare called Messara. Ulurra and Aranare did all the talking in Mycenaean—which she then translated for Mokhat.

It was late afternoon when they got to the Knossos side of Gortys, and Aranare led them up a path onto the right side of the hills which opened out into a high ravine in the Psiloritis Mountains. There they were challenged by a number of small stature people not dissimilar to Aranare, and clearly they knew each other. This little band took them to a cave even further up in the ravine.

Even with the sun in his eyes, Mokhat could see in the distance a familiar figure sitting outside the cave in the afternoon sun. His heart gave a leap and he kicked the sides of the horse to make it move faster. Mokhat yelled at the figure when he was in shouting range, '*P-a-l-a-i-y-a-s!*'

The figure seemed startled, then looked hard at the approaching horseman, finally leaping up and waving frantically.

As his horse reached the cave, Mokhat sprang from it with joy at the sight of his long lost friend, and rushed to embrace Palaiyas. Palaiyas returned the embrace and they hugged each other until it became embarrassing.

'Let me look at you,' Palaiyas said pulling back and staring at his friend. Then he noticed Ulurra trotting up, and scratched his head smiling. 'I was wondering how you would manage to get by not knowing the language. Now I see you've met our palace Hittite speaker. I was going to introduce you to her in the morning; that was before they grabbed me.'

Ulurra jumped down from her horse and came to stand by Mokhat, and bowed to Crown Prince Palaiyas with respect.

'How've you been, you old reprobate?' Mokhat demanded of his friend. 'Did they treat you badly? We're going to have to swap stories of what's been going on while we were separated. But first I have tell you that I've arranged for a boat to pick us up from Kalamaki beach the day after tomorrow, courtesy of Captain Nikmed. You remember him, don't you?'

'Of course! The last time I saw him was when they were putting me on a ship in Tiryns. We passed his ship's mooring and he gave me a curious stare, but we couldn't talk.' Palaiyas led them to some logs that were used as seats, inviting them to sit with him.

'He asked me to say hallo, if we managed to catch up with you,' Mokhat said as he sat down. He patted the seat next to him inviting Ulurra to sit as well. Then Mokhat took a deep breath and continued, 'Now I have some bad news for you that you need to know. It'll affect Tiryns and your whole household; something that has happened to your brother. The morning you were taken, he and I followed you to Mycenae; me to see if I could help, and Amphitryon to talk to the king about his daughter Alkmene.'

'Yes, he told me he was going to go up there to ask for her hand in marriage.' Palaiyas was looking intently down the ravine.

'When we got there, he asked me to wait in the main forecourt outside the *megaron*, while he went inside to talk with the king. A little while later he came rushing out with Alkmene and told me he'd killed the king by accident, and we had to make a run for the gate to get out of Mycenae if we wanted to live. By sheer bravado and luck we managed to get out of the city, then he dashed off to Thebes with Alkmene to seek sanctuary from his uncle; that's what he told me when we parted. I'm telling you this because it is likely to impact badly on your household depending on who succeeds the king of Mycenae. I can't see such an act going unpunished, at least that's my perspective as a member of a royal household.'

Palaiyas was still staring down the ravine, torn between what he'd been told, and what was happening down below. 'Thanks for telling me. I'm going to have to mull this over later. By what I can see, I think we've got trouble from down below.'

Just then a couple of the resistance fighters came running in, shouting loudly in Minoan.

Aranare came over and told them what had happened. 'We're being attacked!' He said urgently. 'The lookouts report there's at least a thousand soldiers down there coming up this way. I'd say they were looking to revenge themselves on us over the ambush we carried out. We must go.'

An elderly stocky man joined them and motioned for them to follow him. Aranare touched two fingers to his forehead in what Palaiyas assumed was a salute and said, 'This is the leader of our resistance and we can't afford to loose him, so his second in command is going to take the two hundred members of our band further up into the mountains, forcing the soldiers to follow them, while we escape. Now quickly, take your stuff and go after him down the ravine. We have this all planned out and we have a safe-hole built for this kind of situation.' The commander led the way and Aranare followed him, as did Mokhat, Palaiyas and

Ulurra, all carrying little sacks with their belongings in them.

They descended the ravine until they could just make out the little dots further down below, strung out in a long line, coming up to where they were. These were the Mycenaean soldiers out searching for them.

The commander led them to the left side of the ravine near a boulder, and without any warning, bent down to the ground and lifted a part of the earth up, at least that's what it seemed like to Palaiyas. In fact he'd lifted a trapdoor covered with grass sods, which made it invisible. There was a rough ladder leading downwards into a box-hole deep underground, and Aranare was the first down it, saying to Mokhat, 'They won't find us down here. We'll wait here until they go past.'

Mokhat was next, then Ulurra, followed by Palaiyas and then the commander, who closed it over himself carefully. At the bottom Mokhat felt his way in the darkness of the elongated hole, clutching at his small sack, until Aranare took him by the free arm and led him to a bench against the earthen wall. They both sat down, and were shortly joined by the others fumbling their way to their seats. They sat in the darkness in silence for a long time, listening for movements from above. Finally they heard a stifled movement from above. It seemed like the heavy hobnailed sandals thumping on the grass sods over the trapdoor—and then they receded, implying that they had passed by. They sat in silence for another lengthy period to allow the soldiers to move well away before Aranare ventured up the rickety ladder to check on what was happening. He shouted down in a whisper, that the soldiers were at the cave. It was safe to come up.

As Palaiyas' head emerged from the hole, he observed in the fading light, in the distance up the ravine, that the soldiers had left the cave, having found it empty, and were now in hot pursuit of the large band of resistance fighters escaping into the high mountains. They would be chasing them all night. They were entirely oblivious of what was occurring behind them.

Mokhat and Ulurra joined Palaiyas sitting on the ground in a circle, their possessions in front of them. They were joined by Aranare and the commander. The commander said something and Aranare translated it as, 'My commander says he will accompany us to the beach. He says that we should make our way in the darkness along the Messara Valley, around Gortys, and then skirt Phaistos, and get to Kalamaki beach around dawn. He would like to know when the ship is expected.'

Mokhat told him that it was supposed to be there just after dawn, and that the timing would be just right.

As Aranare related this to his commander, the old man smiled and nodded his head.

By the time they reached the deserted road at the bottom of the ravine, it was pitch dark and it was a night without a moon. They turned right paralleling the road but staying off of it, travelling on the verge, heading towards Gortys with the hills of the Messara Valley to either side of them.

'We're lucky we have these local guides,' Mokhat whispered to Palaiyas.

'Yes indeed. Fortune has smiled on us for linking us with these Kaptarians. I'd still be in chains without them. My instincts told me they were a good people as soon as I arrived here two years ago. They keep confirming my initial assessment over and over again. We've got all night, so let me tell you how they rescued me this time round. The story of how I was taken to Mycenae, then onto a ship, and then to this island is not worth telling. From Aminiso they had a hundred cavalry escorting me to Phaistos. Can you imagine? A Hundred just for me; mind you, I admit some were replacements for the Phaistos garrison. When we finally reached the road leading to Gortys, we were ambushed by the resistance; over two hundred of them. You saw the place just at the bottom of the ravine.

'These feisty people just erupted from the hedges by the roadside, using slings, arrows, swords, and long hooks to pull the cavalry from their horses. The escort were outnumbered and massacred to the last man. What was strange, to me at least, was that with all the missiles being thrown at us, not one came near me. They seemed to be avoiding me until I managed to work it out. This was all about me—and it was a rescue ambush. That was confirmed when it was all over. I'm sorry so many of our men died in this ambush, but I had no control over any of it. After all, I'm still a Mycenaean, so I regret their deaths. From the locals point, we should never have occupied this island.

'We've been here now some a hundred and fifty years and we've virtually destroyed their once proud civilisation. What that enormous catastrophe of two hundred years ago didn't wreck, we managed to vandalise with our later occupation. You know about the volcano eruption that almost wrecked this island over two hundred years ago, don't you?'

Mokhat shook his head in the darkness as they walked, and then whispered, 'No I don't.'

Ulurra was intently listening to the story that Palaiyas was relating.

'Well, never mind. I'll tell you that some other time. It's part of their folklore. Anyway, now you know why they sent a thousand soldiers to deal with the resistance. Pure vengeance and nothing more; oh, and to teach them a lesson. I'm pretty sure the administration in Knossos will terrorise the local population in Gortys, and probably Phaistos as well. But then the resistance knew what they were getting into with this kind of operation; they've been dealing with us Mycenaeans for over a hundred and fifty years. Well, that's enough about me. What's been happening to you in the last week?'

'Compared to what you've been through, not much. I followed you, and now I'm here walking by your side.' Mokhat was intrigued by the story Palaiyas told, and dejected he hadn't done much to aid in Palaiyas' escape. 'I didn't even have to rescue you as I'd intended. We came over in Nikmed's vessel and the only difficulty was a little bit of rain.'

Ulurra remembered the rain, and having to hide from the downpour. She wouldn't have described it as "a little bit of rain." She remembered more of a short deluge that soaked everything in sight.

'So, do we know what kind of vessel is coming to pick us up?' Palaiyas asked.

'I've no idea what it's going to be,' Mokhat replied. 'Could be a small boat or a large ship. All Nikmed promised was that there would be one on the day appointed. We'll have to trust him to keep to his promise.'

'I've been thinking about our Captain Nikmed,' Palaiyas mused out loud, using Mokhat as a sounding board. 'You told me he was the one that sent you to this tavern landlord, who just happened to be a countryman of his. It sounds to me like he knew the landlord would put you on to where I was. What does all that put together, add up to?'

'That he's involved with the local resistance here? Is that what you're getting at?' Mokhat asked.

'I'm suggesting he's up to his neck in shady dealings of that kind wherever he goes. I'm thinking he's not the simple trader he makes himself out to be. You told me he wasn't surprised when you showed him the Khemet royal seal, and that he admitted he'd done work for them before. So he's part of a spy ring—the only question is whose? Is he working for Ugarit, or is it Khemet?'

'You think he's that deep into it, do you?' Mokhat asked.

'I'm convinced of it,' Palaiyas said sincerely. 'For me the only question is, who is he working for, and can we really trust him?'

'There is one other thing you should know,' Mokhat said earnestly, 'and I should have told you this when you were reintroduced to Ulurra. When I met her in Tiryns, she kept reminding me of someone, and I couldn't put my finger on it. Then when we were coming over to Keftiu on the boat, we got to talking and....here is the surprise, she's Narmus' sister.'

Palaiyas stopped and looked at her, as in shock. 'Strangely, I had the impression—that I somehow knew her, but I dismissed it. Yes! Now I see why she bothered me so much back in Tiryns. I can also see the resemblance. Well I'm stunned, and pleased in a way. Isn't life strange?' He continued walking. Mokhat and Palaiyas hurried to catch up with the three in front. Ulurra hadn't heard the exchange of information between the two friends. Mokhat then told Palaiyas her story of captivity, and his promise to free her. That part of the story Ulurra heard and was pleased to hear it again as a reaffirmation of her coming freedom.

They were walking along the verge of the road coming up to Gortys. They could see the town in the distance and it seemed to be lit up with torches in that dark night.

Aranare said in a whisper to Palaiyas, 'It's started already. The aftermath of the ambush is going to be harsh on the innocent inhabitants.'

'Is that the occupation forces carrying out reprisals?' Palaiyas asked.

'Yes!' Aranare told him. 'They'll go from door to door, pulling one member of the family from each house. If they're lucky, they end up on the slave market, if not, they'll be butchered. For the hundred we killed, they'll take a thousand of ours.' He shrugged his shoulders in the dark. 'We knew what we were doing; we also knew the

317

consequences. If it wasn't for you, Prince, we'd have done something similar anyway, so don't feel too bad about it. It was time we had a go at them, just to let them know we didn't accept their occupation like sheep.'

'I still can't help feeling guilty at this barbarian deed of my people. We're not *all* like that. As a member of a royal house, please accept my sincerest apologies for their atrocious behaviour. I feel ashamed that I'm a Mycenaean.' Palaiyas was deeply affected by what his countrymen were doing to these people.

Ulurra was listening to this with some amazement, hearing a Mycenaean Crown Prince apologise for his own people. This was not the Mycenaeans she knew.

'Sir, this is exactly why we risked our lives to free you,' Aranare said. 'You have the only voice of reason we have ever heard from your royal class. It would be a shame for you to be silenced. We hope that with you free, you will be able to talk some sense into your countrymen.'

'I will certainly try; you have my word on that.'

They continued to go around Gortys and on to Phaistos along the bottom of the Messara Valley using the hedges to stay out of sight. By the time they reached Phaistos, a hint of light was appearing in the east, implying that dawn was nigh. They skirted Phaistos without encountering any problems and came out of the Messara Valley onto a downward sloping path that reached all the way to the sea, according to Aranare. Kalamaki beach was now only a league away and it was all downhill along this twisting path.

As the sun began to rise in the eastern sky, Aranare veered to the right and led the little party off the beaten path, to a small farmhouse that nestled unobtrusively against the downward slope. 'We're going to have a bite to eat with people we trust. I would guess you haven't eaten for a while,' he said over his shoulder.

The commander took the lead to the door, knocked, and opened the door without waiting. There was a startled yell from inside the house, then a few more words followed by laughter. The commander came out again and motioned for the others to come inside.

'Our commander knows these good people, and it is he who invites you to an early breakfast,' Aranare told them.

When the little group of tired travellers had entered, the farmer took one look at Palaiyas and shouted, '*He's a spy!* I know him. I saw him two years ago, here in Phaistos; he's a Mycenaean.' Then he pointed at Mokhat and Ulurra, 'And for all I know, those two are spies as well.'

It took a lot of talk and persuasion from the commander to reassure the farmer that they were not spies. They may be Mycenaeans but they were helping the resistance. These were *good* Mycenaeans, the commander assured the farmer.

Although the farmer seemed to have calmed, he kept looking at Palaiyas, not in a hostile manner, but in amazement that there could be such a thing as a *good* Mycenaean.

Finally they were invited to sit around the kitchen table while the farmer's wife filled their bowls with large helpings of barley porridge from a huge earthenware pot hanging in the fireplace. As they ate, the mood in the little group changed to a more optimistic disposition, suggesting that hunger had been gnawing at the back of their minds for a while. Mokhat and Ulurra had eaten the previous afternoon, but from Palaiyas' appetite, it seemed that he hadn't eaten for some time.

'Did your captors not feed you?' Mokhat asked Palaiyas when they had finished eating.

'They offered, but I refused to take anything from them.' Palaiyas smiled feebly. 'My stubbornness meant I went hungry. My own fault. I was trying to say something to them with my actions, but they weren't listening.'

Aranare reminded them there was a ship waiting for them not too far away and that they should be on the move. Palaiyas went over to hug the old farmer; his way of thanking him for his food. The farmer hugged him back, but kept shaking his head in amazement at this Mycenaean.

After a little while, when they were back on the winding downwards path to Kalamaki, they traversed a gully and after climbing the ridge, they beheld a vast vista that was the sea spread out below them stretching to the distant southern horizon.

'Not long now,' Aranare said excitedly.

Palaiyas and Mokhat both searched the sea for a sight of their ship. The beach was now less than a quarter of a league away and there was a vessel sitting a good distance off shore—but was it their vessel? It was the only one in sight.

'What do you think? Is that our ship?' Mokhat asked Palaiyas.

Ulurra was straining to see the vessel as she walked by their side. Her future seemed tied to her new master and she wondered where he was taking her.

The commander stopped and gazed into the distance, squinting his eyes. He said something to Aranare, who then told Palaiyas, 'The commander says it must be your vessel. It's an *arched* ship from Khemet. Is that what you were expecting?'

Palaiyas shrugged and pointed at Mokhat, 'You'd better ask him; he arranged it.'

When Mokhat discovered what Palaiyas was saying, he said, 'I don't know what we're expecting. I had to leave the choice to someone else.' Mokhat tried to sound apologetic, but failed. He was as excited as a young boy to be leaving this island. He felt he'd been diverted from the task at hand by this abduction of Palaiyas. Hopefully the captain of this vessel could be talked into taking them to Ura so they could continue their search for Satipilli's killer. He felt that a lot of time had been wasted by these diversions.

When they had come nearer to the grey sandy beach, but were still on high ground, the commander halted and said something to Aranare, who translated it to Mokhat as, 'The commander wants you to signal the ship from here—to see if they will answer.'

The puzzled look on Mokhat's face said it all. 'How on earth am I expected to do that from this distance?' Mokhat said incredulously.

The commander pulled out a round piece of bronze from his pouch and handed it to Aranare.

'With this,' Aranare stated and he handed Mokhat the bronze disc.

Mokhat noticed it had been rubbed hard on one side so that it really was a mirror. He understood and was taken aback by the sophistication of the commander's thinking. Mokhat reflected the morning sun at the ship, covering the mirror with his hand so that it gave a three flash signal. He waited and was delighted when the ship flashed back the same signal. By now they could clearly make the ship out because it had closed in to shore, standing a quarter of a league off shore.

The whole group scrambled quickly downwards towards the grey sandy beach. They watched a skiff being lowered from the ship and then making its way towards the shore where they were waiting.

Just before they stepped onto the beach, the commander stopped and said something to Aranare. 'He says there are Mycenaean lookouts operating in this area, and that we're not safe exposing ourselves out in the open until the skiff comes onto the beach itself, and then you three will have to hurry to get on board.'

Suddenly the commander shouted and pointed up the hill to the left. They could see that he was pointing at a group of soldiers running down towards them, their metal glinting in the sun.

Aranare said, 'Quick, you must go to the water's edge and meet the skiff. It might be necessary for you to swim out to the boat to avoid these soldiers. The commander says good luck and asks you not to forget us, but we have to go now before we are caught.' With this, Aranare and the commander disappeared into the bushes edging the shoreline and were gone.

Palaiyas took charge and urged the three of them onto the grey sandy shoreline, towards the water's edge. All three of them were still clutching their little sacks with their personal possessions. The skiff was nearing and so were the soldiers. They could hear them shouting in the distance. An arrow landed near them to emphasise how close the soldiers were. At that point Palaiyas pushed Mokhat further into the cold water and Mokhat grasped Ulurra's hand and pulled her with him. Palaiyas brought up the rear, constantly looking over his shoulder. The skiff was now a short swim away and all three began to swim towards the boat, hampered somewhat by the small sacks, as more arrows landed in the water close by.

The three crew members on the skiff rowed hard towards them, and as the swimmers came close, they pulled Ulurra on board first, followed by Mokhat who managed to swallow a mouthful of seawater and was coughing badly. Palaiyas pulled himself over the side of the skiff into its bottom just as more arrows landed around them. The crew turned the boat and rowed rapidly away from shore trying to get them out of reach of the archers.

# Chapter Thirty Five

The skiff arrived at the large Khemet vessel after some hard rowing by the crew, taking them out of danger from the shore. The little boat bumped the side of the crescent shaped ship and they climbed aboard on the rope ladder that was thrown down to them. When they climbed aboard, they were greeted by the captain, a stocky swarthy fellow with a wide grin on his face.

'Welcome on board,' he said to Ulurra, Mokhat and Palaiyas in broken Mycenaean. 'My name is Mengebet. I've been asked by Captain Nikmed to help you leave this island. I'm told you have something to show me.'

Mokhat looked at Palaiyas and Palaiyas stared back at him in puzzlement. Then Mokhat grasped what the Khemet captain meant. He rummaged in his pouch and pulled out the Khemet royal seal, handing it to Captain Mengebet.

Captain Mengebet stared at it reverentially and handed it back to Mokhat. 'I'm at your service, your royal highness. We will reach Khemet in four days time. In the meantime, make yourselves comfortable. We have reserved three small cabins for you below deck in the stern.'

'Captain!' Palaiyas said forcefully. 'It is important to our mission for us to get to Ura. I must insist that we go there and not to Khemet.'

'I'm sorry; my orders are explicit. They are to return to Khemet before I can go elsewhere. It is more than my commission is worth to disobey those orders. We can go on to Ura from Khemet, but our first port of call is Djanet, which is a little upriver from the mouth of the delta of the great river Iteru. You can get in touch with the Pharaoh's palace from there and have them order me to take you to

Ura. I apologise, but this is not up for discussion, so I would recommend you relax and enjoy your four day voyage.'

Having had his request denied so unequivocally, Palaiyas did as the captain recommended. He put his scanty little wet sack of belongings in the berth at the stern, as did Mokhat and Ulurra, and then settled down to some food and wine with Captain Mengebet. The captain related how he'd been approached by Nikmed and told of the royal seal. With that in mind, he could hardly refuse.

Later in the afternoon, when they'd been on the Big Green for a while, as Captain Mengebet insisted on calling this sea, the three escapees sat themselves near the bow box where the forward lookout was stationed, and reviewed their circumstances. Out of curiosity, and because it would eat up some time, Mokhat and Palaiyas turned their attention on the vessel they were on.

This merchant ship from Khemet looked entirely different from Captain Nikmed's Ugarit ship, or any Mycenaean vessel for that matter. Both Palaiyas and Mokhat made a point of going over it for comparison sake, asking Mengebet for the information. The captain told them it had a crescent shaped hull with the eye of Wadjat painted on its bow to protect it, and the stern was decorated with a carved lotus flower, the royal emblem of Khemet.

There were fifteen rowing oars on either side, used by his crew when the wind was down, and it had two connected oars used as a rudder at the stern. There was a single mast, and on it hung a seven cubit wide horizontal sail. The base of the single mast was embedded in the gangway connecting stern to bow, and it was topped with a bronze finial to which a series of ropes were tied to stern and bow, thus holding the mast rigidly in place.

The ship was ten cubits long and two and a half cubits wide and didn't have a wooden keel like the other vessels from Ugarit or Mycenae, but got its structural strength and stability from a gangway-connecting stern to bow and a

324

huge thick rope fastened under tension at either extremity of the ship. Mengebet told them that this was the way the Khemet shipbuilders had been building their vessels for over a thousand years, and they saw no reason to change the design.

'Now that we've sorted all the business of this vessel out, what are we going to do about getting back to our real objective.' Mokhat sounded peeved at their situation.

Palaiyas was taken aback by Mokhat's tone. 'Let me give you a bit of advice,' he said sharply. 'That which you have *no* control over, you should not concern yourself with, or worry over. Only concern yourself with that which is *within* your control. It's a bit of advice my father passed on to me, and as a friend, I'm passing on to you.'

Mokhat looked at Palaiyas as if he'd been rebuked; which in fact he had been. Disconcertingly, he found that what Palaiyas had just said, made a certain amount of sense.

'I've been abducted,' Palaiyas continued, 'starved and abused. None of this was I able to control or do anything about. We're now on our way to Khemet; well off our intended course, and as you may remember the words of this captain, "he has his orders," and we cannot influence him until we reach Khemet. Mokhat, my dear friend, we will get back on course and discover who it was that killed Satipilli; we may even discover why he was killed in the process, but at the moment, we cannot control where we're going—so relax and enjoy the voyage. Oh! And may I remind you of the voyage out of Millawanda. You seem to have conquered your sea nausea; and that was *within* your control.

Ulurra kept her ears open and her mouth closed as befitting a slave; even though her master had promised to free her in the future. She would believe it when it happened, not before. After ten years of captivity, she was resigned to her fate and had learned to live each day as it came, without looking forward into the future. Now she listened to this banter between friends and found wisdom in Palaiyas' father's words.

Mokhat, on being reminded of his problems with the ship's heaving in the past, suddenly found his stomach giving a lurch, but then he forced his diaphragm down and the nausea subsided. He smiled and said, 'I'm sorry. You're right. I do seem to have got this nausea under control; and you're also right about our mission. We will get to Ura and sort this business out. I want us both to be able to stand in front of King Tudhaliyas, heads held high, and tell him that we have uncovered the reason Satipilli was killed and by whom.

By evening the sea became incredibly rough but the ship managed to corkscrew through the waves, although it was terribly tossed about. The large sail was taken down otherwise the wind would have torn the mast from its fixtures. On advice from their captain, the three passengers retreated to their bunks and stayed there throughout the night; that way at least they were saved from a soaking. The crew used their oars to steer the ship into the warm blustery wind, which was coming from the south.

Sometime in the middle of the night, Mokhat began to feel unwell. He tossed and turned in his small bunk but finally in frustration, he threw his legs out of the bed and swaying, climbed the few steps to the deck. He went to the portside rail and heaved his stomach up over the side. As bad luck would have it, just as he was heaving, a large wave swamped the vessel from the starboard side and threw him into the sea. The two men on the rudder yelled to some of the sailors nearby, and two of them raced to the rail where Mokhat had gone in. They spotted Mokhat floundering not far from the vessel and unheeding of their own safety, dived over the side into the sea. Other sailors rushed to help, grabbing a rope and throwing it over the side for those in the water. This way the two sailors in the sea, with a great deal of struggle, accomplished the difficult task of tying the rope round Mokhat and with a lot of effort from those on board the ship, managed to haul him and themselves back aboard. Mokhat must have swallowed a lot of seawater and lay on the deck seemingly lifeless.

Palaiyas had witnessed the latter part of the rescue, but earlier was slow in following Mokhat, being sound asleep. He barely heard Mokhat pass him, and then had to force himself awake. He followed him, only to be swept against the rail by the same rogue wave that took Mokhat over the side. He joined in when they were hauling on the rope attached to Mokhat and began to pump his chest to get as much of the water out of him as possible when they laid him on the deck. Finally he got Mokhat to heave some of the water out of his stomach, thus proving he was still with them. Then it was a matter of getting him dry and warm.

The two sailors who'd dived in were wrapped in blankets and led away as the captain came to see what all the fuss was about. His chief mate told him the story and Mengebet kept nodding as the details were related to him. He ordered some men to lift Mokhat and take him to his bunk. Ulurra was awake by then and she sat and looked after her master the rest of the night, wiping his forehead, and making sure he was well wrapped up.

By morning the wind had subsided, and the dawn was clear and magnificent; the colours taking the onlooker's breath away. It was a clear crystal sharp dawn such as to be found only at that time of the season when the sun had dipped further south in the sky.

Captain Mengebet had asked for his three passengers to be present when he commended the two sailors, Bari and Mkhai, for their quick thinking and exceptional bravery in diving in to rescue their distinguished passenger. He said he would forward their names to the Pharaoh when they reached Djanet.

Mokhat still felt unwell from his unhappy experience and stayed well away from the unpredictable rail. He stood at Palaiyas' side while the captain commended Bari and Mkhai.

Later that day, the wind picked up again. For the rest of the day and night the weather was atrocious and although there was no full storm, the sea was rough and unpredictable. The three passengers stayed in their bunks for most of the time, occasionally coming out to eat, at least Palaiyas and Ulurra did; Mokhat refused any food and lay miserably in his bed.

On the third day as they neared Africa the climate changed and became calm, and by the fourth day it was simply benign so that when the coast was discerned, the vessel was bathed in glorious sunshine as they approached the great Iteru delta. Palaiyas and Mokhat were joined by Ulurra, gazing at the upcoming land. Mokhat eyed it hungrily, desperate to get off the vessel.

'We'll be ashore soon enough,' joked Palaiyas, as he stared at the looming coastline.

Captain Mengebet came and stood by them. 'We could have had a smoother journey, but the storm was in the lap of Set and when he gets angry, as you saw, he's more of a demon than a god, so I won't apologise on his behalf. We will be docking in Djanet in the afternoon. It is a short passage up the Iteru and you'll find Djanet on the port side. But first we must dock and then I will come with you to the governor's palace and introduce you to him. Do you still want me to take you to Ura?' He looked at Palaiyas for confirmation.

Palaiyas nodded, 'Most certainly. That is where our business lies. We need to get there as soon as possible. If you could send a message to the Pharaoh as soon as we arrive, and give him our greetings and heartfelt thanks for his timely rescue of us from Keftiu, and also ask him to allow you to take us to Ura.'

'I will certainly do that, your highness.' Mengebet stared at his homeland with a longing that was visible to those watching.

'How long have you been away,' Palaiyas asked the captain, not really expecting an answer.

The captain sighed, 'We've been on the Big Green for over two months now. We were in the far west visiting the Sekels on their island, then we went up along the coast to the Rasenna to do some business. Then back down to Keftiu where we picked you up, and back here. I presume I'm safe in telling you all this because of the seal you carry, your highness.'

'I promise, you are safe in telling us.' Palaiyas reassured the captain. He was serious because he perceived that the answer the captain gave was not meant for public knowledge.

They watched the delta loom up and then after some manoeuvring of the two paddled rudder, the ship entered an opening which was the outlet of a substantial river. This was the mouth of the Iteru which flowed from the heart of the continent through Khemet all the way down into this sea. At the mouth of the river the sailors took to their oars because they had to take the ship upriver against the current and they sweated hard to accomplish this. After much time and effort, the ship was finally manoeuvred to the large port of Djanet and tied up on the bustling dockside which was bursting with activity and trade.

Camels, asses, and dockers were moving cargo from the incoming ships and transferring the incoming cargo to large barges for reshipment further to the larger cities upriver. The wharf was extensive and the waterfront long to cope with all the native and foreign vessels. Some of the cargo went into storage in the huge warehouses on the quayside for later delivery. Others were busily bringing outgoing cargo from the warehouses to be stowed onto ships for shipment to distant foreign lands.

# Chapter Thirty Six

Captain Mengebet led the small party down the gangplank into the energetic conurbation, followed by three of his sailors who formed their escort through the city for their security. The short journey led to the outskirts where the governor's palace was situated, and the sentries at the gates saluted the captain through, being familiar with his visits. The entrance of the grand palace opened with a columned portico leading into the enormous vestibule where they found the majordomo, who informed them that the governor was out back in the garden, resting.

They found the elderly corpulent governor under a huge fan that was being wafted by a large slave, trying to cool the governor down as he lay on his couch. The captain deferentially introduced the two foreign princes and Mokhat showed the governor the royal seal. At the sight of that seal, the governor sat up and became overly affable, knowing these two princes had the personal ear of the Pharaoh. He sent one of his aides to get food and drink for the two princes and their servant, Ulurra.

Mengebet told the governor that they only spoke either Hittite or Mycenaean, and that he had to leave immediately to supervise the unloading of his precious cargo. 'The governor says he has various interpreters in his household,' he informed Mokhat and Palaiyas, 'and that I should leave everything up to him.' Mengebet seemed apologetic when he told them this. 'I'm leaving you in his good hands. He also told me that the Pharaoh was up country with his army sorting out some trouble. It may be more like three days before we get a reply from him. These things are out of our hands, and all I can do is urge you to relax and bide your time. I promise you that if the Pharaoh orders me to take you to Ura, we will leave at once. I've asked the governor to send the messages to the Pharaoh and now we will have to be patient and wait for his reply. I'm returning to my ship now but I will see you later this evening.' With that, Captain Mengebet departed.

Ulurra translated for Mokhat what Mengebet had said before he'd left them.

Soon after, a whole retinue of servants arrived with food and drink and it was laid on low tables and more slaves arrived with couches enabling the guests to sit in comfort. In the retinue of new arrivals was a Hittite speaker.

He had a few quick words with the governor, and then this thin elderly member of the governor's entourage introduced himself. 'My name is Menes, your royal highnesses, and I will be happy to be your translator as long as you wish it.'

Mokhat told Menes, 'Thank the governor on our behalf, for his generous hospitality, and we hope we haven't inconvenienced him too much.'

Menes did as requested and the governor waved his hand as if to say, *think nothing of it.* The governor then said something, and Menes translated this as, 'He's happy to have two Hittite princes as his guests, and he will make sure that you are both comfortable while you are under his roof.

Neither Mokhat nor Palaiyas bothered to correct the misconception that they were Hittite princes. It would only complicate matters.

Then the governor spoke to Menes, who translated this for Palaiyas, 'The governor paid out fifty talents of sliver to a Captain Nikmed of Ugarit on your behalf. Was that in keeping with your wishes? He insisted that you had promised him the pay.'

Palaiyas had been told of this by Mokhat and now confirmed that the payment was indeed correct. It was for finding captain Mengebet for them.

After Menes translated this to the governor, it seemed to have satisfied him and he dropped the matter.

By now it was late afternoon and the food kept coming in a stream, out into the garden. It was followed by a group of musicians who played some lively music for those spread out on the couches. The food was delicious and the wine excellent. In this style and surroundings it was difficult not to relax, although Mokhat had that niggling feeling at the back of his mind that they were not doing what they set out to do; but as Palaiyas had told him, the present situation was not under his control.

When the sun had set, a large number of braziers and torches were brought out and the garden was lit up in a most enchanting manner. The stars glittered high in the cobalt sky and the harps and lutes were working overtime to serenade the governor and his guests.

Menes was placed to the right of the governor in between Mokhat, and he leaned over and told Mokhat, 'The governor wishes me to tell you that he has invited a number of the most prominent people of Djanet to a festive dinner tonight to welcome his illustrious guests. We will have this soon in the Banqueting Hall. Ever since Khemet and Hatti signed the peace and mutual cooperation treaty, it is with pleasure that the governor has the opportunity to formally celebrate and share such a settlement with his guests.'

'Sounds like a longwinded bit of smooth talk to me,' Mokhat whispered to Palaiyas.

Palaiyas whispered back, 'I think we would be wise to be careful with this governor so he doesn't get us into something we might regret.'

Just then, captain Mengebet returned and joined them, bringing with him a sense of reality and fresh air.

'I've settled my crew down for the night and offloaded our cargo. I'm now at your disposal,' said Mengebet affably. 'How are you enjoying the governor's hospitality?' Mengebet was still talking in Mycenaean, so only Palaiyas and Ulurra understood. Ulurra had to translate what he said to Mokhat.

'He's laying it on a bit thick, as you can see all around you,' Mokhat complained in jest. 'He's even got some banquet lined up for us later on. Speaking for myself, I could probably do without all this formality. I would much prefer a quiet evening. Do you know if this palace has any kind of a library?'

'But what a library!' said Menes. 'It is one of the finest in Ta-Mehu. Don't be fooled by the governor's appearance. He's as sharp as they come. He's known as a respected scholar amongst the priests of Amun, and that is a high accolade. Better leave it till tomorrow, but I will ask the governor if he would allow you to spend some time in his library if you so wish.'

'I do wish it. It would make the time waiting less heavy. I assume he has Hittite manuscripts?' Mokhat inquired of Menes.

'I'm working on some right now. I will show you tomorrow. I'll just make sure that the governor will allow his guests the use of his library in the morning.' Menes had a quick word with the governor and came back with, 'It would be the governor's pleasure if his guests made themselves at home. He has many Hittite treaties and manuscripts. Tomorrow he will have me show you where the library is.'

Mokhat told Menes to, 'Give the governor my thanks for his generosity.'

This Menes did. Then the governor told Menes to announce that they were all moving to the great banqueting hall, and would the honoured guests be willing to make their way there. The governor rose and led the way; the four honoured guests followed.

The banqueting hall was more like a temple than a place to eat. Slowly over a short period it was filled with the various notables from Djanet. As the multitude arrived, men and women were segregated, unless of course they were married. The seating varied according to their social status, with those of the highest standing sitting on chairs close to the governor, while those slightly lower sat on stools further away, and those of the lowest in rank sat cross-legged on the bare floor at the far end from the governor and his honoured guests.

Prior to the food being served, hand wash basins were provided by the slaves along with a variety of perfumes. Other slaves lit cones of scented fat to spread pleasant smells and to repel the insects. Each notable invited was handed lotus flowers and flower collars as a sign of their coming good fortune.

The governor's aide invoked the goddess Hathor at the outset of the feast and then the slaves began to bring in the dishes. There were considerable quantities of fried fish, roast oxen, lamb, goat, pig, antelope, gazelle, ducks, geese, pigeons, freshly baked bread, fresh vegetables and various fruits. Spices and herbs such as rosemary, cumin, garlic, parsley, cinnamon and mustard, were added for flavour, but these were expensive imports and therefore confined only to the tables near the governor and his wealthy guests. To wash it all down there was an abundant amount of alcohol in the form of wine and beer. For sweets there were cakes baked with dates and sweetened with honey. This was Khemet demonstrating to their foreign guests that Khemet was a land of wealth and plenty, and it was all on display that evening.

Just before the entertainment commenced, four slaves came trooping into the banqueting room carrying a large model of a mummy, a show stopping reminder to the guests of their mortality. Sometime later when all those present had gorged themselves silly, a troupe of professional scantily clad dancing women came in and beguiled the gathering with their exotic performance, accompanied by musicians playing harps, lutes, drums, tambourines, and clappers.

Further entertainment was provided throughout the night by jugglers, clowns, fire eaters and acrobats, and then more musicians and dancers.

It was well past midnight when the three tired guests were eventually shown to their beds in a sumptuous room with a large balcony. Ulurra was in a corner of the huge room with curtains surrounding an artificial cubicle.

Early next morning Palaiyas and Mokhat were woken by a very loud high pitched cry that sounded like a repetitive *lou lou*. They discovered this was coming from the gardens where the governor's peacocks were in splendid throat. Their bedroom with the balcony backed onto the gardens and the weird mewing racket created by these birds made any further sleep out of the question.

Mokhat went out to have a look at the noise mongers and found a male peacock with his beautiful iridescent blue-green coloured plumage strutting about as if he owned the entire estate. His tail feathers had a series of eyes that were stunning when he fanned out his tail.

Breakfast was served in the morning sunshine consisting of hot bread, roast duck and pigeon, dates and a variety of fruit washed down with watered wine or milk. Mokhat backed by Palaiyas, insisted Ulurra be treated as an equal, not as a servant or slave. After all, this was Narmus' sister, and now one of them; a sort of substitute Narmus. She was flattered and somewhat gratified when this was made clear to the governor and his people. She thought it made it more probable that her master would keep his word about freeing her.

After breakfast Mokhat asked to see the library and Menes was sent for. Palaiyas said he'd take Ulurra out into the town to have a look around; see what real life was like, other than in the closeted palace. They would both see him later on at the evening meal.

Menes duly arrived and led Mokhat away to the other side of the palace where the enormous library was housed.

The room with the library had one side completely full of wooden compartments containing rolled papyrus scrolls. Many of the papyrus scrolls were on ordinary wooden shelves placed all around the other walls and some on the two sides of a set of shelves in the middle of the room. It took Mokhat's breath away to see so many manuscripts and he was eager to get at them.

'Your highness, if you will allow me; I will show you what I've been working on for the Hittite king.' Menes took Mokhat to his workbench in a corner of the room and showed him eight manuscripts that he'd translated into Hittite. He picked one out and said, 'This is a very famous piece, well over a thousand years old, from the land of Sumeria called, *The Epic of Gilgamesh*, then from about the same time from Khemet, there is *The Admonitions of Ipuwer*, and from the time of Khufu of the great pyramids, there are two other pieces, *The story of Imhotep*, and *Khufu and the Magician*.' Menes was picking up scroll after scroll showing them to Mokhat. '*The Tale of Sinuhe the Sailor* is around five hundred years old. The story of *The Eloquent Peasant* is set in Henen-nesut, and is around eight hundred years old; and from around the same time there is *The tale of the shipwrecked sailor*. But the oldest story of them all....is from around two thousand years ago, called *The Sebayt of Hardjedef,* which is an instructional tale.'

Menes explained that king Tudhaliyas had asked the Pharaoh to give him a Hittite translation of some of the best epics that the Pharaoh had, which Menes was doing right now, and in return the Hittite king promised to do the same for the Pharaoh with the Hittite epics. It was all to be a part of the cultural exchange which was included in a sub clause in the peace Ishara of Kuruštama between the two empires.

Mokhat was flabbergasted at the amount of new literature he was being offered to read and couldn't wait to get started. Menes left him to go on an errand for the governor and said he would return in the afternoon; in the mean time Mokhat should make himself comfortable on the couch, and if he needed anything to bang the bronze gong on the table and a servant would come running. He didn't tell him how he was to communicate with this servant.

Mokhat began with *The Eloquent Peasant*; a story about a peasant, Khun-Anup, who stumbles upon the property of the noble Rensi, son of Meru, guarded by its harsh overseer, Nemtynakht, set around the city of Henen-nesut. Nemtynakht, was renowned for his misdeeds and tricked the poor Khun-anup into causing damage to his master Meritensa's property by spreading a sheet across some crops near the road beside the farm, then inducing Khun-anup and his donkey to trample over the crops. The donkey then began to eat the grain, whereupon Nemtynakht took custody of the donkey and started to beat Khun-anup, knowing that Rensi would believe the word of his overseer rather than any allegations of trickery and theft from Khun-anup. Needless to say, the story ended badly for Nemtynakht. Being a former priest of Illuyankas, Mokhat read rapidly and was finished with this eloquent fable, now translated so neatly into Hittite.

Next he picked up *The Tale of the Shipwrecked Sailor,* an account of a voyage to the Pharaoh's mines. The papyrus contained the story of a castaway sailor expressing his fears and experiences, the loneliness and the terror of dying in a foreign country. First the sailor tells a tale of a previous voyage of his in which he overcame disaster, including meeting with a god and the king. Then the sailor described how his ship, manned by one hundred and twenty sailors, had sunk in a storm and how he alone had survived and was washed up on an island. There he found shelter and food. While making a burnt offering to the gods, he heard thunder and felt the earth shake and saw a giant serpent approach him. The serpent asked him three times who had brought him to the island. When the sailor could not answer, the serpent took him to where it lived and asked the question three times more. The sailor repeated his story, now saying that he was on a mission for the Pharaoh.

The serpent told him not to fear and that god had let him live and brought him to the island, and that after four months on the island he would be rescued by sailors he knew and would then return home. The serpent then related a tragedy that had happened to him, saying that he had been on the island with seventy-four of his kin plus a daughter, and that a star fell and they went up in flames. The serpent advised the sailor to be brave and to control his heart, and if he did so, he would return to his family.

Mokhat had lost all sense of time as he read these stories. Next he picked out *The Epic of Gilgamesh*. This story revolved around a relationship between Gilgamesh, the ruler of the city of Uruk, and his close companion, Enkidu. Enkidu was a wild man created by the gods as Gilgamesh's equal to distract him from oppressing the citizens of Uruk. Together they undertook dangerous quests that incurred the displeasure of the gods. Firstly, they journeyed to Cedar Mountain to defeat Humbaba, its monstrous guardian. Later they killed the Bull of Heaven that the goddess Ishtar has sent to punish Gilgamesh for spurning her advances. Finally the epic focuses on Gilgamesh's distressed reaction to Enkidu's death, where he embarks on a quest for immortality. Mokhat read of Gilgamesh and his attempts to learn the secret of eternal life by undertaking a long and perilous journey to meet the immortal flood hero, Utnapishtim. In the midst of this quest words are addressed to Gilgamesh which foreshadowed the end of the story: "The life that you are seeking you will never find. When the gods created man they allotted to him death, but life they retained in their own keeping."

Out of the three stories he'd read, Mokhat was most disturbed by this one with its talk of immortality and that anyone should actually make a search for such an elusive concept. It went against nature to seek to live forever. By this time the light had begun to go from the high openings in the library and Mokhat rang the gong. Two servants appeared and he pointed at the lamps on the walls and on the tables. The servants understood immediately and lit them, illuminating the whole vast room. Next he pointed at his mouth and his stomach—and again the servants took his meaning, bringing him food and drink.

Mokhat ate a little before he picked out *The Admonitions of Ipuwer* for his next read. The single papyrus was in the form of a poem with a subtitle; *The Dialogue of Ipuwer and the Lord of All*. In it, Ipuwer describes Khemet as being afflicted by natural disasters and in a state of utter chaos, a topsy-turvy world where the poor had become rich, and the rich were poor, and warfare, famine and death were everywhere. One symptom of this collapse of order was the lament that servants were leaving their servitude and acting rebelliously. It was written in the form of a dialogue between Ipuwer, a noble who was dispossessed by the turmoil, and the Lord of All, meaning the Pharaoh, on the root causes of evil and chaos in their world, and the balance between human and divine responsibility for such chaos. Mokhat enjoyed the stimulation of such a debate.

# Chapter Thirty Seven

When he finished reading *The Admonitions of Ipuwer*, it was getting late and Menes' promise of coming back to see him later in the afternoon hadn't materialised. He heard a muffled movement somewhere near the entrance but it was so insignificant that he ignored it.

He was about to pick up the next papyrus when the entire underworld broke loose around his person. There came a crash behind him and he spun round off his stool, dagger in hand, in time to see a person also with a dagger shaking his head, trying to clear his vision, and what looked like the remains of a vase in fragments on the floor beside him.

Ulurra screeched, *'Watch out! He's trying to kill you.'*

Mokhat didn't need further prompting and took the two paces to the assassin, plunging his dagger into the culprit's stomach, then he pulled it up, ripping the assassin's intestines. The assassin crumpled to the floor in shock, still staring at the dagger in his stomach. Mokhat looked for Ulurra, and saw her near the wall; ten paces away, shaking with anxiety. He went over and engulfed her in his arms.

Almost in tears, she told him, 'Palaiyas sent me to look for you. I saw this odd looking man sneaking around the corridors and followed him to this room. Then I saw you...and he had a knife in his hand. I couldn't warn you earlier because he would have pounced on you. I found a vase and threw it; only then could I shout a warning.' She felt apologetic for not shouting earlier.

'It's all right. You're a brave woman..... and very handy with a vase. You've just saved my life, and for that I'm for ever grateful; both to you, and to Palaiyas for sending you. Narmus saved my life and now *you've* done the same. It must run in the family.' He held her gently in his arms and felt a series of strange emotions welling up inside him.

Servants came rushing in, and seeing the dead body lying there, shouted for the guards. They hurried in swords at the ready, followed by Menes.

'Your highness, what's happened?' He stared at the dead assassin and looked puzzled. 'Who is this man?' he stammered.

Mokhat released Ulurra and turned to stare at Menes. 'Tell the guards that this man lying there tried to kill me, and only my servant's quick reactions here, managed to save my life. Tell them I want to know who he is. Then I want to find the governor and Palaiyas. Is that clear?' Menes' abrupt appearance seemed somehow suspicious to Mokhat.

'Yes your highness,' mumbled Menes, backing out of the room.

Mokhat noted Menes wasn't as shocked as he should have been, but was more puzzled at the scene he found. He followed Menes and found the governor back in his garden with the braziers lit and Palaiyas sitting quietly munching on some roast meat off the bone. Mengebet was tucking into some figs and dates. Mokhat told Palaiyas of the attempt on his life and Menes was made to translate his words to the governor.

Palaiyas told Mengebet in Mycenaean what had occurred, to reinforce his own outrage, and Mengebet looked suitably shocked at this inhospitable act, as did the governor when Menes told him.

'Mengebet?' asked Palaiyas, 'Are there any other Hittite speakers in the governor's household? Could you ask him for me please?'

Mokhat sought Palaiyas' attention and when he'd got it, nodded meaningfully at Menes.

Palaiyas took his meaning and went to stand beside the elderly translator, adding an intimidating note to the situation.

'The governor says there are,' Mengebet replied

Menes said, his voice beginning to tremble. 'Shall I go and fetch them sir?' He said it in Hittite to Mokhat.

'No!' Mokhat replied. 'Tell one of the servants to fetch them all.' Mokhat said this with a strong sense of menace in his voice. 'Palaiyas, tell Mengebet to tell the governor, that this man,' he indicated Menes, 'needs to be taken into custody. I believe he knows something of the attempt on my life.'

'But I *protest*! I swear....I knew nothing of this. Please *believe* me. I'm innocent.' In Hittite, and then in Khemet, 'I've never set eyes on that man you killed before in my life.' Menes was sweating and almost in tears.

'Look at him sweat. That's not the sweat of an innocent,' Mokhat taunted. 'Protest as much as you want, but we will get to the bottom of this affair.'

Mengebet told the governor what Palaiyas had told him and the governor nodded at his guards in the direction of Menes. The guards came and grabbed Menes, locking his arms behind his back, with Menes protesting all the more loudly of his innocence. The guards manhandled Menes, who was screaming in pain, to wherever the guardroom was, removing him as if he were a pile of dung left by the gardeners.

'I fear they may have broken his arms, the way they lifted him,' Mokhat noted to Palaiyas.

'If you're right, it's no more than he deserved,' Palaiyas responded dismissively.

Servants came back and reported to the governor, and Mengebet told this to Palaiyas, that they couldn't find the other two Hittite speakers anywhere in the palace. The governor ordered a search to be initiated throughout the town and the whole Sepat if necessary. Mengebet assured them they would be found. Then he went inside for a chat with the head of palace security.

'What I want to know is,' Mokhat fumed at no one in particular, 'who's behind this assassin? How in the underworld did *they*, whoever they are, know I was in Khemet? First we're assaulted in Hatti, and now here. What in the name of Illuyankas is going on?' Mokhat felt put upon and was venting his frustration at being in the dark about his attacker.

'I could always have a quiet talk with this Menes character, if you get my drift,' offered Palaiyas. 'I managed to outwit that assassin in Ivalanda, remember?'

Ulurra sat, watching and listening, and eyeing Mokhat protectively. Having lost Menes as a translator, Mokhat was again unable to communicate without her help. She would be his voice with the officials here via Mengebet. 'They may not have another Hittite speaker in the palace,' she whispered to Palaiyas, not wishing to interrupt Mokhat, 'but have they a Mycenaean speaker, or are we going to have to rely on captain Mengebet?'

'Good point, my dear,' Palaiyas responded, only half listening to her.

Mengebet came back and waved to Palaiyas to come and join him.

Palaiyas shrugged, stood up and ambled over to the entrance where the captain was waiting.

'I've just come across some intelligence that concerns you directly.' Mengebet looked concerned.

Palaiyas furrowed his brow as if to say, *me, surely not*.

Mengebet continued, 'You are aware that there is a new king in Mycenae?' He waited to see Palaiyas' reaction.

'I heard from Prince Mokhat that there was some trouble in Mycenae. I deduced from what he'd said that a new king would be likely.'

'Elektryon's brother Sthenelus has seized the throne of Mycenae without waiting for the council of nobles to propose him, as they might have done since he was the rightful successor. One of his first acts was to exile your brother Amphitryon for the murder of Elektryon. I'm told that he's dispossessed your family of the throne of Tiryns. He's installed one of his close companions in your father's place. I'm sorry to be the barer of such bad tidings.' Mengebet put out his hand and touched Palaiyas' shoulder in an effort to empathise and comfort him.

'Any news of my family? You clearly have your ear closer to the ground than I have.' Palaiyas felt heavy with the burden of such unwelcome news.

'I'm so sorry…your mother it seems could not stand the trauma and has passed away. Your father has gone to Thebes to be reunited with your brother, and king Kreon has offered him sanctuary.' As Mengebet related this story, his voice dropped into a calm quiet speech to sooth Palaiyas' troubled emotions.

'Anything else?' Palaiyas inquired, hoping to the gods there was no more bad news.

'No, that's it. We've just had a ship dock from Tiryns and the captain rushed this information over to the palace. You have my profound sympathies, your highness. Shall we rejoin the others?' Mengebet led the way back out into the garden to rejoin Mokhat and the governor.

'No longer "your highness," now that my family has lost Tiryns,' said Palaiyas morosely.

A tall, tough, solid looking individual arrived from the direction of where Menes had been taken.

'Ah,' said Mengebet, 'here comes the chief of security. Now maybe we'll find out who this Menes was working for. Take my word for it, he's not someone you want to meet in a dark alley,' Mengebet told Palaiyas.

The new arrival had a lengthy word with the governor, and left the way he came. Then the governor spoke for a while and Mengebet listened attentively.

'The governor has been informed that we've been hosting a Mittani spy ring here in the palace for the past year.' Mengebet looked stunned as he announced this to the three guests. 'Menes has been induced to talk and he's admitted that he takes his orders from Wassukkani. The governor has ordered a purge to root out the entire spy ring. It seems that all the Mittani spies had orders to look out for the two princes and to eliminate them at all costs. Why? He doesn't know. He's admitted there's been a Mittani spy cell operating in Djanet for years, and last year they managed to infiltrate the governor's palace. It's the obvious place to have spies with all the foreign comings and goings of a major Khemet port.' Mengebet stopped at that point, and sat down to ponder on the implications of what they'd found out.

When Ulurra had translated this for Mokhat, he said, 'Well, now we know the *who*...but that still leaves the *why* unanswered?' Mokhat observed. 'I'm still not convinced the Mittani are in this by themselves,' he added. 'Was it the Mittani that had a go at us in Hatti? Somehow I doubt it.' He looked to Palaiyas for help.

Palaiyas was deep in his own thoughts while Mengebet had been talking, dwelling on what had befallen his family. He pulled himself back to the present and turned his attention to the problem at hand. 'Remember what Sflokos said before he died?' He asked Mokhat in Hittite. 'That we should look "closer to home." He suggested we ask Daubum if we wanted to know who killed Satipilli; Daubum is in Ura, which is why we're so desperate to get there. If the Mittani are after us here, then they must be tied into some kind of plot with those in Ura, and with those who were controlling Napat. That surly implicates the Governor of Lukka; you know..., what's his name. What in the name of all the gods have the Mittani to do with Ura? That's what's making all this muddy. With this attempt on Mokhat here by the Mittani, and our troubles in Hatti; there must be a link, but I can't for the life of me see what it could be. We need more pieces of this puzzle to make sense of it.' Palaiyas stopped to take breath while everyone watched with amazement at this long speech in Mycenaean. He was supposedly talking to Mokhat but with all his family troubles on his mind, he'd automatically answered in his native tongue.

Mokhat stood puzzled at what Palaiyas had just said until Ulurra managed to translate it for him.

Mengebet began to translate all that had been said for the governor. When the governor heard all that had been said, he responded, and Mengebet told Palaiyas. 'The governor has a suggestion to make, having heard all you've just told him. Your answers seem definitely to lie in Ura with the Governor of Lukka, Madduwatta. As for the Mittani; it is likely that they are supporting Madduwatta in his mutiny against the Hittite king. If they are, then it would explain their attacks on you. Unfortunately, our governor hasn't got an explanation as to why you should so concern either the Mittani or Madduwatta that they should want to assassinate you so badly. What have you done to annoy either of them?'

Palaiyas looked around at those present. 'Mengebet, I'm about to tell the governor the purpose of our mission. Does anyone here speak Mycenaean apart from us three?'

Mengebet looked carefully at those around him, then shook his head.

Ulurra quickly made sure Mokhat was aware of Palaiyas' move by telling him what was afoot.

'When I tell you what I'm about to tell you, please whisper it into the governor's ear. Don't say it out loud just in case..... Mokhat and I are on a mission for the Hittite king to find out who murdered his chief spy, and more to the point, why. We've been told that our answers lie in Ura, as I've just told you.' Palaiyas stopped and waited for Mengebet to whisper this in the governor's ear, followed by a whispered conversation.

'The governor says that you have your answer. The chief spy found out something that linked the Mittani to Madduwatta. That is what you must determine. What could possibly link the Governor of Lukka to the Mittani?'

Palaiyas tilted his head in thought, and then translated what had been said to Mokhat.

'The only thing that makes any sense is, this Madduwatta wants Mittani help to free himself of Hittite rule,' concluded Mokhat. 'It would suit the Mittani, especially after the bloody nose they got when we had our civil war. They're probably out for revenge—and stirring up trouble *in* Lukka is certainly one way of achieving that. So what did Satipilli find out, that is the real question? Did he have solid proof of Mittani involvement with Lukka? Is that what got him killed?'

Another servant arrived from the direction of where they had taken Menes. He approached the governor, bowed, and told him something; then he left. The governor said something to Mengebet, who then told Palaiyas.

Palaiyas translated for Mokhat, 'It would seem that Menes has just been forwarded to Maat. I'm told that it means he's been brought to account for his misdeeds to the goddess Maat, who weighs his soul when he's passed on. It's a complicated way of saying he's dead.'

'I shan't be loosing any sleep over his demise, I promise you.' Mokhat was dismissive over this traitorous bookworm. 'Do you know, I think Menes must have been lurking outside somewhere, waiting for the assassin to complete his task so he could send a message to the Mittani that their orders had been carried out. Only that way does his sudden appearance make any sense.'

It was late in the night and Palaiyas yawned, prompting Mengebet to suggest they might like to get some sleep. The three guests were led to their room by a servant and they were quickly in their beds and fast asleep.

\*    \*    \*

At breakfast on their third day in Djanet, the governor announced via Mengebet, that word had arrived from the Pharaoh Amenhotep II, who sends his greetings to the two princes, and he confirmed their request that he order Mengebet to take them to Ura.

Mengebet was delighted by the order. 'I told you everything would turn out as you wished. I suggest we sail on the morning tide. My ship is ready and loaded with cargo; I was simply waiting for the Pharaoh's decision.' He seemed relieved to be doing something instead of sitting around waiting for orders.

Palaiyas and Mokhat were delighted with the news and were eager to be off. Ulurra saw it as another step towards her freedom, although she now had mixed feelings about being free of Mokhat. Somehow, saving his life made her feel responsible for him. She was now convinced Mokhat would keep his promise of setting her free in Ivalanda.

'Could you thank the governor for us and assure him that we have nothing but praise for how he's looked after us,' Palaiyas told Mengebet.

Mokhat added, 'Please translate this to Mengebet for me for him to pass on to the governor. With the governor's insight into our problem regarding our mission, he has helped us clarify what we're looking for in Ura. Thank him most kindly for that.'

Ulurra did as Mokhat asked and Mengebet passed this on to the governor. Although the governor seemed nonchalant about the praise, they could see he was highly pleased with the two prince's commendation.

# Chapter Thirty Eight

In the morning breeze, heading out into the Big Green, back on Mengebet's ship, Palaiyas breathed deeply of the fresh sea air. Mokhat, on the other hand, had his teeth clenched with the memory of his previous dip in the sea on the last voyage. He had reluctantly concluded he was not made for this mode of transport.

'It should take two to three days depending on the weather,' Mengebet told them while scrutinising his men on the double rudder.

'Ura, here we come,' Palaiyas said enthusiastically with regard to being back on their intended mission.

'Ahm! Yes, well.' Mengebet was trying to say something but wasn't certain how it would go down. 'There's just one snag. We have to go to Ugarit first.'

Mokhat was left out of this conversation because he didn't understand a word of it; it was all in Mycenaean.

'Ugarit?' burst out Palaiyas. '*Why* Ugarit?'

'I have an urgent message to deliver to King Niqmaddu of Ugarit on behalf of the Pharaoh, and he is the ultimate commander of this ship. I'm sorry, I should have told you earlier, but I've been putting it off.' Mengebet tried to look apologetic. 'We'll stop off there for as short a time as possible; just to dock and hand over the message and then we're out to sea again.'

'You're right of course. The Pharaoh's business must come first on *his* vessel. It would be churlish of me if it were otherwise. Of course we don't mind.' Palaiyas said this as he shrugged his shoulders. He was still behaving like a prince of Tiryns; magnanimous when forced to back down.

'As your friend cannot understand what we're saying, I would kindly ask you to keep a close watch on him at all times. I fear he will not make a good sailor no matter how long he sails on the Big Green.' Mengebet meant this in a kindly way.

Palaiyas nodded in agreement, 'I take your meaning. Although, simply as a friend, I would have done that in any case. Thank you for the reminder.'

'I think I'll go and lie down,' Mokhat told them in a dejected voice. He zigzagged down to his bunk and stayed there for the remainder of their voyage.

'I think it for the best,' murmured Mengebet, watching Mokhat's retreat to safety. 'We'll be going up the Retenu coast, passing Tyre, Sidon, Gebel and Arvid, before coming into Ugarit. If the weather stays fine it should be a delightful experience. I've always liked this part of the coastline.'

*   *   *

On the sunny morning of the third day they sighted Ugarit to starboard. It had been an uneventful journey with fine weather conditions and a benign sea. The wind had been there for the vessel and the oars only came out now that they were heading inland towards the grand port of Ugarit.

Captain Mengebet stood on the foredeck eagerly looking at this familiar foreign port, straining to find a space on the crowded quayside. The two burly sailors on the rudder were doing an excellent job of manoeuvring the ship in conjunction with the ships mate who was shouting detailed directions to the rowers.

Palaiyas and Mokhat, with Ulurra at his side, were standing at the rail looking at the new scenery with anticipation. It was something new to look at after the two days of staring at the ocean. As the Khemet vessel approached the Ugarit dockside they noticed someone on a distant vessel, already docked at a wharf further up, waving frantically at them.

Mengebet spotted the animated individual waving at them and shouted to Palaiyas, 'It seems you may have a warm welcome from someone who instigated your rescue from Keftiu.' He pointed at an individual who resembled Captain Nikmed, walking quickly down the wharf towards where their ship would dock. Their vessel docked and the gangplank was put in place, just in time for Captain Nikmed to stomp on board.

'Well, I never! Blessed to my Rephaim...I thought you were in Khemet.' Nikmed came and embraced Mokhat and Palaiyas, and nodded politely at Ulurra, the servant. 'I had a deadly shock when I recognised this vessel, and then spotted you two at the rails, coming in to *my* harbour. What has brought you to Ugarit—surly not to see *me*?' He chuckled quietly.

Finally, Mokhat had someone whom he could talk to in Hittite. 'And why shouldn't we come to see you? Don't you want to see your old friends?' Mokhat was all smiles.

Palaiyas, still a little peeved at this digression in their journey, got to the point. 'We've really been waylaid by our good captain here,' he stood aside to let Mengebet and Nikmed shake forearms in greeting.

Mengebet said something in Khemetian to Nikmed, of which none of the three other listeners could understand. This prompted Nikmed to yell ashore, which brought an Ugarit officer to the boat. Mengebet pulled out a scroll from a pouch by his side and handed it to the officer.

'There,' he said to Palaiyas, 'it's done. I've delivered the Pharaoh's message. We can set out again whenever you wish.' He stood expectantly, looking at Palaiyas.

'Well what do you say?' Palaiyas asked Mokhat. 'Do we have to go immediately, or can we stay a moment and thank Captain Nikmed here properly, for rescuing us from Keftiu?'

'It would simply be *impolite* NOT to thank Captain Nikmed,' Mokhat exclaimed. 'We should find a tavern and pour a libation in his honour. Tell our Khemet captain we're going to stay for a short while.'

Palaiyas explained to Mengebet that they had an obligation to thank Nikmed properly, and that surely as a fellow captain, he would understand. Mengebet smiled, shrugged his shoulders and nodded to Mokhat.

'So captain, where can we buy you a drink here in Ugarit. After all it's your home port.' Mokhat was in his element, now that he had someone to converse with.

Nikmed led the way off the Khemet vessel, followed by Mokhat, Ulurra, and Palaiyas, while Mengebet brought up the rear.

Nikmed pointed at the far distant hill inland where the bustling city of Ugarit crowned its prominence. 'That is my Arzenu, my land. Earlier today I made an offering in the Grand Temple to Baal the "king," son of El, on your behalf. I was asking Baal to take you under his protection, to ensure your safety. And here you are safely in Ugarit. That surely is no coincidence. I was intending to make another offering to Dagon, the god of fertility and wheat, in case you hadn't made it; to make your journey in the underworld less arduous. Now I see I have no need of doing that.'

'We appreciate the first offering, and are happy you didn't need the second,' responded Mokhat, in a light-hearted mood.

Nikmed led them to a dockside tavern where he was well known. The landlord greeted him like a long lost relation, and for all the group knew, he may have been a relation. A room with a large table was theirs for as long as they needed it, Nikmed told Mokhat and Palaiyas. The best wine was served in a flagon, with a variety of snacks on a number of platters, and as they relaxed they managed to reacquire their land legs.

Nikmed said in Hittite, 'Clearly I don't need to ask if my fellow captain managed to get you safely off of Keftiu since you're sitting here in front of me, looking non the worse for wear. But what brings you to Ugarit? I thought you would be in Ura by now.'

Ulurra translated this for Mengebet, who, for a change, was now unable to understand what was being said.

'Hmm! Sorry, but that may be my fault,' Mengebet said to Nikmed in Mycenaean. I had an urgent message for your king from our Pharaoh, so we had to drop off here. I'm still taking them to Ura on the next tide.'

'Look, my friend,' Nikmed told Mengebet, 'Why don't I save you the bother. My next stop is Ura; I'm going to Ura on business and I can take them there for you. I have cargo to deliver, and cargo to pick up there. I'm sure you have better things to do than ferry our guests around the Big Green.'

Ulurra told Mokhat what was being discussed and Mokhat's ears pricked up. From past experience, he felt far safer on Nikmed's ship than on the Khemet vessel.

'It makes perfect sense to me to use captain Nikmed, since he's heading for Ura anyway.' Mokhat was using his pleading eyes to urge Palaiyas to agree to the switch in boats.

'How do you feel about this, Captain Mengebet?' Palaiyas asked the Khemetian captain. He didn't want to upset him, especially with all the help he'd given them up to that point.

Mengebet smiled, 'I've no objections, especially if you're more comfortable going with Captain Nikmed.'

'Then that's settled,' Nikmed voiced emphatically, closing the subject.

Mengebet said to Palaiyas, 'If I'm not needed anymore, then would you mind if I rushed off. If I go now I can just catch the tide.' He got up from the table and touched Mokhat's hand to get his attention, then waved at him as if he were leaving. He turned to Nikmed and said, 'Good to see you Nikmed; say hallo to the wife for me.' And with that short exchange, he was gone.

'What just happened?' a puzzled Mokhat asked, looking after Mengebet.

'He's rushing off to catch the tide,' Palaiyas told him. 'I assume he's going back to Khemet. I mean there's no point in him hanging around here now we've got Nikmed to take us to Ura.'

'Oh! I suppose you're right,' Mokhat agreed between mouthfuls. 'Try this sausage, it's excellent.'

'So, how have you faired without me?' Nikmed asked Mokhat, seeing he was in such a good mood.

'They had a go at me in Djanet; tried to kill me,' Mokhat replied offhandedly. 'As you can see, they failed.'

Nikmed was shocked at this news. 'Do you know who the culprit was?'

'We've managed to put some of the pieces together. I can tell you that in Djanet it was a Mittani assassin. It would seem that our antagonists in Hatti were to do with Madduwatta, the Governor of Lukka. We're not entirely certain how those two are linked, but it must have something to do with our search for a certain killer we're after. We think the Mittani are stirring up trouble in Lukka to avenge their bloodied nose in our civil war three years ago. They don't want us interfering in their business.'

'Sounds a bit messy, if you ask me; at least it does to a simple cargo ship captain.' Nikmed was trying to be modest, and failing badly at it. Both Mokhat and Palaiyas knew quite well how sharp this simple captain was.

'So, captain, tell us, how have you spent the fifty silver talents you got in Khemet? We heard you collected it from the governor.' Mokhat was in a cajoling mood.

'Now you're talking family business here. One moment I had the talents; next moment the wife had the money. She deals with all the bookkeeping and the finances. I'll be lucky if I see a new shirt for all my troubles.' Nikmed chuckled at Mokhat. He wasn't giving anything away.

'So captain, when do we sail?' asked Palaiyas, impatient to be back on their journey to Ura.

'This afternoon, on the afternoon tide, if that's alright by your highnesses.' Nikmed picked up his goblet of wine and drained it.

Ulurra refilled it for him. She'd been quietly listening to the conversation, and now that they were so close to Hatti, she became homesick and eager to be back in Ivalanda. Once they reached Ura, she was practically home, and the closest to freedom she'd been in the last ten years of captivity.

'We can stay here, eat drink and be merry, or I can take you for a little sightseeing? Which would your highnesses prefer?' Nikmed asked, settling nicely into his seat, almost suggesting the answer.

'Frankly, I'm not bothered either way,' announced Mokhat.

Palaiyas just shrugged and said, 'I've seen far more lands and cities recently than I care for. How about ordering another flagon of that excellent wine and some more nibbles.'

'Good! That settles it. Instead of sightseeing, I'm going to entertain you by relating to you a tale from one of Ugarit's great epics called *The Story of Keret.*'

Mokhat's ears pricked up at the prospect of hearing another epic. He'd got the taste for them in the governor's library in Djanet, and it nearly cost him dearly; still he couldn't resist a good yarn. Now he sat up, in attentiveness, much to Nikmed's delight and encouragement.

'Well,' Nikmed continued, 'This is a tale of misfortune that befell a king of a distant land because he didn't keep a solemn promise he made to a goddess. It is in the manner of the Khemetian tale of *The Sebayt of Hardjedef.*

'King Keret of Khuburu, said to be a son of the great god El himself, was struck with many misfortunes. Although Keret had seven wives, they all either died in childbirth of various diseases or they deserted him, thus it was that Keret had no surviving children. Keret was the only one to survive of eight brothers, and he had no family members to succeed him, so he was watching his dynasty come to an end.

'Keret prayed and lamented his plight. Then in his sleep, the god El appeared to Keret, and he begged El for an heir. El told Keret that he should make war against the kingdom of Udum and demand that the daughter of King Pubala of Udum be given to him as a wife, as a price for peace, refusing any offers of silver and gold.

'Keret followed El's advice and set out for Udum with a great army. Along the way he stopped at a shrine of Athirat, the goddess of the sea, and prayed to her, promising to give her a great tribute in gold and silver if his mission succeeded.

'Keret then lay siege to Udum and eventually prevailed and forced King Pubala to give his daughter, Hariya, to Keret in marriage. Keret and Hariya were married and she bore him two sons and six daughters. However, Keret broke his promise to the goddess Athirat to pay her a gold and silver tribute after his marriage.

'After a number of years, when Keret's children were all grown up, the goddess Athirat grew angry at Keret's broken promise and struck him down with a deadly illness. Keret's family wept and prayed for him but to no avail. His youngest son, Elhu, complained that a man, who was said to be the son of the great god El himself, should not be allowed to die in this manner. Keret asked that only his daughter, Tatmanat, whose passion was the strongest, should be the one to pray to the gods on his behalf. As Tatmanat prayed and wailed, the land first grew dry and barren, but then eventually was watered by a great rain.

'All of this time, the gods had been debating Keret's fate. Upon learning of Keret's broken promise to Athirat, El took Keret's side and said that Keret's vow was unreasonable and that Keret should not be held to it. El then asked if any of the other gods would cure Keret, but none were willing to do so. Then El performed some divine magic himself and created a winged woman, Shatiqtu, with the power to heal Keret. Shatiqtu cooled Keret's fever and cured him of his sickness. In two days Keret recovered and resumed his throne.

'Then Yassub, Keret's oldest son, approached Keret and accused him of being lazy and unworthy of the throne and demanded that Keret abdicate. Keret grew angry and cast a terrible curse on Yassub, asking Horonu, the master of demons, to smash Yassub's skull.

'Thus it was that Keret, over time, lost all of his children in one way or another, with much help from the malevolence of Athirat—all except for one daughter, Tatmanat, who became his sole heir.' Nikmed was finished and sat back, waiting for a reaction.

Palaiyas was puzzled as to why Nikmed chose to tell them such a pointless tale. Ulurra, on the other hand was enthralled by the story and had thoroughly enjoyed it.

'Hmm! Interesting,' said Mokhat thoughtfully. 'It's true we've had a bit of misfortune in this mission, but I can assure you, none of it was down to any impropriety, or us reneging on anything whatsoever.' Mokhat had immediately caught the symbolism implied in the tale, and was at pains to reassure Nikmed that they were blameless. He'd determined earlier, when Nikmed told them of his offerings to Baal on their behalf, that he had a credulous streak in him, and this tale reinforced that assessment. Nikmed was using this story to ask if the two princes had offended the gods in anyway.

'I'm glad to hear that. I just thought I'd ask. Well, I think it's probably time to get back to the ship or we'll loose the tide.' Nikmed got up and went over to the tavern landlord and had a quiet chat with him.

Palaiyas caught up with Nikmed. 'Ask him how much I owe him?'

Nikmed shook his head, 'I'm afraid your money isn't any good in here. I've told him I'll roast him alive if he accepts a shekel from you.' Nikmed smiled mischievously.

Palaiyas was about to get angry at being so outwitted, but then thought better of it. After all, without the captain's ship, they'd be stuck in Ugarit. 'Have it your way, but when we get to Ura the drinks are on me, and no arguments.'

Nikmed spread his hands, as if to say; *me argue? Wouldn't think of it.*

When they climbed aboard Nikmed's ship, the familiarity made them feel immediately at home. Even the eye painted on either side of the high prow felt reassuring.

Mokhat had been wondering about this eye business and finally asked Nikmed, 'Why do you have an eye painted on your ship? Mengebet explained that his eye of Wadjat protects the vessel from danger and also wards off any evil spirits. It is a symbol of protection, royal power and good health. But you're not Khemetian, so what does your eye represent?'

'Nikmed smiled at the question, 'I was wondering when one of you would get round to asking me that. All my passengers ask me the same question. I have the same reply for all of them. The name Wadjat comes from 'wadj,' meaning 'green' which is why they call him 'the green one' and it means the 'risen one'; it is taken from the image of a cobra rising up in protection. We have a great respect for the ancient Khemetian civilisation. We have traded with them for well over a thousand years, and it came from them.

We liked what we saw and copied it. I hope that it doesn't shock you too much.

'Now, before we sail, I have an obligation to perform. On behalf of my ship and as a duty to my sailors, before each journey, I must make an offering and say some prayers to Baal Zaphon, in the expectation of a safe and profitable journey.'

# Chapter Thirty Nine

'On the port side over there, is the island of Alasiya,' Nikmed pointed out to Mokhat and Palaiyas. 'It is the source of much copper, without which you would not have your swords and daggers. I sometimes stop off at Enkomi, its capital. I have a lot of friends there. Sadly we must bypass Enkomi this time.' He sighed deeply, suggesting he had someone on the island he would have liked to visit.

This was the morning of the second day out from Ugarit. The journey was scheduled to last two to three days, depending on the weather and sea conditions, Nikmed had informed them. So far the conditions had been good and the sea had behaved itself; at least Mokhat thought so. He'd had some more of that *ziggiberis* root that Nikmed had fed him the first time round, and it had worked its miracle yet again. Ulurra kept looking to starboard, seeking the coastline. They'd passed Kizzuwatna yesterday and now were moving up the Hittite coastline. She felt happy and seemed to mentally free herself of those years as a slave, bound to someone else's servitude.

'How long do you think it will be before we manage to reach Ivalanda?' she asked Mokhat quietly.

He understood she had been nursing those thoughts ever since he'd told her she'd be free once they reached Ivalanda. Gently he said, 'If we reach Ura tomorrow, we may need a couple of days to finish what we set out to do; that should put us back in Ivalanda in about a weeks time. Bear in mind this time schedule assumes nothing happens to delay us. Be patient—you will get there, I promise.' In reassurance, he put his right arm around her shoulder, and she didn't resist.

Palaiyas had been chatting with Nikmed, but now wandered over to Mokhat, and as he approached, Mokhat removed his hand from her shoulder.

'The captain says we're doing good time with the wind being exceptionally kind to us.' He'd seen Mokhat remove his arm and decided to ignore it, but noted the possible implications.

'That's good. That should put us in Ura by tomorrow at the latest.' Mokhat looked up at the full sail. 'I assume we'll play it by ear when we get there. We're going to have to be careful since we'll be in the lion's den. If Daubum has any power there and he spots us, we're dead—you know that?'

'You're right of course,' Palaiyas agreed. 'I think it might be worth considering a disguise of some sort.'

'How about we resurrect the priestly garbs,' suggested Mokhat. 'That way most of our faces and bodies will be covered. Ulurra can act as our handmaiden. She's going to have to have shredded clothing if she's to be that poor. A little mud on her face, and such should do it. What do you think?'

'Say no more, I'm thoroughly convinced. I can see it already,' chuckled Palaiyas.

\*   \*   \*

In the middle of the afternoon they were sitting out on the deck, eating their midday meal on one of the covered cargo hatches, when a lookout suddenly shouted that he'd sighted a number of sail to starboard. Nikmed dropped his food and rushed off to have a look.

'Can't be that serious, surely, that he had to drop his food,' joked Palaiyas.

Nikmed shouted various instructions at his crew, which had the steersmen trying to manoeuvre the ship away from the oncoming vessels. He came back to them looking somewhat worried. 'If I'm right, we may have a big problem.'

'Why, what's the matter man. It's only some ships out on business,' Mokhat suggested.

'Yes, and *we're* their business.' Nikmed was frowning. 'If I'm right; those are pirates. They'll be after my cargo—and my ship. This area is notorious for pirates. Frankly, I should have taken a wider route round this part of the coast. You'd better make sure you have your swords at the ready. We'll make a run for it; usually I can outrun them, but this time I've spotted an unusually large vessel amongst them, and that my be our biggest headache. I swear on my Rephaim, I don't know where they got it from. They shouldn't have anything that big.'

As the afternoon progressed, the big pirate ship seemed to gain on Nikmed's vessel. No matter what he did, the other matched his course and upped a notch on his speed. Soon, the large pirate ship was close enough for them to see the grinning crew on its deck. They were making visual signs at Nikmed's vessel; using their daggers in a slicing motion at their own throats and then pointing at Nikmed's vessel. Clearly they were intent on slitting the crew's throats.

All fifteen crew members on Nikmed's vessel had armed themselves with sword and dagger, getting ready for the encounter. That it was now coming, of that there was little doubt. Ulurra was clutching Mokhat's arm with fear. He was trying to shield her behind him. After some more futile attempts to outrun them, finally the pirate vessel bumped Nikmed's ship and grappling ropes were thrown to pull them together. Nikmed's crew hacked off the ropes only to have more thrown aboard.

Arrows began arriving and took their toll on Nikmed's sailors. Some of the missiles narrowly missed Mokhat and Palaiyas, but tragically a large needle shaped bronze spike thrown by one of the attackers imbedded itself in Nikmed's chest. He fell to the deck looking shocked at being hit. Mokhat knelt by his side trying to help him, but it had struck near his heart and Nikmed lay there, a final plea in his eyes, before he died.

When the pirates jumped aboard, Palaiyas began the fight of his life. No matter how many he managed to put away, more came to replace their fallen comrades. Ultimately, he didn't stand a chance. They jumped on him and wrestled him to the deck, tying him up. Mokhat put up a valiant struggle but was hampered by trying to protect Ulurra. He was soon overpowered by sheer numbers and trussed up with his arms and legs securely tied; as was Ulurra.

Nikmed's death had dispirited the crew but they put up one serious fight, sending a sizable number of pirates to the underworld before they were finally overpowered.

After the battle, only five of the crew remained alive, trussed up like Palaiyas, Mokhat and Ulurra, that included the poor old cook. Eight prisoners lay piled on the deck as if they were bundles of rags.

The pirate chief was a burly fellow with jet black hair and bedecked in gold ornaments. He had gold round his neck, in his ears, on his fingers and on his wrists. He towered above the pile of prisoners, swaggering up and down on the deck. Then he called the pirates together with a loud shout. 'Well lads, what shall we do with these merchants? Shall we feed them to the fishes?'

Palaiyas shouted at the chief, 'Touch a hair on my body and you will have to answer to the King of the Hittites.'

'*What have we here; a loud mouth*?' the pirate chieftain boomed at the prisoners.

Mokhat joined in loudly with, 'Not only King Tudhaliyas, but Pharaoh Amenhotep of Khemet will send a fleet after you to seek vengeance for abusing his envoys. You'll be hunted down like the dogs you are. Take heed before you make a serious mistake.' Despite being tied up, a part of Mokhat was overjoyed that the pirates were all Hittite speakers. He actually understood what the people were saying again.

What stopped the pirate chief in his tracks was hearing the names of Tudhaliyas and Amenhotep being used by these two prisoners. He watched them lying there while he scratched his head, then scratched his beard, then shook his head and laughed out loud. 'Well I never. You're either serious, or you have the balls of a demon. I know you can fight, but are you being devious or just plain stupid?'

'Take me seriously, you big oaf. I am Prince Palaiyas of Tiryns and beside me is Prince Mokhat of the Kaska. Harm us and all the underworld will erupt in your face. The Hittite King will send a fleet to hunt you down, as will the Pharaoh.'

The big chieftain shook his head as if to clear it. Then he shouted at his men, 'Pick those two up, let me have a good look at them. If they're princes, they should look like princes. If their rogues, I'll soon tell the difference.'

Hands grabbed Palaiyas and Mokhat and roughly stood them up. Palaiyas glared at the chieftain, almost with disdain. Mokhat held his head up high in defiance.

'Cut their bonds,' commanded the chief. 'Let's see what they have to say for themselves.'

Puzzled but compliant, the pirates did as their chief commanded. Clearly they were terrified of him and jumped to obey his orders.

Palaiyas rubbed his wrists to regain his circulation, then walked over slowly to where the chieftain stood. He looked him in the eyes and said, 'You seem to have some sense after all. I made no false claims as to what would happen to you had you carried out your threat to throw us overboard. We are envoys of the Hittite King on a secret mission on his behalf. Mokhat, come and show this oaf the royal seals.'

Mokhat walked over to stand beside Palaiyas and removed the royal seals from his pouch round his neck. He showed them in the palm of his hand to the pirate chief.

The chief picked one up and squinted at it, 'Well I'll be; you're certainly full of surprises, aren't you.' He put that one down and picked up the next one and peered at it closely. He bawled out loud to his cronies, 'I'm sorry lads, these two stay. We might turn a good profit on their ransom. The rest you can have,' he indicated the other prisoners with a wave of his hand.

'Not so fast,' Palaiyas interrupted. 'That woman down there is his personal aide,' he motioned at Mokhat, 'and we require her to complete our mission. She stays! If you need a ransom for her, then so be it; but she's only worth money as long as she's intact, if you get my meaning.'

'So be it,' declared the pirate chief loudly. 'Take these three aboard my vessel. We'll take them back to Bastiniya with us. We'll send out the ransom demand in the usual way.' He turned and began to inspect Nikmed's vessel. Just then, the rest of the pirate fleet caught up with them and more pirates clambered aboard.

The dead were thrown overboard, as were the four live unfortunates of the crew, their hands still tied behind their backs. They kept the cook so he could work for them. 'No sense in wasting such a talent,' the pirate chief had exclaimed.

Palaiyas, Mokhat and Ulurra were taken on board the large pirate ship, and they were surprised to find it was a former Mycenaean vessel. They spent some time below deck lamenting Captain Nikmed's sudden and untimely demise. Then they felt an embarrassing relief that they had survived while he had not. It was Palaiyas who finally reminded them that all this was out of their control, and that settled the matter.

It was well into the night before the pirate fleet docked in the small port of Bastiniya, welcomed by a hoard of townspeople holding torches, looking for spoils of the day's takings.

The big pirate chief led a procession away from the quayside, heading up a hill to a small mansion just outside of town, which he'd appropriated when the pirates moved into the small port. Inside the reception room the pirate chief made himself comfortable slouching on a large couch that was one of many spread in a circle. This is where he entertained his *guests*. The chief settled himself and invited Palaiyas and Mokhat to use the other empty couches. Ulurra was sent to the kitchens.

'Might as well make yourselves comfortable while you wait for the ransom to be paid. From my experience, it could be a long wait.' He yelled at one of the servants cowering near the door to fetch some food and drink.

Palaiyas thought he might as well try to make use of the situation. 'Can I ask you a question. Do you know anybody called Daubum?'

That got the chief's attention. 'Daubum? What do you know of Daubum? How is it you've heard of him?' The chief was glaring at Palaiyas as if he wanted to do him some mischief.

'He's the reason we were on that ship you hijacked. We were going to Ura to have a chat with this Daubum. So what do you know of him? We're all grown up; you can tell us.' Palaiyas was goading the chief into revealing the information.

'He's pure scum, and nasty with it. If you think I'm bad you haven't met Daubum—or have you?' The chief almost spat those words out.

Palaiyas raised his eyebrows. 'No we haven't met him —but we're certainly going to. We need some answers from him, whether he likes it or not. So who is this *nasty* fellow?'

'He's Madduwatta's chief spy.' Again the chief was spitting out the words. 'He's the reason we're here and not in Ura. That's where we were before this shitbag threw us out with his tricks and diversions. He stirred up the town's population against us and made us believe that an army of Ahhiyawan soldiers were due to arrive any moment; that he'd made friends with the Ahhiyawan king and invited them to come and *cleanse* the town of *pirates*. There's a cunning demon for you if there ever was one. Fool that I was, I believed him. If I ever get my hands on him, he'll plead for me to kill him.' Pure hate and anger were plainly visible on the chief's face. 'You still haven't told me what *you* want with him.'

'As I explained to you earlier, we're on a mission for the King of Hatti and we need some answers to our questions from this Daubum.' Palaiyas was weary of giving out too much information.

'What kind of questions? Who knows, I might even have the answers. Try me!' The chief was curious and cajoling.

'You might as well tell him,' Mokhat advised. 'We're so close, and he really might have something more to tell us. This is the first time we've come across anybody who knows him that well.'

'Well..., all right....I'll give it a shot. Have you heard of someone called Satipilli?' Palaiyas waited, certain the chief wouldn't know the Hittite spy chief.

'Hmm! You are swimming in muddy waters now. You know Satipilli's *dead* don't you?' The pirate grinned roguishly. 'Some weeks back.'

Both Palaiyas and Mokhat were shocked to hear this pirate's grasp of what was happening in the outside world.

'We should do; we found him outside Ivalanda with Sflokos' dagger in his chest.'

Now the pirate's eyebrows were raised in surprise. '*You* found him?' He stopped and began to scratch his beard, then switched to stroking it. 'This whole situation is beginning to get more curiouser and curiouser. So what's this got to do with you searching for Daubum? You still haven't answered my first question.'

Mokhat intervened, 'We believe Daubum had something to do with Satipilli's murder. He might even have ordered it. We want to know if he did—and why? And so does the king in Hattusas. He's the one who sent us to find out the truth of the matter. So do you have something to add to this or not; or were you just bragging?'

Again the pirate stroked his beard in thought. 'I heard something to the effect that Satipilli had been incarcerated in Ura's deepest dungeon. Then he went missing....until he turned up dead. It doesn't take much brains to connect Daubum with Satipilli's death. Him and that northern lout he uses as his main tool and sidekick.'

Mokhat screwed up his face, 'You don't mean Napat, do you?'

'I'm beginning to think someone sent you to me.' The chief was getting jittery. 'How come you know his name?'

Mokhat smiled, 'We've both been followed by that hoodlum ever since we left Hattusas. We've only just recently put the pieces of the story together. I've managed to kick his arse the last time we met, which was outside of Ivalanda.'

'It certainly is a most peculiar coincidence that's brought us together like this. You weren't sent by Daubum to attack our ship were you?' Palaiyas asked, trying to counter the pirate's suspicion.

'If I had been,' said the chief angrily, 'both of you would be dead by now—you surely must see that?'

'Yes, I suppose so. But as you're suspicious of us, so we're somewhat suspicious of you. Let's compromise instead and call both our suspicions *a coincidence*, alright?' Mokhat paused for a moment to gather his thoughts. Then he said, 'Look, this may sound weird but I've a suggestion for you; well more of a proposition. Why don't *you* take us to Ura and let us finish our job?' Mokhat took a wild chance that this might just come off. 'That way we'll get rid of Daubum for you. That's what you want isn't it?'

That got the chief stroking his beard more earnestly than ever before. 'How do I know you'll do that? I've only just met you and I've only your word for what you've told me. What assurance do I have you'll keep to your end of the bargain?'

Palaiyas was getting impatient with the way this was going. 'How do we know *this* or *that*? We could keep going round in circles like this until next year. You'll have to trust us, that's all. Remember, you grabbed us, not the other way round.'

'All right, *your highness*, keep you hair on. I'm just weighing up the pros and cons of the next move.' The chief seemed to have settled down and gave signs of having come to a decision. 'I'll do as you ask. I'll take you to Ura, but I'm coming all the way with you. I want to be there when we nab Daubum. It's my way or no way at all, am I clear? Do you agree? And if there's any killing to do; I'm the one doing it.'

Mokhat sighed with relief. 'As long as we get the answers to the questions we have for him. Then you can have him; he's all yours.'

'Agreed!' Boomed the pirate chieftain. 'We'll forget the ransom then.' He chuckled, 'I must say, this is the first time that my prisoners have really turned into proper guests. But then there's a first time for everything, don't you think?'

'Let's seal this bargain with a toast,' Palaiyas suggested. He raised his goblet, 'Daubum! Good riddance to bad rubbish,' was his toast.

'Good riddance to bad rubbish,' responded Mokhat.

'Good riddance to bad rubbish,' said the pirate chieftain.

Then they all drained their goblets and had the servants refill them.

# Chapter Forty

The seven pirate ships set out around noon the next day, stuffed full with armed ruffians, intending to lay off Ura just as the sun set in the west. They would make a night approach which would give them maximum surprise. A night attack with twelve hundred armed pirates would cause panic and no one in Ura would expect the pirates to be bold enough to attack such a large port.

The pirate chieftain was relying on Madduwatta's overconfidence as part of his strategy. Mokhat and Palaiyas had both donned their disguises, but they were not that of priests—instead, they dressed up as pirates and so became invisible, and it was more likely that they would avoid being targeted by other pirates if they were dressed like them.

The chief pirate was going into known territory for him; he knew Ura as well as anyone could. One of the reasons he'd agreed to this venture was that it was a homecoming for him. He considered Madduwatta the usurper, the one who had taken his home port away from him. This was payback time and he was looking forward to it.

Under the cover of darkness, the ships sailed into Ura quietly and docked at an almost empty quayside.

'Something's not right here!' Exclaimed the pirate leader. 'This dock is usually overflowing with ships so that people have to fight to get a berth on the dock.'

On the quayside people were running around shouting, seemingly in some kind of a panic.

'You're right,' agreed Palaiyas. 'What in the name of all the gods is going on? They haven't even noticed that we've arrived.'

'Ulurra,' Mokhat took hold of her wrist, 'I want you to stay on the ship. This could get brutal and I want you out of harms way.' Mokhat told her this in as commanding a voice as he could muster. 'I will come back and get you when we've finished this business. I won't leave you, I promise.'

As the pirates began to disembark from their vessels, people came and stared at them, *in hope*. They thought this was a rescue mission instead of an attack on the town. The chieftain grabbed a couple of the townspeople and demanded to know what the panic was all about.

'It seems we've come at an inconvenient time,' the chieftain grimaced as he told Palaiyas. 'The Ahhiyawan army is *really* at the western gates of the town this time. The governor has seriously upset their king and he's here to teach Madduwatta some manners. Now what do we do?' He asked the two princes becoming somewhat hesitant. For the second time those damned Ahhiyawans were making him doubt his plan would work.

'We continue with the plan,' replied Mokhat with resolution. 'It may work in our favour. I suggest you keep around a thousand of your men here near the ships, ready to make a run for it, and bring two hundred with us while we search for Daubum, if he hasn't fled already. While we're here we might as well look for him; see if we can squeeze some answers out of him.'

The chief agreed and they went inland, up into the town proper. Cautiously they crept along the streets, aware of people piling their belonging onto carts and heading north and east, fleeing from the oncoming destruction of an invading army. As they entered the main square, they grabbed another of the townspeople and asked him if he knew what had happened to the governor.

They were told Madduwatta was heading northwards out of town with his family and the remnants of the entire administration, running for it towards Ivalanda. Some of his army were acting as a rearguard. Some of his thugs were still out in the town settling scores with the townspeople who'd opposed the governor.

They even spotted a group of thugs on the other side of the square beating up a helpless victim.

'Hey! Look over there,' whispered Palaiyas, 'Isn't that Napat...I'm sure it's him. There's about ten of them, but that big lug sticks out like a sore thumb.'

'By all that's holy, your right!' agreed Mokhat. 'Quick send some men round either side of the square. We'll have him if we're quick.'

The pirate chief gave the order and fifty men went to the left, and fifty to the right, trying to encircle the gang that had left a number of corpses lying in the square. The rest waited until the encirclement was almost complete, and then they headed straight for Napat's gang.

As soon as Napat realised that a large group of armed men were coming towards him, he broke off and tried to make a run for it, but he was caught by those that had circled round him to cut him off. He fought like a man crazed, but was overwhelmed by sheer numbers and was soon tied up, just as the pirate chief reached him. Palaiyas and Mokhat were only a few steps behind; they stared at Napat—and he stared back at them. Slowly, it dawned on him that these two pirates were in fact the men he'd been sent to follow and kill.

Napat kept shaking his head as if his eyes were deceiving him. '*No...no...no.*' He kept repeating the same word over and over, in utter disbelief.

'Where's Daubum,' demanded the pirate chief. 'Come on you piece of shit, speak or I'll cut your tongue out.'

'No...it can't be. Not here...not here.' Napat said over and over—but his eyes looked up the hill towards a house, then back at Mokhat, and he shook his head again almost in despair.

'That's good enough for me,' said the pirate chief. 'I know where he's looking—and I know why he's looking up there. It's where the gang's hideout is. Daubum is holed up in his little hideaway up there; he uses that building as his headquarters. You six, take this scum back to my ship, I'll deal with him later, after I've got his boss.'

The pirate chieftain led the group of pirates up the street to the house he'd mentioned; the house Napat had been looking at. They went through the gate and into the garden. There they met more ruffians who attempted to stop them. It was desperate, but they had to fight their way inside the house against a determined gang of men who seemed intent on defending the place. Others tried to block their entrance at every turn. It was fortunate there were a sufficient number of pirates to deal with them. They found Daubum hiding in the cellar—inside a clothing box under some sheets. They only found him because the pirates wrecked the whole place looking for him. They tore the building apart and only by breaking every stick of furniture did they stumble on Daubum. One pirate was hammering on the clothing box with a chair and only stopped when he heard noises coming from inside. Once they flushed him from his hiding place, it was only Palaiyas' shouting that stopped the pirate chief from killing him there and then.

'*You promised me that I would be able to question him,*' yelled Palaiyas at the pirate chief.

Reluctantly, the chief sheathed his dagger and had Daubum tied to a chair, then moving to the other side of the cellar and sitting down; he watched carefully at what would happen next.

Mokhat walked round the bound spy chief sizing him up. 'Finally I get to meet the scum that thinks he can kill me with impunity.' Mokhat slapped Daubum hard on both cheeks, causing some blood to flow.

Palaiyas stood in front of Daubum watching and smiling, making sure that Daubum knew his game was ended. More light was lit in the cellar so they had a clear look at Daubum's eyes. If he was going to lie, they wanted to be able to see the lie coming out.

Despite Mokhat hitting him, Daubum was watching Palaiyas, not Mokhat. He'd assessed that Palaiyas was the dangerous one.

Mokhat went over to have a quiet chat with the seated pirate chief. He whispered something to him, and then nodded to Palaiyas.

Palaiyas now took over. 'As you can see, your attempts on our lives failed miserably and have in fact rebounded on you. The answers you give me will determine whether you live or die—they will also determine how much pain you suffer. It's all down to you.' Palaiyas watched Daubum like a hawk. Every little squirm, every blink of the eyes, every twitch or movement even though he was trussed up tight.

'What do you want to know,' Daubum said sullenly, clearly not too eager to cooperate.

'Why did you try to kill us? Why did you kill Satipilli? Who ordered you to do all this? I want the answers in that order, and may the gods help you if you lie to me.' Palaiyas had removed his dagger from his sheath.

Mokhat thought Palaiyas was as angry as he'd ever seen him. He came back to stand by Palaiyas' side, watched Palaiyas use his dagger to stroke Daubum's chin…not too gently, just to remind the him of what he'd said.

'Who said I tried to kill you?' Daubum said with a sneer.

Palaiyas made a cut down Daubum's cheek, 'Ups, sorry the knife slipped,' he said grimly. 'Play games with me and you'll end up in slices while you're still alive, begging for me to kill you. I'm sure you know how it goes.'

Daubum said reluctantly, 'I was trying to deter you from pursuing your mission. Had you turned back I would have left you alone.'

'That's better.' Palaiyas stared hard at the spy chief.

'Who's your contact in Hattusas?' Mokhat demanded.

'As for Satipilli, he found out that Artatama was helping my boss.' He'd ignored Mokhat's previous question and gave the answer he wanted to.

Palaiyas persisted now he had this spy chief talking. 'What did he find out exactly?'

'Satipilli had intercepted a Mittani courier and got hold of his written instructions for Madduwatta. The governor wanted that back; I got it back for him.' He was almost smug when he told Palaiyas that.

'What did you do with the "instructions"?' Palaiyas had cut Daubum on the other cheek for being smug.

'I destroyed it of course. What, you think I should have kept it for you?' That wise crack cost Daubum another cut.

'Keep a civil tongue in your head. You're talking to a prince, not one of your riffraff. So who got to kill Satipilli? I assume you didn't dirty your hands?' Palaiyas was now stroking Daubum's chest with his knife.

'He died in the dungeon, here in Ura—I stuck a dagger in his chest to divert suspicion. Then had him dumped where you would find him, still trying to put you off going any further.'

'Clearly you don't know us.' Palaiyas scoffed.

'Clearly,' repeated Daubum. 'As for who ordered me to do all this; it must be evident, surely. I take my orders from my boss—the Governor of Lukka.' There was that arrogant tone again. That cost him some more cuts. Palaiyas knew Daubum was a living corpse. The pirate chief had made that clear at the outset. He had to squeeze as much information out of him before he handed him over to the pirate.

'Why did Madduwatta seek help from the Mittani?' That was still not answered to Palaiyas' satisfaction.

'Who knows? He's a megalomaniac. He's power hungry—Madduwatta wants to be a king. He's obsessed with his grandiose plans to become royalty. Artatama was only too happy to send him aid. He's really angry at Hattusas for chasing him all the way back home during the war. As for Madduwatta, right now he's running for his life. If you hurry you can catch up with him—in Ivalanda.' Daubum grinned mischievously.

'You're a slow learner,' said Palaiyas as he cut him some more. 'If you don't control yourself, you'll end up in shreds.'

There was quite a bit of blood covering Daubum from all the cuts and Mokhat looked away at this butchery, not because he felt nauseous, but it was just unpleasant. Killing was one thing; torture was quite another. He knew this had to be done because the next item on the agenda was Daubum's death by the pirate chief. He'd whispered in the pirate's ear that Palaiyas would definitely leave Daubum to him—but that he had to make Daubum believe that he might survive if he cooperated.

Palaiyas stood up taking a pace back from stooping over Daubum and nodded at the pirate chief.

Daubum suddenly understood he'd been given a false promise, and began to struggle on the chair, tipping himself over onto the cellar floor. He'd realised that he was being toyed with and that the pirate chief was ultimately in charge of his fate—and that could only end up one way. He struggled on the ground until he was exhausted, then lay still.

The pirate chief came and stood over him. 'So, you smart arse, you thought you could make a fool out of me and get away with it, did you?' He motioned for his fellow pirates to untie Daubum from the chair and lift him up. 'I'm going to take you back to Bastiniya with me. I want to have a long chat with you. Mind you, unlike my friend here, I can't promise you anything.' He looked at his chief mate and said, 'I'm putting this cur in your charge. If you lose him I'll skin you alive. Stick to him like tar, or you'll regret it.'

With this the large party of pirates that were left after the fight for the house, now made their way into the street and were intent on heading back down to the dock.

Palaiyas stopped and said to the pirate chief, 'You have what you wanted, as I said you would. Our bargain is kept—agreed?'

'Agreed,' replied the pirate chief.

'We'll come back to the ship with you to collect the woman,' Mokhat said, 'and then we're heading off north to Ivalanda. We need to hurry before the Ahhiyawans arrive.'

At that point, yet another bunch of pirates arrived at a run, looking for their chief.

One of them came and told him, 'Boss, that big fellow's escaped. And we've lost her as well. We've been looking for them both all over the place but we can't find them.' The man was clearly afraid of what might happen. 'She ran off, now we don't know where she is.'

'What are you babbling about?' demanded the chief.

'The big fellow you sent down to the ship—he burst free and laid into some of our men, then he ran off. And that woman that was with them,' they pointed at Mokhat and Palaiyas. 'She's gone. Jumped ship and ran off as well.'

Mokhat intervened gruffly on hearing this. '*You lost her*? What do you mean? She's running around in this chaotic town, is that what you're saying? How long ago?'

'About an hour ago,' replied the pirate, looking in fear at his boss. He was right to be afraid because his boss was fuming.

The pirate chief grabbed the one that had told him of these disasters, picked him up by the scruff of the neck and threw him on the ground, then he roared his frustration out loudly.

Mokhat was looking around wildly, 'We must find her. She'll get herself killed,' he complained to Palaiyas.

'Nice to have met you chief, and thanks for your help, but we have to find this woman,' Palaiyas said to the pirate.

The chief didn't even notice; the pirates were off dragging the trussed up Daubum after them, back down to their ships, following their scowling boss, while Mokhat and Palaiyas went back down in the direction of the town square looking for Ulurra.

Palaiyas was ahead, walking down a side street, mulling over what Daubum had revealed. He'd watched the pirates scurrying off downhill towards their ships while Mokhat was walking behind him, when suddenly there was an almighty woman's scream from behind them.

'*Your highness...!*' Mokhat heard, and swivelled around to where the scream came from just in time to see two men creeping up on him with swords raised. He parried the nearest would-be killer's thrust, and lunged at the second would-be killer, plunging his dagger in the throat of the second man as that man's sword thrust past him. Palaiyas had turned and swiftly ran back in time to finish the first would-be killer who was just turning to have another go at Mokhat.

'By the gods, that was close,' breathed Mokhat. Then he saw who had screamed at them. Mokhat spotted Ulurra standing in a doorway not three cubits away, crying.

Palaiyas held back, looking at the would-be assassins, while Mokhat rushed over to where she was standing and engulfed her in his arms. 'There, there, it's alright. We've dealt with them—but that's the second time you've saved my life. I really am going to have to do something about that,' he whispered in her ear.

She sobbed on his shoulder, more out of fright than anything. 'I...I...I came looking for you. I thought you'd gone off without me. I'm sorry; I got such a fright when I saw those two about to kill you.'

Palaiyas walked up calmly. 'We were just looking for you,' he said to Ulurra with concern as Mokhat released her from his arms. 'Anyhow, we must hurry and make a move or we'll get caught by my Ahhiyawan friends, and after Sflokos, we won't be safe with them.'

'Yes, you're right,' replied Mokhat. 'Come Ulurra, we have to head up north....to Ivalanda.' He noted the surprise that came upon Ulurra's tearful face. 'Any chance of finding any horses?' he asked Palaiyas.

'All the horse will have been taken by those fleeing from town. No! We'll have to walk.' Palaiyas moved quickly, sword at the ready, walking up the street northwards.

# Chapter Forty One

**P**alaiyas spotted the silhouette of a group of soldiers on the northern outskirts of Ura, sitting on their horses by the side of the road, watching the exodus of the population from the town.

'Shh!' Palaiyas grabbed Mokhat and pulled Ulurra down near the ground by their clothing. 'See those,' he pointed at the soldiers. 'Mokhat, can you recognise their uniforms? I can't make them out it's so dark.'

Mokhat crept closer, then stood up and hailed them, 'Where's your officer?' he shouted at them.

Palaiyas understood they couldn't be Ahhiyawans, either that, or Mokhat had gone insane. He stood and brought Ulurra upright, then both joined Mokhat.

The soldiers looked down at the two pirates with a woman, and unsheathed their swords. 'Advance closer but without your weapons so we can see you better,' said one of them, seemingly in authority.

There was a moment of silence, then, 'Is that you Onasiyas?' asked Mokhat in a surprised voice.

The soldier on the horse looked down not recognising who had called him by his name. 'Do I know you?' he inquired doubtfully, peering down at the pirate.

'You should!' replied Mokhat. 'Is your friend Feliyas with you? Got anymore assassins for us?'

That had the man on the horse startled. 'Is that you, your highness?' Captain Onasiyas dismounted and walked forward to look at Mokhat more closely. 'Well bless my soul, it *is* you. I wouldn't have recognised you in that pirate outfit. Is Prince Palaiyas with you?' he asked eagerly after his fellow Mycenaean.

'Here I am,' said Palaiyas, joining Mokhat, followed by Ulurra. 'Good to see you again. It's been a long time.'

'Not really! Its only been a month, surely,' said Onasiyas. Then he remembered his duty, 'What are you doing here? Don't you know this is a war zone?'

That brought out a loud chuckle from Mokhat and a loud laugh from Palaiyas.

'Don't we just know it. Why do you think we're running from it?' Palaiyas said, still grinning widely. 'I must say, it's a stroke of luck us finding you here. We thought we'd have to walk back to Ivalanda.'

'The whole garrison is down here, but we're heavily outnumbered.' Onasiyas turned and led his horse and them back to his mounted troops. 'Attarsiyas has his whole army with him. We've sent for reinforcements but they won't be here for at least two weeks. From our scouts, we've just had a report he's entered Ura. It won't be long before we have to make a run for it. I only have orders to skirmish with them. Brigadier Mekiner is waiting further up the road with the main force. He's going to try and deter them going further into Hittite territory.'

'What about Madduwatta? Did he come through here?' asked Mokhat.

'Yes, a while ago,' scoffed Onasiyas. 'Him and his whole retinue; wives, family, hangers on and the like. He's asking General Tipali for sanctuary. He's pleading innocence—he's done nothing, so he claims, to warrant this attack by his neighbour. From the reports General Tipali's received in the last three weeks, he's not so sure.'

'I've got more for him on Madduwatta. He's a complete scoundrel. We've finally managed to complete our mission, and Madduwatta is at the bottom of it all. I have a few choice bits for General Tipali, I can tell you,' Mokhat said in disgust.

'I think the general has something for you too, your highness. He was going to send it on to Hattusas, but since

383

he'll be seeing you soon, he'll probably give it to you personally. It concerns Satipilli. We've found some documents amongst the ex-governor's belongings. He's just confided the short version with a few chosen officers from the intelligence unit. I'll let him fill you in on the whole sorry tale.'

Mokhat was intrigued. What more could be added to the information they already had? Surely they had the whole story now.

Onasiyas sent one of his troopers to round up three horses for the new arrivals. There were always a few spare horses with any outfit just in case one of the troop's horses became lame or got injured. The spare horses arrived and Mokhat was pleased to be mounted after all that walking.

Palaiyas shrugged and climbed on his mount, as did Ulurra on her mount. Onasiyas eyed her but said nothing. If they wanted to, they would tell him who she was, otherwise what these royals got up to was none of his business.

'I'm going to send you up the road with one of my men, up to the brigadier. He'll know what to do. When all this is over and we're back in Ivalanda, we'll have to have a drink to your safe return, if you think that's suitable, your highnesses.' Onasiyas wanted to hear their story but didn't want to be too pushy by asking out right. He was hoping they would tell him over some wine. How come the two princes were dressed as pirates? He was dying to know.

'You can count on it,' responded Palaiyas.

'Include me in,' said Mokhat.

One of Onasiyas' troopers had detached from the main group and was waving for Mokhat and Palaiyas to join him. The three mounted riders swung their horses round to go along with the soldier who was already cantering down the road towards where the brigadier had stationed himself.

On arrival at the brigadier's camp, Palaiyas estimated the brigadier had around four thousand men under his command, and Onasiyas had said they were heavily outnumbered by the enemy. It all seemed extremely bad news for the Hittites. Thanks to the antics of a self delusional governor, the country was at war with its neighbour.

'Ah there you are, you bunch of scoundrels...' shouted the tall heavily built brigadier, then stopping and staring at the new arrivals. 'Don't I know you?' He asked Mokhat, who was still dressed in his pirates outfit.

'Yes, brigadier. We met about a month ago in Ivalanda. I'm Prince Mokhat and that's Prince Palaiyas,' Mokhat said pointing at his friend.

'What on earth are you doing dressed like a pair of pirates? Where have you been? I thought you were supposed to be in Millawanda.' The brigadier beamed at them as if they were long lost relatives. 'Mind you, with what's going on there you're lucky you're not in Millawanda, eh?'

'I'm sorry brigadier, but we need to get to Ivalanda as soon as possible,' Palaiyas said, coming straight to the point. 'We have to talk with your general. He seems to have something for us. Then we need to get back to Hattusas and report to the king on what we've discovered. Any ideas?'

'Right!' The brigadier grasped that these two were in a hurry—on the king's business. 'I'll give you an escort of twenty men. That should keep you out of trouble. Do you want to start right now or will the morning do?'

Palaiyas looked at Mokhat questioningly. 'What do you think? Shall we start immediately or can this wait till morning?'

'What? Are you out of your mind? Of course it can wait. Look at her, she's almost asleep on her feet.' He meant Ulurra.

'It can wait till morning,' announced Palaiyas. 'Any food? We could do with a bite to eat; we've been travelling all night.'

The brigadier clapped his hands and a couple of soldiers peered through the tent flaps. 'Get some food and drink. Oh, and make sure there's a free tent for our guests for the night.' He turned back to his guests. 'So, your highnesses, where have you been? Are you able to tell me?'

After some food and drink, Mokhat and Palaiyas told the brigadier the short version of their travels, and as the story unfolded, the brigadier's mouth slowly opened in astonishment.

'You've been to Khemet?' he said with his eyebrows raised. 'And to Keftiu? All since I last saw you?' He had trouble taking such a journey in. Finally he said, 'I'm not a sailor and I prefer to keep my feet on dry land.' It was said with conviction.

Mokhat nodded in agreement, understanding those sentiments perfectly. 'If we may now, we'd like to turn in. it's been a long day.'

Palaiyas, Mokhat, and Ulurra, all stood to take their leave of the brigadier.

During what was left of the night, just as dawn was breaking, a huge commotion broke out in the army camp. Orders were being shouted, horses were neighing in protest, and all the ruckus and yelling woke Palaiyas, Mokhat and Ulurra. The trio had barely dropped off into their slumbers.

Onasiyas popped his head into their tent and shouted, 'We have to move, the Ahhiyawans are upon us. Grab your swords, you may need them. Oh! And good morning.' He grinned at them and was gone.

The camp had been dismantled and everything loaded on wagons. Cooks were handing out cold rations as fast as they could. The officers were mustering their men into battle order, facing south, and the wagons were already rolling to the back, heading further up north leaving the cavalry to hold the line.

Onasiyas found them and said, 'The brigadier has ordered me to escort you back to Ivalanda. Are you ready to move?'

Palaiyas, Mokhat, and Ulurra, were all mounted and Mokhat nodded at Onasiyas. 'Lead on, captain,' Mokhat shouted.

The small column of twenty cavalry led by Onasiyas spurred their horses out of the former camp and headed north in a hurry. It took them a day's hard riding to reach the city of Ivalanda. There were clear signs of preparation for war even as they approached the city in the dusk. Patrols were numerous and cavalry exercises were in full swing, even this late in the day. The place was swarming with soldiers, and more were arriving all the time from the east. Chariots were practicing their battle drills. The area all around was lit up with many torches throwing an eerie light on the snow filled landscape.

Over to one side there was a group of elaborate colourful tents set up with a lot of civilians standing watching the army drills. A lot of loud noise was coming from the biggest tent.

'My guess is that's Madduwatta's entourage,' Onasiyas pointed them out to Mokhat and Palaiyas. 'Seems like Tipali's locked him out of the city. At least, I hope he has.'

They arrived at the main gates where jittery guards stopped the column even after the sentries had recognised the captain. Orders were orders. No one was allowed through the gate without challenge.

As the column passed through the gates, Mokhat turned to Ulurra and said gently, 'I hereby fulfil my promise —I set you free. You are now a free woman, Ulurra. Do as you will.' And that was that, and Ulurra just sat on her horse looking dumbstruck, letting the horse follow the rest of the horses.

After dismounting at the former governor's mansion, the trio were led by Onasiyas to the upstairs room where General Tipali and his staff were pouring over the map of the border region. Ulurra was in a bit of a daze, still sticking with Mokhat as if he'd not said what he'd said.

General Tipali looked with outright contempt at the two pirates entering the room and was just about to yell for the guards when he stopped himself. 'Is that *you*, prince Mokhat?' He squinted at Mokhat and then relaxed. He looked at Palaiyas and smiled. 'This won't do...no...this won't do at all.' He turned to one of his aides and told him to fetch a couple of uniforms from the stores. 'You can't walk around dressed as pirates, your highnesses, you really can't. You'll get yourselves into trouble...and who would blame a soldier for running through a couple of pirates, heh?' He smiled broadly and came over to shake their forearms. 'Glad you came. I was just about to send something meant for you, to Hattusas.' He turned to his staff and said, 'We'll resume this briefing in the morning. Full vigilance throughout the whole night, gentlemen. Double guards and full strength patrols out to the south and west. I don't want any surprises from the enemy.' Then he turned to his second in command, 'Send colonel Haliya down to reinforce brigadier Mekiner at the southern border. I want those invaders stopped before they get into Hatti proper. Do that right now, don't wait for the morning.' Tipali returned his attention to Mokhat and Palaiyas. 'Now, your highnesses, I'd like to show you something we found hidden amongst the former governor's possessions.' He led the way out to the next room.

The aide who'd been sent to fetch the uniforms returned. He held one out to Mokhat and in the other hand, to Palaiyas. They were the uniforms of full colonels in the Hittite army. They fitted both the princes as if they were made for them.

'That's better,' Tipali announced once he'd seen them properly dressed. 'Take those pirate outfits and burn them,' he ordered the same aide who'd brought the uniforms in.

'Now, if you wouldn't mind,' he walked over to a side table and held out a package for Mokhat. 'It's addressed to captain Narmus.'

On hearing her brother's name, Ulurra fainted.

'What's got into her,' Tipali demanded, irritated.

'She's Narmus' sister. It's all just got too much for her.' Mokhat couldn't entirely explain without going into a long story. Ulurra was probably under enormous strain after getting the long sought freedom he'd promised her.

'By the way, where is Narmus?' Tipali asked. 'I thought he went with you.'

'I'm sorry, general, Colonel Narmus died in the line of duty about three weeks ago,' Palaiyas told Tipali, leaving Mokhat free to deal with Ulurra. 'If I may, I'll take that,' and Palaiyas held out his hand for the package Tipali was still holding.

The package was heavy and contained a number of clay tablets. Palaiyas had Tipali read them for him. The first one instructed Narmus to take the tablets to the king in Hattusas with haste and in secrecy. The others explained that Satipilli had intercepted a Mittani courier who was carrying detailed instructions to Madduwatta on what he had to do to earn all the gold that had been sent to him from Wassukkani. The latter was in the form of a Khemet like scroll written on papyrus. It was signed by Artatama, crown prince of Mittani.

'Thank the gods and bless Satipilli for his forethought, may he rest easy in the underworld,' exclaimed Palaiyas. 'Mokhat, this is exactly what we needed to back up our verbal report.' Palaiyas was searching for Mokhat and found him at the back of the room, with Ulurra lying on a couch. He was talking tenderly to her, and Palaiyas smiled and shook his head. 'I knew this was coming,' he said to a puzzled Tipali.

'What was coming?' Tipali asked.

'I think Prince Mokhat has found himself another partner.' Palaiyas said this tenderly as to a close friend, without regret.

General Tipali looked at Mokhat and smiled. 'Good for him. She's Narmus' sister, you say? How is it she's with you two then?'

Palaiyas told Tipali a shortened version of what had happened to them since they last saw each other. When the general heard of Sflokos' death, he grinned with pleasure, and thanked Palaiyas for doing the Hittite army a big favour.

Mokhat led Ulurra over to Palaiyas and said, 'Since we're close friends, I think you should be the first to know. I've asked Ulurra to be my wife—and she's condescended to take on an old reprobate like me under her wing. When we get back to Nerik, there will be a royal wedding to which you are cordially invited—and no excuses.'

Ulurra stood there blushing, looking radiant. 'Freed and trapped again, all in one day,' she joked, 'and I wouldn't have it any other way,' she said to Palaiyas.

Palaiyas smiled, 'I knew this was coming, you lucky old man. My sincerest congratulations—and of course I'll come. I wouldn't miss it for the world.'

'Well let me be the second one to congratulate you, Prince Mokhat,' put in Tipali. 'May your problems be all little ones,' and he winked at Mokhat and patted Ulurra's wrist in a fatherly manner.

\*　　\*　　\*

For three days Mokhat escorted Ulurra around Ivalanda as she looked for the remnants of her broken family. She found a distant cousin and that was all, even with all of the enormous help that the local administration was ordered to give her.

On the morning of the fourth day they had decided to depart for Hattusas when Tipali's aide found them at breakfast. 'The general sends his compliments and asks that you join him in the war room, upstairs.'

Mokhat and Palaiyas left Ulurra to finish her food and hurried upstairs to Tipali. They found the general standing with a fat man who was looking around him in a perturbed manner. There was another military man standing abreast of the fat one.

'Ah! Prince Mokhat and Prince Palaiyas. Good of you to join us.' Tipali was formal and quietly fuming. 'You may not have met our erstwhile Governor of Lukka here, but I'm aware you've heard of him.'

At that Madduwatta shuffled nervously.

Mokhat stared daggers at the cause of all the recent chaos.

Palaiyas didn't even bother to look at him. 'If I were the king,' he said regally, 'I would have this scoundrel publicly flogged and then executed in the main square here.'

Madduwatta mouth opened in shock at these words. 'I protest. How dare this man talk to a governor like this. Who does he think he is?' He pulled his stomach in and lifted his head as if he was the injured party.

'This is *Prince* Palaiyas....and that outranks a mere governor any day; and I'm afraid my sympathies lie with him,' Tipali told the fat governor. 'However, it would seem the king has other ideas.' Tipali spoke to Mokhat and Palaiyas. 'A dispatch has just arrived from Hattusas.' He was handed a clay tablet by his aide. 'They must have broken a record to get this to me. I must first tell you that Governor Madduwatta has sent a plea to King Tudhaliyas for sanctuary for himself, his wives, and children, and for his retinue of followers and remaining troops, and for permission to travel to Purushanda to get away from Attarsiyas' vindictive pursuit of him. He sent the message as soon as he came under attack. This is the king's reply.' Tipali read:

"You were under an oath of the god to stay in Lukka and govern it for the benefit of My Sun, yet you sought war with Arzawa, your neighbour to the north and upset, Ahhiyawa, your neighbour to the west. It was thus that your neighbour to the west chased you out of Lukka along with your wives, your children, your troops, and your chariotry.

"It is with a great deal of reluctance that My Sun is going to save you from the blade of Attarsiyas. My Sun will offer you sanctuary outside the gates of Ivalanda to save you, Madduwatta, along with your wives, your children, your household servants, and along with your troops and chariots. My Sun is prepared to give you grain, and seed in heaps, to sustain you. He is prepared to give you beer and wine, malt, rennet, and cheese in heaps, to sustain you. My Sun will save you from hunger. If he does not, dogs would have devoured you from hunger. Even if you had escaped from Attarsiyas, you would have died from hunger.

"Know this, Madduwatta, that you are now deeply in debt to My Sun, and he expects you to behave in a manner expected of a true vassal. Fail this expectation and your life will be forfeit."

Tipali finished reading, and looked daggers at Madduwatta. 'You, former Governor of Lukka, are to stay where you are until further notice. If there is the slightest trouble from your camp, I will have the lot of you thrown into our dungeons. Have I made myself clear?' He stared at Madduwatta for confirmation that he had understood.

Madduwatta's Chief of Staff, General Vasanitti, nodded quietly his assent, and only then did Madduwatta follow with a mumbled, 'Yes.'

# Chapter Forty Two

$T$he three riders with their fifty soldier escort rode into sight of Hattusas on the morning of the fifth day, to the sight of the tall thick grey walls that fortified the twin hills on which it stood. It had taken five days since leaving Ivalanda to get them this far. As the little column approached the open southern crest of the hill, the sentries atop the crenulated ramparts shouted down to their counterparts below that riders were approaching from the west.

The riders cantered along the access road that swung sharply into a lane set between the two flanking bastion towers, leading to the southern Sphinx Gate. The arched gateway led into the tunnel built into the wall, and through into the Upper Town, and the riders were soon through it trotting along the cobbles streets of Hattusas. They were armed with the answers the king had commissioned them to obtain more than a month ago.

Now that they were in Hattusas, both Mokhat and Palaiyas heaved a deep sigh of relief. It had taken them well over a month to get at the answer to Satipilli's murder and they'd travelled nearly the whole of the known world to achieve that. But they had got to the bottom of *who* and *why* he was killed. They even had Satipilli's own written proof to show the king. Now it was merely a matter of getting to the castle to report their findings.

As the column rode through the streets, Palaiyas said, 'I must go and see Mahera…and my child. I can't put it off any longer. I'll bring them to the castle as we agreed, and then they come to Nerik with us.' He waved and rode off to find his long suffering wife.

The small column of soldiers continued along the main thoroughfare of the Upper City that crossed from east to west, heading towards the familiar narrow corbelled arches of the citadel gates, still flanked by the portal sculptures. Through the arches into the lower paved courtyard and to the official access to the Upper Palace proper. Their escort had halted at the stables while Mokhat and Ulurra continued to the palace entrance. They dismounted and servants rushed to take their horses back down to the stables.

'It's strange but comforting coming here,' Mokhat said to Ulurra. 'I feel that after all I've seen, I'm finally coming back to reality.'

Ulurra squeezed his hand in reassurance. Ever since leaving Ivalanda, she had put her trust in this man she was to marry, and was now bound to him and this new adventure.

At the top of the main staircase the servant held the door open and the king's chamberlain waited inside to welcome them and take them to the royal reception room.

'Welcome! Come inside out of the cold. The king waits impatiently up in the antechamber. He's most keen to see you

'It's good to be back again.' Mokhat and Ulurra followed the elderly chamberlain up the wide stairs to a private room behind the throne room. Ranks of bronze torch-holders lit their way.

They found Tudhaliyas sitting at his table, pouring over some wax tablets, quietly reading. He lifted his head and saw Mokhat behind the chamberlain and rose to his feet. 'I'm happy to see you, Prince. It's been a while. I hope you have some answers for me. I'm informed you do. Warm yourselves by the fire.'

'Your majesty,' Mokhat responded, 'may I introduce my fiancée, Ulurra from Ivalanda. As soon as we get to Nerik I will make her my wife.'

Ulurra bowed her head as low as custom demanded and stayed silent.

'I'm to congratulate you then. Good for you—and about time you made that commitment. We all have to sooner or later. And where's Prince Palaiyas?' Tudhaliyas asked smiling.

'He sends his apologies and requests I make the report as if he were present. He's not seen *his* family here in Hattusas for some time and is collecting them to take them to Nerik with us.' Mokhat tried to look apologetic.

'Never mind. Now sit and tell me what have you found out? Let me see, it must be about fifty days since I last saw you.' He motioned to some chairs and watched as Mokhat and Ulurra settled themselves. Then he sent his servants to fetch some wine and goblets.

'Your majesty, you are already aware that Madduwatta was planning a rebellion against you?' Mokhat waited to see how much the king knew already.

'Yes, and I'll deal with that scoundrel in my own way, but you can be sure he will get his just deserts, I promise you.' Tudhaliyas sat back to listen.

'Your majesty, Satipilli died at the hands of Madduwatta, urged on by Artatama. It may not have been by Madduwatta's hand directly, but he was the culprit as surely as if he'd stabbed him himself. Behind Madduwatta was Artatama of the Mittani, who was seeking revenge for what he perceived was his humiliating defeat at the Battle of the Wide Plateau. Satipilli had intercepted a Mittani courier who was carrying instructions to Madduwatta of what they wanted him to do to earn the gold they had paid him. Satipilli's tablets relating what had occurred were found amongst the possessions of the former governor of Ivalanda. This is what got him killed. I have the Mittani scroll here for you to use against the Mittani when they deny causing you mischief.'

'So you're saying *the **Mittani*** were ultimately behind Satipilli's death? My chief spy was killed by the machinations of that scoundrel in Wassukkani?' Tudhaliyas was fuming. 'This is intolerable. I will have to find a way of *teaching* them a lesson. I can't have that young *rascal* Artatama causing me trouble this way.'

'So, sire, you now have the *who*, and the *why* of your chief spy's death. That was our given mission—and I ask you —have we *fulfilled* it?' Mokhat knew they had, but did the king agree?

Tudhaliyas sat for a moment while he contemplated his answer. 'Yes, I think you have. In *full*, and you and Palaiyas have my admiration and gratitude. I knew I could count on you. You two seem to have a knack for this kind of commission. I hope the task was not too arduous?'

Mokhat's mind suddenly flipped back to thoughts of the storm and the Khemet vessel; and him being thrown into the sea to drown. He shuddered silently and replied, 'Arduous, *no* sire, not *too* arduous. I'm sure Prince Palaiyas would agree with me.' He smiled graciously. 'I now have one final task to perform.' Mokhat pulled out the pouch from round his neck and removed a pair of royal pottery seals. 'I return these seals with thanks—they have proven to be of great service and I am grateful for the forethought in allowing us to use them.' Mokhat handed them back to the king. 'And please give my fond regards to Queen Nikal on both our behalves.'

The servants had brought in the goblets of wine and now filled them.

'I give you a toast, and an official thank you for completing a difficult assignment.' Tudhaliyas stood and lifted his goblet, as did Mokhat and Ulurra. They downed the wine and sat back down.

'I assume you could do with some food.' The king waved his hand for servants to bring forth food.

# Epilogue

It was another week before Mokhat set foot in Nerik and embraced his brother Kasalliwa, the king of the Kaska. He introduced Ulurra to the king, and his older brother was overjoyed at the prospect of a royal wedding and a new sister-in-law. Coincidentally, as if they were somehow in cahoots, Kasalliwa repeated Tudiliyas' words that it was high time Mokhat made that commitment and settled down to producing an heir.

Palaiyas had finally come to his senses and brought his family back with him to Nerik and made a solemn vow not to leave them again. Mahera took to Ulurra as if they were long lost sisters and they found they had much in common. Ulurra dotted on Mahera's daughter and tended to spoil her. Both were kind-hearted women who'd had endured difficult lives and had tied their destinies to well meaning adventurers.

End

# Murder in Hattusas

## Sasha Garrydeb

Murder in Hattusas is the 1st Volume of the Hittite Trilogy.

At the close of the Old Kingdom in 1420 BC, the realm of the ancient Hittite Empire is in chaos. Muwatallis, the king has been assassinated in the capital, Hattusas, by the feared Kaska Assassin's Guild. Muwas, the dead king's brother blames the two sons of the previous king, Huzziyas, and he insists he be the one to succeed his brother. The two sons of Huzziyas, Kantuzzili and Himuili, insist the next king be Tudhaliyas, son of Himuili, since rewarding Muwatallis' previous assassination of Huzziyas, is unthinkable. Neither side is prepared to give way, and the scene is set for civil war. Tagrama, the High Priest of the temple of the Storm God Taru, tries to broker a peace, but is up against outright stubbornness.

Muwas then hires Harep, of the same Assassin's Guild, to kill Tudhaliyas. Only Mokhat, the former spiritual adviser to the Assassin's Guild, knows what Harep looks like, and he is determined to stop all the damnable assassinations. He's had enough of the Guild's murdering ways.

Muwas calls upon his Mittani allies, the Mittani King Saustatar, who sends his son Artatama with an army to Muwas' aid. The Kizzuwatna King Shunashura changes allegiance and abandons the Mittani in favour of Kantuzzili's faction, sending an army to help Tudhaliyas.

The Pharaoh Amenhotep II threatens to invade Mittani unless they pull their army out of Hatti. Saustatar refuses.

When Tudhaliyas meets Nikal, he falls for this daughter of the Kizzuwatna king. They announce their engagement. Harep, the hired assassin, makes a number of attempts on Tudhaliyas' life, but is foiled. The major Battle of the Wide Plateau settles the civil war but in the mean time, Harap manages to kidnap Nikal.

The protagonist, Mokhat, is in search of himself after his sordid ministrations to a bunch of murderers. It is a bronze-age thriller, which includes a romp through the Hittite landscape, a civil war, and chariots in battle. This is a tale of love and adventure set in the most fascinating recently discovered culture of the ancient world. Volume 2 is due for publication in February 2011.

A must for all fans of the Hittite civilisation.

# The Wizard of Kálar

Sasha Garrydeb

On the distant planet of Kálar the two hundred year old life cycle of the Schánda once again menace the idyllic lives of the Bólani, a small tribal village of forest dwellers living in their hollowed Lándo trees.

The schánda stand half a cubit high, have a two hundred year life-cycle and normally live up on the northern edges of the tundra of the planet of Kálar. They are an insect, something like a cross between a spider and a scorpion. The adult form has no poisonous stinger and isn't carnivorous. Then the mating urge mutates the schánda into a massive swarm of ferocious carnivores. It doubles in size, grows the stinger and large claws in its fourth and final moult, then begins its long march from its home-ground in the North of Kálar, south to its mating grounds on the shores of the Golden Sea.

In its path live the small peaceful Bólani tribe who make their homes in living Lándo trees in the forest. Around the same time as the schánda begin their journey, the Bólani's collective unconscious, an imbedded memory of these carnivorous insects, triggers nightmares. They dream of an unstoppable carnivorous procession intent on eating their way to their mating grounds, heading their way.

The Bólani must gather their possessions and flee ahead of the encroaching swarm. They escape south to the shores of the Golden Sea just ahead of the voracious insects. Their long march to the shores of the Golden Sea takes them through a series of adventures with small blood sucking insects, vicious storms, predatory birds, unfriendly villages, lakes of volcanic lava, and desert worms. Only the skill of their apprentice wizard, Morác, saves them from disaster—

transforming his powers in the process. Even when they reach the Golden Sea their problems are not at an end. Imprisoned by a coastal tribe and then buffeted by storms on their flimsy rafts the dynamics of the tribe are changed forever before they finally manage to return to their small forest village back up in the far North.

This is an eco-fantasy tale stretching the imagination beyond the solar system.

# Worlds Beyond Ours

Sasha Garrydeb

In the fourth millennium humans finally invent the warp-drive and set out to explore the Galaxy. The first mission is sent to our nearest star, Alpha Centauri, and the starship returns to a stormy acclaim by earth's population. It then comes as a shock to our planet when aliens visit earth and announce that the Galactic Federation intends to lift its quarantine around the Solar System. Since humans now have warp drive capability, would they like to join the Galactic Federation?

This story brings humanity for the first time into contact with a variety of alien life-forms: elfin-like creatures, dinosauroids, insectoids, and many more, when Earth's Embassies are sent to other worlds. As the humans fan out from their home world they encounter a number of adventures which shape humanity's future for generations to come. Wonders like floating cities in the sky, terraforming other planets and genetic advertising.

The story at the end comes full circle when it culminates in another first contact, but this time from our neighbouring galaxy for this Galactic Federation.